BETWEEN TWO SCORPIONS

BETWEEN TWO SCORPIONS

A DANGEROUS CLIQUE NOVEL

JIM GERAGHTY

DISCUS BOOKS
ALEXANDRIA, VIRGINIA

ISBN: 978-1-7337346-1-5 (paperback)

"To all cliques of close-knit friends, past, present and future."

CHAPTER 1

CAFÉ VERNUNFT
BERLIN, GERMANY
SATURDAY, MARCH 6

Not even a ticking bomb under the next table could have distracted the eyes of Rafiq Tannous when Katrina entered the café.

He felt a great sense of relief upon her arrival.

She was an angel sculpted by the devil—tan, lean, Eurasian eyes set in an unforgettable face. Rafiq found it amusing the way she tried to blend in and failed so thoroughly. Every man in the room would remember her as head-turning and looking like she was "from somewhere else"—with guesses ranging from Mongolia to Turkey to Peru to Lebanon. Her name and surname, Leonidivna, suggested she was Russian, but Rafiq concluded she was far too dark. One of Rafiq's sources had once implausibly insisted she was one of the last Bukhari Jews out of Uzbekistan.

Wherever she had been born, she was American now, a long-ago contact at the CIA, and the only person Rafiq was certain he could trust.

She spotted him instantly and strode through the café on stylish black leather flat-bottomed boots—she was always prepared to run, and never chased someone in heels if she could avoid it—and stood for a moment before sitting, sizing him up. Rafiq Abdel Tannous had always been rotund, but now he was obese, and unshaven. A half-hour earlier, Rafiq's cab driver had called him "DJ Khaled" and Rafiq didn't understand the reference. A bit of chicken remained stuck in his beard. Realizing his napkin was now a mess of stains and grease, he wiped his face with his hand. He offered his other hand, and she ignored it—the left hand was considered unclean in his culture, and for all he knew, in hers, too. She pulled out her seat, angling herself to move quickly to the door if needed.

"Don't waste my time," she warned. "You lied to us before, Rat."

Years ago, the source with the initials and nickname "RAT" had been useful, selling information about arms deals in Lebanon to Katrina and the CIA. Then she found he was turning around and telling what the Agency knew to Hamas, Hezbollah, and anybody else who was willing to line his pockets. She had informed him of the end of their working relationship by leaving a pile of rotting fish heads in his bed. He hadn't dealt with anyone in the CIA for a half-decade. But a week ago, he had walked into the US embassy in Beirut and begged them to send a message to his old handler, Katrina. He needed her to meet him in Berlin in a week at "the Stasi restaurant."

Café Vernunft—German for "reason"—was part of the complex of buildings that used to house the Stasi, the infamously ruthless secret police of East Germany, and the museum dedicated to the history of the organization was just across the street. The restaurant's chairs and tables were allegedly reused from the old headquarters. For all Katrina knew, a cold-blooded interrogator may have previously sat where her cheeks were resting. She suspected the restaurant selection was Rat's twisted idea of a joke.

"Months ago, I started working for a man who I think is plotting terror attacks against the United States," Rafiq blurted out. He had her attention.

"I'm risking my life just telling you this," Rat continued his sales pitch. "This man, goes by the name Akoman, isn't some wannabe. He's Iranian, walks and talks like he's government. Big spender. First, he needed me to move some money for him. Then he asked for information about planes and chemicals. I kept copies of everything I gave him. I'm pretty sure he's got somebody in Mexico who can get him across the border. Then I warn him about you guys—how the NSA hears everything. He says not to worry, he's got somebody on the inside."

Katrina kept her poker face. But in her head, she checked a box: Rat's last comment aligned with perpetual rumors within the halls of both Langley and Fort Meade about there being at least two serious moles.

"I think he's got plans to hijack planes, bomb cafés, poisons, chemicals. This is big. You have to believe me."

He paused and leaned forward and continued in a whisper. "I'm going to need money and protection, for myself and my woman."

When Katrina glared at a man, she made him feel like he had just jumped into a bathtub of ice water. Rafiq flinched when he realized how far from the mark his sales pitch had landed.

"I *know* you, Rat. You've lied to us before and you're a greedy bastard. You put guns in the hands of the worst people on the planet. I should have left something much worse in your bed. Something like scorpions."

"That was a long time ago. I'm a changed man," he insisted, and she couldn't help but roll her eyes.

"Do you have any idea how many times I've heard tips like this?" Katrina asked. "The old Threat Matrix was full of this sort of stuff. 'There's a nuke on a train headed to Pittsburgh.' 'There are four sleepers in northern Virginia getting ready to bomb the DC Metro.' Nine times out of ten, it's just rumors from somebody looking for a payoff."

She looked around the café, starting to fill up as the dinner hour approached. Shoppers with bags, businessmen with briefcases, students with backpacks—any one of them could be surreptitiously watching Rat. One guy, probably Turkish, in a Fenerbahçe jacket, had looked over at them twice—difficult to tell if he was taking an interest in what he could overhear from Rat, or whether he was just checking out Katrina. If the Germans were watching Rat, they hadn't told the CIA.

"Please!" Rat whispered desperately. "This isn't just about money. Right after I helped Akoman make his arrangements, I ran into a monk on the street. I helped him up and he just asked me, out of the blue, what I thought awaited me after I died. I took it as a sign."

Katrina allowed herself to laugh. In her experience, arms dealers rarely grew consciences in midlife crises.

"Here's how this is going to work," she declared evenly. "I'm going to see if anything you told me checks out. Iranian, alias 'Akoman,' asking about sneaking into the country from Mexico. If it checks out, we'll discuss this further."

"I'm telling you, this Akoman is a dangerous man," Rat whispered. "I need protection."

Katrina laughed again, a reaction that was only half-calculated. "Everybody needs protection," she shrugged. "We can discuss that when I know you aren't lying to me."

"I'm not lying," he said solemnly. "You know how to reach me."

"I know how to *find* you," she corrected. "And if this doesn't check out, Rat . . . I will . . ."

She let the implied threat hang in the air a moment, then got up from the table and headed for the door. Rat frowned; he had ordered and eaten with the expectation that she would pick up the check.

Katrina suspected Rat's duplicitous habits had finally caught up with him, and he wanted the CIA to protect him from whoever he had double-crossed this time.

She pushed the cafe door open and turned toward Ruschestrasse, where her husband and partner, Alec, was sitting in a car, listening through the microphone on her lapel. She would give their boss, Raquel Holtz, an earful when she got back to the States. Raquel had pitched the meeting with Rat as a quick "working vacation" for them in Berlin, then in the face of Katrina's reluctance, Raquel asked again as a personal favor. Rat's message indicated he would only meet with Katrina. Katrina thought it was simply because he had enjoyed staring at her cleavage in their meetings all those years ago.

What a waste of time, Katrina thought. She was about to turn the corner onto Ruschestrasse when—*DOOOOM!*—she felt like someone played the lowest key on the piano of the world. Katrina felt the thunderclap of an explosion behind her, and the shock wave knocked her down to her hands and knees. She turned and saw that the Café Vernunft was now a cloud of black smoke. She heard a twisted chorus of screams. Every window for a block in every direction had simultaneously shattered. The reverberating echo of the blast sang over the car alarms going off and the shouts and cries from other pedestrians. After a moment, bloody patrons stumbled and staggered out of the screen of smoke.

Katrina rose to her feet and immediately ran back to help the elderly woman who had collapsed a few meters behind her. Within a few moments, police and ambulance sirens sliced through the din.

"Bombing cafés," she whispered to herself. Maybe Rat wasn't full of it after all. She stepped closer to the café, then froze in horror at what the clearing smoke now revealed.

An overturned baby carriage and a bloodied mother, holding her child, both sobbing with shock.

CHAPTER 2

Within moments, Katrina's partner in work and marriage, Alec Flanagan, was out of the car and by her side outside what remained of Café Vernunft. The pair helped a bleeding man through the smoldering doorway. By then, police, firemen, and paramedics were descending upon the scene; Katrina had already checked; Rat hadn't made it. She had left him sitting at the table, probably close to the middle of the blast.

"Not a coincidence," she declared.

Alec nodded, and started muttering a mental checklist. "Okay, what do we know? Somebody would have been here close to monitor the detonation. We gotta call this in. You've got to get to the SCIF" – the Secure Compartmentalized Information Facility in the CIA's Berlin Station – "but I can dig around. Wait, who knew Rat was in Berlin? Who knew he was meeting here? Where was he staying?"

She started the car, steered around the approaching fire trucks, ambulances, and news vans, and headed in the direction of the American embassy. After a minute, Alec took out his phone and dialed.

"Dee, Katrina and I are fine. Somebody blew up the café. Listen, I need to know where Rat was staying, and I need to know it now."

CHAPTER 3

Rat's accommodation was a once-grand, now-dreary thirty-six-room hostel in Neukölln, where the pale yellow paint was fading unevenly, now resembling a smear of mustard that had been left out on a cookout table all day. Dee—their NSA-trained teammate and hack-of-all-trades—had confirmed that a credit card matching the name of one of Rat's known aliases had rented one of the hostel's few solo rooms in the establishment, on the top floor.

Once part of the American sector when Berlin was divided, locals now called the neighborhood "Little Istanbul." After Katrina dropped him off and continued on her way back to the SCIF, Alec passed more headscarves than high heels on the streets approaching the hostel; his pale skin was only slightly more common than the tan hues of the Turkish, Arab, and Lebanese immigrants and their children. More than a few Syrian refugees had ended up living in store backrooms, or multiple families crammed into small apartments. Those on the street spoke with a nervous energy to one another and into their phones; the bombing across town meant trouble was coming their way in the days and weeks to come. They were veiled, but the suspicions were not.

Alec didn't belong here, by any measure. He was trained as an analyst specializing in terror financing but had spent years jumping into the field with the ops side, against the better judgment of just about everyone. Katrina's reputation within the

Agency was sterling; his... *wasn't.* Despite widespread skepticism and more than a few encounters that had gone very wrong very fast, he had managed to keep himself in one piece.

So far.

Alec grabbed the hostel door as a man in a blue and yellow soccer jacket departed. He straightened his posture and walked through the lobby with a look of authority; he had learned you could walk right into a lot of restricted areas just by looking and acting like you belonged. He quickly realized the effort wasn't necessary. The front desk clerk never looked up from his phone, watching coverage of the bombing elsewhere in the city. Alec looked around the lobby and started wondering how he could get anyone else out of Rat's room and get rid of any potential witnesses. He spotted a fire alarm just a bit down the hallway, just out of the clerk's line of sight. Alec figured he could pull the alarm, which would clear out anyone else in Rat's room, as well as any witnesses to see him entering it

He had almost gotten to the alarm when it suddenly went off by itself. For a second, Alec wondered if he had set it off with his thoughts.

The clerk started shouting instructions in German, and heads started to pop out of the hostel room doors. Alec realized someone else must have just pulled the alarm.

Not a coincidence, Alec concluded.

He stepped into the stairwell, and quickly found himself trying to run against the tide of the guests descending the cramped staircase. He blurted out "Excuse me, pardon me, coming through, excuse me" as he squeezed past a cavalcade of college students, folks who looked like they might be Syrian refugees, and assorted odd fellows exiting the building. It didn't matter, no one could hear him over the alarm and chaos of the panicking residents. As he reached the third floor, Alec realized that he smelled smoke and the people coming down the stairs had genuine fear in their eyes and were shouting. This was no prank.

Alec coughed as bit as he climbed through a thin haze of smoke, and it was much thicker and worse when he reached the fourth floor. He dropped to the floor, and realized the smoke was streaming out of a door that was open a crack at the end of the hallway - Rat's room, Dee had said. Everything he knew about fires told him that opening that door was a quick way to get barbecued; but if Rat had left any useful evidence, it was in there—probably burning up at that very moment.

He crawled on his belly down the rest of the hallway. He brought around his legs and kicked the door open. A horrific *fwoosh* brought a wave of flame and heat as the fire within the room voraciously devoured the new oxygen from the open doorway. Alec grimaced, figuring he was making things worse.

He wished he had a bandana; he tried to tie his handkerchief around his face to make a mask, and it barely fit. He held the handkerchief in place, crouched as low as he could and peered around the corner into the burning room.

He saw nothing good, to the extent he could see anything at all. A metal wastepaper basket was practically melting; the room's curtains were ablaze. The fire had spread to the wallpaper—a mercy killing of a hideous pea-soup-colored paisley pattern from the 1970s—and what was left of the bed roared like a Yule log. Alec scanned the floor and found three pieces of paper that had not yet been reduced to ash. He grabbed them, stamped out the burning edges, and stuffed them in his pockets.

But within moments, the heat grew overwhelming, and he backed out of the room, rising to a crouch. He took a last look and froze in horror.

The burning bed had a body in it.

It was far too late to save whoever it had been; from what Alec could see, she had been bound by the arms and legs and gagged—not merely arson, but murder. He crossed himself, turned, and ran back into the hallway…

…where he nearly knocked over an old woman who had been struggling to get to the stairwell.

Alec swore. The old woman yelled something in a panic—maybe in Arabic, maybe in German, in between awful, cholera-worthy coughs. He coughed himself and concluded he couldn't just leave her here. He reached out and, much to her surprise, threw her over his back.

Alec's knees nearly buckled when he tried to walk with her doubled over on his shoulder. Apparently, her breakfast had been bricks and cement. She yelled, and not in gratitude.

But step by step, he struggled his way down the stairs. The first set of steps wasn't so bad. By the second one, her yelling and wiggling was making it tougher. By the third one he was convinced she was deliberately trying to knee him in the chest, and by the fourth, he was certain he had pulled something and couldn't tell if the sweat was from carrying her or from the fire. He gasped for air and reassured himself that he was almost done. He looked up at the stairwell wall.

Two more floors to go. The old woman was howling now, and Alec understood *schnell* and *dicker mann*, which he was pretty sure translated to something like, "faster, fatso."

The fifth, sixth, seventh and eighth sets of stairs were worse, and by the time he reached the hostel's front door, his legs felt like jelly, the adrenaline was wearing off, he had sweat through his clothes, and he happily handed over the old woman to two burly German men. The first fire truck was emerging from around the corner.

The old woman had a coughing fit, then started spitting out rapid-fire German and Arabic, pointing at Alec and sounding upset. Alec looked at one of the burly German men and asked in English, "Do you know what she's saying?"

The burly, mustached German listened for a moment. "She says that you should have asked permission before touching her. You're an infidel, and she's a believer."

"Oh, you're"—he inserted a bunch of German swear words—"welcome!" Her face softened a bit.

"Are you fireman?" the old woman asked.

Alec looked at her and exhaled. "Nope. Forensic accountant."

CHAPTER 4

Katrina was in the SCIF of the CIA's Berlin Station, giving her boss, Raquel, a completely different message than she had planned when she left the café.

"Thank God you're all right," Raquel said, making a mental note to yell at Katrina later for not letting her know she was alive sooner.

For nearly two decades, Raquel Holtz's position and title floated around on the ever-reorganizing organization chart of the CIA's Counterterrorism Center. Over that time, she and the small group of officers she supervised established relationships and roles with many corners of the US government involved in national security—the National Security Agency, the Federal Bureau of Investigation, the Defense Intelligence Agency, the office of the Director of National Intelligence. Raquel's deviously ingenious system was to collect funding from as many places as possible, with every agency believing she and her team were submitting expense reports to the other.

"This wasn't terrorism, or at least not *just* that," Katrina said. Her residual shaking from adrenaline had finally stopped once she entered the SCIF. She closed her eyes and shook the image of the overturned carriage from her head again. "That bomb was meant to kill Rat. He said he needed protection; he said 'Akoman' was after him. I think this Akoman plugged a leak, and made it look like garden-variety jihadist terrorism."

Katrina was interrupted by the loud beeping signal that the SCIF door was opening. Alec entered, smelling like a fireplace and looking like a mess.

"What happened to you?" Katrina gasped, rushing to him. "Are you all right?"

"You would have been proud of me out there," Alec groaned. "As Marv Albert would say, I was *on fire!*"

She nearly choked when she caught a whiff of his jacket. "I don't know which is worse, your judgment or your jokes. What did you find at the hostel?"

"Hostility," he said flatly, thinking of the old woman. "Rat said he needed protection for a woman, right?"

Katrina nodded. She had listened to the surreptitiously collected audio three times with Raquel.

"Whoever she was, she's dead," Alec said, his voice a low mumble. "Somebody got there before I did, torched the place with her in it. Destroyed everything Rat had except this."

He held up three crumpled papers with burned corners. "Looks like a blueprint and part of an operating manual for some plane. I can't figure out the writing on this last one. Maybe this guy Akoman is planning a hijacking?"

Katrina carefully examined the papers. "Stupid decision-making, good results," she declared. She kissed his smoky hair. He smiled.

"Don't take any stupid risks again." She looked very closely at the papers, then looked up. "Do you have a crayon?"

Alec stared back at her. "What do I look like, a kindergarten classroom?"

She didn't answer; she just turned toward the SCIF door. Within a minute, the pair and the Berlin station chief were hurriedly sticking their heads in the doorways of embassy offices asking if anyone had any crayons. After the mom of a toddler pulled one from her purse, Katrina returned to the SCIF and rubbed a red crayon over one of the sheets from Rat's room.

"Hey, no reason for our forensics teams to go over that document, go ahead, just rub all over it," Raquel clucked sarcastically from the screen. But within a moment, Katrina smiled, and held it up.

"Rat wrote on a piece of paper on top of these documents," she said gleefully. "Left an impression on this sheet. Look, see? He wrote F-R-A-N-C-I-S ..."

"Francis."

"N-E-U-S-E."

"Neuse."

CHAPTER 5

BEA
Trident
OPERATIONS MANUAL
VOLUME 1
FLIGHT MANAGEMENT
896

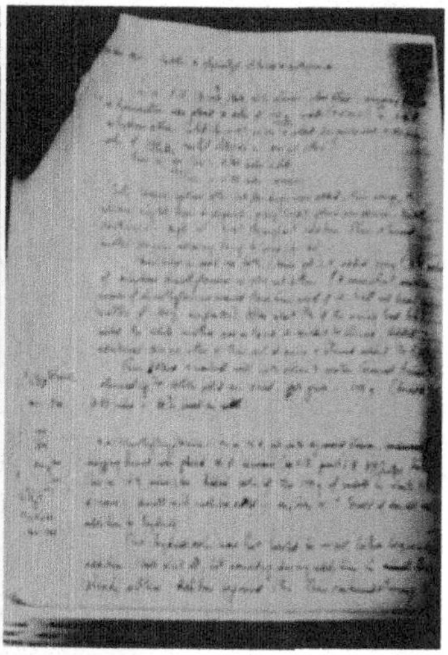

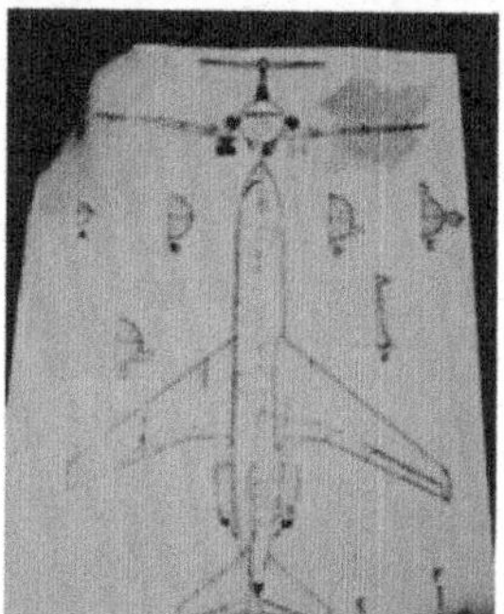

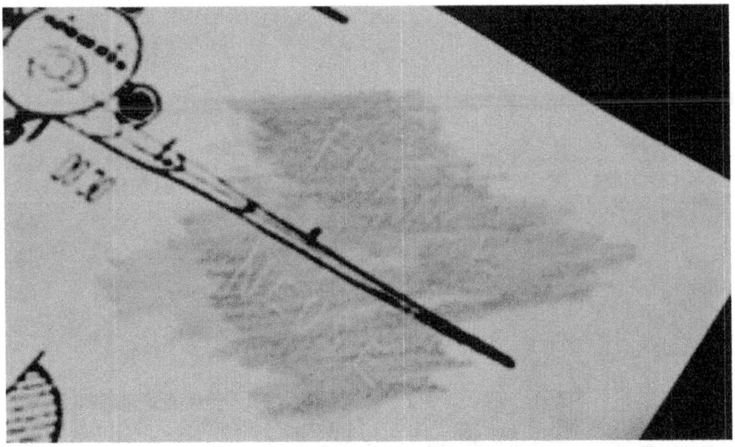

"I'll have Dee tell NSA to begin a full-spectrum search for anyone using the alias Akoman," Raquel declared through the SCIF's connection. "Friendly services, INTERPOL. I'll have Elaine check domestic databases, too."

Raquel knew the claim that an Iranian had committed a terror attack, and that he was preparing more against the United States, would hit a wall of skepticism. The US government and its European allies didn't see eye to eye on the issue of Iran's regime anymore. Without any incontrovertible proof, the Europeans invested in the tenuous peace with Tehran would be skeptical that an Iranian had just blown up a slew of Germans as they dined in a café. Raquel's team could not withdraw from any savings account of accumulated goodwill or trust; they had built a reputation for going their own way and disregarding the assessments of other branches of the intelligence community.

"If you say you believe Rat, then I believe you, full stop, to the end," Raquel said. "But whatever report you write about Rat's warning, there's a good chance it will get ignored or just lost in the noise," Raquel warned.

"Unless I take matters into my own hands," Katrina said quietly.

"We," Alec corrected. "Our own hands."

CHAPTER 6

This was not the way anything was supposed to turn out, Katrina thought, staring out the window as the cab took her and Alec to the Tegel international airport in Berlin.

It wasn't just this particular mission to Germany. She hadn't wanted to spend her entire career in counterterrorism. Years ago, taking her first steps in the adult world, the path ahead seemed so clear for both her and everyone else. When you're twenty-one, the world looks like your oyster.

Then one Tuesday the world changed, and Katrina found herself as one of only a small handful of agency employees who could speak Uzbek like a native, and her career path was more or less determined by fate. Weathered, gray-haired men who had worked in Central America—the Balkans and Iraq on missions no one ever was allowed to read about—suddenly were telling her that they needed her to get on a plane to some mountainous tribal region and help them negotiate with some warlord to change sides.

That felt like a long time ago. Someone had spun the world off its axis; no one in her world could remember the last "slow news day." Instead of calming after a crisis, the world just seemed to accelerate into the next one, often forgetting yesterday's outrage or travesty as quickly as a vigorous shake erased the image on an Etch A Sketch. Terrorism, provocative threats, bluster, saber-rattling, political coalitions collapsing, alliances on the verge of collapse. Massacre, candlelight vigil, empty international joint communiqué; lather, rinse, repeat. Katrina's faith was tested more than ever, now serving under her third consecutive deeply frustrating president, a man she instantly assessed as an ill-informed, erratic demagogue.

As things got worse, people cared less, Katrina thought. It wasn't just the madmen, zealots, and political allies of the Taliban who now controlled their own nuclear arsenals. It was the sense that the unthinkable had become commonplace, the wildly abnormal the "new normal," the temptation to tune out and just refocus on Kim Kardashian's rear stronger than ever. "LOL NOTHING MATTERS" was a cynical joke on social media to deal with the day's latest madness, but somehow Katrina Leonidivna hadn't yet made peace with the idea that nothing mattered.

Yet.

Day by day, year by year, the optimistic vision from Katrina's youth unraveled. She and Alec were thinking about having children, and she heard that ticking clock a little louder each year. That assumed Alec would stop running into burning buildings and rushing into harm's way, determined to prove that he could keep up with her.

CHAPTER 7

The Mexican man known as Jaguar had found the waiting the worst; Akoman's communications methods traded security for speed. He had written the update about the café bombing and the hostel fire and sent it off to the hotel in Ashgabat. He wanted to get out of Berlin; there was always a chance someone who survived the bombing would remember a lean Latin man forgetting his backpack under a table. Jaguar wore a blue and yellow jacket of Istanbul's Fenerbahçe soccer team, hoping that if anyone did remember him, they would describe him as a swarthy Turk. Tezcatlipoca knows, Berlin had enough of them.

He stayed in his hotel, watched television, worked out in the hotel gym, and ordered from room service. He itched to reach out to his love, Esmerelda, but an assignment like this required minimal electronic or phone communications of any kind. Akoman had demanded he travel with no computer and only put the batteries in his phone for short periods a few times during the day. He indulged himself by looking at a picture of Esmerelda before going to bed each night. He knew the NSA's electronic eyes were everywhere.

Finally, two days after the bombing, the front desk called his room and informed him a DHL Express envelope had arrived for him. They sent it up, and Jaguar opened it; a slim postcard slid out.

I AM SORRY TO HEAR OUR FRIEND HAS PASSED,
BUT GLAD YOUR TRIP IS GOING WELL.
I URGE YOU TO COME VISIT ME. USE THE PATH I RECOMMENDED.

Jaguar tried to book a hotel through his phone but found it a pain. He went to the hotel's business center and used one of the hotel computers to book a flight to Ashgabat, Turkmenistan.

CHAPTER 8

MONDAY, MARCH 8

After a rapid burst of crisis-driven expansion two decades ago, the CIA Headquarters campus in Langley, Virginia struggled to cope with too many analysts and support staff crammed into too few workspaces. Each year, America's intelligence community expanded into more generic-looking office complexes throughout the Washington area. Throughout the region's suburbs, Washingtonians waved at their neighbors who dressed professionally, carried a strangely unlabeled photo ID card in a lanyard, and each weekday reported to office buildings with a lot of dishes and antennae on the roof, and unusually tight security provided by private firms. Asked where they worked, thousands of seemingly ordinary Americans would respond with an acronym or a perfectly generic name that sounded like it could be a federal agency, think-tank, or university department: "Special Collection Service." "International Analysis Center." "Office of Screening Management."

Raquel Holtz's team operated in building LX-1 in the Liberty Crossing Intelligence Campus on Lewinsville Road in Tysons Corner, not far from the intersection of the Capital Beltway and the Dulles Toll Road. The team deliberately changed its name in every administrative reorganization of the intelligence community, selecting randomly from a collection of important-sounding words that never quite defined their duties or jurisdiction. Alec had once suggested "Liaison for Analysis of Counter-Terrorism Organization, Support and Enforcement," and had almost persuaded Raquel until she realized the name was an elaborate effort to create the acronym LACTOSE. When she refused, he accused her of being intolerant.

As soon as she had concluded her videoconference with Alec and Katrina, Raquel tried to get a meeting as high up the chain of command as possible. She wanted CIA Director William Peck, but settled for a meeting the next morning with Deputy Director Richard Mitchell and Peck's executive assistant, Patrick Horne. She braced herself at the door of the secure conference room at Langley. Horne was likely to be a problem, carrying a grudge against Alec that went back many years.

She laid out everything Rafiq Abdel Tannous had told Katrina, and Alec's account of the hostel blaze.

"You want us to prioritize finding this Akoman character," Mitchell guessed, in a tone that suggested Raquel had just asked for a pony for her birthday.

"Yeah, but there's more. I don't think Rat's comment about this Akoman having a mole is something we can ignore. So in addition to whatever CTC or JTTF or anyone else wants to do on hunting Akoman, I want you guys to give my team a lot of blank permission slips, unlimited access to the NSA Follow the Money databases, as much funding for travel as we need, and no questions asked until Akoman's neutralized, one way or another."

Mitchell smirked at the audacity of her request, while Patrick scoffed. "All because some guy who we know is a liar—somebody who is nicknamed 'Rat'!—claimed there's a mole."

Raquel shook her head. "No, because a guy walks into our embassy in Beirut, sets up a meeting in Berlin, and then when he shows up, he gets blown to Kingdom Come. How many people in the agency knew where he would be?" She had already calculated at least a half-dozen CIA employees had known about the time and location.

"If this Akoman was the bomber—and let's remember that three jihadist groups are all claiming responsibility for the blast—he could have had Rat followed," Patrick noted. "And you don't know how many people Rat told about the meeting."

Raquel's temper was about to flare when Mitchell raised his hand.

"You do know what the Seventh Floor calls your team, right, Holtz?"

She didn't blink. "The Island of Misfit Toys."

"Oh, I hadn't heard that one, but that one's good, too," Mitchell said. "No, the word I keep hearing is 'clique.' A dangerous clique. You never want to tell anyone else what you're doing."

"We work the way we do because we've learned some hard lessons," Raquel said, hoping she came across as reasonably wary instead of paranoid. "Every couple of years, somebody comes along and leaks every secret we have. Snowden, Assange, Ames, Hanssen ... Heck, go back to Kim Philby. Bad enough we've got a slew of millennials who wake up one day and decide they don't believe in keeping secrets anymore and that information wants to be free."

Mitchell nodded begrudgingly. "Admittedly, we've recruited some ... real winners."

She smiled at his subtle joke. "Reality Winner!"

"Look, sir, you and I have talked about this before. The CIA was built to watch a big, obvious foe—the Soviet military," Raquel said, beginning an argument she had had with many officials on the seventh floor over the years. "Now our foes operate in small cells—ISIS, al-Nusrah, Boko Haram, Haqqani, the New People's Army. We need our own small, nimble groups. Find problems and eliminate problems—any luck and you eliminate the next OBL when he's just starting his career."

Patrick smirked. "I think everyone was a little more sympathetic to that idea before you poached one of our best, Katrina Leonidivna, from the Global Jihad Unit, and wasted her career on wild goose chases. Her hubby's a walking liability, not smart enough to be an analyst, not tough enough to work in operations."

He's never going to let that grudge go, Raquel thought.

But Patrick wasn't done. "And his buddy, the trigger-happy former Army Ranger? You might as well be working with Ted Nugent."

Raquel bristled. "Ward Rutledge was honorably discharged and applied to the clandestine service for a paramilitary operations position. Patrick is wildly exaggerating what the Army psyche evaluation called an 'irrational exuberance' for using explosives."

"And your super-hacker, Alves, doesn't think 'secret' applies to her and breaks down the rest of the intel community's firewalls for kicks."

Mitchell shifted in his seat uncomfortably. "Is that true?" He suddenly recalled rumors about a "Dominica Alves," the granddaughter of a Cuban exile and CIA informant against Castro, tearing up the NSA's internal security protocols a few years ago.

"If you tell Dee she can't do something, she takes it as a challenge," Raquel shrugged. "I'll talk to her about it. Sir, Patrick's just upset because the one time he joined Dee for a meeting with the FBI, she showed up in one of those fake FBI caps and t-shirts that the tourists buy."

"Our colleagues at the bureau didn't think it was funny!" Patrick groused. "She could have blown their cover!"

"What undercover FBI agents wear FBI t-shirts?" Raquel exclaimed incredulously.

"Island of Misfit Toys indeed," Mitchell decreed. "You're so outside the system and established chains of command and conventional procedures that you might as well not be in the agency at all."

Raquel shrugged. "Hey, we'll take help from FBI, NSA, DHS, military intelligence . . . the whole point is to leave us off the organizational chart."

Mitchell tapped his fingers on the table, then reclined his chair, looking at the ceiling, exhaling for a long time. While Mitchell's tired eyes counted the tiles on the ceiling, Patrick made a *what the hell is this crap?* gesture and expression to Raquel. She made a *you're an idiot* face back at him.

They stopped the moment Mitchell sat up and returned his gaze to them. "Fine. Patrick, pass all of this along to CTC and anyone else who you think could use it. Raquel, do what you need to do, just keep Peck, Patrick, and myself in the loop through secure channels."

CHAPTER 9

A year earlier, Raquel had secured an office suite and access to certain classified files at the Liberty Campus complex, which housed the Director of National Intelligence's office.

If Ward Rutledge was taller, his colleagues would describe him as a mountain of a man, but he was only a foothill: stocky and stout, built like an undersized middle linebacker, clad in ball caps and casual clothes, face and neck hidden by an unruly red beard. If he were born farther north, he would have been nicknamed Yukon Cornelius, for resembling the character from the Christmas special. His knuckles had small scars from tattoos removed long ago. The Army needed him to blend in and keep a low profile, and tattoos were rare, often illegal, and easy to remember in places like Mesopotamia, the Maghreb, and the graveyard of empires.

Like a flash-fried steak, Ward looked tough and a little seared on the outside but was tender inside, and upon seeing Alec in the office for the first time since he returned from Berlin, Ward nearly knocked him over with an embrace and inspected him head to toe.

"Thank God you're not a crispy critter!" Ward said, slapping him on the back shoulder, sending a reverberating impact through Alec's body. "The hell were you thinking? Is this what happens when I'm not around to watch your back?"

"I'm fine," Alec grimaced, trying to not show that Ward had left his shoulder sore. "You know me, when it hits the fan, I'm a regular mad dog."

"Yeah, all the menace of an Irish setter," Ward scoffed. "No, really, buddy, new rule: everywhere you go, I go. Anything ever happened to you, I'd be crippled by guilt, knowing I let you go into harm's way with the combat skills of a puppy."

Alec grunted appreciation, but Ward continued, undeterred. "Katrina's nearly barbecued by a bomb, then you head right into a burning building. What next, fire-walking? Gonna do some Tony Robbins stroll-across-hot-coals-while-unleashing-the-giant-within routine?" He stepped closer and lowered his voice. "How's she doing?"

Alec took his time with his answer. "You know her, tough as nails. But . . . she's wondering if she could have saved more people."

***

The combination coffee and espresso maker in Raquel's office came equipped with two ceramic burr grinders and two heating systems and was capable of brewing two coffee drinks at the same time, with no need to move the cups from start to finish. It was huge, sleek, black and silver, and had enough complicated controls to easily blend in with the bridge of the starship *Enterprise*. If the machine were any more advanced, it would become SkyNet.

The coffeemaker cost the ungodly retail price of $7,500, the exact sum of the difference between a pile of cash stolen from a terrorist hideout by Alec and Ward two years ago and the amount that was actually turned in and still sitting in a vast and secure government warehouse of evidence. The pair considered the coffeemaker an investment for the unusual hours they sometimes needed to keep.

In her office, Raquel raised her mug.

"To my team members coming back in one piece," she toasted casually. "I should have sent Ward to watch your backs."

Katrina shook her head. "This was supposed to be a quiet, low-profile meeting with an old source. Ward's as subtle as the Kool-Aid Man."

Raquel chuckled at the not-altogether-impossible thought of Ward bursting through a wall and greeting everyone with a raucous, *"Oh, yeahhh!"* She studied Katrina's face. "Please tell me you're not blaming yourself for Rat's death."

"No, I'm just mad at myself for being so certain he was lying," Katrina said softly. "That's cynicism interfering with judgment. That's assumption."

"That's a judgment shaped by experience," Raquel corrected.

"No, that's bad analysis," Katrina corrected. "We don't know the sheep are sheared on both sides," she said, referring to an old joke from their mutual mentor, Harold Hare. Raquel laughed.

Hare was a brilliant, unorthodox deputy director of the CIA who had given Raquel the authority to set up the team with Alec and Katrina. Hare was everything they thought a director should be, an agency lifer with a theatrical personality, thoroughly uncharacteristic for a spy, complete with elfin grin and winks. Hare was forever quoting aphorisms, fascinated with other cultures' myths and legends, and enjoyed a magic tricks as a hobby. He was like the ultimate cool grandpa, cracking corny jokes one moment and telling a maybe-that-ought-to-be-classified tale from the Agency's Cold War days the next. Alas, Hare was passed over for promotion and shuffled out the door after the last director retired.

"We do this to save lives, not end them," Katrina said quietly. "Didn't save enough people in Berlin."

"There wasn't any more we could do," Raquel answered firmly. "Rat ran with a dangerous crowd for a lot of years. He knew the risks."

"His girlfriend probably didn't," Katrina answered. So far, nothing had turned up on the identity of the young woman who was found, bound and burned to death, in the hostel fire. Katrina feared the woman had little knowledge of Rafiq's dirty business, and had simply fallen for the wrong man, traveled with him to a strange country because he said he was taking her someplace safe, someplace better.

Katrina's eyes drifted to the world map of the wall of Raquel's office, and her gaze settled on Uzbekistan. She had been born there, one of the last generations of Bukhari Jews, immigrating with her parents to New York City. *Not that different from the burned girl,* Katrina thought. Taking a leap into the unknown, leaving all family, friends, neighbors, and lives behind in the hope that someplace far away could bring a new life and new hope.

Growing up hated by the Soviet authorities and their Muslim neighbors, Katrina's father, Abraham, said he felt as if they were growing up in between two scorpions. That was life, he and his wife, Ziva, sometimes lamented after a bit too much vodka: no true good or evil, just natural forces battling for dominance. Katrina's CIA career had brought her in contact with plenty of scorpions, and when push came to shove, she walked away in one piece and they didn't. But winning those fights came at a cost. More nights in the past year, she found herself staring at the ceiling late at night as Alec snored beside her, wondering whether she had become just another scorpion.

CHAPTER 10

The ten o'clock meeting began a few minutes late when the team's favorite FBI special agent, Elaine Kopek, was held up by the usual delays from the building's security checkpoints. Once the team's connection to the FBI's Joint Terrorism Task Force, Elaine had been transferred to a much cushier, less stressful managerial job in the Office of Public Affairs. Raquel had sent along everything Alec and Katrina had found in Berlin to her counterparts at the Bureau and the National Security Agency.

"Okay, first problem," began Elaine. "The airliner blueprint and operating manual you recovered from Rat are practically antiques. There are no more Hawker Siddeley Tridents flying anymore. Stopped making them back in the late seventies, stopped flying in the nineties. Five are on display in aviation museums around the world, none in any condition to fly, and none in the Western hemisphere. One was Mao's personal plane and is on display in the Military Museum of the Chinese People's Revolution in Beijing. If this guy Akoman wants to try to steal it..." She pantomimed waving. "Good luck, pal."

"So much for the planned hijacking theory," Raquel muttered.

"The page of notes looks like research into the chemical formula of 3-quinuclidinyl benzilate. NATO calls it BZ, also known as Agent 15," Elaine continued. "Our government tested it at Edgewood Arsenal in the sixties, one of the more ignoble chapters of the Pentagon's medical research history. BZ is an incapacitating agent that causes hallucinations, heart palpitations, and panic attacks. Scary as this sounds, this information is easily obtained on the Internet, and as far as chemical weapons go, this is ... meh. Not even lethal, really."

She turned to her third folder. "The BZ formula is a little interesting in light of the name Francis Neuse ..." Elaine continued, opening and displaying a file. "Francis Gordon Neuse, age 71. Psychologist, pharmacologist, follower of and successor to Timothy Leary and John C. Lilly. Bit of a celebrity a while back, turned into a bit of a psychedelic drug new-age guru. No known links to Iran or terrorism, though I found it interesting that he traveled to Afghanistan in the late seventies to sample the opium. Criminal record is a long string of minor busts for possession of controlled substances, never did serious time. Ex-wife filed a missing person report on him about two months ago. Whereabouts unknown, but passport and FAA records have him boarding a flight to São Paulo, Brazil, eleven weeks ago."

Alec leaned forward, in a mix of intrigue and confusion. "Huh."

Elaine nodded to Dominica "Dee" Alves, the team's liaison to the NSA.

"The name 'Akoman' does not match any known name or alias of anyone of interest to our intelligence community or any of our allies," Dee reported, not hiding her disappointment. "It is the name of a demon in Zoroastrianism, basically their Satan figure: 'the evil mind,' 'embodiment of vile thoughts and discord,' head-spinning-in-*The-Exorcist* stuff. It is also the name of a Ukrainian heavy metal band."

She turned a page, and seeming to sense a coming objection, she declared, "Yes, Alec, I looked hard. There's the usual Hezbollah presence in Mexico, but there's nothing in NSA's extensive collection of data about an Iranian trying to sneak across the border."

Elaine and Dee looked at each other, each silently communicating that they thought the other would have found something to confirm Rat's claims.

Raquel looked around the room in disappointment. "So . . . nothing Rat told us checks out?"

"Hello? The hostel fire?" Alec piped up. "Somebody blew up Rat and then kills his girl right after he tells us all about this Akoman guy? Come on, that can't be a coincidence."

"For what it's worth, the Germans don't think they're connected," Raquel said.

"When it comes to terrorism, the Germans are the mayor of Amity!" Alec exclaimed. "'There's no shark in the water! Stop scaring the tourists! Everything is fine! Nothing to see here!' If you tell the Germans that all their outreach to Iran is for nothing, and that Tehran might be sponsoring terror attacks that killed Germans on their own soil, of course they're going to insist this is all a bunch of coincidences!"

"No part of this is coincidence." When Katrina spoke in that tone, it wasn't merely an assertion.

Raquel nodded. "I'm getting one of you and Dee cleared for the NSA's Follow the Money servers. Tomorrow, you'll be spending quality time with Rat's bank records. Maybe there's something in there that leads to this Akoman."

CHAPTER 11

TOP SECRET/ /NOFORN,ORCON//MR1

FAX COVER SHEET
Central Intelligence Agency

Washington, DC 20505

March [redacted]

To: Raquel Holtz, [redacted]
From: Merlin [redacted]

It is very very good to hear from you, old friend. I have five responses to the recent events you describe.

1. Keep everything you're working on close to the vest. You heard correctly; that classified report from last year concluded that there are at least two moles at the highest levels in Langley. This is why a group like yours is needed. No one pays attention to you and your team by design. The perception of your unimportance is your camouflage.

2. Trust your gut, and trust Katrina's. If it feels like a storm is brewing... they say before an earthquake, all the animals disappear. Scientists at the US Geological Survey speculate this is because they can somehow detect precursor vibrations from the building pressures in the fault lines between tectonic plates; a spiritualist like myself would say this is because all living things are connected, and the animals can listen to the earth in ways we have forgotten. Listen to the sounds.
3. [redacted]
4. The day before you reached out to me, I heard from an old friend on the Iran desk that five agents under surveillance left the United States in the past two weeks. Then I started asking around. We have thousands of suspected foreign terrorists and suspected spies under surveillance. In any given month, the number entering and leaving the United States is about the same. But last month fifteen more departed than entered—way outside normal parameters.
5. The owls that lived in my barn disappeared last week. It's the wrong time of year for migration. I don't think their departure is what it seems.

The animals are disappearing.
—Merlin

CHAPTER 12

WEDNESDAY, MARCH 10

The highlight of Katrina and Alec's night featured both of them stripping off their clothes, brief difficulty getting off Katrina's boots because the zipper was stuck, tooth-brushing and a quick mouthwash, a mutual shower, mood music, knocking over a scented candle and getting hot melted wax all over the bedside table, a brief interlude as Alec put another pair of boots back on Katrina, rolling around the bed, falling off the bed, a burst of aggressive hip gyrations on both their parts, her lipstick in no less than seven distinct parts of his body, one distinct red handprint on her left butt cheek, one sore right hand, mild bruising on all four wrists, serious scratches on his chest and back, and a desperate need for a towel afterward. Both Alec and Katrina felt like eons of stress and tension and anxiety had been beaten, bitten, thrust, and squeezed out of them, and for once, every trouble in the world felt light-years away.

"Good to be back home," she said quietly. He got up, groaned slightly and thought about how he could be sore in places that would be difficult to explain, and started putting the pillows and blankets back on the bed. Both of their phones rang simultaneously.

They shared a look. Anytime both phones rang at the same time, it was work, and it was never good news.

"Tell them we're still in afterglow," Alec grumbled. Katrina saw it was Raquel and answered.

"Did you see what's happening? Are you watching television?" Raquel asked tensely. "Turn to any news channel."

Katrina mumbled a curse and clicked on the television in the bedroom.

"Why are you doing that?" Alec groaned. "Anytime someone calls up and asks, 'are you watching this?' it's never good news!" He saw his phone was Ward. He hit ignore and texted he could call back in a few minutes. "Just once I'd like it to be, 'hey, are you watching television? The game just went into overtime!'"

Katrina clicked through the channels until she found one of the cable news networks. She stopped upon the sight of a beautiful veiled woman, sitting in shadow, with ornate symbols painted behind her. She sat, cross-legged, in a dark room with a backdrop of bloody handprints. Her English was strongly accented.

"You brought this on yourselves. You are not safe. This is a response to your arrogance and oppression."

The chyron on the screen clarified: THIS IS A LIVE SIGNAL FROM WPIX AND WWOR IN NEW YORK CITY. During the woman's long pause, the anchor's voice interjected. "Again, this is some sort of pirate signal that is overriding two of the television stations in the New York area. We don't know-" He stopped when the woman began speaking again.

"Your helpless leaders will call us liars, but we are giving you a gift, the greatest and rarest gift in our decadent age of adamant denial. We are giving you the truth. You cannot be saved."

Katrina changed from CNN to Fox and to MSNBC and found all three cable channels were carrying the message live. The CNN chyron changed to WOMAN CALLS SELF "ANGRA DRUJ."

Alec smirked. "Who's this 'Angry Drudge' chick, and why is she on every news channel?"

"Persian accent," Katrina said with certainty. "Iranian."

The message from Angra Druj continued.

"Your fear is rational. You are fated for much pain and suffering. You have failed; your struggle now is coming to accept that. You are doomed and your fate is sealed by our hands. In the days and weeks to come, we will teach you that you are an insignificant plaything. The Voices reveal and prove this. The power of random chance and the frequency of tragedy in life proves that we are right. No one watches over you, no one protects you; you sense, in your sleepless nights, that a terrible fate awaits you, getting closer each day. Everyone can hear the doubt in your voice as you deny this."

She paused, looking down. During her silence Alec made a variety of vulgar gestures at the screen, inviting Angra Druj to commit undignified acts with his anatomy. Katrina shushed him as Druj started speaking again.

"You have denied this truth, and now we open your eyes. We searched your country and picked five of you at random. There was nothing unique about them—they are not in the ranks of your armies, or high of power or stature. We found their names in the phone book."

Katrina wondered how many people still used phone books. Sharp-eyed viewers noticed Angra Druj glancing down at a piece of paper in front of her.

"Hector Ramirez, Columbus, Ohio. Worked in construction… Helen Rai, Grosse Pointe, Michigan. Florist… David Glass, lawyer, Brooklyn… Mai Ng, manicurist, Los Angeles, California… John Brown, cab driver, Chattanooga, Tennessee…"

Angra Druj stopped glancing down at the paper and stared into the camera.

"Today, we sliced their throats open."

Across the country, viewers gasped and swore at their screens.

"We will continue this ritual," Druj promised. "There is nothing you can do to stop us. The next to die will be Smith, Johnson, Williams, Brown, and Jones. You are not safe. You will know us. You will know Atarsa."

The message ended. Confused anchors returned to the screen, attempting to explain again how the evening news on two local New York City stations had been interrupted by some pirate signal, and debating whether the boast of five murders could be true.

Over the phone, Raquel piped up. "Think this is what Rat was warning about?"

Katrina grunted affirmatively. "Akoman's supposedly Iranian, and an Iranian woman voices this message. But it's weird, this doesn't fit the Islamists. They wouldn't use a woman as the messenger."

Katrina switched the phone to speaker. "They're saying that the two local channels up in New York started broadcasting the local news, but for some reason, viewers at home saw this woman rambling." Raquel said.

"Max Headroom!" Alec chuckled. "Back in '87, some nut in a Max Headroom mask interrupted the signal for two broadcast stations in Chicago. Never caught the guy, some really whacked-out message."

Alec gleefully detailed how the guy in the Max Headroom mask set up signaling equipment between the channel's studio and the downtown transmitters atop the John Hancock building and Sears Tower. By increasing the power of the signal from his equipment, the channel's transmitter sent out a hijacked message instead of the intended programming.

"A low-tech solution that feels high-tech," Raquel said. "Why not just upload the message onto YouTube?"

"Because if you want to get Americans' attention, you have to interrupt their television programs," Katrina said.

***

The signal first reached the dwindling audience for non-major-network local news in the New York City viewing area. But a few moments later, the New York offices of the major cable news networks realized what was going on, when their monitors of the competing local news picked up the same signal. Once they figured out that this was some sort of threatening pirate broadcast, they began simulcasting it, attempting to explain to viewers that the local stations weren't broadcasting it themselves. Misunderstanding the explanation, some viewers believed the major cable news networks had been hacked, too.

When Akoman first imagined his plan, he described the ghostly veiled face of Angra Druj, looking down upon Americans from the giant screens on Times Square, appearing on every screen in the television store, jamming every channel and every broadcast simultaneously. His technical team disappointed him by telling him that was not technically possible, despite all of those scenes he had seen in movies. But they assured him that once Atarsa announced they had murdered five Americans in their homes, television networks around the world would give Akoman the rough equivalent, replaying and analyzing the video in a relentless deluge of coverage.

CHAPTER 13

THURSDAY, MARCH 11

Ward Rutledge lived with his wife, Marie, and six children on a farm outside Williamsburg, Virginia, not too far from the CIA's training facility nicknamed "The Farm." Most weeks, he only came up to Liberty Campus for Mondays through Wednesdays, not counting the multiple times a year he had to go overseas and arrange for something bad to happen to someone bad. But within an hour of the Atarsa broadcast, he was making the drive back up to Liberty Campus. Raquel hadn't ordered or asked him; he kissed his wife, made sure she was armed, grabbed his go bag of clothes and toiletries and hit the road.

He entered the office late that night to find a pile of updates from the FBI on the agency's secure internal communication system. The NYPD had found on a rooftop the broadcast equipment Alec described. The perpetrators had left a basic live remote broadcast setup, with the dish pointed exactly at the Empire State Building, the broadcast tower for the two networks. The building's tenants described seeing a maintenance crew bringing in equipment earlier in the day. All of the equipment had been wiped clean with bleach, destroying both fingerprints and any residual DNA.

"She said, 'the next to die will be Smith, Johnson, Williams, Brown, and Jones.' They're taunting us by naming the next victims," Ward said with visible irritation. "There's got to be something we can do with that."

"I already checked, there are roughly eight and a half million people with those last names in the United States," Dee chirped. "This is a scare tactic. Everybody with those last names is now looking over their shoulder."

"Five of the most common last names in the country," Katrina said. "They've done research, studied Americans, tried to figure out a way to frighten every Mr. and Mrs. Jones in suburbia."

"Well, they got my attention. Marie's maiden name is Williams," Ward growled.

CHAPTER 14

"I don't know if money is the root of all evil, but evil rarely works pro bono," Alec observed. He and Dee stretched, cracked their necks and knuckles, and settled in, back to back at twin workstations, for another day of marathon sessions of reviewing electronic financial records, examining Rat's plentiful financial transactions from his many accounts and looking for anything that pointed to Akoman.

The National Security Agency has a branch named "Follow the Money," conducting extraordinarily far-reaching surveillance results on bank transfers, credit card transactions, and money transfers, encompassing hundreds of millions of datasets. For years, the NSA had secretly monitored and copied the internal data traffic of the Society for Worldwide Interbank Financial Telecommunication, a cooperative used by more than eight thousand banks worldwide for their international transactions. This caused a brief controversy after the Snowden revelations, and many powerful banks demanded the agency stop metaphorically scuba-driving in that ocean of allegedly private information without a warrant. The NSA sent secret certified letters promising to stop... and then resumed full-spectrum monitoring.

Short of withdrawing cash, physically carrying it, and depositing it into a new account manually, few methods of moving money could escape the myriad NSA snooping programs: Tracfin, Dishfire, XKeyscore, ICREACH, BullRun, PiggyBank, SafeWord, and URSOL. The old hawala systems, once the favorite of terror groups, still existed but had shrunk and now charged higher commissions. Pressure from governments and legal authorities forced more of them to log their transactions, provide photo identification, and check names against blacklists. If those records were electronic, the NSA could obtain them if it really wanted to, and it often did. The biggest international money transfer firm in Africa now took fingerprints of new customers, sensitive data that the all-seeing eye eagerly vacuumed up and stored.

After four hours, Dee blurted out a surprised, "Hello!"

She motioned Alec over. "See this account from Rat? Starting six months ago, he starts moving money, roughly twice a week, increments of eight thousand to nine thousand dollars. He probably thinks it's safer because the Bank Secrecy Act requires banks to report transfers of more than ten thousand dollars in cash."

"Haha, sucker, we're watching everything," Alec chucked.

She continued. "Within a few months, that's a more than hundred grand. That account, registered under the name 'J.C. Lopez,' set up a debit card that made withdrawals in . . . São Paulo, Brazil."

"Francis Neuse disappeared after flying to São Paulo," Alec recalled.

She began typing furiously. Within moments, she revealed that the account associated with the debit card had financed a busy shopping spree, including leasing a boat, a wide variety of lab equipment, and numerous cash withdrawals. "J.C. Lopez" spent his money from this account almost as quickly as it came in. Finally, Alec and Dee came across the oddest expenditure, a hefty sum to the Butantan Institute, a vaccine maker.

"Cooking up some kind of bioweapon?" Dee asked. "Related to that BZ stuff?"

Alec consulted the Institute's website. "Maybe, but this institute specializes in something different." He looked up.

"Snake antivenom."

CHAPTER 15

NINETY MILES OFF THE COAST OF BRAZIL
TUESDAY, MARCH 16

Alec stood on the deck of the Brazilian Navy Macaé-class patrol vessel *Babitonga*, eyes transfixed at the ominous destination before him, Snake Island.

As their destination grew closer and larger, Katrina approached and watched him. His eyes began to wince, his jaw tightened, and his face twisted to an expression of grim. Sweat trickled down both sides of his face. Then Alec leaned over the deck and with a loud and painful-sounding heave, suddenly and violently deposited all of his breakfast into the sea.

After two days of frantic analysis of what Rat's mysterious client, "J.C. Lopez," had bought in São Paulo, all the data pointed the team to this spot.

The official Brazilian name of Snake Island was Ilha da Queimada Grande. Ninety miles off the coast of São Paulo, with an acreage the size of Vatican City, the subtropical island was home to zero humans and more venomous snakes per square meter than any other place on earth. The island was the only home on the planet for the golden lancehead pit viper, a three – to four-foot yellowish snake that boasted the deadliest venom in the world.

The snake infestation kept most humans away for as long as any Brazilians could remember. The government built a lighthouse in 1909, but humans left the island for good once it was automated in the 1920s. For generations, only the Brazilian Navy set foot on the island to repair the lighthouse. They had great difficulty finding volunteers.

The island became a legend, with one horrific tale after another of desperate, confused, drunken or foolhardy sailors ending up on its shores and dying terrible, painful deaths from snakebites. Four years ago, a local research firm negotiated with the Brazilian government to build a facility on the island, planning to study the snake venom for medical purposes. But the facility was abandoned close to completion, as the firm went bankrupt and snakes continually bit the construction workers. The construction firms tripled their standard wages, but still had great difficulty finding people willing to work.

Raquel and Dee had reviewed the most recent pictures of the island from the National Reconnaissance Office, and determined that for several months, someone had been there. Boat traffic came every few days and the abandoned research facility had light and heat at night. Raquel's team concluded that Rat transferred money from Akoman to "J.C. Lopez," likely in an effort to finance chemical weapons research at the facility on the island. They sent a complete dossier of their findings to the Director and DNI, the US Naval Support Detachment based in São Paulo, and the Brazilian government, requesting action to verify their suspicions.

Once again, they had great difficulty finding volunteers.

Within a few days, the Brazilian government declared the naval patrol vessel *Babitonga* would be happy to take an American team to inspect the facility. They would provide the ship's doctor and the best experts in venom treatment.

They just weren't willing to send any Brazilian personnel onto the actual island.

Katrina, Ward, and Dee joined Alec on the deck, watching the island get closer. They couldn't see any snakes sunning themselves on its rocky shore. The knowledge that several thousand snakes were all hiding in the grasses and trees and in between the rocks simply made it worse.

Alec heaved again. Ward handed him a napkin.

"Nerves?"

"Seasick," Alec insisted with a wheeze.

Ward nodded skeptically. "It's nerves." He reached for a pair of binoculars.

"Snakes," Alec sighed. "Why did it have to—"

"There's one clear path up to the lab," Ward interrupted him, peering through binoculars. "We go up that path in daylight like this, we're sitting ducks."

Katrina secured her gloves and picked up a pair of goggles. "You'd rather try sneaking through the jungle with all the snakes whose venom can melt your insides? Want to go at night where we can't see the snakes dropping on us from the branches, the way they attack the birds?"

Ward shook his head.

"Then we go up the path during daylight," she declared.

"I'm not going up there!" Dee piped up behind them. "I know my job. I'm the hacker. You guys do the shooting and the snake-handling. If you guys find a computer up there, you bring it down here to me."

The captain of the *Babitonga*, Joaquim Barbosa, approached, laughing and not disguising the fact that he was eavesdropping.

"I doubt you will find terrorists there," Barbosa said. "My guess is animal smugglers. It's a booming business. Not even the scientists come here much anymore, getting too dangerous. They say that as prey gets scarce, the snakes get more aggressive. I've been to this island twice before. Went with my men the first time, wouldn't do it the second. Look ten times before you move and a hundred times before you step. Remember, even if administered immediately, the antivenom does not always work."

With that ominous warning, a Brazilian corpsman shouted that they were close enough. Birds from the island flew overhead, and the buzz of insects was audible from the shore.

"I read the island's cockroaches are the size of a child's foot," Ward said. Alec dry-heaved.

The Brazilian sailors began preparing an inflatable boat that would take the American team to the island's rocky shore, with two Brazilian sailors and a doctor who specialized in treating snakebites. Ward laid out their gear. He would carry a modified AR-15 rifle. He offered one to Katrina, but she concluded it would be too heavy and didn't fit her frame. She put on two holsters for Glock 45s around her thighs. He handed Alec a Glock 37, but Alec looked at it in disappointment.

"Oh, come on, buddy. You know I prefer a nine-millimeter."

"You're gonna need something with more knock-down power," Ward declared. He debated explaining that the .45 caliber rounds used in the Glock 37 had about twenty percent more muzzle energy than the nine-millimeter rounds. This meant more kinetic energy going forward, as well as more energy kicking backward each time the trigger was pulled.

"Yeah, well, I'll remind you of that when I'm trying to compensate for the kickback next time we're under fire."

"It's not like you're that good a shot either way," Ward teased. "I want any shot you *do* make to do as much damage as possible."

Ward also wore twin holsters, one with a Glock and one with a Ruger Redhawk revolver, which strongly resembled Dirty Harry's infamous .44 Magnum Smith & Wesson. The assembled Brazilian Navy men let out an involuntary "ooooh" as Ward drew it from the holster and loaded it.

Alec nodded in acquiescence. Ward assembled the rest of their gear: A container of eight doses of broad-spectrum antivenom, each in needles ready for use. Signal flares. Two first aid kits. Survival knife. Flashlights. One by one, they joined the

Brazilian sailors and doctor in the inflatable boat, and moments later it gently descended to the Atlantic waters.

A few minutes later, the boat stopped at the rocky shortline. The three Americans looked at one another, each waiting for the other to make the first move toward the island. Alec looked, noticed Katrina's hesitation, wiped the sweat from his face, and took a deep breath.

"All right, we can do this!" Alec barked, suddenly rising to his feet and clapping his hands. "In every life, sooner or later you've got to face your fear, go nose to nose with your dweller on the threshold. Indy hated snakes, Bruce Wayne hated bats, and Paul Atreides warned us fear is the mind-killer. We just gotta take a stroll on an island of snakes. This will be a great story for our grandkids, if it doesn't put them in therapy."

He took his first two steps onto the island, stopped, looked back, and gave a sarcastic thumbs-up. Everyone laughed, even all the Brazilian sailors watching from the *Babitonga*, and Katrina and Ward stepped up towards the shore to follow.

Alec made it seven more steps before the first snake darted its head out of a crack in the rocks beneath him and bit him in the calf.

CHAPTER 16

A lot of things happened at once: Alec let out a scream that most men would deny ever making, and collapsed to the ground, reaching for his leg. Katrina screamed Alec's name. Ward raised his rifle, lined up the scope to his eye, and fired two shots—the sound of the shots reverberated up and down the shoreline, and there was a spark of a ricochet by the rocks near Alec's leg. Alec, stunned, looked down. The head of the snake and another four inches of it dangled from his pant leg, ending in a bloody mess. One of Ward's shots had split the snake in two.

Katrina leaped onto the island, holding a gun at what was left of the snake. She grabbed Alec by the back of his shirt and started yanking him back toward the inflatable boat. *That's why you do all those weights*, Katrina told herself, *not to have Michelle Obama arms, because you never know when you'll have to drag two-hundred-something pounds of foolhardy husband out of a mess.* Alec's eyes clenched as tight as possible, face contorted into an extreme grimace, like a raisin. He could occasionally scramble in a crab walk, sometimes kicking his legs frantically, sometimes an arm flailing as he felt waves of pain shooting up his leg. Katrina holstered her gun, grabbed him by the belt buckle with her other hand, and felt Ward coming forward and grabbing her husband as well. They more or less threw him back onto the inflatable boat.

The Brazilian sailors had already prepared the antivenom dosages. As Alec flopped into the boat, the two sailors tore open his shirt and they about to inject Alec with a needle the size of a steak knife when the doctor shouted at them to stop.

"What are you waiting for?" Ward screamed.

The doctor, with rubber-gloved hands, delicately pulled the snake's head off of Alec's pant leg.

"This is not *Bothrops insularis*," he said, repeating his observation in Portuguese. "Not the golden lancehead pit viper." He carefully held up the head. "*Dipsas albifrons.* Greenish color around the head, not yellow. Different species. Not venomous."

Everyone exhaled, except Alec, who merely gurgled. "It still hurts," he gasped.

"You must have startled it, it mostly eats snails," the doctor unhelpfully said as he prepared to clean the wound and apply antibiotics.

"Must have mistaken you for a snail from your speed, Alec," Ward assured his friend.

Alec groaned a request for painkillers, calming when his hand met Katrina's. He looked up at her and blinked *thank you.* After a moment, she turned her head, back up toward the path.

"Hell of a bad omen," Ward murmured.

"Good omen," Katrina corrected. "Your shots could be heard across the whole island. No one came looking to see who was here." She stared at bushes and trees and crevices, a million perfect hiding places for the deadlier breeds of serpent. "Now we just need to figure out some way to drive the snakes away from us."

Below her, Alec gurgled, "Call Saint Patrick."

The inflatable raft returned back to the *Babitonga*, where Alec's leg could get properly bandaged. Katrina was calculating how they could make a second assault on the island when she turned and saw Ward dragging a crate to the center of the deck. He cracked it open, and upon confirmation that it contained what he had hoped, his face broke into a gleeful smile.

"Oh, yeah!" he shouted with glee. He lifted one of the Brazilian navy's flash-bang grenades.

As Ward chuckled, Katrina envisioned him as Kool-Aid Man.

***

For the next twenty minutes, Ward and Katrina gradually crept up the path to the abandoned laboratory, every few minutes throwing a flash-bang grenade onto the path ahead of them. Each blinding light and deafening boom set off a furious movement in the trees, grasses, and underbrush, scattering the snakes away.

The laboratory, had it ever been completed, would have been a gorgeous modern temple of research, an ivory sanctuary in the dense green trees halfway up the island's lone peak, and a monument to science and man's ability to colonize even the most hostile environment. Alas, storms, humidity, mold, and the rest of nature's flails had tortured the half-completed structure. Some force had ripped the doors from the hinges, and vines conquered the entrance. The vines strongly resembled snakes, and within the entryway, incomplete electrical wiring hung from the skeleton of the ceiling... also resembling snakes. Katrina felt like she was stepping into an H. R. Giger painting designed to make her think everything around her was a snake.

"How about I throw a bunch of flash-bangs in and burn the whole place out?" Ward offered.

"How about we try not to burn up any actual intelligence?" Katrina countered.

They proceeded down a dark hallway, hearing hisses and slithers behind the walls. Despite the ominous sounds, Katrina carefully studied where the vines had been stripped away from the doorframe before them.

Someone had tried to chop away and clear out the overgrown chaos that had overtaken the main chamber of the laboratory.

The pair turned on tactical flashlights, illuminating a lair worthy of Rotwang, Caligari, or Moreau. Three giant, door-sized tables were covered with compressed gas cylinders, glass containers, bottles connected with rubber hosing and duct tape, tubes, hundreds of bottles of substances both labeled and unlabeled, Pyrex containers, jugs, coffee filters, thermometers, cheesecloths, rubber gloves, a gas mask, aluminum foil, a Bunsen burner, measuring cups, hotplates, and laboratory beakers. The jumbled equipment covered part of the floor as well, creating a ton of perfect hiding places for the island's vipers. Ward and Katrina trod slowly and carefully, until turning a corner. She gasped, he let out a short, muffled burst of profanity.

The far corner of the room featured a desk and large chair, with a figure seated, head thrown back, mouth wide open, eyes staring at the ceiling.

"Dead at least a few days," Katrina pronounced.

The corpse was a mess. Each stark-white hair on the head seemed to have a mind of its own and pointed in a different direction, creating Einstein-esque chaos atop his dome. He had probably once been handsome and tall; his eyes were a cloudy pale blue, still piercing in the face of the team's flashlights. But the wrinkles in his face had deepened to canyons; his eyelids heavier. He had tried to shave, and had several days' growth in the shaved places, longer chunks in other areas. He wore a white dress shirt—long since yellow and brown from sweat stains, smeared with grime—yet buttoned up to the top button. His pants, once khakis, were torn at the calves. The feet were covered in yellow and yellowish-green blisters. Neither Katrina nor Ward succeeded in suppressing a shudder at the aftereffect of the viper bites.

Ward reached into his vest pocket and removed a printed-out copy of a passport photo. He held it next to the corpse's head

"Dr. Neuse, I presume?"

Katrina kneeled down and examined the corpse's hands. The right hand held the chair's armrest, fingernails digging into the wood. The left pointed toward the empty desktop.

"This guy could have used some antivenom," Ward said with a shake of his head.

"Even without chemicals, he points," Katrina murmured, closely examining his left hand and the index finger directed at the desktop. She banged the desk a few times, hoping to scare out any hiding snakes. Once certain it was free of hostile reptiles, she looked closely at the desk, around it, behind it, and then finally got on all fours and looked under it.

Hidden under the desk was a sheaf of five papers, covered with increasingly frantic writing and doodles.

Katrina recoiled as she turned to the last page.

Katrina studied the papers for a few moments, attempting to decipher the decaying scrawl, when something that had been bothering her became too strong to ignore.

"Do you smell something?"

Ward accidentally knocked over one of the glass bottles in the lab, but it didn't break.

"I'm standing in Frankenstein's meth lab, in front of a rotting corpse, I smell a lot," Ward said, turning back to her. He opened his mouth to speak, then suddenly inhaled.

"No, I mean something different, something chem—" she stopped. She felt it on the back of her neck. Something had touched her and pulled back. She looked up and saw Ward's eyes, bulging like a pair of ping-pong balls, staring behind her head. She could hear it, sense it, feel it.

Ward put his finger to his lips, carefully slung his rifle over his shoulder and moved his hand slowly toward the holster on his belt. Katrina contemplated whether she could turn and grab the snake, or just leap away. With his eyes, Ward instructed her to not move, and he had just put his hand on his sidearm when—*BLAM!*—the lancehead viper, shot through its head, tumbled to her feet like a rope, the rest of its body limp. She let out a short scream and stumbled back a few feet, sending glass beakers skidding across the floor.

In the doorway stood Alec, dripping wet from head to toe, and holding up a smoking handgun. He hobbled closer on a heavily bandaged leg.

"What are you doing here?" Katrina gasped. A wave of odor hit her like an ocean wave hitting a child at the beach. "And what's that smell?"

"Cleaning chemicals," Alec announced. "Snakes smell with their tongue, and they're really sensitive ... so I went to the first lieutenant's storeroom. Figured if I doused myself in enough cleaning solution, douse my boots in ammonia, I'd keep 'em away." He held up his smaller gun to Ward. "Good thing one of the Brazilians lent me a nine-millimeter, huh?"

"Nice shot," Ward said with a nod. "I'd hug you, but you smell like you've been waterboarded with Pine-Sol."

Katrina went to hug him, then hesitated and covered her nose and mouth. "Sweetheart, dousing yourself in cleaning fluids can't be healthy. Don't poison yourself, I still plan on having your baby someday."

Alec looked around at the mess. "What do you guys think, he was working on some sort of chemical bomb?"

Katrina held up Neuse's journal. "Worse," she declared. "How about some sort of debilitating fear drug?"

December

I don't know when they will let me go. If they will let me go. I am Francis Neuse, and they said they were fans of my work. They wanted my help with some ground-breaking new pharmaceuticals for mind expansion. I have always been an explorer and felt a need to chase the horizon.

The woman at the airport in Sao Paulo was one of the most beautiful woman I had ever seen. Camila? Carmella? So hard to remember now - but I remember her accent was Mexican, not Brazilian - Spanish, not Portuguese.

On the ride from the airport, I felt woozy, confused, passed out. Must have been out a long time. <u>She</u> was gone. In her place where men with skull masks, all yelling, angry, threatening. I was in this lab; I am on an island. They warned me snakes are EVERYWHERE and they will abandon me here if I do not do what they say.

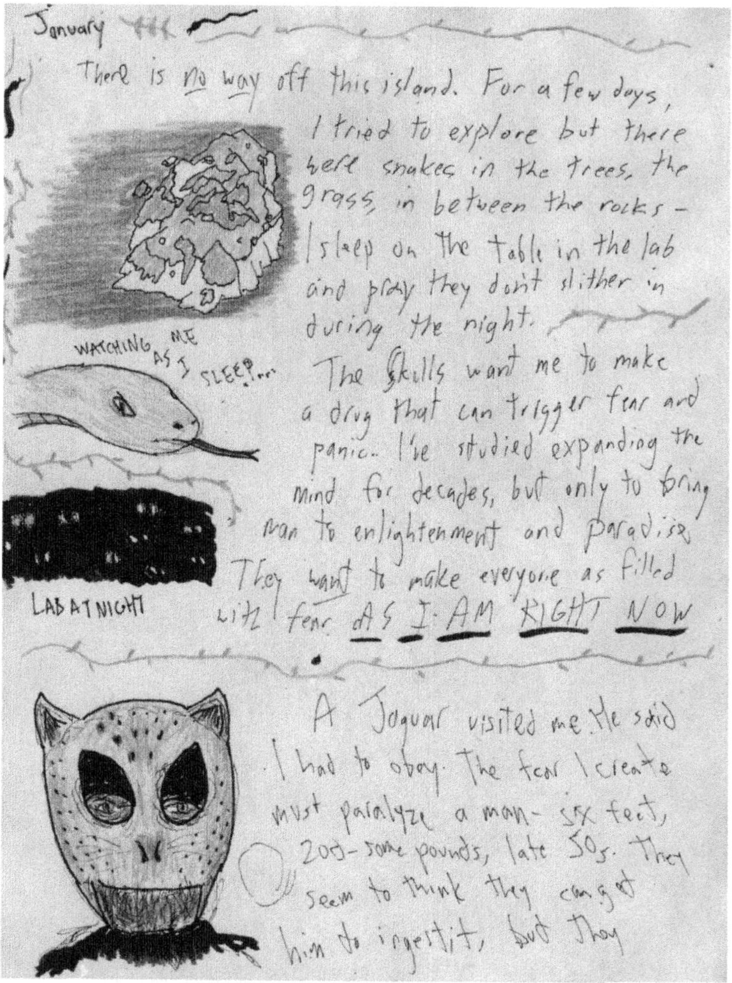

January

There is no way off this island. For a few days, I tried to explore but there were snakes in the trees, the grass, in between the rocks – I sleep on the table in the lab and pray they don't slither in during the night.

The Skulls want me to make a drug that can trigger fear and panic. I've studied expanding the mind for decades, but only to bring man to enlightenment and paradise. They want to make everyone as filled with fear AS I AM RIGHT NOW.

A Jaguar visited me. He said I had to obey. The fear I create must paralyze a man – six feet, 200-some pounds, late 50s. They seem to think they can get him to ingest it, but they

WATCHING ME AS I SLEEP....
LAB AT NIGHT

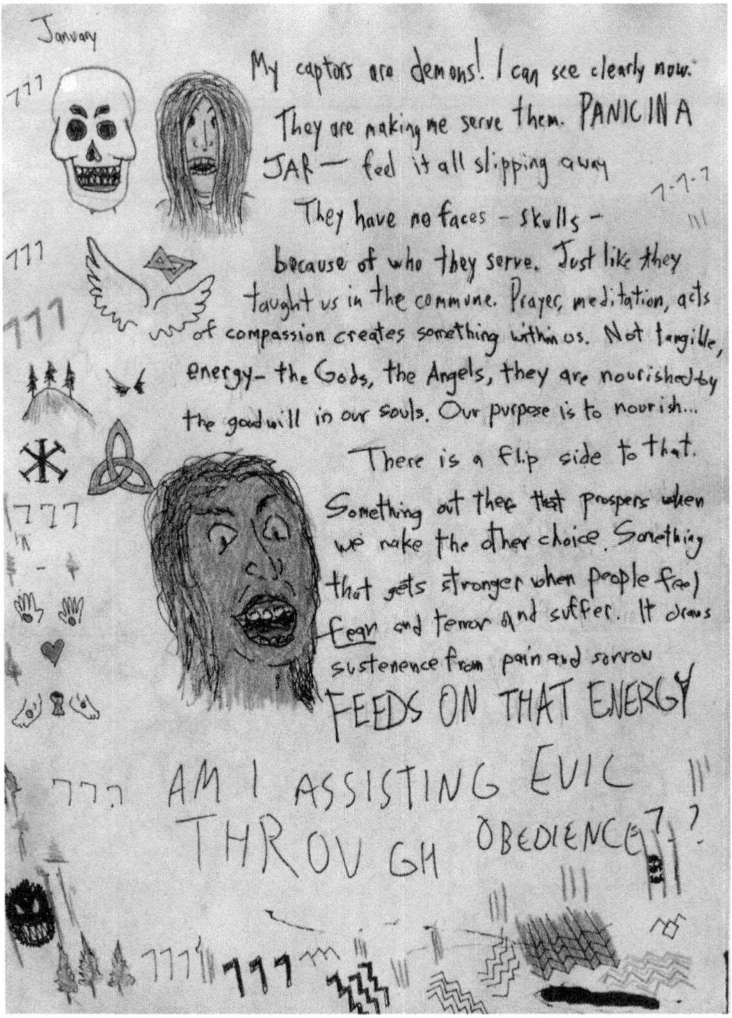

January

My captors are demons! I can see clearly now.
They are making me serve them. PANIC IN A JAR — feel it all slipping away

They have no faces – skulls – because of who they serve. Just like they taught us in the commune. Prayer, meditation, acts of compassion creates something within us. Not tangible, energy – the Gods, the Angels, they are nourished by the goodwill in our souls. Our purpose is to nourish...

There is a flip side to that. Something out thee that prospers when we make the other choice. Something that gets stronger when people feel fear and terror and suffer. It draws sustenence from pain and sorrow

FEEDS ON THAT ENERGY

AM I ASSISTING EVIL THROUGH OBEDIENCE??

February?

Something beyond this world, diety, being, Angels, consciousness, stronger from peace, love, Kindness. — wants us to do the right thing — TUG FROM BEYOND — I DID NOT LISTEN ENOUGH

Other side — prospers when we make the other choice — fear, cruelty, pain, — feeds on

Schizophrenics hear them

Lurking

WATCHING

WAITING FOR WEAKNESS

HIDING IN DIVISIONS

IT IS HERE

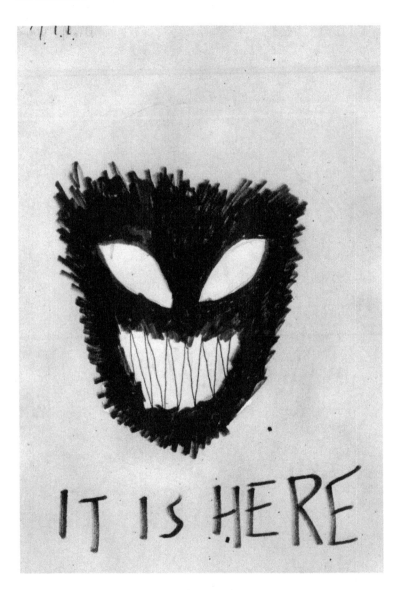

CHAPTER 17

TOP SECRET/ /NOFORN/ORCON//MR1

FAX COVER SHEET
Central Intelligence Agency

Washington, DC 20505

March [redacted]

To: Raquel Holtz, [redacted]
From: Merlin [redacted]

Francis Neuse! Believe it or not, I went to one of his talks, incognito, probably more than two decades ago now. I was working in [redacted] a lot at the time, Silicon Valley, cyber-security, that sort of thing. [redacted] Out there in California, the line between high society and the indisputably insane is a thin, permeable membrane; Jerry Brown used to hang around with Reverend Jim Jones of Kool-Aid fame. The Beach Boys hung out with Charles Manson. William Ayers and Bernardine Dohrn helped spring Timothy Leary out of prison. (This was before they got tenure.)

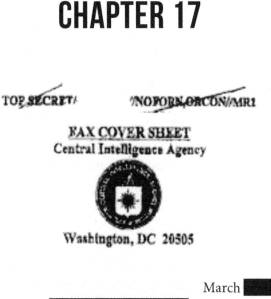

One of our consultants was really into [redacted], and he kept raving about Neuse. At this point, we were looking for any analytical edge, and if the tech geniuses at the dot coms were trying LSD as a form of creative steroids, we weren't ready to completely dismiss the idea if they could prove it worked.

They talked me into going to one of Neuse's talks, and I was completely unprepared for what a loon he turned out to be. Riveting speaker, though. He would lead the audience, step by step, so gradually down the path of his nutty ideas, that most didn't notice they were nodding along to talk of magic and pseudoscientific nonsense. He said all geniuses are considered madmen at first, and he argued that human society had missed so many potential insights and breakthroughs, as those who had been dismissed as mad in the past may have simply been misunderstood geniuses. He said he had studied Tesla, alchemists, occultists, theosophists, Turkey's whirling dervishes, every holy man in Tibet and Nepal, the rumors of the dugpas, qi, you name it. I remember him insisting that he had, in the past, slipped into some world beyond ours, or another world draped over ours like a tablecloth on a table, speaking almost like poetry—I remember this phrase, "with a curtain of the symbolic color through whose folds I pass"—this was about moving to this other world.

He believed that the barrier between these other worlds and ours was quite thin; he seemed quite convinced that most interruptions to electrical currents reflected interference from this other world. He also believed that this other world of souls and dream-like symbols could be seen by people, and that this explained sightings of ghosts, angels, UFOs, and the monsters under the bed.

The crowd of new-age crystal wearers seated around me ate all of this up with a spoon. I saw a man attempting to impose a theological logic upon his LSD hallucinations. But I did like one thought I had when I left his event that evening. Every time I've had a good feeling about someone and it proved well founded, or a feeling of ominous distrust of a stranger and it panned out, I chalked it up to instinct. Francis Neuse would have argued that in that first instant of warmth or wariness, my mind had caught a fleeting glimpse of that person's soul.

—Merlin

CHAPTER 18

CIA HEADQUARTERS
LANGLEY, VIRGINIA
FRIDAY, MARCH 19

It was an old trick, but Raquel was desperate; she hung around the elevator that CIA Director William Peck used and ambushed him as soon as he and his personal detail emerged. Like a school of fish turning in unison, the men on the detail moved with great purpose; the rumor around the intel community was that Peck was pre-taping an appearance for the Sunday's *Meet the Press*.

"Director, I need five minutes of your time," Raquel said, striding toward him. A defensive lineman in a dark suit stepped toward her with a palm raised, as if directing traffic to stop, but Peck put a reassuring hand on the detail man's shoulder.

"Holtz, thank you for crawling out of your hiding place over at Liberty Campus," Peck said in what was supposed to be a playful taunt but didn't really hide his contempt. "Would whatever you're about to tell me help explain why the German government keeps asking me about American agents in Berlin the night of the café bombing?"

"Only tangentially, sir," Raquel said, not skipping a beat, and wondering just how much of what she had told Mitchell and Horne had actually made it to the director. "This is part of my team's continuing effort to investigate potentially overlooked avenues and sources of intelligence. We think the group responsible for the New York broadcast has been researching a variation of BZ, a chemical agent that can cause hallucinations and panic attacks."

Peck stopped, reached for the folder, and gave it a glance.

"Brazil?" She nodded. He continued walking and reading, and she walked with him. She began to speak, but he held up his hand. He read and walked, only once letting out a giggle and asking, "Alec got bit by a snake?"

"Yeah, he's fine, physically. Of course, each time he retells the story, the snake gets bigger."

Peck laughed. By the time they were crossing the seal in the main lobby of the headquarters building, he was handing her back the file.

"Very dramatic," he concluded skeptically. "Snake Island. Long-lost mad scientist. A secret formula that paralyzes people with fear ... maybe if you guys hadn't been such a clique, and you had gotten the IOC or CTC to sign off on this analysis, I'd give you more than five minutes."

"Sir, whatever you think of my team or myself, I'm begging you to put that aside and focus on—"

"On what, some nut-job's diary says demons with skulls for faces made him cook up a drug formula for panic attacks? You worked the Threat Matrix, you know this sort of lunatic chatter comes in all the time. Everybody and their brother here runs into some big talk that ends up being nothing and tries to get it the PDB.," – the President's Daily Briefing, considered the most important and prestigious work of the CIA. "We hear crazy stories and claims every day. Take a number."

"Sir, I thnk—"

"We have official channels, Holtz," Peck declared. "Use them."

CHAPTER 19

NBC NEWS STUDIOS
4001 NEBRASKA AVENUE
WASHINGTON, DC

"Chuck, let me be clear," CIA Director William Peck said, leaning toward the host of *Meet the Press*. "This group, Atarsa—which is, apparently, is the name of the symbol behind her—is high on theatricality, but low on resources. They have a flair for dramatic spectacle, but we should not overstate their ability to threaten the American people."

A bit more than an hour earlier, Peck and his security detail arrived at the NBC News studios in Washington, a complex that combined impressively modern technical equipment such as giant satellite dishes and a looming broadcast tower with sadly boxy and outdated 1950s architecture, the color and shape of a group of wet cardboard boxes pushed together.

Peck had pushed for doing the interview remotely, but bringing the host and a camera crew to the agency's headquarters in Langley presented all kinds of security headaches. The host and all of his producers pledged to bend over backward to make an in-studio interview work. They never got around to mentioning their insistence wasn't just the better chemistry of a face-to-face interview; the network's producers had noticed that certain administration officials would claim they couldn't hear the question or were getting static feedback during remote interviews, just as the questions started to get difficult. The network's tech guys could never determine any cause for the conveniently timed, seemingly one-sided technical difficulties. Occasionally a slower-witted guest would be asked by the host, "Can you hear me?" and answer, "No, I can't."

A high-profile guest like the CIA director couldn't be expected to settle for the green room Keurig. Peck was ushered in directly to the host's office, decorated with memorabilia from campaigns going back decades. After a few moments of chuckling about the DUPONT '88 poster, the director shifted to small talk about his grandchildren's soccer team and the host countered with tales of his children's grammar school exploits. Both concurred that winning a war against ever-evolving terror groups was easier than getting kindergarteners to spread out and stop clumping together around the ball. After the casual, off-the-record coffee chat, Peck followed the eager staffers to makeup, was outfitted with a lapel microphone and earpiece, and stepped onto the set.

Peck recited his memorized talking points. "At times like this, we harness our resources, look for innovative solutions, and work in close cooperation with our allies for a multifaceted approach that adapts to changing challenges."

The host stifled the urge to congratulate the director for setting the new Guinness Record for "Most Buzzwords and Clichés Stuffed into a Single Sentence."

After a few minutes of back and forth, the host had wondered whether he should stop the interview or take a break; there was more than a little glint of sweat on the director's forehead. His voice was growing louder, and he was speaking faster, hiswordsrunningtogetherlikethis.

"How certain can you be that this group won't be able to kill more Americans?"

"We can't be certain, because we can't protect everybody!" the director exclaimed, to the surprise of everyone in the room—including himself. "The expectations upon us are immeasurable, impossible—we're expected to know what everybody in the world is doing all the time, everywhere! If it's not al-Qaeda, it's ISIS, when it's not ISIS, it's the Khorasan Group, or the Haqqani Network, or the Brotherhood of Eblis, or Hadramout—"

"But, Director," the host interrupted. Unbeknownst to him, Peck had begun listing nascent terror groups that the US government had never discussed before.

"It's like everybody's walking around in this trance, completely oblivious to reality and how the world really works!" Peck spoke louder, eyes starting to bulge. "How are we supposed to protect people when they choose to go hiking over the Iranian border? Why do Americans walk around thinking these countries are as safe as going to the local mall?!" The host stared, marveling that one of the highest-ranking officials in the US government, the keeper of the nation's secrets, was starting to sound like a ranting Larry David.

He tried to steer the conversation, "So you seem to be suggesting that Americans need to get used to—"

"We sit around debating if this kind of chaos is the new normal—what the hell is normal anymore? The other day the Azeri trade minister is at a closed-door lunch meeting with the Saudi ambassador, just reaches across the table and stabbed the ambassador with his knife! Nobody knows why! Just happens! Guy goes nuts without warning, nearly starts a war! What are we supposed to do about that?"

The host stared back, marveling that the rant was becoming a full-blown meltdown. Usually these sorts of off-the-cuff rambling tirades were reserved for the president.

"Are there spies in our ranks? Probably! CI branch theorized there were two moles on my senior staff last year! How am I supposed to watch my back twenty-four/seven? Are they gonna get me in my sleep? Walls, borders—we've got thousands of people coming into our country every day, any one of them could be a bug. People aren't what they seem. Most people can't see them, but I'm starting to see! Walking around like sock puppets, something's pulling the strings, hand up their—"

"Okay, I think we should take a little break," the host said nervously, looking at his producers and seeing their same stunned, frozen reaction. But Director Peck's voice just grew louder, more frantic, his gestures manic and wild.

"You can see the tentacles everywhere, reaching into everything, and nobody wants to do something about it! It wants the end of all of us! *Don't you see it? We're not safe! None of us are safe!*"

CHAPTER 20

The word spread like wildfire through America's intelligence community; by the time NBC News reported that CIA Director William Peck had been taken to Sibley Memorial Hospital in Washington because of "chest pains, as a precaution," hundreds of people around the globe already knew that he had some sort of breakdown while taping the interview. Their job, of course, was uncovering official secrets, and those skills were easily reapplied to their own government.

Raquel's professionalism and empathy almost completely overcame any lingering resentment of Peck's snide dismissiveness from earlier in the day. *Almost.* She couldn't help but wonder if a severe bout of karma triggered Peck's sudden, overwhelming panic attack just hours after she had warned him about the possibility of a terror group cooking up some sort of fear drug. Once Patrick Horne had begrudgingly confirmed to Raquel that the rumors were true, she sent four GET OVER HERE RIGHT NOW texts.

"Director Peck wasn't hospitalized for heart palpitations," she told the team once they had gathered back in the office. "He had a full, all-out psychotic breakdown with the cameras rolling."

The team stared back in disbelief for a moment, until Alec burst out with inappropriate laughter. "I mean, that's terrible. Not even he deserves that."

"They had to give him a sedative and restrain him on the way out the door. They think he was drugged." Everyone exchanged an uncomfortable look after the final word.

"Let me get this straight," Ward rumbled. "The CIA director goes on television to tell Mr. and Mrs. America, 'Don't worry about this Atarsa thing, we got this,' and right at that moment, somehow they drug him and he starts screaming about lizard people?"

Raquel gave him a grim nod. "Bugs were controlling people like puppets," she paraphrased.

Ward winced. "Man, we're going to get some insufferable I-told-you-so's from Alex Jones."

"They're running every conceivable test on him," Raquel continued. "If Atarsa has created a modified version of Agent 15 or BZ, then there's a million different ways you can hit somebody with this. Peck could have inhaled it, drank it, eaten it, had it applied to his skin if he shook someone's hand."

"And they could use the same stuff just about anywhere else," Katrina surmised. Since they had returned from Brazil, she had been brainstorming the most dangerous places someone could have a chemically induced debilitating panic attack, and thus, she concluded, the most likely targets for Atarsa. Her list was a catalog of nightmares: train engineers, airline pilots, police officers, surgeons, anyone in a crowded location like a sports arena, nightclub, or Times Square on New Year's Eve . . .

But her teammates quickly came up with other frightening possibilities.

"The floor of the New York Stock Exchange," Dee suggested. "Literal panic selling. Could make the Flash Crash look mild."

"Truck drivers?" Alec asked, thinking of the jackknifed tractor trailer that had made a mess of the Beltway that morning. His stomach grew queasy. How did they know Atarsa hadn't been using the panic drug on people already?

"Children," Ward interjected. Everyone stood in grim silence at the thought.

Raquel broke the gloom. "With Peck out until further notice, Mitchell is now running the show, and he was always . . . more tolerant of our old tricks than Peck."

CHAPTER 21

The second message from Atarsa lasted only a few moments, interrupting those viewers in the Philadelphia area who still watched television off antennae. It was ghostly: Angra Druj's face, fading in from static, staring at the viewers with a smile.

"We got to him."

Then the screen returned to the reality show.

***

SATURDAY, MARCH 20

Katrina's nightmares didn't always align with impending disasters, but over the years she grew to interpret them as a warning shot, her subconscious sensing some sort of danger headed her way. The one the night after Peck's nervous breakdown felt as clear a warning as a flashing neon sign.

Like all dreams, it just began, with no sense of how she got here. In her dream, she was outside some nondescript Rust Belt city. She was driving a car with Alec in the backseat. (Sometimes the symbolism of her dreams wasn't too hard to interpret.) The highway was empty, except for abandoned cars on either side of the road.

She knew something terrible had happened, and she had to get away. She looked up and down the road, at the fast-food places in the distance, and she could see bodies hanging from the golden arches and kingly crowns and other icons of the roadway.

She pulled off the highway and found herself parking in front of a Friendly's restaurant. She got out of the car into the parking lot, even though she didn't want to, and immediately Alec started wandering off. She tried to yell a warning but couldn't, her voice wouldn't work. She turned to the Friendly's and saw the windows had been replaced with signs:

OUTSIDERS NOT WELCOME HERE
WE HAVE FOUND SEVERAL INFILTRATORS
WE WILL KILL ANY MORE WE FIND

Even though she didn't want to, she walked closer to the restaurant and realized the locked door had been covered by wanted posters: a whole town of people, elderly, children, teenagers, all suddenly wanted and suspected as sleeper agents and sentenced to death.

SLEEPERS AGENTS AND BUGS
THEY ARE HERE TO KILL US
DO NOT TRUST THEM
KILL THEM

She heard noises from the other side of the restaurant—someone or a group of people, undoubtedly hostile, were on the move. The wind howled, and she looked down, seeing her feet were buried by a pile of little white insects that were crawling up her legs, climbing up her body . . .

That was the last thing she saw before she awoke, suddenly and violently, bolting into a sitting position and thrashing her arms. On the way up, her right arm had managed to whack Alec in the nose, and he groaned in pain. After a moment of realizing it had been a dream, and that she had just struck him, she wiped the sweat from her forehead and apologized profusely.

Alec rubbed his nose. “I’d wear a hockey mask to bed, but that would just make the nightmares worse, wouldn’t it?”

CHAPTER 22

Jaguar, a.k.a. J.C. Lopez, a.k.a Juan Perez, a.k.a. Juan Comillo, was on a plane about to land in Ashgabat, Turkmenistan—the farthest he had ever traveled from his native Mexico.

Juan Comillo grew up knowing exactly what he wanted to be: a heroic lawman. His father was a lawyer and his mother a former model, and they enjoyed a comfortable life in San Juan Teotihuacan, a town just northeast of Mexico City, noted for the spectacular Mesoamerican pyramids and ruins of Teotihuacan next to the modern town. By his teen years, Jaguar knew mere police work wouldn't be enough for him—even though it certainly involved enough danger from the country's perpetual war with drug cartels. No, he set out to join Centro de Investigación y Seguridad Nacional, Mexico's intelligence agency.

His shining transcript from Universidad Nacional Autónoma de México—with a year abroad at the University Texas at Austin—and obsession with all aspects of law enforcement made him a star recruit for the agency.

At CISN, Comillo learned everything he could about almost all of the dark arts of espionage. He proved ruthless in a fight and sharp-eyed on the street, a keen analyst. What his bosses and family could not know was that the clear view from his new position—seeing how his country really worked—was slowly eating away at his worldview. Once determined to serve his country, he began to wonder if he still had a country.

He gradually and painfully learned modern Mexico was rife with corruption, an afterthought in international affairs, and pushed around with impunity by its northern neighbors. Far too many of its citizens left and headed north for a better life. Some police and prosecutors fought hard for order, but their efforts were whack-a-mole at best; knock down one dealer, gang, or kingpin and another would quickly replace him. Battles against poverty, ignorance, and violent crime were marked by frequent setbacks.

The Catholic Church, the faith of his childhood, seemed hapless and helpless in the face of these dire challenges. Overwhelmed with crime, corruption, and despair, they assured the faithful that everything would be better in the afterlife. To Juan, it increasingly felt like a message of surrender. He found himself haunted by his college readings of Nietzsche, the dismissal of Christianity as a "slave morality," more focused on good or evil intentions than good or bad consequences. Jaguar concluded that whatever the modern leaders of Mexico had intended, the consequences of their leadership were disastrous. The economy stumbled, torn between rapacious greed at the top and inflammatory populist crusaders, quick to turn around and enjoy the high life once they had tasted some of it for themselves.

He had been raised to detest the cartels, but the more he studied them, he found himself begrudgingly admiring them. Some far-off madman had once declared that given a choice between a strong horse and a weak horse, people will always choose the strong horse. In his country, Comillo began to conclude the cartels were the stronger horse—arguably the true government in some portions of the country.

After close to a decade of service, Juan Comillo resigned his government job and went into "the private sector"—working for the cartels under the nom de guerre "Jaguar," a career path that he found was not that unusual. He found himself wealthier—able to purchase a nice condo in Xochimilco, not far from the canals in Mexico City, as well as a cheap apartment for use as a safe house—but still haunted by the state of his homeland.

What maddened Jaguar was that the cartels had everything before them to complete the takeover of a country that some analysts argued was on the cusp of becoming a failed state. They had enormous financial resources and an intelligence network that penetrated every urban neighborhood or small town. They commanded not-so-virtual armies. One analysis concluded the cartels commanded 100,000 men through their network of allied gangs and informants; the Mexican Army had 130,000 soldiers. But then again, some men would be counted among both groups.

What's more, for all of its flaws and weaknesses, Comillo saw that Mexico had two things other people needed. It had drugs that Americans wanted and needed and would pay dearly for, and it had the access to the United States that the rest of Central America coveted.

Jaguar said to anyone who would listen that Mexico could demonstrate its leverage quickly and easily. Give the American DEA and Mexican government what they say they want and stop the drug shipments. He proposed launching a brief "strike" of drug shipments to get every American user to go into a paralyzing state of withdrawal and desperation. Jaguar had done the research; the US National Institutes of Health estimated that 27 million Americans had used an illegal drug in the past month, a number only increasing as opioid addiction became disturbingly mainstream.

The cartels had more than enough financial reserves to survive a "work stoppage." Within a few weeks—two months, tops—the consequences of a national forced withdrawal would be clear all over America: overwhelmed emergency rooms and drug treatment centers, gangs and drug dealers shooting each other in the street over remaining drug stashes, amateurs trying to cook their own meth and blowing up their houses.

"Let's show them exactly what a drug-free America would look like," Jaguar would declare with a smile.

Jaguar proposed that after a good month of chaos north of the border, the cartels could make an offer no one could refuse: Everyone on both sides of the border would accept that the cartels were merely giving Americans what they wanted, a chemical escape from their miserable, hopeless lives. The DEA would find something else to do, the border posts would be left open, and the cartels would be free to sell their product to anyone who wanted to buy it. To Jaguar, legalization was moot; he didn't care if cocaine, heroin, and crystal meth were sold at the corner store or the alley behind it, as long as the distribution networks and customer base operated unmolested. Americans would finally realize that they needed Mexico more than Mexico needed it and behave accordingly. The Mexican government would recognize the cartels held the whip hand.

When Jaguar discussed this idea, most of his cartel employers smiled, nodded, and ignored him, or pointed out the minor flaw that getting the three major cartels, four regional cartels, toll collector cartels, and hundreds of gangs to cooperate on a stoppage was nearly impossible. They pointed out that drug cartels from other regions of the world would eagerly step in to fill the vacuum—or perhaps even big pharmaceutical companies. Under Jaguar's plan, America might remain every bit as addicted, with the Mexican cartels simply losing their customer base.

One spring night, years ago, Jaguar walked through the Templo Mayor Archeological Zone in Mexico City. The glories of his country's pre-colonial past still captivated him, much as it had as a boy. He marveled at how the city had grown over the ancient sites, and how people had unknowingly walked atop the sites of rituals and sacrifices for centuries. Only a random discovery in 1978, while digging a subway tunnel, uncovered this long-forgotten chapter of his ancestors.

He strolled past the excavations of the twin temples—one to Huitzilopochtli, the god of war, and to Tlaloc, the god of rain or water. He paused at the tzompantli shrine or wall of skulls—a stone square of rows arranged with carvings of human skulls. A stone eagle represented Huitzilopochtli; devoted followers would bring human hearts and place them before the giant bird.

Models within the museum depicted the complex in ancient times, including a spire in the center devoted to worship of Quetzalcoatl, the feathered serpent sky god.

He exited the museum and walked toward the Museum of the Ministry of Finance and Public Credit—an awkward name for an art museum, one that recognized the building's previous occupant. Before that, it was owned by the Church. Some of the artwork and artifacts within the museum paid tribute to what stood atop that spot before the church's arrival: the Temple to Tezcatlipoca.

Both young Juan Comillo and adult Jaguar felt a chill and bit of excitement at the thought of the Aztec God Tezcatlipoca, whose name translated to "Smoking Mirror." Smoking Mirror was the deity no mortal dared disrespect. He was the punisher, the arbitrary, the dark, the powerful, the merciless. His realms and symbols communicated pure intimidation: the night sky, obsidian, discord, war, the color black, and of course . . . jaguars.

Outsiders oversimplified Smoking Mirror as a devil character, Jaguar thought. He was also the deity of beauty, temptation, sorcery, and the change that comes from conflict. He was everything strange and terrifying about the world to the Aztec people, yet the world could not have such beauty, peace, growth, and change without the forces he represented. Smoking Mirror was not a benevolent, distant, smiling old man in the sky. He was a deity for modern adults—mysterious, occasionally cruel, demanding, unforgiving, and caring not one whit about how human beings treated one another. Juan Comillo saw little or no sign of the Christian God in the world, but Smoking Mirror's fingerprints were all over it.

And then, standing there, above the site of Smoking Mirror's temple that night, Jaguar had a vision that filled him with adrenaline. Suddenly, he wasn't standing in Mexico City and the modern day. It was some future time—Jaguar couldn't tell if it was just a few years away or generations from that moment—when all of the buildings around him were covered in ornate carvings of the Aztec gods.

Directly in front of Jaguar, the Museum of the Ministry of Finance and Public Credit would be gone, and a new temple to Smoking Mirror stood in its place. He turned its head. Mexico City Cathedral, a block away, was torn down and replaced as well; the new temple stretched out more than twice the length of the Plaza de Constitution. With walls of black obsidian, shining and lit by torches, the pyramid rose over the rest of the city, with all of the other temples of Templo Mayor restored as well. But Smoking Mirror's was the largest—and indisputably the most important. He heard chanting within and could smell blood. Where the Cathedral's entrance had once stood was a pit—a giant circle, lined with a complete circle of human skulls. And directly beneath that circle was another. And another. And another, hundreds, and Jaguar could not see the bottom from where he stood. He knew that many had opposed the rise of this new order—and their eyeless skulls and open jaws would stare out from that pit forever, a warning to anyone who dared oppose the country's new Aztec regime.

Jaguar knew that in that future moment, whether it was a year or a generation away, Smoking Mirror would no longer be this forgotten legend, confined to storybooks and archaeology textbooks. He and the other Aztec Gods were real, restored to their central role in the life of his countrymen, steering the people on their path, and bestowing protection upon the followers who made the appropriate sacrifices.

The vision ended, and Jaguar looked around, noticing strange looks from several people in the square, pointing and whispering to one another. He looked at himself, everything seemed normal. An old vendor finally approached and asked if he felt okay. Jaguar nodded affirmative and asked why the old man had asked. The vendor, keeping his distance, said that Jaguar had been staring at the museum, unmoving and unresponsive, for about fifteen minutes. Jaguar sheepishly apologized and moved on, ready to burst from excitement about his vision.

He chuckled the whole way home. American Chicano activists in the 1960s and 1970s had spoken of "Aztlan"—the name of the ancestral home of the Aztecs—to refer to the lands of Northern Mexico taken by the United States in the Mexican-American War. They had begun a largely fruitless movement claiming all of the American Southwest and West and either returning it to Mexico or forming an independent state. Despite leadership conferences and campus protests by groups such as MEChA, the Movimiento Estudiantil Chicano de Aztlán, not much had come of it, other than a resolution renaming the group Movimiento Estudiantil Chican@ de Aztlán, after concluding that the term "Chicano" was gender-exclusionary.

What Jaguar saw in his vision was not Aztlán, a silly crusade of hapless activists, trying to persuade prosperous Latino Americans to secede from the world's superpower and align themselves with a chaotic basket case of nation. What he saw was a strong, orderly, prosperous, culturally ascendant society that was the envy of its neighbors—one that would make the like-minded and - blooded to petition to join Restaurada Imperio Azteca—the Restored Aztec Empire.

Jaguar only told a few people about his vision, and other than Esmerelda, no one believed he had seen the future—even after archaeologists discovered another, bigger rack of skulls while excavating a courtyard behind Mexico City Cathedral in 2015. In years of work, the archaeologists had uncovered thousands of skulls of men, women, and children. The accounts of the Conquistadors described towers of skulls, displaying more than 100,000 human sacrifices, but historians had concluded that those were mythical, or at most a wild exaggeration. Now the historians were not so sure.

Jaguar had done considerable work for the Zeta cartel in recent years, finding the men they sought, and ensuring the men they wanted to disappear were never found. Working with them, he knew the best ways into the United States. He knew the drug trade inside and out and could navigate the dangerous waters of freelancing and territorial disputes. Better to remain a free agent, for hire to anyone, enjoying the fruits of a reputation as a quiet, thoroughly professional operator. The work had brought him considerable creature comforts, such as his luxury condo and boat, and now, a strikingly attractive girlfriend, Esmerelda. Everyone mistook her for a model or actress, but Jaguar knew she was like him, a survivor. Most other men were entranced by her eyes, her lips, her cleavage; it all distracted from her true nature that was more akin to a coiled cobra.

Jaguar built up a reputation as a thorough professional, usually quiet, until an employer asked or provided an opening for his seemingly crazy ideas of bringing the United States to its knees through a drug smuggler work stoppage, or the Mexican government and Catholic Church someday being replaced by the return of the Aztec Empire and its ancient gods.

He continually studied the art of leverage, intimidation, and interrogation. He saw what men did when exposed to 3-quinuclidinyl benzilate—the banned chemical weapon Agent

15, rumored to be available from the right unscrupulous source in either Libya or what was left of Syria. He learned "infrasound"—sounds lower in frequency than 20 hertz per second—could instill a prisoner with anxiety, dread, and fear. (One theory suggested that the sound wave hitting the cornea created false or illusory visions out the corner of the eye, leading to ghost sightings.) The discontinued drug Compazine, designed to treat schizophrenia, could induce panic attacks in certain patients.

He learned which drugs could make a man talk and which ones could silence him forever.

He learned his effective work using these materials had attracted the interest of someone named "Akoman." Hezbollah vouched for him to the Zetas; the Zetas reached out to Jaguar. Akoman apparently was quite generous with his finder's fee.

Jaguar met him nearly a year ago. Akoman waited for him in a Mexico City café, unbothered by the early summer heat.

Akoman was tall and lean, with a long, tan face, and black mustache and goatee. Jaguar had a hard time nailing down his age—late thirties? Forties? A well-kept fifty? He could be Turkish, Iranian, Armenian, or Azeri, Jaguar calculated. If Hezbollah had vouched for him, he had to be Iranian, he concluded.

Akoman rose and gracefully removed a white trilby—a narrow-rimmed fedora—revealing a shaved head. He wore a collared short-sleeved shirt with a black-and-white zigzag pattern and tan khakis—just stylish enough in the café they had chosen for their meeting but not too much.

"You come highly recommended," Akoman said in English, and Jaguar suspected from his accent that his potential employer had been educated in a British school.

After both men had exchanged pleasantries, Akoman asked Jaguar if, given basic health information about the target, he could engineer a dose of a drug that would quickly induce a panic attack. The pair discussed dosage and delivery methods. Jaguar didn't ask the target's identity, just age, body mass, known allergies, general state of health, and so on. He answered the questions honestly, pointing out that physiology and pharmacology were complicated subjects, and that even expert doctors couldn't guarantee a particular reaction.

Akoman had brought some of his own research—translated, Jaguar surmised from the grammar and phrasing. Akoman wanted to give a dose to a fifty-some male, Caucasian, between two hundred and two hundred fifty pounds, no known health ailments beyond potential hypertension from a stressful lifestyle. The great challenge, Akoman finally elaborated, was that this was not an interrogation. The target had to be given the drug secretly and unknowingly in a public place. There wouldn't be a second chance.

Their conversations continued, gradually elaborating on potential options. Akoman generously compensated Jaguar for every "consulting session." They concluded their best chance of cooking up a drug to achieve Akoman's goal would require a pharmacological specialist. A bit of web searching turned up an aging hippie who promoted recreational use of LSD and other hallucinogens.

Akoman had a spectacularly simple method for secure communications. He was wary about electronic communications, e-mail, texting, even using the phone. He said he was familiar with the far-reaching methods of America's National Security Agency and preferred the ultimate in low-tech evasion: the postage system.

"Mail can be read," Jaguar cautioned. "It is not unheard of in my country, or the United States for that matter, for someone to open your mail."

"Oh, I prefer postcards," Akoman chuckled. "Let them read. If you seem to have nothing to hide, no one cares."

So they communicated by postcard, offering regular updates, using general language about "the weather," "meetings," "friends," and how the "medication" was working. When things had to be more specific, they used a pictogram of doodles in the margins. Jaguar, the trained intelligence professional, marveled at the effectiveness of hiding in plain sight. As far as he could tell, their communications never metaphorically pinged the radar screens of any intelligence or law enforcement agency. Their postcards just swam in the schools of junk mail fish.

Months later, Akoman and Jaguar acquired their pharmacological specialist, and after initial difficulties, he proved sufficiently motivated to assist them. Jaguar met Akoman's associate—a remarkably quiet, short gentleman who went by the name Azi Dhaka. After they had acquired their "panic in a jar," Jaguar helped Dhaka across the border, where he disappeared, as scheduled, in Houston. Jaguar offered a great deal of advice about how to operate within the United States without running into local law enforcement, and Dhaka merely listened intently, nodded, and offered a curt "thank you." Jaguar began to suspect Akoman and Dhaka knew almost everything they needed to know already.

CHAPTER 23

At Langley, Acting Director Richard Mitchell had actually used the term "all hands on deck" in his first address to CIA employees. But several long days of research proved surprisingly fruitless. Every available staffer within the Agency's walls spent the day reviewing previous intelligence files for anything resembling the actions of the group now called Atarsa. So far Atarsa seemed sui generis—borrowing bits and pieces of ideas and methods from a wide variety of past terror groups, and then executing a spectacularly high-profile method of communicating threats to the American public.

Much to the confusion of the analysts, Atarsa hadn't yet followed up their initial threatening message with attacks on Smith, Johnson, Williams, Brown, and Jones. Some argued that this indicated that the group had an initial plan, but something had gone wrong. Others wondered if Director Peck was a target of opportunity for the group. But the Deputy Director of Analysis pointed out that a plot to successfully poison a CIA director required exceptional planning and resources. Peck's toxicology report came back with some traces of 3-quinuclidinyl benzilate, but the medical analysis suggested he had been hit by some sort of new, intense hallucinogen. The scribbled notes in Francis Neuse's diary offered some intriguing avenues of investigation for the medical staff treating Peck, who was gradually becoming calmer and more lucid with each passing day.

Despite their recovery of Neuse's diary, Raquel's group was repeatedly told by the Terrorist Threat Integration Center, the International Operations Center, the Directorate of Operations, the Seventh Floor, and the FBI's Joint Terrorism Task Force to shut up and go away. Politely.

CHAPTER 24

MONDAY, MARCH 22

That night Alec dreamed he was being chased by owls and snakes that flew through the air. But sleep did the trick; the subconscious mind sorted through his chaotic visions and experiences of recent days and he awoke at four a.m., inexplicably energized and inspired.

Alec got dressed, kissed Katrina as she slept, then hopped into his car. Within twenty minutes he was bursting through the office door.

He found Dee sleeping in her cubicle, a windbreaker upon her chest as a blanket. *Her husband must be an exceptionally patient man*, he thought. Then again, a little workaholism was a small price to pay for life with a bubbly blond curvaceous genius. For about ten seconds, he watched her sleep. The excited look on his face faded a bit; he studied her closed eyes and knew she deserved rest for her relentless work in the past weeks. He departed the office, went down the hall, and returned a few minutes later with two cups of *meh*-at-best coffee, quickly brewed in the office machine. He gently jostled her arm.

"Dee! Dee! Wake up! I've got it!" She awoke with a start, looked around in panic for a moment, then realized where she was and that it was Alec. He held up the cup of coffee.

"I'll get you a cappuccino when Starbucks opens in a few hours," he apologized in advance. She sipped and winced, but the quick shot of caffeine got a few more neurons to snap into place and start connecting.

"I'm running every search algorithm I can on the NSA intercepts for the past six months," she began. "We're talking an ungodly amount of data—"

Alec held up his hands in a *stop* motion and grinned with pride. "We may not need all that. We've got the best clue of all. Neuse."

"What?"

"The dead guy we found on the island. The NSA has a backdoor into Google searches, right?"

It was if someone had flipped a switch; Dee reverted to rote public relations rhetoric. "Alec," she said, straightening her posture. "You know that sort of baseless allegation from scurrilous foreign intelligence disinformation operations and their puppets is vehemently denied by the intelligence community. The PRISM system is operated in complete accordance with all relevant US laws—"

Alec waived his hand. "Yeah, yeah, and there's no Area 51, all the witnesses saw was the planet Venus and swamp gas and a weather balloon, and the secretary will disavow all knowledge of your actions. Listen, we need to know anyone who googled Francis Neuse in the three months before his kidnapping." Alec had already checked on his home laptop before heading to work; Neuse's public profile had virtually dried up in the years since Timothy Leary died.

She nodded. "I can do that, but... he was still a semi-public figure. You're probably going to get, I don't know, dozens of people, maybe hundreds."

"And how many people who used a particular computer to run a Google search on Neuse would also be doing similar research into pharmacology, fear-inducing drugs, that sort of thing? Maybe even looking for a remote island on Google Maps?"

Her eyebrows shot up. "Significantly fewer."

"And what happens if you match anything you find with the financial information we found for 'J.C. Lopez'?"

Dee blinked, and suddenly looked irritated. "You have no idea how embarrassed I am that you thought of this first."

CHAPTER 25

Jaguar was certain he wasn't being led into a trap. But that didn't mean he felt particularly secure in his decision to accept Akoman's invitation to meet, halfway across the globe.

Turkmenistan was the North Korea of Central Asia. If it were not for the country's enormous oil and natural gas reserves, the country's entire paranoid kleptocracy would have come crashing down years ago. Citizens received free gasoline, and certain sectors of the economy boomed, thanks to giant contracts with Russia, China, and Iran. The country's abundant resources reached the Caspian Sea through canals.

But for most of the country, that free gas came at a steep price. Controlled by Moscow during the Cold War, citizens of Turkmenistan somehow missed out on any genuine liberation after the Soviet Union collapsed. Sure, independence arrived in 1991, but the country just replaced the oppression of communism with a thoroughly bonkers cult of personality. The Communist Party changed its name to the Democratic Party of Turkmenistan and maintained the same monopoly on all government power. There was no press freedom, routine oppression of activists and antigovernment speech and little to no outside scrutiny. Some argued that Turkmenistan welcomed fewer foreign visitors than any other country in the world.

The country had just two presidents since 1985—first Saparmurat Niyazov, who guided the country from despotic Communist rule to his despotic independent rule, and his successor, Gurbanguly Berdymukhamedov. Jaguar wondered if he had been named when a bag of Scrabble letters spilled in random order.

Niyazov and Berdymukhamedov weren't relentlessly barbaric or cruel, but they had some infamous moments. In 2005, Niyazov exercised his dictatorial power by closing all hospitals outside the capital and all rural libraries. Sometimes the pair were just weird, such as their shared pride that the capital city featured more white marble buildings, memorials, and sculptures than anywhere else on earth. When the sculptures weren't marble, they were gold; an enormous golden statue of the president greeted visitors, a twisted mirror-universe version of the Statue of Liberty.

Jaguar was on guard as a foreign national entering a country with a paranoid, unpredictable state security system. Akoman had assured him repeatedly that he would be treated with every conceivable hospitality during his visit.

Turkmenistan practiced "permanent neutrality" in all foreign affairs—although the government was sometimes flexible in its definition of neutrality. Their most important decision in the past decades was letting the United States use Ashgabat Airport for refueling and shipping supplies into Afghanistan. But a long border with Iran ensured the regime felt the need for good relations with Tehran, as well. Jaguar increasingly suspected that Akoman had friends in high places in both Turkmenistan and Iran.

Jaguar knew his fake passports were as good as they got—that is, authentic ones, duplicate identities he had created at CISN, meaning he legally existed under a half-dozen names in Mexico's census. Once the border patrol officer at the visa counter checked his name, he waved over porters and treated him like a distinguished guest. A driver was waiting for him, and he was rapidly ushered into downtown on roads that seemed surprisingly empty for a capital city.

Jaguar checked into the similarly eerily quiet luxury hotel downtown and took a lengthy nap.

Within a few hours, Jaguar's jet lag had passed. Akoman's postcard had left a clear schedule for his trip out of the city. He drove in a prearranged rental car north of the city, into the vast Karakum Desert. Akoman's last postcard told him to head down this road; his destination, their meeting place, was described simply, "you will know it when you see it."

Late afternoon turned to dusk, and then Jaguar finally saw it... on the horizon, the left side of the road seemed to be on fire.

As he approached, he realized it was a circle of glowing fire—a giant crater. Jaguar wondered if he had somehow stumbled on a meteorite strike. As he drove closer, he realized the circle burned perfectly, with more fires burning within the crater. No smoke, though, which was strange. And then the smell hit him. Sulfur.

No one remembered exactly how the Darvaza crater was formed, but the most common story was that a Soviet drilling team had been exploring, searching for oil, and had found a pocket of natural gas. It turned out to be a bubble, and the drilling rig sank into the hole. The Soviets saw the pit filling with methane and noxious gases and lit it to burn it off... and the crater just kept on burning. All through the night, the next day... and for the next forty years.

The crater was massive—225 feet wide and about 100 feet deep. The heat, if one stood close enough, could cause blisters. Even at night, the area seemed surprisingly well lit, as if a thousand tiny campfires burned around the circle. As Jaguar got out of the car, he heard it—the roar, like a jet engine, all of these high-pressure gas-burning plumes burning simultaneously. Yet there was no smoke; the air shimmered with heat distortions.

The endlessly burning crater was unique and had been, until a few years back, a bit of a tourist attraction with nicknames like "the Pit of Fire" and "the Gates of Hell." A combination of

Turkmeni government paranoia and terrorist threats against Americans traveling abroad had slowly choked off the flow of tourists. Jaguar stood, transfixed, mystified, impressed, until he sensed figures approaching the darkness beyond the crater.

Akoman waved. Another man stood behind him, only partially illuminated by the light of the flames.

"Welcome, my friend," Akoman said.

Jaguar nodded.

"You remember my associate Azi Dhaka," Akoman said. Jaguar nodded and Akoman offered a bit of a chuckle. "Now you see why I felt quite confident you would have no problem finding this place."

"This is an amazing place," Jaguar said, squinting as a wave of heat and a gust of wind brought more sulfur smell.

"They called it the Gates of Hell. Perhaps that is fitting, considering what we will bring to our enemies. Come, we have a tent upwind."

It was a long walk into the desert to their tent, the light of the flame crater behind them, seeming to head into pitch black, the dry, salty sand crunching underneath their feet. Then a tent was opened, revealing light within; Jaguar wondered how his hosts could so easily operate in such complete darkness. Waiting inside was a beautiful woman—well, her eyes seemed beautiful behind the sheer veil. One of the ornate lanterns within the tent had green glass, and for a split second, the woman looked otherworldly, as if her skin were green or scaled. After a moment, Jaguar's eyes adjusted, and her skin appeared normal, tan, quite beautiful.

"This is Angra Druj," Akoman said, without further elaboration. She nodded a silent greeting and removed her veil. Jaguar tried not to stare and failed. Jet black hair, dark eyes, full lips—he guessed she was Lebanese. The folds of her robe loosened slightly, revealing she wore something shiny and taut across her curves, so tight she seemed to have been sewn into it. He had not expected his generous Iranian employer to be lounging with a serpentine supermodel.

Once inside the tent, Jaguar's hosts offered him tea. They discussed their recent travels and went over the details of their recent operations, any potential mistakes or opportunities for their foes to detect them.

"Jaguar, you have proven quite helpful to our endeavors," Akoman said. "Our efforts will be entering a new stage quite soon. Your assistance will not be forgotten. Besides your financial compensation, we invited you to get a sense of your . . . other interests and plans. Our mutual friends mentioned you were a man of bold vision."

Jaguar reacted with pleasant surprise. The only person who had ever asked to hear more about his radical proposal to win the drug war was Esmerelda.

He laid out how he envisioned the cartel "work stoppage" would lead to chaos in America's cities, and how the US government would be forced to accept an unimpeded drug pipeline to its citizens. Akoman, Azi Dhaka, and Angra Druj listened quietly, smiling, nodding, but never quite giving Jaguar a good sense of what they really thought. When he finished, there was a long moment of awkward silence.

"That," Akoman finally said, "is brilliant."

CHAPTER 26

MONDAY, MARCH 22

Within a few hours, the NSA had identified one Google user whose search history matched someone planning a kidnapping of Francis Neuse. A traceroute command identified the IP address. The user had made a fairly good effort to mask his actual location, but his technology was at least one upgrade out of date. (The NSA had already logged the IP address when the user there searched for information about anonymizing services. Yes, if you express interest in hiding your web activity from the National Security Agency, they are automatically alerted to the fact that you don't want them to know what you're doing.) Subsequent searches included research into nickel-carbon material, the kind that one would use to build a homemade SCIF that would be impenetrable from the usual forms of electronic surveillance.

The result was that the NSA stated, with ninety-four percent certainty, that the searches about Neuse came from a laptop computer connected to the Internet via a private wireless connection in a fourth-floor luxury condominium in Mexico City, right on the border of the neighborhoods of Coapa and Xochimilco. That was Mexico City's southern borough, full of relative greenery and not far from an ecological park full of polluted canals.

The condo was registered to Juan Lopez, a self-employed "contractor." A cursory search of his finances with various banks in Mexican banks found significant resources, nine accounts in separate banks with a little less than $100,000 in each account.

***

By midday, Raquel had begun wondering just what Dee had meant with her hastily scrawled "Had to run to Fort Meade, be back soon" Post-it note on her door, and where Alec was.

The sound of music in the bull pen of cubicles outside her office offered some answers. She emerged from her office and was treated to the sight of Alec and Dee dancing in front of the door to her office, waving around the printed-out documents confirming that "J.C. Lopez," the figure who had financed and organized the kidnapping of Francis Neuse, was in fact Mexican citizen Juan Lopez.

"I can't wait to catch this guy," Raquel deadpanned. "Then we can really punish him by making him watch you dance."

Both Alec and Dee simply danced more outrageously.

"Even if Juan Lopez is an alias, we now have a passport photo, address, and bank accounts to go with that alias," Alec beamed. He held up his hand for a high-five. "NSA tracks 'em, CIA whacks 'em."

Dee left him hanging for a moment, then relented. "I cannot believe I didn't think of the Google search." She smacked his hand. They turned to Raquel.

Raquel nodded and smiled. "Spastic dancing aside, this is good work." She entered her office, and they followed, uninvited. Raquel furrowed her brow and recognized an expectant look in Alec's eyes.

"What I *should* do is pass this to Mexico City station and let them begin an effort to track down Juan Lopez, but you're going to flip out and tell me not to do that, aren't you, Alec?" Raquel asked.

They finally stopped dancing. Alec closed the door.

"Well, if the alleged mole everybody's whispering about is in Mexico City station, Juan Lopez is just going to disappear, isn't he?" Alec asked. "And even if there isn't a mole in that station, the list of people we can trust down there is short. We've both read the NIEs on Mexico." He was referring to the CIA's National Intelligence Estimates, comprehensive studies of a country's interal problems and possible threats. "It's Cartel-istan, with practically the entire government compromised. The only reason the drug lords haven't formally taken over is they don't want the aggravation of trying to run the public pension programs."

Dee nodded. "I hate to indulge Alec's usually baseless paranoia, but if you tell Mexico City station, there's no guarantee they won't tell someone in the Mexic—"

Raquel held up her hand and put a finger to her mouth, and Alec stopped. Raquel rose from her desk seat, walked to the door and opened it.

Ward was directly behind it.

"Stop trying to eavesdrop and just come in," she said. She looked beyond him. "Katrina!"

Katrina entered, and the quartet stood before her. Alec excitedly explained how he and Dee had figured out that J.C. Lopez was Juan Lopez, but Katrina interrupted him and put a finger to his mouth. She picked up the printout of the passport photo.

"This is Juan Lopez?" she asked. Dee nodded. Katrina closed her eyes.

"Café Vernunft, Berlin, about two weeks ago," she said slowly. "I was talking with Rat. This man was sitting two tables down from us." She tapped the photo. "He was wearing a Fenerbaçhe jacket."

She opened her eyes again, having concluded her séance with her own memory. Alec grinned madly.

"That's my girl!" he cheered, pumping his fist in the air. "Just identified the Berlin bomber!" He turned to Raquel, who was folding her arms.

"Let me guess, you want me to send you four to Mexico to find this guy."

"I wouldn't mind running into him again," Katrina said quietly. "He's got a lot of blood on his hands."

"Whoa, whoa, whoa, I'm not going to Mexico!" Dee exclaimed, shaking her head. "Snake Island was bad enough. I belong behind a keyboard."

Alec nodded. "Dee can help us more back here. But we're the ones who tracked him down. We found Francis Neuse. We have momentum."

"Only Katrina speaks Spanish," Raquel pointed out.

"Yo hablo Espanol!" Alec said indignantly. Dee's skeptical guffaw didn't help his case.

"We can be on a flight tomorrow morning. We get into his place, collect everything we can, and *then* tell Mexico City station and the Mexican government. No worries about them withholding any useful intelligence that way."

CHAPTER 27

TUESDAY, MARCH 23

Jaguar was relieved to return to Mexico City. After the first night in Turkmenistan, Jaguar half-jokingly wondered if the trio of Akoman, Angra Druj, and Azi Dhaka were some sort of aliens who had read extensively about how to host a human being but had never actually done it before. They were respectful and indisputably generous hosts, but something about them seemed off. The would pause midsentence when speaking, then exchange long looks to each other that seemed to replace spoken communication.

Once the trio elaborated on their ambitious plans, he understood why he was being brought into their confidence. He had been flattered that they hadn't laughed at his plan to force Americans to submit to the cartels, and he treated their blueprint to shake American society to its core with similar respect. If they pulled it off—and it appeared the American security agencies had barely amounted to a speed bump so far—Akoman and his gang would shove America's social fabric into a wood chipper. The trio seemed to recognize they were asking him to take a greater risk and kept offering cash incentives to keep his border-crossing services at the ready.

He had returned to his condo and begun unpacking his clothes—including one outfit still stinking of sulfur from the nights by the flaming crater in the desert.

He couldn't wait to touch Esmerelda again. She was quickly rising in the ranks of the local all-female gang, Las Calaveras, the "sister gang" of Los Craneos. As the Craneos were expanding their power and reach, they had turned to Las Calaveras to manage some of their existing drug-related operations and neighborhood surveillance. But Jaguar had asked her to help oversee his "special project" in São Paulo. She had hated her one visit to the island and left other trusted associates with the skull masks to interrogate and intimidate Neuse.

Esmerelda was on her way back from there, and he found himself feeling impatient. The first time she had visited Brazil, Esmerelda had returned with a Carnival costume and given him a one-woman carnal parade that night. His Turkmenistan trip proved exhausting by the time he finished, and he found the locals cold, prudish, and suspicious. He felt like it had been far too long since he had gazed upon exposed midriffs, short shorts, plunging cleavage, or other examples of fashionable flaunting by Mexico City women that brightened his day.

He had been distracted, picturing Esmerelda in ever more elaborate outfits when his phone buzzed with a text. Ah, finally, Esmerelda!

He checked his phone and immediately swore. The text from Esmerelda read "9999."

He threw his sulfur-smelling clothes in the closet. He went to a wall safe behind a picture frame and removed a backpack, full of cash of varying currencies, several passports, and two burner phones. He put one of his guns in his back of his pants, hidden by his jacket, and strapped another into his ankle holster. He opened up a foot locker in his closet, removed a gym bag, and hoisted it over his shoulder. Within three minutes, he was out the door, locking it, and heading to the street, unsure if he would ever return to his condo.

He took the stairs, waved to Manuel the condominium doorman, and headed down the street, slowed only slightly by the weight of the backpack and gym bag. To anyone else, Esmerelda's text looked like an accidental butt-dial. Jaguar knew four nines meant trouble. He headed to their prearranged rendezvous point, a trendily faux-downscale cantina a few blocks away.

***

For as long as she could remember, people told Esmerelda that she was beautiful. It was a blessing early in life, growing up in one of Mexico City's poorest and roughest neighborhoods, but by her earliest moments of puberty she realized how mixed that blessing could be. Beauty guaranteed a man's head would turn, but all too often, they had harsh tempers, raised hands, and malevolence in their hearts. She learned to fight at an early age. She had stabbed three men by the time she was sixteen.

Juan the Jaguar was different. Most men she encountered—brutes, thugs, creeps—were painfully simple. Juan had layers. She had seen his public face—ruthless, cold, all-business. In Mexico City's underworld, full of machismo and boasts and threats, Juan was quiet, using no more words than the moment required. Juan's reputation demonstrated he could afford to be a gentleman; he didn't need to brag because his work spoke for itself. Fist, knife, gun—whatever you came at Juan with, he was faster and would leave you bleeding on the floor.

Esmerelda found Juan's second layer familiar, but hilarious and endearing because it contrasted so completely with the first. Once alone with her, Juan the Jaguar would drop his ruthless, predator-of-the-night pose and offer almost goofy purple-prose poetry about how mad her beauty drove him. Sometimes he would be romantic, sometimes wildly, hilariously perverse. She inevitably laughed at how the man who had earlier in the day ruthlessly strangled a police informant would spend the evening kissing her behind and talking directly to it, talking about how he had spent the afternoon trying to decide if he liked the left cheek or right cheek better.

But what really attracted Esmerelda to Juan was his sense of mission. He had shared his plan for the cartels, his love of Aztec mythology, his sense that the Smoking Mirror had given him a vision of their country restored to power and greatness. She had shared with him her own beliefs, a devotion to Santa Muerte, "Saint Death," the Saint of Last Resort. Usually depicted as the Virgin of Guadalupe with a skull for a face, Santa Muerte offered her followers protection, blessings, and deliverance of vengeance in exchange for sacrifices—poured alcohol, blown marijuana smoke, blood, and body parts of enemies or those who doubted or rejected her. To many outsiders, the cult of Santa Muerte sounded twisted, but it hadn't taken long for it to become the fastest growing faith in Mexico, a favorite of cartels and those victimized by them. The Catholic Church denounced the worship of her as heresy, but that had only fueled her curiosity.

Juan the Jaguar said he didn't partake of Santa Muerte rituals; he thought but didn't dare tell his love that he saw it as a Catholic perversion of the pure Aztec rituals. But she wondered if Santa Muerte was already protecting him and guiding him.

Some fool had tried to rob Esmerelda and Juan the Jaguar, about a year ago. He emerged from an alley, raised the cheapest, oldest pistol imaginable, but didn't even have time to demand their money. Neither she nor the assailant saw the knife or where it came from—Juan's hand rose to the attacker's neck and suddenly his jugular was spraying, everything turning red. The gun dropped from his hand. He collapsed and stared, wide eyed, wondering how Juan could have had such a knife hidden in a sleeve or pocket. It was only two and a half inches, but its thick, dark, kukri-like curve was perfectly sharp, built for gasp-inducing, intense puncturing power. The tip of the blade worked through the front of his neck like it was nothing.

The attacker was down, dying before him, but Juan wasn't finished. He didn't say anything, but Esmerelda could see from the rage in his eyes that he intended to make an example of his attacker. He began hacking away at his chest, turning it to a crimson mess. The last gasp of life left the assailant, eyes still staring at the sky, face frozen in shock, mouth open in a silent scream. Then with his bare hand, Jaguar tore out a chunk of flesh, leaving the heart exposed. Another round of hacking. And then, with witnesses still staring in horror and disbelief, he pried the attacker's heart out with his knife. He held it up for everyone to see.

No one thought of intervening. No one even dared scream. Residents who had seen fights and beatings and shots fired found Jaguar's rough justice horrifying and mesmerizing. He made a full circle, blood dripping from the heart in his hand, staring at the assembled crowd, and almost daring anyone to object. Then he dropped the heart, gave Esmerelda a look, and they made a quick exit from the scene.

They didn't need to rush. No one dared call the police. It was an hour before a cop saw the body in the street and began the slow process of removing it.

***

Juan sat, nursing his drink in a corner booth of the cantina. He knew that Esmerelda would not send another text. He had taught her that the NSA could catch just about anything typed or spoken into a phone; no matter what trouble had come, she was not to elaborate any key details electronically. The seemingly innocent butt-dial "9999" was their signal for trouble, most likely law enforcement. If police had arrested Esmerelda, he would likely know soon, a discreet message from any of the local and national police he bribed intermittently, or some of his old friends in CISN.

Finally, she entered, wearing a low-cut black top, tight jeans, and boots. He knew she was trying to be subdued—no red lipstick, none of her preferred jewelry, her long black hair pulled back into a ponytail. It didn't matter much; men's heads still inevitably turned as she walked through the bar. Juan couldn't help but chuckle. Her irrepressible sexuality often ruined his efforts to not stand out in a crowd, but her pleasures were too good to pass up.

They removed the batteries from their phones—Juan had heard how the phones could be turned on remotely and used as eavesdropping and recording devices—and she leaned in close. She offered a brief kiss, and Juan swore at their troubles for disrupting what should have been a passionate reunion.

"Terrible news from São Paulo," she whispered in Spanish. "The Brazilian Navy escorted an American team to the island."

Jaguar's face hardened. Up until now, everything had run smoothly, although the imprisonment and intimidation of Neuse seemed to be generating diminishing returns. Neuse's long history of experimental recreational pharmacology had left him twitchy, eccentric, and unpredictable even before the abduction. Several months of extreme isolation, punctuated with intermittent terrifying death threats by captors in skull masks and the constant threat of fatal snakebites had shaken his sanity like a snow globe.

After two minutes of carefully looking around the room, Jaguar concluded they were not being watched—or at least surreptitiously. Men were still stealing glances at Esmerelda.

"Americans... There's a big difference if they found a crazy man or a corpse," he concluded.

"Even if he's not dead, our friends said he was acting crazier each time they went out there," she said. Esmerelda didn't want to be naïve or optimistic, but she felt Santa Muerte wouldn't let misfortune wreck their lives so suddenly. "You said the old man hadn't generated anything useful since the first sample."

Jaguar nodded. Once it became clear that not even Neuse could construct a functional fear drug that could be dispersed as an aerosol, they settled for the next best thing, a powder that when added to ingested liquid that could trigger a panic attack. After the last visit, a month ago, Jaguar determined he didn't need to see Neuse anymore. The plan had been to leave him with just enough food and water to sustain him to the next visit; he would have to earn more by generating results.

"Testing the panic syrup on the man who created it was probably a mistake," Jaguar conceded.

He drummed his fingers against the table. Could this be from Akoman's work already? On the plane, he had seen the news coverage of America on high alert for terror attacks.

No, Jaguar thought, it was not a coincidence.

The drumming fingers made a fist.

"We have to assume those Americans have Neuse, and that he's told them everything."

"He's a crazy old man, no one will listen to his stories of being abducted by the devil and his demons." Esmerelda cooed, attempting to calm Jaguar's building frustration. He calmed slightly, put his hand on hers, and wondered if she understood which particular kind of frustration was bedeviling him the most at that moment.

"Countries are run by crazy old men," Jaguar shook his head. "They may believe him, they may not, but for now we must proceed as if everything has been compromised. I can't go back to the condo for a while. Stay away from your home, too. We'll use the little place in Tepito." It was a barely furnished dump, but it would suffice for carnal relief, he concluded. "Tell Las Calaveras I want them to watch the neighborhood around my place in

Xochimilco, look for any Americans snooping around. And tell them to get rid of the skull makeup."

"They'll never give that up," Esmerelda said skeptically.

"Theatrical flair is going to catch up to them someday," he said. She laughed, and he watched her tongue in her mouth.

"Considering your favorite mask, that's ironic," she teased.

Jaguar put a hand on the gym bag by his feet. Damn it all, he thought. He was supposed to be having acrobatic sex with Esmerelda in his bedroom right now. He had covered his tracks, used every precaution, and none of it mattered. Now he would have to watch his back, wondering what American intelligence knew.

CHAPTER 28

XOCHIMILCO
MEXICO CITY, MEXICO
WEDNESDAY, MARCH 24

Alec and Katrina had not been to Mexico City in more than a decade; their last trip had been passing through to a wedding of friends. The intervening years had not been kind to the sprawling mega-metropolis, now the largest city in North America.

One in four Mexico City residents reported being the victim of a violent crime in the past year—a mugging, home invasion, assault, or threat. Less than eight percent had gone to the police, believing that the police would do nothing, or victimize them again. Some locals believed that even those abominable statistics understated the scope of the problem; somehow the official numbers recorded only sixty or so kidnappings within Mexico City in the past year while the prosecutor's office claimed to have investigated about eighty during the same time period. The rate of "express kidnappings" had increased dramatically; a cab driver or other seemingly benign figure would brandish a weapon and make the victim go to an ATM and withdraw the maximum allowed. These "kidnappings" usually lasted only a few hours; some managed to escape their captors and flee. Particularly shrewd thieves kidnapped a victim close to midnight, so that they could force the victim to withdraw the daily maximum from the

ATM just before midnight, and then a second time again after a new day had begun. The few victims who did report their crimes to the police usually said the investigative process treated them as if they were the criminals.

Overall, the crime rating for Mexico City was "critical" with the State Department's travel warning cheerfully informing visitors, "beheadings, lynching, torture, and other gruesome displays of violence as well as high numbers of forced disappearances have become routine occurrences in various parts of the country, including the Mexico City metropolitan area." The list of recommended security precautions included, "Replace two lug nuts on each wheel with specially keyed bolts that locks or can only be removed with a special attachment to the tire iron."

"They will steal your tires," Alec shook his head.

Katrina shrugged. "In the Soviet Union, people stole windshield wipers for the rubber."

Ward couldn't stifle his laughter at the State Department warning. "'Although Mexico employs strict gun-control laws, criminals are usually armed with handguns,'" he read aloud. "Gee, it's almost like those gun control laws don't work, huh?"

Before getting on the Dulles-to-Mexico-City flight, Katrina had assigned Dee to look into the banking and other electronic records of any staff of the targeted building, hoping to find an indication that someone took bribes. Dee said she found something almost as good, flirty texts between the married doorman and his neighbor's teenage daughter. Katrina printed out the texts, along with the birth record of the girl next door and the cell phone number of the doorman's wife.

Despite being given no details about why they were in Mexico, the Agency's Mexico City station had left Katrina, Ward, and Alec an armored SUV that would stand out wherever it went—pretty much useless for surveillance, but handy if they ran into trouble. Ward took it and was instructed to try to find an inconspicuous parking place that would allow him to arrive on scene quickly. Katrina hadn't trusted the red-bearded walking armory to handle covert surveillance. Better to have him entering explosively at the first whisper of "Hey, Kool-Aid Man!" She left first, and told Alec to follow, ten minutes behind, on a different route. She didn't mention that she could blend into the crowd like a local and get ignored, while her gringo husband could not.

Despite the urban menaces plaguing much of Mexico City, Coapa was a nice neighborhood. Xochimilco had a large park not far away, full of relative greenery and a canal that must have once been scenic but was now rather polluted. The map indicated the park included something labeled the "Island of the Dolls."

"The guides don't do it justice, nobody's tried to rob me yet," Alec muttered to Ward through his lapel microphone as he walked through Coapa around the dinner hour. The street had mostly two and three-story buildings, some small internet cafes, bars, corner markets, a *farmacia*, and the universally ubiquitous 7-Eleven.

Vendors began packing up their wares from tarp-covered stalls set up on the sidewalk. Alec understood perhaps every third word he heard; like many Americans, he was convinced he "more or less" spoke Spanish because could order off the menu, understand the words that were phonetically similar to English, listened to Shakira, and occasionally stopped to ogle an attractive anchor on Univision while clicking through the channels.

"Hey, Alec," Ward's voice snickered in Alec's earpiece. "I looked up what the name of this neighborhood means. In Nahuatl, Coapa translates to 'nest of snakes.'"

"Haven't we had enough snakes?" he groaned. "Why did it have to be—" he paused as he saw someone step out of an alley up ahead, looking his way as if she expected him, "—skulls."

She was stunning, remarkably tall for a Mexican woman. The skin around her eyes was painted black, as was the tip of her nose. Her lips, which would have looked puffy and kissable with standard red lipstick, were painted white with black lines, looking like teeth; the "teeth" extended to the sides of her mouth. Beyond the skull makeup, she was striking and almost beautiful. Some of it was her hair, curled up in an almost old-fashioned bob. Alec couldn't quite make out the words on her neck tattoo—or for that matter, her arms; both were covered in tattoos. She wore a white t-shirt with Santa Muerte on it, tight enough to demonstrate she had curves to go with her menace.

The Agency's Mexico City station warned that one of the reasons this neighborhood was relatively quiet was the rule of a gang, "Las Calaveras"—which translated to "The Skulls." A mostly-female gang was pretty rare, and it was theorized that they were an offshoot of a larger gang with a similar taste in war masks, "Los Craneos." As the Craneos had expanded their smuggling and distribution operations well beyond the city, Las Calaveras had stepped in to take over the day-to-day management of protection rackets, keeping rival gangs away from the turf, and other criminal operations. It was hard to tell where the graffiti ended and the public murals began, and the implied threat for crossing the gang was not subtle.

Alec fully expected to be ambushed as he approached the address, a luxury condo complex, but the skull-painted woman just watched him. A lookout, he concluded.

Alec tried to look like he wasn't rushing as he walked the last few blocks to the lobby of El Grande, a relatively new four-story luxury condominium with terraces and balconies surrounding a green courtyard. He used his standard counter-surveillance techniques, used an indirect route, and saw no sign of the skull-faced woman following him. The door buzzed upon Alec's approach. Katrina was already waiting for him, standing before a nervous-looking doorman, a mustached sheepdog of a man.

"This is Manuel, who's going to let us into the unit," Katrina nodded, adding something in Spanish. Alec understood "gracious," "kind," "appreciation," and "easier alternative than having a Federal Police unit kicking down the door."

"Señor is out, and has been out for several days," the nervous Manuel objected. "I should really call my supervisor—"

"Manuel," Katrina offered a grin. "We've been over this. If your wife saw those texts…"

Manuel looked sheepish. "Just do whatever you have to do quickly."

"Let's take the stairs," Katrina nodded.

CHAPTER 29

"You were followed," Katrina said quietly, not quite inquiring.

"I noticed her and lost her," Alec said.

"Yeah, I've heard that before," she sighed. As soon as the station report indicated a female gang was active in the area, Katrina suspected that Alec and Ward would underestimate them. "Remember that old German counterterrorism team advice: 'Shoot the women first.' Any woman in a male-dominated group like a terror cell or gang has to work ten times as hard to be accepted—tougher, smarter, more ruthless—"

"I suspect that applies to women on counterterrorism teams, too."

"Obviously," she said dryly.

"Yes! Yes! Yes!" Alec and Katrina heard in their earpieces as they stepped into the hallway. They shared a glance; Katrina repressed the urge to respond, "I'll have what she's having."

"Dee, please tell me hubby isn't visiting and demonstrating hydrostatic calisthenics," Alec said softly into his microphone.

"I'm in, I'm in!" Dee boasted. "This guy had some of the best private computer security firewalls I've ever seen. Mr. Juan, tear down this wall!"

Alec and Katrina tried to act normal as Dee continued her excited cheers of victory in their ears, as Manuel jingled the keys on his chain and prepared to open the door to the fourth-floor condominium.

"How does a folder labeled 'Identidades' sound? Oh, man. Jackpot. Bingo. Jacko. Bingpot! Juan Lopez, Juan Garcia, Juan Sanchez—this guy has a lot of aliases. Got photos. Dang it, he's handsome."

Manuel the doorman opened the door to the condo. Alec and Katrina casually kept their hands on their not-so-concealed pistols and entered. On a desk in the corner, the resident's computer hard drive under the desk was already alive and humming, evidence of Dee's ongoing hacking intrusion.

"Señor?" Manuel called out. No one answered. There was no indication anyone had been in the condo for some time. He nodded and let them in. Alec put a twenty-dollar bill in Manuel's hand.

"Muchas gracias, señor," Alec said. Katrina shot him a disapproving look; she had just finished threatening the man. He shrugged. "I never know how much to tip in a foreign country."

It took only a few moments of searching for Katrina to find postcards postmarked from Ashgabat, Turkmenistan in one of the desk drawers. She found several photos of the man he surmised was Juan Whatever-His-Real-Surname-Was, and a strikingly beautiful woman. She looked on the back for a date.

What threw Alec was how normal the place seemed. He perused the bookshelf—Alec always believed you could learn a lot from a person from the books they read and cared to keep—and found a terrific collection of works on the Aztec, Mayan, and Inca empires in Spanish and English. The artwork on the walls was similarly expensive and spectacular.

"I have art envy," Katrina sighed. They progressed to the master bedroom.

They had been searching for barely two minutes when the condominium's landline phone rang. Alec and Katrina looked at each other.

"Dee, can you trace the call coming to this unit's landline right now?" Katrina asked aloud. She grunted an affirmative reply. Katrina nodded to Alec and he picked it up.

"Hola!"

"Why are Americans walking around my home?" Jaguar asked in English. His voice purred, a little irritated that he was suffering a home invasion, but rather pleased that his home alarm system had alerted him, and his countermeasures were already underway. Alec put his hand over the bottom of the phone.

"Silent alarm," he cringed and whispered to Katrina.

"Cupping your hand over the phone does not impede my home surveillance equipment," lectured Jaguar.

"Oh, yeah?" Alec looked around the room for anything like a lens and raised a middle finger to the mirror. "How many fingers am I holding up?"

"That's rude, American," Jaguar answered.

"You're the Juan I've been looking for," Alec said, glancing around, determined to spot the hidden camera. "How about you and I meet, amigo, and we'll talk about why you kidnapped Francis Neuse, how you poisoned the director, who you're working for, and you and I go from there like men? Mano a mano.'"

Katrina rolled her eyes as Alec tried to bait Juan's machismo. She suspected the phrase "mano a mano" probably represented most of Alec's Spanish vocabulary.

Jaguar laughed. "They call me the Jaguar, not the rat. You seem quite proud to have found one of my homes. I assure you, American, you will never find me, but some night, when you least expect it, I will find you."

"Buddy, you're bragging to the wrong guy," Alec shot back. "Last week I found J. D. Salinger, D. B. Cooper, and Amelia Earhart. Together."

"I'm going to find you, and I'm going to—"

Alec hung up. Katrina looked at him in surprise.

"He'll call back."

A moment later, the phone did ring. Katrina shook her head in amusement. "You're terrible undercover, but a master of getting under someone's skin." Alec smiled and answered the phone.

"Listen, American—"

"No, *you* listen!" Alec said, smiling as he spotted a small circular lens atop a picture frame next to the bedroom door. He strode close, fairly certain Juan the Jaguar was watching him through the lens. "Whatever you've done with your life until this moment, know that it has not prepared you for this. Sure, it's bought you a nice place, nice woman," Alec held up the picture of Esmerelda. "You've got skull-faced women watching your neighborhood for you. You thought it made you untouchable, beyond anyone's reach. But here I am, walking around your bedroom, talking to you on your phone, rifling through everything you own, learning all about you. I want you to send a message to your friends, the chick in the video up in New York, the guys who helped you grab Neuse, all of 'em. It's an important message. Make sure they get it. You ready?"

Jaguar grunted. "What?"

"It's like they said in their video," Alec declared, stared into the camera lens. "You … are not safe."

Alec reached out and pulled the camera out of the frame. He dropped it on the ground and he stomped on it a few times for good measure. He looked at Katrina, certain she would be impressed.

Katrina rolled her eyes again. "Are you finished?"

They quickly rifled through the house, grabbing anything that could be useful. An older laptop computer, the picture of Esmerelda, a comb for DNA samples. Everything was sealed in plastic bags and dumped in messenger bags around their shoulders. In the closet, Alec pulled out a set of clothes.

Katrina frowned. "We're supposed to be looking for metaphorical dirty laundry."

Alec stuck his nose in a black shirt and recoiled. "Smell that."

"No," Katrina said firmly.

"Sulfur," Alec said. "Maybe he's been working with chemicals or something. Bomb-making?"

"Bag it," she concluded, checking her watch. He placed it into a messenger bag. "Time to move, Alec," she said insistently.

She turned to the door, where Manuel was still waiting patiently and unnerved by what he had heard. He began saying something in Spanish—to Alec's ears, it sounded something like, "señora, you must leave, I shouldn't have let you in here"—when he turned to face someone out in the hall and registered a look of shock and horror before bullets tore through him.

CHAPTER 30

Manuel fell backward; in the time it took Alec to draw his gun, Katrina had closed the distance to the door and was crouched down in a squat by the doorway. She held her gun with two hands and readied herself to quickly, instinctively survey the "the slices of the pie"—each section of angle around the corner. In one fluid motion measured in milliseconds, Katrina scanned from the floor to the ceiling; as she saw feet, she shot above it, center mass. She shot three, four, five, six times in rapid succession. One stray shot from the approaching assailants hit the ceiling; another hit the floor before them.

The two Calaveras who had shot Manuel were bold and, in retrospect, stupid. While Jaguar would undoubtedly appreciate their lethal punishment of Manuel for letting two Americans barge into his home—even Mexican police had to get a search warrant—he wasn't the real target. The pair hadn't realized that Esmerelda had selected them to go up first to measure the intruders' skills. From the stairwell, Esmerelda and three other Calaveras crouched and heard nothing after the eight shots—their gang sisters had not even screamed or groaned in passing. Esmerelda exhaled. This was going to be difficult.

***

Just a few minutes earlier, a furious Jaguar had called Esmerelda and told her that he had seen two Americans, a man and a woman, searching his home on his surveillance system. The man had the *cojones* to taunt him once Jaguar had called on the phone. The Calaveras said that they had spotted one suspicious-looking American earlier that night and watched him enter the building and talk with the doorman and what appeared to be a local woman.

Jaguar told Esmerelda to get the Calaveras to deal with the intruders; he hadn't specified alive or dead.

Esmerelda was no fool. Americans sniffing around Jaguar's building, and now two of her gang sisters dead after eight shots had been fired in the hallway. These were not ordinary intruders, and she would be cautious. Right now, somewhere in the building, some resident was calling the police and reporting gunshots. Eventually, the cops would come.

***

Inside Jaguar's apartment, half the Americans were similarly calm.

"Two women, armed, handguns, skull makeup," Katrina said, safely crouched back within the doorway. "Both down." Her voice was calm, but her heart was pounding.

Alec was less calm. He grumbled into his lapel microphone.

"Nice job, backup!" Alec fumed. "Where the hell are you?"

"On my way, but I'm seeing a bunch of women with skull masks converging on your position," Ward reported. "I'll be there to get you out in two minutes. Maybe three. Wait, I think one spotted me." He swore. "Make it four. Okay, five." Ward's feed was just a steady stream of profanity.

Alec stared at Katrina incredulously.

"I feel like I'm watching my Uber driver go in the wrong direction," Alec muttered. He wiped the sweat from his brow. "Dee, do you read me?"

Back in northern Virginia, Dee sat before giant monitors, trying to simultaneously refocus the drone camera and track which phone calls from the condo building were calling the police.

"Alec, I think you guys have five, maybe ten minutes max before the police respond to reports of shots fired," Dee reported.

"How's that tracking on the number that just called the condo's landline? It was our Juan, calling himself the Jaguar," Alec said, checking, unnecessarily, that his gun was fully loaded and that the safety was off. "Bet he's close."

"Triangulating location, almost have it," she said. The audio connection was suddenly interrupted by the loud, sudden *pop pop pop* of gunfire.

"We're all right! We're all right!" Alec reported. "Katrina's offering them steel-jacketed discouragement."

Katrina removed a compact mirror and used it to peer out into the hallway. She saw the door to the stairwell at the end of the hall open a crack, then quickly close—just enough noise for Alec to hear.

"More of 'em?"

"Others down the hall, hiding in the stairwell," Katrina said. In the mirror, she spotted the door opening. "Amateurish."

She again rotated around the corner and made use of the fact that the hallway so tightly limited the space for the approaching Calaveras. Once again, she methodically fired another six shots, as casually and easily as most people typed on their phones. Five of her shots hit their mark in center mass, knocking the three women into one another and tumbling into a bleeding pile in the stairwell doorway.

"Nice shots," Alec guessed without looking.

"I know," she replied.

She was back at it again. Lethal shots had become a habit that proved impossible to permanently break. She momentarily thought of her last night in Pakistan years ago, when the job was done, and a more-than-slightly inebriated group of men from the British SAS serenaded her with a farewell rendition of Queen's "Killer Queen." They mangled the lyrics a bit, but their salute was clear: *"She's a killer queen, gunpower and kerosene, dynamite with an M-16, guaranteed to blow your mind anytime! She's like the Baroness, puts the sex in Semtex, if you're on her list, you'll dieeee!"* Men trained to kill were in awe of her, and that fact periodically left her awake at night.

"Cover me!" Katrina said, and Alec peered out the doorway. Esmerelda was raising her gun above the three women bleeding in front of her and swearing in Spanish. Alec aimed - his shots were a bit high, hitting the door above Esmerelda, forcing her to duck back behind the doorway.

It took Katrina just moments to reload. "Go!" she said, hitting Alec on the shoulder and pointing to the other end of the hallway, past the elevators, where a second stairway awaited.

"They might be coming up the other—" Alec's warning was too late: Katrina stepped into the hallway and sent another shot that seemed to send Esmerelda stumbling back and falling down ten stairs to the landing. "Move!" Katrina barked.

Alec inhaled and took giant leaping steps down the hallway. He was more than halfway down the hall when the door started to open, and he glimpsed one skull-like face emerging—he raised his weapon, but before he could fire, he heard bullets whizzing by his head—

—and two more Calaveras were shot as soon as the door opened. Alec looked back, realizing Katrina had been shooting from behind him. Holding her gun with two hands, she methodically shot both assailants twice each.

"Next time, duck lower," she instructed.

Alec stood, stunned, angry, flabbergasted, and more than a little terrified at his wife's lethal power. What's more, none of this seemed hard to Katrina. She just aimed and shot, and her aim always seemed to be true.

He was shaken out of his shock by his earpiece. "I've tracked the call to the room from a cell phone, and it's really close!" Dee shouted.

***

Katrina and Alec scrambled back down the other staircase and headed toward the rear entrance that led to an alley behind the building. Alec ran toward the door, as Dee recited something about the signal from the cell phone moving rapidly, suggesting he was on foot or maybe on a bike. Alec burst through the condominium building's rear door, out into the alley, greeted by a giant street art mural of the Virgin of Guadalupe.

Alec heard Dee say, *"Right there!"* and her voice was cut off by the sound of concrete breaking away from the mural. Two bullets, then a third and fourth, hit the mural, sending concrete powder raining upon Alec's head.

He turned and saw an image that had terrified many unlucky targets of the cartels in the past several years: a giant, man-sized jaguar was roaring at him.

CHAPTER 31

A millisecond later, Alec's eyes refocused and he realized it wasn't a man-sized jaguar, and the roar was the sound of guns firing. It was a man in a realistic jaguar mask. Clad in a black leather motorcycle jacket and pants, he held a pair of Belgian-made FN Five-seven handguns and let out an animalistic shriek.

Many times, Jaguar's otherworldly cry and visage had paralyzed his foes with fear. But that night his aim was uncharacteristically bad, bullets defacing the Virgin painting around Alec instead of going right through him.

Even worse for Jaguar, Alec's semi-panicked instinctive response was to raise his gun and blast away wildly. Jaguar had to suddenly slide to duck below the barrage from Alec, rolling to his left and twisting until he had ducked behind a small dumpster. Much to Jaguar's surprise and irritation, the smug American who had taunted him on the phone wasn't frozen in fear or running away. Alec just ran furiously in his direction, continuing to try to put shots through the dumpster. Alec fired his last shot, ejected the cartridge, and then leaped for cover towards the dumpster, crashing into it. The large metallic box had wheels on the bottom, and Jaguar found the dumpster slamming into him, knocking him down from a crouch and momentarily trapping his lower legs underneath it. He howled, reached around the corner of the dumpster and emptied his clip into the spot Alec had run a moment earlier. But Alec had already ducked behind the other side of the dumpster, huddled in a crouch, and slammed another clip into his gun.

Katrina emerged from the doorway, heard the sound of gunfire, and gaped at an absurd sight: Alec was crouching and firing above the dumpster, just above Juan the Jaguar's head. The Jaguar crouched and fired around the side of the dumpster. The two men were no more than six feet away from each other, firing furiously in the general direction of each other, missing every time. She had seen it before, how peripheral vision could disappear in the intense adrenaline of a gunfight.

Katrina added her fire to the barrage against Jaguar.

Jaguar realized that he was under fire from two directions. He swore in Spanish as he retreated, backing up, and then scrambled on all fours around the corner toward the next street, Ignacio Chavez. He finally rose to a human stride and began to race away. Where the hell were the Calaveras?

***

"Dee, stay on that phone's signal!" Alec said, running down the alley into the street, spotting the dark figure running in the opposite direction. He heard police sirens.

"Heading south—no, wait, he just cut east," she said, following the dot on the map on her screen. Headed toward … Avenue Canal Nacional!"

Katrina caught up with Alec, then passed him. "Come on!"

"I hate it when they run," he huffed and puffed. "This is why I shoot them, so I don't have to run after them." He stopped for a second, feeling a pain in his side. "Wait a minute, why are we running? We brought an SUV!" He pressed his earpiece. "Ward? Ward, where the hell are you?"

An ominous moment of silence followed. "Ward?"

He heard gunshots through his earpiece.

"Sorry, had to turn off comms for a second," Ward said. "One of the Skull girls tried to jump me. I'm over in … where the hell am I? A block north of the condo complex." Alec sighed. Too far away.

"Come on!" Katrina huffed into her earpiece. "He's almost into the park!"

***

A few moments later, Alec and Katrina stood by the edge of the pitch-black expanse of the Xochimilco Ecological Park. They glanced back and heard the sirens of police responding to the condo complex, where they would find quite a few members of the Calaveras gang, dead from gunshot wounds.

They heard a splash. The brightly colored gondola-style floats and barges were all tied; during daytime, the water looked too murky and polluted to be home to many fish. No, it was a much larger animal that had disturbed the surface of the water. The night had been cloudy, with a forecast for rain, but for the moment, there was just enough ambient light from the city to show the movement, down the canal, too far away for any shot to be worthwhile, even with Katrina's marksmanship.

Alec and Katrina hustled in that direction. Alec looked at the sludge floating on the surface of the water and shuddered at the thought of jumping into that heavily polluted waterway in pursuit. *They'll be pumping us full of antibiotics for weeks*, Alec thought.

He turned and watched as Katrina dove in without hesitation. He grimaced and realized that he couldn't fail to follow. He jumped in, too, making more of a cannonball. He was surprised to hit the bottom, and realized that the canal wasn't deep at all, maybe six feet or so.

Their heads surfaced, and Alec did his best to not think of the multitudes of bacteria that were likely making their way into his body at that moment in every possible orifice. He wished he had night vision goggles. But Katrina just turned her head, listened, and pointed. "That island over there."

They swam, noticing how overgrown and lush that island appeared. The trees seemed to be bursting with strange, large, lumpy fruit. As they swam closer, Alec began to wonder if they were sleeping birds, or some other strange animal. Monkeys? No, they didn't seem to move, beyond swaying with the branches. There was movement by the tall grasses by the shoreline, and the figure, almost certainly Jaguar, crawled on all fours and disappeared into the bushes by the shore.

Katrina gave Alec a *come on* head shake, and the pair approached the shoreline. Alec was ready to curse the darkness, until he realized that at least for now, the darkness was his best protection. If it was a bit brighter, Jaguar, now ashore, could simply try to shoot him. Every moment in that canal water was basically an open invitation to flesh-eating bacteria or dysentery or God knows what. Once ashore, would Jaguar have a clear shot at them? Would the water jam Jaguar's gun? Would it jam his own gun? Too many variables, even for his appetite for risk.

They crawled ashore. Alec didn't feel that much better out of the filthy water; the thick tangle of trees and vines gave Jaguar all the cover he needed and then some. The moonlight and ambient light of the city couldn't penetrate the branches and leaves. At any moment, two shots could ring out, and if Jaguar's aim was true, that bacteria wouldn't have time to do any more damage.

Katrina suddenly reached out and grabbed Alec, digging her fingers into his forearm so hard it hurt. Alec froze, wondering if he had just touched some tripwire or some other danger. He glanced over at his wife and saw a terrified look on her face, one he saw so rarely he could count on two hands the number of times he had seen it in more than a decade. This woman had just been brave enough to jump into sewage without a moment's hesitation—what on God's green earth could have stopped her in her tracks here?

After a moment of his eyes adjusting further to the darkness, he realized what she was looking at: the motionless body of a small child lying on the sand before them.

Wait, no. Not a child, a doll. A weathered, dirty old doll with one artificial eyelid closed and one open, staring creepily in their direction.

They exhaled together. Weird and creepy, but not, as they had both momentarily thought, the heart-stopping sight of a dead infant right before them.

Then the clouds parted again, and the moonlight illuminated the tree in front of them.

On every branch stood a child's doll—ten, twenty, dozens, all staring vacantly, some from empty eye sockets, some missing limbs, some hanging from strings and ropes almost like nooses. Some just heads, and some eerily realistic.

Katrina's eyes suddenly widened in terror and grasped her hands over her mouth just in time to stifle a scream. She had kicked down doors in some of the world's most ruthless terrorists, but an endless jungle of creepy dolls staring back at her kicked her amygdala into overdrive. The wind picked up and the frozen smiles swayed, seeming to silently laugh at the hapless mortals beneath them.

Alec reached out and tried to put a reassuring hand on her shoulder—never mind he had nearly peed himself a moment ago when he saw all the creepy doll faces staring at him—and after a moment she downgraded to much milder nerves.

They peered and silently crept to where they had seen Jaguar climb ashore. Alec was half-prepared to see the tracks of a giant cat; the idea that the feral, ferocious, purring Juan Lopez was some sort of were-jaguar would have somehow made sense in light of the surreal events of recent days. But the shore revealed no footprints of any kind at all. Alec and Katrina shared a glance of disbelief.

She nodded, an indication that it was time to swim back to shore, and slowly started moving toward the water, continuing to scan the woods for any sign of Jaguar. Alec didn't mind leaving, and it wasn't just the persistent sense that the dolls were watching him. Just minutes earlier in the alley, feeling the adrenaline and the thrill of the chase, he felt unstoppable. The fact that Jaguar had somehow missed four shots at him—pockmarking what had been a rather impressive street art vision of the Virgin of Guadalupe—must have used up his last bit of luck for a while. Here, with all the dolls watching him, he sensed any risk would go against him.

Or maybe that was just the infectious brain-eating bacteria talking.

CHAPTER 32

Fifteen minutes later, Alec and Katrina sat quietly in the backseat as Ward drove them to one of the Agency's safe houses. He made the traditional sudden turns to throw off anyone following them, but neither he nor Alec saw any indications they had picked up a tail. Katrina closed her eyes, seeming to do some sort of meditation to calm down from the adrenaline of the hallway gunfight, the chase through the Mexico City streets, and the bizarre, twisted sights of what they later learned was a macabre local tourist attraction, the Island of the Dolls.

Ward explained as they drove that apparently a young girl had drowned near the island many years ago, and shortly after the tragedy, the island's caretaker had found the girl's doll on the shore. He hung it from a tree in tribute, and the locals started doing the same out of sadness for the girl. The island caretaker felt haunted by the girl, and he continued to hang dolls and toys from the trees to bring her soul to rest. The caretaker lived on the island for fifty years… until the day he drowned, in nearly the same spot the girl did.

"That story is the opposite of helpful," Alec responded.

He checked the messenger bag at his feet and the plastic bags within it. Thankfully, the two dips in the awful-smelling canals hadn't damaged the evidence they had recovered from Jaguar's apartment.

Reassured, Alec reached for Katrina's hand. She opened her eyes, startled.

"Thank you," Alec whispered.

Her look softened—perhaps one iota. He leaned over and whispered in her ear. "You're amazing."

She looked out the window.

"It's not like I grew up dreaming of being really good at killing people," she said firmly.

Alec nodded in understanding and looked out his own window.

A moment later, he couldn't help himself.

He leaned over and whispered in her ear, "But you were *so awesome*!" This made Katrina laugh. "Better to be really good at this and alive than really bad and dead."

"I suppose," she said, shaking her head. "Better to be judged by twelve than carried by six."

Alec leaned forward. "Ward, you had to see this! There were like, six of them—"

"Alec!" Katrina said, laughing a little.

"Six of them, and Katrina just *pop pop pop*—like Annie Oakley, Lara Croft, and Princess Leia rolled into one!" Alec gushed. "Each one comes up, *click-chick BOOM*. Dust, bitten. Farm, bought. Pining for the fjords!"

Ward smiled. "I'd expect nothing less!"

"Don't encourage him!" Katrina fumed. She was having a perfectly good moment of angst disrupted by Alec's joy at having survived the gunfight.

"I don't even think—did you even miss? Do you have, like, magic bullets that just go around corners?" Alec continued, now venting his jealousy a bit. "I think I hit a door. You hit six of them, with, like, four bullets somehow, and I hit a door. I'm the one who should be in a bad mood!"

Katrina shook her head. “Yes, I missed.” Alec stared at her skeptically. “Three times. Out of eighteen shots.”

Ward laughed from the front seat. Katrina continued to shake her head, trying to not smile or laugh at the absurdity of trying to sound modest. “And Alec?”

He stared back.

“I didn’t hit six of them, I hit seven,” she corrected. Alec and Ward roared with laughter.

CHAPTER 33

MEXICO CITY
THURSDAY, MARCH 25

At the CIA station in Mexico City, everything recovered from Jaguar's apartment was photographed, documented, and prepared to be securely sent back to Langley; it was unlikely to provide a lot more than Dee's electronic ransacking of Jaguar's home computer, but experience taught everyone to be thorough. Alec, Katrina, and Ward got in late, and slept late.

By midmorning the station chief strongly urged them to be on the next flight back to Washington.

The Mexico City police had no idea who shot up the Calaveras gang, killing five and seriously wounding two others, but even in a city with horrific rates of violent crime, a mass shooting in a luxury condominium stood out. Even the Centro de Investigación y Seguridad Nacional perked their ears up at word that an Anglo man believed to be American was seen entering before the shooting started. The fact that all of the security cameras in the building had simultaneously failed and some sort of hacking had wrecked the operating system only made the investigating detectives more curious.

But no forensic technician would ever match the rounds from the gunfight to the Americans' SIG Sauers; they were permanently relocated to the embassy furnace.

The Mexico City police were used to uncooperative witnesses. They would go through the motions, knowing that the real investigation would be conducted by the men of Los Craneos, the "brother gang" to the all-women Calaveras. The men swore vengeance; glasses of tequila were poured on the floor. The more driven Craneos knocked on the doors of Jaguar's neighbors, demanding answers. The terrified neighbors told the gang members that when they heard the first shots, they hit the floor.

On the other side of the city, Jaguar stewed, sitting on a bed in his own safe house, with a terrified Esmerelda lying on the bed beside him. She had been there when the ambulances arrived; she had seen her sisters taken to the hospital. Two might pull through. The Craneos were on the warpath, demanding answers, and while they didn't know of Jaguar's particular hideaway down a back alley in Tepito, he couldn't spend the rest of his life hiding.

How could he explain to the gang that he had inadvertently brought all this trouble to their door, with five of the gang's women dead and two more hanging on the edge? Somehow it would have been easier to explain, easier to forget if it had been just another bloody turf battle between gangs or rival cartels. But those were fought in the streets, not in the hallways of luxury condos. Two assailants—mostly one woman, from Esmerelda's account—wiping out a good chunk of a gang in one night?

But to tell the Craneos, "*lo siento, mis amigos*, my work for this mysterious patron living in Turkmenistan brought the CIA to your door"—well, there was an excellent chance the Craneos would kill him out of misplaced rage. Or Esmerelda.

A man and a woman... Jaguar contemplated that unusual detail from the shooting. There were a handful women in Mexico capable of such ruthlessness in a fight, accurate enough with a gun to cut through the Calaveras and walk away unscathed. "La China," an infamous woman assassin, had killed 150 people in a ten-year span for the Damasco cartel in Baja California. She had been arrested way back in 2015, but it was plausible—even likely?—that she had some protégé or someone as good as she was.

Jaguar picked up one of his burner phones and called the demonic thug who was the Craneos' boss de la dia.

"It's Jaguar," he spoke, not waiting for a reply. "I've been working all my sources the moment I heard. Do you think the Damasco cartel would come after you? This matches their old methods."

That grain of suspicion was all Jaguar needed to plant in the gang's collective mind. Within an hour, and with a half-dozen additional calls, the Craneos had convinced themselves that the Damasco cartel, who had never respected them, were audaciously attempting to break into the Mexico City territory. Even worse, their opening move had been ruthless, reckless, and personal. A new cartel war was underway.

"The Damascos will never see our counterattack coming," a Craneo boasted to Jaguar.

Indeed, because they have no idea I'm using them as the scapegoat, Jaguar thought.

He hung up the phone after the last call. He turned to find Esmerelda in the other room, blowing marijuana smoke to the small statuette of Santa Muerte she had installed. She poured a complete small bottle of tequila at the feet of the statue.

Esmerelda turned and gave Jaguar a relieved smile. "I told you she would protect us if we were loyal."

Jaguar nodded and repressed all of his theological objections to his love's devotion to Saint Death, the twisted occult folk saint that the Catholic Church abhorred.

Only when she settled into the bed did Jaguar let himself silently roll his eyes at her rituals. If only she would put aside these silly superstitions and accept a real deity, like Tezcatlipoca.

"We'll have to disappear for a while," Jaguar said. "We'll go to San Miguel." He had always enjoyed his visits to the picturesque mountain town, full of artists and American expats. Life would be quieter there; he had enough cash reserves to live off the grid for a long, long while.

He curled up and let his hand settle on Esmerelda's bottom and smiled. A long, long while with nothing to do but her.

***

Once the commercial jetliner from Mexico City to Dulles International Airport passed into American airspace, Alec exhaled . . . and smiled. He noticed Katrina didn't share his good spirits and nudged her.

"Cold trail," she mumbled.

"Just for now," Alec said confidently. "We'll get these guys. We're at ten thousand feet. Soon enough we'll put them six feet under."

Katrina shook her head. "There's no pride in . . . doing that. You and Ward take a necessary evil of our work and forget that it's an evil."

"I'll work on that, as long as you don't forget that it can be necessary," Alec shrugged. "It's the business we're in."

"No, we're in the information business," Katrina said firmly.

"Are we?" Alec asked. He sipped his drink. "I'd say we're in the consequence business. Bad people do bad things because they think they can get away with it, and we show up at their door, demonstrating the consequences."

Katrina pursed her lips. "Judge, jury, and executioner?"

"We don't go around looking for trouble. We are a reaction. Don't start none, won't be none."

Ward leaned in, uninvited, from across the aisle. "Did you ever think that maybe the world would be a little better place—a calmer, more respectful, more peaceful place—if everybody was a little more concerned about return fire?" he asked quietly. "An armed society is a polite society. That makes us Miss Manners with laser sights."

Alec gave an approving nod. Katrina was unimpressed.

"It's not like we come up behind guys when they're standing at the urinal!" Alec objected in an offended whisper. "When these guys decide to go out guns blazing, it's not our fault!"

"Of course," Katrina said. "Neither of you would walk up to a man and shoot him without warning. That violates Ward's sense of honor and your self-image as a Christian. You both think of yourself as the good guys. But deliberately provoking a man into a gunfight you know he'll lose—you guys are fine with that. That way you can look in the mirror and tell yourself that he made the choice, not you."

Katrina could tell from Alec's eyes she had hit a bull's-eye once again.

"Those of us who think our purpose is to obtain information want these guys alive, so they can talk. Sources, moles, defectors—there was a time when that was our bread and butter. The whole point was to learn secrets, to inform policymakers, to help make a safer world. Three straight presidencies now, work becomes more paramilitary ops, more drone strikes, more of your so-called consequences." She looked out the window. "How sure are you that it's really making everything safer out there?"

Alec stared ahead, offended.

"I didn't make this world," he said. "I'm just trying to fix it."

CHAPTER 34

TOP SECRET/ /NOFORN/ORCON//MR1

FAX COVER SHEET
Central Intelligence Agency

Washington, DC 20505

March [redacted]

To: Raquel Holtz, [redacted] CIA
From: Merlin [redacted]

Tsk-tsk, Raquel, what kind of kids are they hiring at Langley these days? It took barely a day of working contacts and favor-trading to find the attached police reports attributing various cartel-related deaths and disappearances to "The Jaguar." They do know the difference between "killed by a jaguar" and "killed by 'the Jaguar,'" right?

A lot of Mexico's most notorious assassins operate under a nom de guerre—El Sicario (The Hitman), El Sangres (The Blood), El Ponchis (The Cloak), El Nino (The Boy), and Los Antrax (The Anthrax).

I'm not entirely surprised about the trail leading through Mexico. Back when I was in a position to do something about it all, our neighbor to the south worried me.

In American eyes, Mexico is the land of the Treasure of the Sierra Madre, El Dorado's cities of gold, land of Zorro, the Magnificent Seven. It's the place where the food is magic, as in *Like Water for Chocolate*; tequila's a magic potion that makes you take leave of your senses. (Does it put a mask on you and change your identity? Or does it take the mask off, and reveal what's always been underneath?) Mexico's the land just beyond the border where you can break rules you wouldn't break at home. If America's really xenophobic, it's the peculiar kind of xenophobia that drives us to put everything in a burrito and get smashed on margaritas on Cinco de Mayo.

But there's always been this fearful undercurrent in the way America sees Mexico: the beautiful curse at the heart of Steinbeck's *The Pearl*, D. H. Lawrence's *The Plumed Serpent*, Orson Welles' corrupt small-town police captain in *Touch of Evil*, the unstoppable hit man in *No Country for Old Men*, the Aztec Temple hidden underneath a truck stop in *From Dusk Till Dawn*. (My grand-nephew made me watch that one.) Montezuma's revenge is always lurking out there. The danger has always been there, and the locals just live with it; luxurious Mexican homes feature interior courtyards, not front lawns. Sturdy, protective walls face the street. The danger comes from outside: from the slums, the jungles, the deserts, the mountains. Go too far and there's no law that can protect you. To live comfortably and safely is to live in sealed-off enclaves; the rest of the country is conceded to … it. The dark.

What happens if you mix the worst of America with the worst of Mexico? What if the interaction between both sides of the border begat both the beautiful and, separately, something darker, twisted, curdled? (I'm not just talking about the goat-sucking Chupacabra urban legend.)

D. H. Lawrence's *The Plumed Serpent*, written in 1926, gets dismissed as fascist, and it has more than a little Kipling-ish "white man's burden, oh, look at these silly natives, careful, those godless savages will seduce your white woman with their sensual voodoo" vibe to it. But the subtext isn't that hard to pick up: that something malevolent and bloodthirsty still stirred in this land, quenched for centuries by human hearts and ritual sacrifice of children, and whatever setback it endured with the arrival of Cortés, it was still lurking beneath Mexico's surface, searching for the chance to break through into a rational, scientific modern world that long ago gave up its capacity to understand it.

I looked up something about Lawrence; he did this big tour of Mexico, hitting all the Aztec ruins and the floating gardens at Xochimilco before writing that novel. His traveling companion, the poet Witter Bynner, wrote:

In the great quadrangle of Quetzalcoatl, we saw Lawrence stand looking and brooding. The coloured stone heads of the feathered snakes in one of the temples were a match for him. The stone serpents and owls held something that he obviously feared.

Now, as far as I know, nobody's seen a giant feathered serpent running around Mexico devouring the internal organs of hapless sacrifice victims. But not all monsters have scales.

The American demand for drugs in their myriad forms and the Mexican supply would be the opening that Lawrence's dark force sought. If you were a malevolent force sustained by ritualistic human sacrifice, wouldn't a cartel—with a head, a voracious appetite for blood, and claws dug deep into everything—be the perfect form for you? Someone like Francis Neuse would ask if the monsters of legend had adapted to the modern, secular age by simply becoming ethereal influences on human behavior.

A few years back the Archbishop and Cardinal attempted an exorcism of the whole country in San Luis Potosí. I don't think it worked yet.

—Merlin

CHAPTER 35

THURSDAY, MARCH 25

In the early evening hours, Atarsa struck again.

Smith, Johnson, Williams, Brown, and Jones died that night, although within a few hours, the misleading nature of Atarsa's threat was clear. Those were the names of the perpetrators, all of whom were killed that night in the course of their attacks.

They timed their attacks to begin simultaneously across the country, across different time zones. Calvin Smith, age thirty-one, pulled out a knife and began stabbing anyone he could in the lobby of the Marriott Hotel in the Renaissance Center in Detroit, Michigan. He killed one man and one woman before being shot by a police officer.

Ezra Johnson did the same at the entrance to the Empire State Building in Manhattan. All six of his victims survived and were stable in local hospitals; an NYPD officer put him down quickly with a shot to the chest.

Zed Williams walked into the Cartier store on Rodeo Drive in Beverly Hills and stabbed the first customer he saw, causing fatal wounds. A store security guard was cut badly while wrestling him to the ground. Moments after police entered, Williams cut his own throat and died shortly thereafter.

Reginald Brown attempted the same outside Quicken Loans Arena in Cleveland. A passerby shot him with his firearm after Brown injured four people, two critically.

Nathaniel Jones picked a hospital in Charlotte, North Carolina, aiming for immobilized, vulnerable victims. He killed four people before a hospital security guard shot him. Like Williams, his last act was a slice to his own throat, ensuring he would not speak and betray his cause.

Having stabbed random victims to death in their houses, Atarsa attempted mass stabbings in crowded public places. All of the perpetrators were men, between the ages of nineteen and thirty-one; Brown was African American, the others were white.

All of the men, at six p.m. Eastern, three p.m. Pacific, removed common kitchen knives out of their pockets or bags and began stabbing the closest person. The death toll was only seven people, with eleven injured. But that evening, the networks preempted their regular programming for live coverage.

The wall-to-wall coverage might have seemed excessive except that all of the perpetrators had used GoPro cameras to record video of their attacks, and the footage was uploaded to the Internet as it recorded. Some unknown perpetrators then hacked the Emergency Broadcast System, sending text messages to tens of thousands of Americans: UPDATED GOVERNMENT WARNING ON ONGOING TERROR ATTACKS, CLICK HERE. Upon clicking the link, the phones were redirected to video of the attacks from the perpetrators' view.

CHAPTER 36

Watching a screen above the bar in the Dulles International Terminal upon his return from Mexico, Alec wondered whether Wolf Blitzer was going to need to breathe into a brown paper bag soon.

"Absolutely horrifying, truly disturbing," the bearded anchor declared. "We're warning people not to click on the links if they receive a text from the Emergency Broadcast System. The Department of Homeland Security is saying, emphatically, that they are not sending these texts. Let's turn to our chief terrorism analyst, to see what he makes of this ghoulish dimension to the attacks—"

Katrina and Alec watched as the chief terrorism analyst managed to work in a reference to the time he had tea with a long-dead terror mastermind decades earlier.

Then the chyron at the bottom of the screen changed: WARNING: GRAPHIC. "We're going to show you what that link will take you to—and we warn you, the video you're about to see may not be appropriate for some viewers. Viewer discretion is advised."

Katrina threw her hands in the air. "I can't believe these idiots are broadcasting the video of the attacks," she fumed. "Just go ahead and save them the trouble of hijacking any signal, just show it for all of us to see."

"If it bleeds, it leads," Alec said, quoting an old journalism adage.

"They know our media culture," Katrina said. "They've studied us."

***

Katrina wanted to go straight to Liberty Campus, but Raquel had told them to go home, sleep, eat, and report the next morning to Dee; Raquel herself would be out of town. The entire intelligence community was working around the clock after the night's attacks. So far, the clues to the identity to Angra Druj, Akoman, or anyone else associated with Atarsa—beyond Juan Lopez—were few and far between.

***

FRIDAY, MARCH 26

When Alec arrived at Liberty Campus in the morning, Ward was waiting for him, eager to complain about how his hotel wanted two forms of ID to check in the previous evening.

"Cops are out everywhere, people are calling 911 because they see people in their backyard, two Metro stops shut down over abandoned packages," Ward shook his head. "And now this guy wants a passport *and* a driver's license to check in to my room. I'm friggin' exhausted. Yeah, pal, *I'm* a terrorist."

"In the clerk's defense, with that beard, you're either Taliban or Amish," Dee pointed out.

"You notice there was way less traffic here this morning? Marie's a teacher, and she said a third of the kids aren't in her class this morning," Ward continued griping. "It's Williamsburg, not someplace dangerous like Damascus or Kandahar or Camden. The whole country's in a Category Five freak-out."

Katrina had managed to pull some of the morning's traffic. The attacks in Manhattan, Detroit, Cleveland, Beverly Hills, and Charlotte had global repercussions. No less than three Islamist groups insisted the Atarsa attack had really been their work. All embassies and consulates abroad had been urged to take additional security precautions. The French embassy had inquired about postponing a visit by their president in the coming weeks.

The CIA's Counterterrorism Center and FBI's Joint Terrorism Task Force had launched an extensive search for additional clues to any remaining Atarsa members, but their managers were already offering a grim assessment. Atarsa clearly had been planning this series of attacks for a long time. So far no common link had been found among Calvin Smith, Ezra Johnson, Zed Williams, Reginald Brown, or Nathaniel Jones; there was no indication they had ever met each other. None of the men had been on any watch list or with any known links to terror groups; all were American citizens. Four of them had minor juvenile records, for petty theft, fighting, and threatening teachers in their high school years, but all of those charges had been dropped and were long ago. The men had few friends, but no recent histories of violence or indications of extremist views.

Some analysts contended the fact that all five Atarsa members had been killed in the attacks indicated that this was the grand finale of the group's plan, but others argued this suggested that Atarsa had multiple American-born members willing to die, and that these could be sacrificed in high-profile attacks. What's more, the use of the GoPro cameras and fake DHS text messages suggested a technological sophistication that was rare for a terror group.

Alec turned his attention to the pile of evidence grabbed from Jaguar's apartment; he began with the postcards from Turkmenistan.

"Jaguar was talking to somebody in Turkmenistan. Do we know anybody who's a threat in Turkmenistan?" He looked around to the doorway out of habit and realized he hadn't heard from Raquel yet that morning.

"Hey, where is Raquel today, anyway?"

"Up in New York."

CHAPTER 37

Each day, thousands of New Yorkers crossed the intersection of Third Avenue and Fortieth Street without knowing they were walking by the location of the lone representation of the Iranian government within United States territory.

The US severed diplomatic relations with Iran in 1980 during the hostage crisis. All diplomats were expelled from the Iranian Embassy, at 3003 Massachusetts Avenue on Embassy Row in Washington; the embassy and separate residence of the military attaché and cultural attaché spent the next generation empty, being maintained by the US State Department. When the Iranians absolutely needed to talk to the United States, they sent the message through the Pakistani embassy; when the US government absolutely needed to speak to the Iranians, they sent the message through the Swiss. For a short time during negotiations of the Iranian nuclear deal, American and Iranian officials met and negotiated face-to-face regularly, but any discussion of reestablishing ties ended with the next presidential election.

The Iranian consulate to the United Nations provided Tehran with their only venue for spies with diplomatic cover. When an older, distinguished gentleman and a large, beefy colleague departed the consulate building to approach a black BMW with diplomatic plates, Raquel lowered her newspaper and stood in their path.

"Mr. Karroubi?"

To most of the world, Hossein Karroubi was just another diplomatic bureaucrat in Iran's consulate. Raquel knew he was the New York station chief for Iran's foreign intelligence service, VEVAK.

"If you want to spare your country an enormous amount of sorrow, you and I need to have a conversation. Right now," she said, with the directness of an arrow in flight.

He frowned. "And you are?"

"In your line of work," she said, knowingly. "There's a Shake Shack across the street. Let's sit and talk. Ten minutes."

He looked around uncomfortably, presuming he was under surveillance—from America and, perhaps, his own country.

Karroubi's beefy comrade stepped significantly closer to Raquel. The top of her head came to his pectorals. He leaned in, with more than a little menace and declared, "Where he goes, I go."

Raquel almost laughed at him. "Sure, bring the goon. I understand how intimidating I can be."

They crossed the street, entered, and sat in a booth, skipping the line to order. When no one objected, Karroubi presumed everyone in the entire restaurant was undercover FBI counterintelligence personnel. He was prepared to scream bloody murder, showcase his diplomatic credentials and, if need be, sprint back to the Iranian soil of the consulate.

"I know you saw that threatening message broadcast out to the city a two weeks ago," Raquel began.

Karroubi stared back. "And?"

"The woman in the video spoke with an accent that was Persian," Raquel stated. "Indisputably."

Karroubi shrugged. "Possibly. I don't know who she is."

Raquel leaned forward. "I think you do."

Karroubi frowned. "This is the sort of paranoid demonization of foreign cultures that have made your country so hated around the world."

Raquel was undeterred. "She's Iranian."

Karroubi was an old pro, and not easily intimidated. "If you have evidence of that, I would very much like to see it."

"Does the name Akoman mean anything to you?" she inquired.

Karroubi made a show of rubbing his chin. "That is the name of a demon from Zoroastrian mythology. Is the CIA preparing a strike against ghosts and goblins?"

Raquel ignored his mockery. "Do you realize what an enormous favor I'm doing for you and, by extension, your country right now?"

His confusion was not feigned. "I do not understand."

"Hossein," she used his first name here, a deliberately presumptuous gesture. "There's an Iranian woman running around directing maniacs to kill Americans and making videos of it. A lot of people are going to conclude your government is behind it, whether or not they actually are. The only thing that's going to stop it is if we show evidence you helped us catch the bastards."

The Iranian scoffed, nodded to his beefy compatriot, and started to slide out of the booth.

"I don't jump at the first threat from the CIA," he said tersely.

Raquel raised her voice a little. "If you think this woman isn't your problem, you're sorely mistaken. If these attacks continue, you will get the blame!" She pointed directly at him. "There are going to be a lot of cries for revenge."

"Any attack on my country would be—"

Raquel cut him off, showing a bit of frightening fury in the middle of the burger shop, loud enough to get patrons turning around. "Take a good look at Tehran next time you're there, because if you don't help us, it means war, and your hometown's gonna look real different, real quick. Don't think your not-so-secret nuclear program is going to save you. Throw a nuke at us, we'll throw a lot more back at you. We've got about five thousand warheads. You'll run out of people long before we run out of nukes."

Raquel's casual suggestion of nuclear war genuinely shocked Karroubi. He looked around, and saw the other patrons were staring and frowning. What was she thinking? What had he been thinking when he agreed to an unscheduled meeting with an American claiming to be with its intelligence agency? He and his bodyguard shook their heads in exasperated surprise and quickly headed for the restaurant's front door, dreading an FBI team that never appeared.

CHAPTER 38

About fifteen minutes later, Raquel was in a seemingly nondescript office a few blocks away, behind a series of extremely imposing and complicated steel-frame locked doors. This was one of the National Security Agency's most important facilities in New York, the one that managed the thorough electronic surveillance of all of the UN consulates in the city.

Raquel hadn't expected Hossein Karroubi to say much or be cooperative. If he had offered anything useful on Atarsa, Akoman, or the woman in the video, it would be a pleasant surprise.

But the public meeting with Raquel and her bold accusations and not-so-veiled threat had instantly given him something he needed to communicate to his superiors as soon as possible. Raquel had watched Karroubi and his bodyguard quickly return to the consulate.

At the NSA, they had confirmed he had gone to the consulate's SCIF, which had the allegedly secure electronic, phone, and other data lines to Tehran.

Those lines of communication weren't quite as secure as the Iranians thought. And when the NSA teams knew that communications would be coming and had advance warning to focus all of their technologically advanced surveillance equipment on one building, one room, one set of cables, one set of satellite dishes, and so on, the Iranians would have been better off using carrier pigeons.

Karroubi was genuinely rattled by Raquel's suggestion that the US suspected the Iranians were behind the Atarsa attacks, and that all-out war, including nuclear weapons, were being discussed. It seemed wildly disproportional and completely unlike anything he had seen in the American government since—well, the bad old days, when the city had been devastated by terror. Yes, the American president periodically furiously denounced Iran with for its aggression in foreign policy, but in Karroubi's experience, those storms blew over quickly. His messages back to VEVAK headquarters weren't quite panicked, but he emphasized that he needed further guidance and, ideally, any indication of whether the Americans could have really determined that the woman in the video was Iranian. Her accent was, indeed, distinctively Persian.

Running VEVAK's operations in the Great Satan was a big responsibility, and Karroubi's ties to the top level of VEVAK went back years. His bosses communicated to him with trust.

VEVAK had indeed identified the woman calling herself Angra Druj in the video: Sarvar Rashin, an Iranian citizen who dropped off the grid several years ago. Not much was known about her, other than the fact that she wasn't Muslim; she practiced the Zoroastrian faith.

It was the second part of the response from Tehran that made Karroubi gasp for the first time in so long that he couldn't remember.

According to VEVAK, Sarvar Rashin had been the lover of Gholam Gul, who up until seven years ago had worked in VEVAK's Department of Disinformation, in charge of creating and waging psychological warfare against the enemies of the Islamic Republic. Gul ran into official disapproval of his relationship with Rashin—a non-Muslim woman—and left VEVAK on cordial terms, promising to join Hezbollah. Gul, too, had dropped off the grid after a short stint of work for Hezbollah.

VEVAK believed he operated out of Turkmenistan and Cyprus, but had no current bead on him, beyond his alias.

"Akoman."

Tehran hadn't ordered this, but they had trained the man who was running the attacks against Americans. Would the US government blame Iran for the attacks? Would the populace? Would some unscrupulous voices within the American government try to turn the Iranian regime into a politically convenient scapegoat? If he were in their shoes, he might, Karroubi thought.

Suddenly a war between the United States and Iran didn't seem quite so unthinkable.

Despite the shudder-inducing thought, Karroubi noticed that his superiors hadn't even considered telling the Americans about Rashin and Gul.

CHAPTER 39

SATURDAY, MARCH 27

In the Friday afternoon intercept of the Iranian communications, the names "Gholam Gul" and "Sarvar Rashin" rocketed around the intelligence community—not just to the relevant offices of the NSA and CIA, but throughout the fourteen other American agencies, and then overseas to the other four partners of the "Five Eyes." Long-forgotten colleagues sent Raquel messages of congratulations. Within a few hours, MI6 sent word that British travel systems had a record of a woman with a Lebanese passport passing through Heathrow on her way from Beirut to New York five years ago. Her passport photo matched the eyes and other visible parts of her face from the Atarsa videos.

Facial recognition software, previously hindered by Rashin's veil, finally had a better image to work with, and overnight, a second passport with the same face and the name "Zahra Amadi" popped up in the database searches. This woman had traveled to the United States several times. Then the same search yielded a Jordanian passport under the name "Zahra Amadir," and, shortly thereafter, a Moroccan passport under the name "Fatima Zahra Amadi," and a Turkish passport under "Zara Ahmadi." In each picture, she had a slightly different haircut, makeup, even just-barely-noticeable weight changes. Altogether, the four faces on the screens looked like they could be sisters.

By Saturday morning, the good news was that American intelligence knew four of Sarvar Rashin's aliases. The bad news was that they had no idea how many more she had, meaning she could have slipped into almost any country under any name.

Raquel had driven back from New York, because LaGuardia, JFK, and the Acela to Washington had all been delayed with various security scares. She got in late and wanted to sleep late.

She awoke to a text from Katrina. The message asked her to meet at J. Gilbert's around lunch. Katrina knew Raquel was likely to have to go to either Liberty Crossing in Tysons Corner or the actual headquarters building in Langley, and the restaurant was roughly halfway from either of them.

Raquel at least got to have coffee with her husband, Vaughn, and then hopped in her car again, hoping the traffic wouldn't be so bad on the weekend. She saw Katrina waiting for her in the parking lot, leaning on her deep blue Nissan 370Z Coupe. It was a slight splurge that Katrina justified by telling herself she never knew when she might need to practice evasive driving with a top speed of 102 miles per hour. Raquel could tell from Katrina's face that something was terribly wrong.

"What's up?" Raquel said, as soon as she opened the door. "What's wrong?"

Katrina stared back for an uncomfortably long time.

"I want to resign."

CHAPTER 40

J. GILBERT'S

They didn't dare go into the restaurant; the place's probably overhyped reputation as a spy hangout meant you never knew who was listening, from a tourist to a blogger to a Russian agent.

Raquel stood for a moment, struggling to think of the least harmful reaction.

"I would hate to see that happen," she began.

"I said I want to resign, not that I will resign," Katrina said, almost too softly to be heard over the passing traffic. She folded her arms and leaned on the roof of her car.

"Is this because of Mexico?" Raquel probed gently.

Katrina exhaled. "Mexico, and Germany, and Pakistan, and Afghanistan, and all of the other places I've gone over the years." She inhaled, and Raquel wondered if Katrina was fighting the urge to cry. "It's not because I can't handle it."

Raquel took her spot, right next to her, leaning over the roof of the car like it was a back fence.

"I know that," she began. "I don't ever want you feeling like I or anybody else take you for granted."

"Coming over here as a kid, not speaking the language. Stuck in New York before it got cleaned up. Living in a tenement with my parents, watching them clean houses. My Jewish father chopping pork all day because it's the best job he can find. You learn as an immigrant that nothing is given to you. You have to earn everything. Go to school, run into bullies. Gangs. People forget what New York was like before. People thought I was crazy, a teenage girl, walking around alone at night."

She wiped an eye.

"And it just kept going. Get into Stuyvesant. Take karate. Guys get handsy. Break some fingers. Full ride to Georgetown. School of Foreign Service. Professor wants to hook up with me. Trust fund frat boys. And then there's this one guy who's an accounting major who keeps making me laugh."

Raquel smiled. Whatever crisis Katrina was experiencing at the moment, remembering the good times represented a glide path.

"The world's our oyster. But he's determined to apply to Langley. Won't get over something about his dad and the IRA and some girl he knew that disappeared. And I say sure. Then the recruiter is practically begging me." She took a deep breath. "And I'm still waiting to hear from the Foreign Service, so I think, sure. This is another path. Fix the world. Make it a better place. Protect those who need protecting. I go down to the Farm and everybody says I'm great at this. And I never really stop to ask, 'Is this really what I want to do with my life?'"

Raquel put a hand on her shoulder.

"Then that Tuesday happens, world changes. They need Uzbek speakers. Suddenly I'm in Afghanistan, translating deals to get warlords who have done God knows what before we arrived to switch to our side against the Taliban." She paused again. "You read the reports. I'm walking around with a Beretta, then a Glock 19, and then I'm drawing one of them when a negotiation goes bad. And then I'm using it. And then I'm using it a lot. Men are dead because I pulled the trigger. And I go back, thinking... what is Alec going to think of me?"

Raquel looked confused. "Come on. You had to know Alec would always love you."

Katrina looked sadder than before. "Oh, it wasn't that. He was jealous. Never said it outright, but while I'm out there, he's spending months staring at international bank records, finding rich foreigners who are funding terrorism and trying to get somebody to extraordinary rendition them. He thinks I'm making a difference, and he isn't. I keep going places. Proving myself. He's going stir crazy in offices. And then you come along, with this idea for a special group. Outside the system. A little clique doing things our own way."

Raquel studied Katrina's face. "Are you more worried about yourself, or Alec?"

Katrina looked at her, and then the sky, and then back at Raquel. "I can handle a lot. I've proven it. You put me in a bad situation, I've got as much chance as anybody else on earth to walk out alive. Right now, it feels like only one thing scares me. Not bombs, not snakes, not shootouts with cartels. You want to know what really scares me?"

Raquel waited.

"Being a widow... the one who has to go on afterward." Another deep breath. "If I wanted this, I could have married a Navy SEAL or a cop. I picked the preppie goofball accountant with the heart the size of Connecticut. He's not supposed to be the guy running into a burning room or getting bitten by snakes or shot at. I'm not supposed to be the one worrying about whether he's going to come home alive. I can handle the danger to me. I don't know if I can handle the danger to him. I don't want to handle the danger to him."

Raquel nodded in understanding. Then after an appropriately long pause, sprung the trap.

"How do you think he felt all those times you were out there?"

Katrina grumbled.

"He's stronger than you realize," Raquel said. "Otherwise I wouldn't have him doing this. You're a virtuoso. He improvises.

You execute the plan. He rewrites it on the fly. That's why you two work well together. Yin and yang."

Katrina was about to respond when their phones buzzed simultaneously with a text. They both exhaled with dread and checked their phones.

It was Alec: GOT IT GOT IT GOT IT FOUND EM FOUND EM FOUND EM COME TO THE OFFICE QUICK NOW NOW NOW

Both women couldn't help but laugh at the message's tone.

"You going to resign?" Raquel asked. She felt only mildly frustrated that they would have to skip lunch, and debated grabbing takeout.

"No," Katrina sighed. "I just... I told you what my father used to say about Bukhari, right? That living as Jews between the Communists and the Muslims was like living between two scorpions."

Raquel nodded. "A burden few Americans can really understand." Raquel wondered if what her friend was really struggling with was a sense of guilt—an easier, better life in America than her parents had enjoyed in the old country.

Katrina unlocked her car. "Scorpions just sting, it's just their instinct. It's not good or evil, no malevolence, just their nature, it's what they do. I just... " She opened the door. "I don't want to wake up one morning and feel like I've become a scorpion."

They got in their cars, and Raquel wondered if Katrina had ever read Kafka's *The Metamorphosis.*

CHAPTER 41

LIBERTY CROSSING INTELLIGENCE CAMPUS
TYSONS CORNER, VIRGINIA

Alec had a smug smile on his face when Raquel and Katrina got to the office.

"Suppose I said we had figured out Atarsa's base of operations."

Raquel paused. "Where?"

He held up a plastic bag containing a well-worn, heavily wrinkled black shirt, removed it, and grinned widely. "Somewhere near Darvaza, Turkmenistan."

Off her frown, he held the shirt up to her face.

"Jesus, that stinks!" she exclaimed. "What is that, rotten eggs? Sulfur?"

He nodded enthusiastically, eyebrows approaching the stratosphere. "So I started looking for sulfur sources in Turkmenistan."

"VEVAK believes he operated out of Turkmenistan and Cyprus ..." Katrina murmured, weighing Alec's stinky evidence. "That doesn't really narrow it down, Alec. Turkmenistan is one of the world's largest producers of sulfur. Jaguar's Mexican, and his home country has got at least one sulfur mine, too."

Alec smirked and shook his head.

"Jaguar's a world-class bad-guy, kidnapping Americans, producing hallucinogenic drugs, living in a luxury condo in Mexico City. He's living the high life, baby!" Alec reviewed, snapping his fingers and waving his arms like one of Steve Martin and Dan Aykroyd's "Wild and Crazy Guys." "How many sulfur mines do you think this guy hangs around in? Look at this shirt—it's a nice shirt, beyond the stink. This is not a sulfur miner's shirt. He didn't go digging somewhere. He went *here*."

He pointed to the flat-screen monitor behind him.

"The Darvaza crater," Raquel read off the screen. Alec handed a map printed off from Google.

"Some giant fire pit that never burns out and apparently smells like sulfur. It's out in the middle of nowhere, but just off a major highway. Two villages nearby. Good place to disappear if you're Gul and Sarvin Rashomon, Starvin' Marvin, whatever her name is."

Raquel finished reading the website about the Darvaza crater, and looked at the map for a long time. She even picked up the shirt again and gave it another sniff, then winced.

"Okay," she said quietly. "Might as well check the latest satellite photos."

***

Two hours later, they gathered around the report from the National Reconnaissance Office.

"NRO is the best," Alec murmured.

NRO had looked along the highway that ran alongside the Darvaza crater, fifty miles in each direction. They found a half dozen small campsites and structures that could represent a remote site for Atarsa's base of operations. But by comparing them to archived images, they could determine that only one had been continually active for several months.

"Twelve hours ago, one truck, at least two structures, could be tents, some stuff around them, maybe crates," summarized Dee.

"Ladies and gentlemen, Atarsa headquarters," Alec announced confidently.

"Not so fast," Dee interrupted. "No satellite dishes. Could have them inside the tent at that time, or maybe they just don't have them. No guards, no sign of any security at all." She looked at Alec skeptically. "That could be anybody in there."

"If a drone isn't an option, we need another way to get eyes onto that site," Katrina said. "We monitored the compound in Abbottabad for months before the Osama bin Laden raid."

"We know what…" Alec paused to check her name on the paper. "Sarvar Rashin looks like from her video messages and the alias passports, and we've got an old passport photo of Gul from the time he flew through Amman," Alec continued. "All we need to do is get a person to that site to look inside those tents. Send us."

All of the women looked at Alec like he was crazy.

Raquel shook her head. "Don't get any ideas. I'm just letting you look at these images to indulge you. The decision to send anybody into the North Korea of Central Asia is way above my pay grade."

Katrina didn't feel much relief. It made no sense to send Alec to Turkmenistan, but it made at least some sense to send her.

Alec was undeterred and followed Raquel as she left the office suite. "You've heard of dress for the job you want, not the job you have, right? Why not make the decisions for the job you want?"

CHAPTER 42

CIA HEADQUARTERS
LANGLEY, VIRGINIA
SUNDAY, MARCH 28

Alec wasn't invited to Raquel's big meeting on the CIA's seventh floor with Acting Director Mitchell. There she laid out everything she and the NSA team had learned from the Iranian consulate's communications, Alec's theory about the Darvaza crater, and the potential Atarsa hideouts along the desert road.

Acting Director Mitchell decided CIA stations in Cyprus and Northern Cyprus would be instructed to hunt down any leads to Sarvar Rashin and Gholam Gul's location. The US Treasury Department would trace every account ever associated with Rashin and Gul, and any known aliases. The FBI was instructed to put out a BOLO—be on the lookout.

But then the point was raised about how to proceed if Gul and Rashin were still in either side of Cyprus' tense border or in Turkmenistan, and whether it was best to try to cooperate with local intelligence agencies and counterterrorism authorities. Raquel gently reminded the table that the raid that killed Osama bin Laden hadn't been cleared with Pakistani authorities.

The deputy director of operations suggested a CIA team should be involved in any effort to capture or eliminate the pair, and the Department of Defense liaison in the back of the room cleared his throat and pointed out that this was precisely the sort of work SEAL Team Six and Delta Force trained to do.

The director of the Clandestine Service noted that Turkmenistan was a particularly difficult place for covert operations, either Agency or military, because of the paranoid local counterintelligence services, who still demonstrated old Soviet habits. This led to a lot of debate about whether the US had a reliable ally in the region from which to base a special forces mission; Uzbekistan was ruled out; the rather oppressive regime had told US forces to leave about fifteen years earlier after the Bush administration objected to a brutal crackdown full of human rights abuses. After that, the country realigned itself closer to Russia and China.

Bagram Air Base in Afghanistan was an option, but tricky; the Taliban and a fractured band of hostile warlords effectively ruled much the country outside of Kabul, and the remaining US forces in the country debated whether the best historical comparison to their situation was Saigon 1975, Tehran 1979, Somalia 1993, Benghazi 2012, or Mosul 2014.

Azerbaijan was more promising, and still periodically expressed interest in NATO membership, but NATO was wary every time fighting flared up the country's internal dispute with the breakaway region Nagorno-Karabakh.

The Department of Defense still used Ashgabat Airport in Turkmenistan for a refueling stop for C-17 and C-5 cargo planes between NATO air bases and Bagram Air Base. The US government paid considerable "air navigation fees" and "air company infrastructure charges" in exchange for an extremely loose Turkmeni definition of "humanitarian aid," which included Turkmen officials choosing not to notice several shipments of humanitarian small arms and humanitarian ammunition heading to Afghanistan to assist with humanitarian assaults on the

Taliban. A small US Air Force team of about a half dozen to a dozen personnel managed the refueling operations.

Acting Director Mitchell said he would take their findings to the White House and said he would ask the Pentagon to begin prepping plans for an attack on the site suspected to be the Atarsa camp.

CHAPTER 43

Katrina came away from the seventh-floor meeting with a sense of progress. She was almost relaxed for much of dinner, and afterward she threw herself into a form of stress relief she felt she had neglected too long.

After she and Alec had climaxed, she rolled over. She thought she had heard her phone buzzing a few moments earlier, when the pair were too distracted by the moment's passions. Two messages from Raquel, one after another, both indicating urgency.

She picked up the phone and simultaneously clicked on the television in the bedroom.

"Why are you doing that?" Alec groaned. He knew eventually Katrina would tune to a news channel, which would just remind them of all the troubles in the world.

"Raquel called, I just want to know if—" she stopped.

Angra Druj, a.k.a. Sarvar Rashin, was on the screen again, but the image was different. New.

Katrina's gasp turned into a sigh. "I'm going to kill that woman," she murmured, staring at the screen.

A few minutes earlier, the local CBS affiliate in Washington had begun the eleven o'clock news with an update on the day's Metro station shutdowns and other police responses to suspicious packages. Then, as in New York weeks earlier, the signal intrusion began. The image was going out to broadcast customers, not cable, but within a few minutes the local affiliate program directors concluded the Atarsa message was news, and that all of their viewers should see it. They switched to the incoming Atarsa message.

Rashin sat, still veiled and in shadow, with the same ornate painted symbols and bloody handprints behind her. But the camera had moved, she was a little closer to it now.

"This ... does not stop," she said. "It will not stop. It will continue for the rest of your days. You have put your faith in false gods. You will be punished tenfold." She picked up a knife and ran it slowly across her left hand.

"Our knives will come for you all, including the children," she said matter-of-factly.

Then the video of her changed to a series of video snippets. Each one appeared to have been recorded on a phone and began at an unidentified person's feet and the pavement. Then the camera rose, and the hand of the person holding the phone held up a small sheet of paper with the Atarsa symbols on it. As the camera softened the focused on the piece of paper, the sites of the recording came into focus. Some of the sites were instantly recognizable—first Ground Zero in New York City; the Sidwell Friends school in Washington, DC, then Independence Hall in Philadelphia. The final three were unclear until Twitter and Facebook exploded with people recognizing their hometowns—Church Street Marketplace in Burlington, Vermont, the city hall in Peoria, Illinois, and the Wren Building at the College of William and Mary in Virginia.

The signal continued and then was interrupted. The confused anchors realized they were live again, and began excitedly trying to explain to viewers what they had just seen. Within a few moments, the national news bureaus interrupted the local coverage, dissecting the video, and warned viewers that Atarsa appeared to be telling Americans they were ready to strike both iconic landmarks and smaller cities.

But unlike the New York messages, this time there was a second interruption, beginning about twenty minutes later. Washington's ABC affiliate, broadcasting from a different tower, had its signal hijacked.

Angra Druj returned again, but she simply stared at the camera and chanted softly for a good two minutes, with few words discernible other than the occasional "help you."

Finally, after one of the longest and most unnerving awkward silences in television history, Druj said, "It is coming, and there is nothing you can do to avert it. No one can help you."

Then the signal switched to a series of recorded images. The first was particularly unnerving video of a distant yellow school bus, pulled off to the side of a road in a grassy field, tilted on a hill and on fire. No people could be seen outside of it; it was unclear if anyone was inside. The smoke continued to billow from the bus for thirty seconds; the only sound was a roaring wind. There was no clear indication of where or when the video had been recorded.

Then it was a rapidly cut sequence of video segments of terrifying airplane crashes from Taiwan, a 747 crashing in Afghanistan, a smaller plane from Iceland, and rapidly edited computer-generated footage reenacting a mid-air collision over Staten Island in 1960. Until this was later identified and clarified by the armchair experts on Twitter and the in-studio terrorism analysts, for a few moments people wondered if Atarsa had broadcast several deliberately crashed planes in sequence.

"Come follow us," Angra Druj whispered.

The video concluded with a flashing sequence of rapidly blinking red and blue lights that many viewers said caused immediate headaches, dizziness, and nausea. A subsequent forensic investigation indicated that this was similar to the strobe-like effect in a 1997 *Pokémon* cartoon that had sent nearly seven hundred children to the hospital with seizure-like symptoms.

***

Ward called Alec in between the two videos, and began the call: "Did you see that last one? The hand with the Atarsa symbol? It was right in front of the Wren building, right there in Williamsburg!"

Ward swore an elaborate blue streak before Alec could interrupt.

"All right, buddy, all right, calm down," Alec said. He grabbed underwear. What a mess, literally caught with his pants down. He had to get Ward thinking clearly again. A terror video filmed in your nearest town was ominous but not an imminent threat. "You've trained Marie and the kids on how to use a gun. They know how to protect themselves. You and they don't live that close to the campus or the historic district."

Ward was calmer, but still angry.

"It feels like it's right at my damn door."

"That's exactly what they want you to feel," Alec said. "But they're not. We're the ones who are hunting them. They're showing this to freak people out, and they're doing this because they can feel us getting closer. We've already put a bunch of 'em in the ground. You're the apex predator."

Ward's mood changed. "Damn right."

They continued exchanging theories about possible avenues of investigation when the network began broadcasting the second message. "Gotta go," said both men simultaneously, hanging up.

Alec and Katrina watched the second video, and then squinted when the screen became simply rapidly-flashing red and blue lights.

"Gee, cable networks, you better hope nobody watching at home is epileptic," Katrina swore. It felt like America's media was inadvertently doing half the work of the terrorists for them.

"Blipverts," Alec said, referring to a long-ago television show that he now found unnervingly prescient. "Atarsa is going to do the impossible. They're going to get Americans to turn off their televisions."

CHAPTER 44

LIBERTY CROSSING INTELLIGENCE CAMPUS
TYSONS CORNER, VIRGINIA
MONDAY, MARCH 29

"I've heard through the grapevine that the White House wants a military response," Raquel announced as soon as they were all gathered in her office the following morning. "The decision's been made to seek out Turkmeni cooperation on this."

She held up a hand, anticipating and interrupting Alec's objection. "At this point, if you want to go to Turkmenistan, you've got to ride on a missile like Slim Pickens."

Alec looked as if was going to vomit. "That's a huge gamble, hoping no one in the Turkmeni government warns Atarsa," he groaned. "How likely is it that Gholam Gul set up a terrorist operation over there and no one in the world's most paranoid government noticed?"

Around the table, everyone concurred the risk of Atarsa being warned about the strike was considerable.

"Send Katrina and me to check out the sites," Alec insisted. "We've never worked there before. No one there knows our covers."

"Did you hear what I just said? The Pentagon is about to create some new flaming craters of its own! Besides, you're the last person I should send," Raquel said. "You don't speak the language, you don't know the territory, you don't blend in."

Alec fumed. "I swear to God, Raquel, if you don't send me, I'm just going to get a tourist visa, pay to fly there myself, hunt these two down, and if I have to, I will kill them with a fork!"

"Turkmen eat a lot of dishes without cutlery," Katrina corrected under her breath.

Raquel shook her head. "Alec, you do not understand what we're dealing with! A covert operation over there is not an option," she said with irritation. "The reports from our station in Turkmenistan might as well be written by Orwell."

"The point is, every place we've gone, we've found something," Alec said. "The seventh floor has the Counterterrorism Center, the FBI's Joint Terrorism Task Force, everybody and their brother kicking down doors—or more likely, waiting for the warrants giving them permission to kick down doors—and we've been one step ahead of them because this is it." He gestured to the rest of the team. "This is us. This is our committee meeting. We decide to do it and we do it. We don't coordinate with other agencies. We don't sit around and wait for permission. We just show up and do it. We are a small, quick-moving, active cell, the same way the bad guys are."

Raquel exhaled.

"No fair using my own speeches against me."

Katrina stirred.

"Any chance we could ask the Turkmenis to let us assess the damage after the military strike?"

***

The diminutive Azi Dhaka stopped his truck a long distance from the highway. He let his eyes adjust to the darkness once his truck's headlights were off, grabbed his bag, and listened to the wind whip through the dusk sky. Off in the distance, he saw the burning flames of Darvaza, and began heading to the tent.

As he approached it, he saw the indentations in the sand, marking where Akoman and Angra Druj had knelt and prayed. Had a local spotted them, they would have remarked they were praying incorrectly by not facing Mecca. They knelt toward the crater and beyond it, barely visible on clearest of nights, the few faint lights of the village of Erbent. But neither one had spoken to a local in weeks.

He paused at the entrance to the tent. The remote, isolated location for their tent gave Akoman and Angra Druj a lot of privacy, and he knew they indulged their passions quite regularly. He had accidentally walked in on them once, and they hadn't stopped upon seeing him. Alas, he suspected, he had arrived too late tonight.

He drew back the tent's curtain entrance and found the pair under a blanket. Both emerged, unclothed and unashamed.

"No postcard from Jaguar or the Queen Termite," Dhaka reported. "Otherwise, the news is good." He reached into his bag and removed a slightly dog-eared copy of the most recent issue of *The Economist*, obtained from the gift shop of Ashgabat's nicest hotel for foreign visitors. He tossed it onto the bed, and Akoman and Angra Druj saw the cover depicting the Statue of Liberty crouching and covering her eyes, under the headline, ONE NATION UNDER FEAR. Akoman picked it up and gave the cover a satisfied nod.

He looked up at Azi and recognized the tension in his face. As far as Azi was concerned, their plot relied on too many disconnected people following precise instructions upon vague, easily missed signals. Akoman stepped closer and looked into his lieutenant's eyes, communicating a distilled essence of confidence. Everyone had been taught their part long ago, he knew. Everyone had gone their separate ways, confident they had never attracted unnecessary attention. Everything was proceeding as he had foreseen. The Voices were devouring their nourishment. The Queen Termite had performed her role perfectly so far, and they needed to trust all of the remaining Atarsa members would fulfill their missions.

Their silent, communicative look was interrupted by the alien sound of Akoman's satellite phone ringing. A communication like this was intended only for the direst emergencies. Akoman picked it up and recognized the number. All three exchanged looks of grim concern, but Akoman didn't answer, merely grabbing clothes and his bag.

***

By the afternoon, Raquel had ensured that Katrina and Alec could be sent on the next available US Air Force flight to Ashgabat, Turkmenistan, to join the Turkmeni military and intelligence services for assessment of damage by US air strikes. They were to pack bags and get themselves to Ramstein Air Base in Rhineland-Palatinate, Germany as soon as possible.

Raquel turned to Ward and Dee.

"Don't think that I let you guys get completely left out," she said. "I turned to the terror financing guys and found a job for you." She handed Ward a sheet of papers.

"Numbers? Bank records?" Ward recoiled. "What do I look like, an accountant? That's Alec's job. It was my understanding that there would be no math involved."

"One of Sarvar Rashin's known aliases is Zahra Amadi—apparently one of the most common first names and surnames in Iran—it's their Jane Smith," Raquel said. "It created roughly a million hits for the Treasury Department—"

"Kind of like Juan Lopez!" Dee piped up as she leaned over and started bringing up search programs on her computer.

"But Treasury found the name Zahra Amadi on an account that two years ago sent a half-million dollars to a now-closed US nonprofit, the New Beginnings Foundation."

"What's so special about this one?" Ward asked.

Raquel handed Ward another pile of printed-out documents. "Founded six years ago, it ran a volunteer service to provide emotional support to troubled youth. It suddenly closed its doors last year, citing financial difficulties, even though it seemed to be humming along, with twenty offices in US cities."

Ward looked up at her skeptically. "I'm your Rambo, and you're telling me to be a forensic accountant."

"The FBI and Treasury are going to be busy sorting through a ton of Zahra Amadis, God knows when they get to this one. I liked this one the moment I saw it. You want to find the Atarsa guys here in the States? Follow the money!" Raquel emphasized.

He grumbled. "Deep Throat never actually said that."

CHAPTER 45

DULLES INTERNATIONAL AIRPORT
VIRGINIA
TUESDAY, MARCH 30

Alec called his parents from the departure lounge. He and Katrina were scheduled to take a commercial flight to Germany and then catch an Air Force flight to Turkmenistan. He had been meaning to call them for a while, but he always found their conversations awkward, as his description of his life inevitably ran to conversational brick walls. CIA employees generally told their families and close friends the vaguest and most general gist of their daily work, revealing nothing classified. Alec found himself trying to explain overseas trips with Katrina to obscure locations and coming back with odd injuries. He lied about the details, and his parents knew he was lying, and he knew that they knew that he was lying.

Alec's father, Joseph Flanagan, was a retired and once quite successful banker, icon of the Westport, Connecticut community, active in the Chamber of Commerce and Knights of Columbus and coaching soccer. He and his wife, Aneta, had three sons, Michael Patrick, Martin Ryan, and Doran Alexander. Michael followed in his father's footsteps into the world of banking; Joseph tried to nudge Martin into the priesthood and Doran into police work, two iconic professions of Irish-American families. Neither set of nudges worked out the way Joseph expected, as Martin had become a musician, specializing in the theme music for professional wrestlers, and Doran's interest in police work eventually led him to the gates of Langley.

The Flanagans were prayer-before-dinner, attend-mass-every-week Catholics, and Joseph tried his best to instill in his children an intense pride in their Irish heritage. The boys' great-grandfather fled the Potato Famine and arrived at Ellis Island with "eighty dollars and three suitcases," as Alec could recite from memory. Early in his adult life, Joseph reconnected with some distant relatives left behind in Ireland and became an active American supporter of Irish nationalism.

Doran had grown up with dinner-table stories of the noble struggle to unite Ireland's thirty-two counties, the awful brutality of the Protestant/Unionist authorities and gangs, the horrible barricades dividing neighborhoods and the inspiring, impassioned murals of defiance. The Flanagan home became a small personal museum of Irish-American history, complete with the requisite portrait of John F. Kennedy on the mantel above the fireplace. Joseph Flanagan was a generous donor and fund-raiser for NORAID, the Irish Northern Aid Committee. His name came up in a mid-1980s investigation of the organization diverting funds for IRA arms purchases, but he was never charged with any crimes. Joseph dismissed all of the allegations as complete nonsense—adding that even if the charges had been true, it would only have been because the freedom fighters had been so unfairly outgunned.

But Doran—who began to insist people call him "Alec" in high school—kept seeing inconvenient facts in his parents' narrative. He asked how anyone calling themselves Catholic could possibly build a car bomb. His father could quote a lot of Saint Augustine and Thomas Aquinas and "just war" essays, but he just grumbled quietly when Alec pointed out that the Enniskillen Remembrance Day parade bomb had killed a pregnant woman—a rather glaring violation of Catholic pro-life principles. Aneta scolded her husband and son for bickering.

But all of the Flanagans carried stubbornness in their DNA and more than a bit of "Irish Alzheimer's"—an ability to forget everything except a grudge. Alec pestered his father about the Provisional IRA's decision to work with and buy arms from Libyan dictator Muammar Gaddafi. His father would counter with morally problematic alliances throughout history, including the World War II–era American alliance with the Soviet Union. Alec reminded his father that the Libyan dictator had once pledged to attack "Americans in their own streets."

Alec became increasingly convinced that his father's romantic vision of a united, happy Ireland had led him to a moral inversion. In the son's eyes, the IRA's attacks looked nothing like a war of national liberation. It was garden-variety terrorism: bombing the Brighton Hotel, firing homemade mortar shells at 10 Downing Street, leveling Canary Wharf in London, detonating a 3,300-pound bomb in downtown Manchester.

Over the years, Alec's arguments with his father grew angrier and more heated; he declared the IRA as bad as the nut-jobs who had tried to blow up the World Trade Center. For a while, Alec thought he might join the FBI, to be one of those cool-under-fire investigators who found all the clues and caught the killer and celebrated with coffee and cherry pie. He envisioned himself dismantling the IRA's fund-raising network in New England—and imprisoning all of his dad's rotating cast of long-lost friends from the old country with unexplained scars and the occasional missing finger.

Alec scoffed at teenagers who thought rebelling against their parents meant playing loud music.

But Alec's law enforcement ambitions faded after one of his classmates disappeared in his junior year of high school. To Alec, Sarina Locke was the artistic girl who seemed so much mature than everyone else, who seemed to have endless knowledge about obscure bands and movies and books that no one else did, who seemed to have spent all of her time away from school in some cooler, sophisticated, more exciting and dangerous universe. If high school was an extended waiting room, with the pleasures and dangers of adulthood locked behind the door to the next room, Sarina had somehow snuck into that adjacent chamber of mysteries and come back, willing to teasingly hint at what she had seen and experienced, but never quite tell the whole story.

She and Alec weren't dating, but they had grown considerably closer when she suddenly disappeared from her parents' house one autumn night. Many believed Sarina had run away from a troubled home, with the town rumor-mill reporting that her irregularly employed father was an alcoholic and that her mother was emotionally disturbed and had recurring "problems with drugs." Alec never believed it—he had certainly never seen her unhappy enough to just disappear without a trace—and found himself wondering about every stranger he had seen in town in the days, weeks, and months preceding her vanishing.

Sarina Locke's disappearance brought two weeks of media hysteria to Westport, a brief appearance by the FBI reviewing any possible leads for kidnapping, and an investigation that was thorough by anyone's standards except those of a quietly distraught sixteen-year-old. Sarina Locke was never found, no solid leads were ever generated, and no one was ever charged with any crime in connection to her disappearance. The New York City television station vans left the park in front of town hall on Main Street. Alec looked on in bewilderment as the yellow ribbons faded and eventually fell from the trees after months of exposure to the elements. The window signs came down and the community meetings and newspaper articles stopped. Everyone else's life went on; Sarina's parents divorced and moved away and young Alec never heard exactly where.

By the end of his senior year of high school, Alec walked around with silent, seething anger, feeling like Sarina had been erased and everyone around him had volunteered for selective amnesia, forgetting she had ever walked those halls, fought with her stubborn locker, forgot her homework, or worked on the decorations for the fall dance. At the end of the school year she disappeared, Alec took one of Sarina's pieces of artwork from the art room. It was a self-portrait, from an assignment to try to copy the style of Gustav Klimt, using a lot of gold paint. She had initially tried to paint herself in a near-copy of Klimt's *Judith and the Head of Holofernes*, right down to Judith's sheer top and exposed nipples. The art teacher insisted Sarina use some more gold paint to make it "school appropriate." Sarina's self-portrait still sat in a cardboard box in Alec's attic. He spoke about his memories of her with Katrina once in a great while.

Alec left his hometown thoroughly disgusted with the way his classmates, teachers, neighbors, and friends managed to move on from tragedy and forget about it, and with what he perceived as the police's complicity in the communal decision to forget. Alec feared police work would lead to a slow, steady erosion of his capacity for outrage, and knew he would never be an FBI agent. The bureau seemed too bureaucratic and rule-bound, too comfortable with leaving someone else's world-destroying tragedy unsolved in a box of cold case files. No, he knew his impatience and growing disregard for rules would only be accepted in the infamous, legendary, glamorized organization specifically assigned to break the laws of other countries: the Central Intelligence Agency.

Years later, when he was well situated in the Agency and with considerable resources of the intelligence world, Alec tried to restart a personal investigation into Sarina's disappearance, but he was no more successful than the local police. He did find himself intrigued by the number of mysterious disappearances reported across the country in the years before and after her vanishing.

He thought the nineties were a dark time in America that no one seemed to want to acknowledge, no more than his old hometown had wanted to acknowledge the unsolved crime that claimed a high school junior. His temper would flare if someone described that decade as a big national party, a rollicking cavalcade of presidential sex scandals, dot-com profits, and wildly embarrassing dance crazes.

To Alec, those years were series of ill omens, all blindingly obvious in hindsight: One plane crash after another off the New England coast. An Egyptian airliner suddenly diving into the sea, a calm pilot at the controls. Some guy in Milwaukee caught eating people. Cults committed mass suicide; fashion adopted the look of heroin chic; a certain bloody nihilism permeated the breakthrough of independent film. The sex scandals weren't always the stuff of political farce; a murder-minded Lolita on Long Island become a national antihero, the biggest stars in Hollywood feared the revelation of their names in the black book of an infamous madam, and Los Angeles crowds cheered a wife-beating double-murderer on the run. Something dark and twisted was working its way through the American psyche in those years, and Alec convinced himself that this amorphous darkness was tied into Sarina's sudden disappearance. That darkness waxed and waned since then but had never really left.

The really amazing thing, Alec realized, was that ominous portents like the destruction of Khobar Towers, the bombing of two American embassies, and a speedboat full of explosives blowing a sixty-foot gash in a US Navy destroyer just got lost in the noise. Everybody slept, everybody tuned out, everybody chose to forget the unpleasantness. But Alec wouldn't let himself forget. He smiled, he joked, he greeted the absurdities of life with goofy puns and deadpan snark. Very few people knew that behind all the laughter, he was looking for somebody rotten enough to remind him of the composite portrait of malevolence that he imagined had taken Sarina, and when he found a suitable candidate, he dished out punishment with relish.

He and Ward had discussed Sarina once, early in their friendship and at length; after that, they rarely felt the need to revisit the topic. Ward understood completely. He had been in Oklahoma City the day of the bombing, too young to do anything to help, but similarly scarred by the sights and sounds and smells. Like Alec, Ward would be forever determined to find the next man with evil in his heart.

Despite their country-mouse-and-city-mouse differences, Alec and Ward completely understood that barely audible whisper in their ear in their solitary moments: someone, somewhere had to pay for those tragedies.

In the disappearance of a Connecticut girl without a trace and the sight of children's bodies pulled out of wreckage in Oklahoma City, both men understood the how cruel the fallen world could be. Both men, having once been hurt so badly, could only cope by finding someone sufficiently morally culpable and acting out the Johnny Cash lyric: "I will make you hurt."

Ironically, Alec's work never quite brought him across what remained of the IRA, the Continuity IRA, the Real IRA, or the latest reconstituted offshoot, Nua Éireann Arm. Someday, he figured.

CHAPTER 46

K STREET
WASHINGTON DC
WEDNESDAY, MARCH 31

Ward was surprised to see that so many charities and nonprofits had their DC offices in a three-block-by-four-block radius near K Street: Special Olympics, Reading Is Fundamental, Fight for Children, Oxfam America, the Muscular Dystrophy Association, US Fund for UNICEF, CARE, and the relatively new Better Tomorrow Foundation. Philip Shuler, formerly treasurer for the New Beginnings Foundation and the man listed as the primary contact on all of its tax forms, now worked as director of development at the Better Tomorrow Foundation.

"Better Tomorrow, New Beginnings, these all sound the same," Ward said, shaking his head.

Cabinet officials from a previous administration founded the Better Tomorrow Foundation a few years ago. In addition to the black-tie annual gala, the foundation ran a slew of major conferences and other events on trendy charitable causes: mental health and counseling clinics in struggling communities, cancer treatment for refugees still escaping the Syria Toxic Zone.

Ward opened the door and entered. No one was in the small waiting room that offered the standard quasi-comfortable chairs, a coffee table, the nonprofit's glossy brochure featuring smiling Third World children, windmills, solar panels, and several black tie–clad figures holding a large check that included a lot of zeroes. A not terribly busy receptionist looked up at Ward.

"May I help you?" she asked.

"I need to see Philip Shuler," Ward said.

The receptionist explained to Ward that he would need an appointment.

He not-so-subtly bumped his holstered gun against her desk.

"I'm with the American government. Let me show you the latest addition to the FBI most wanted list," he said, holding up his phone. "You know those threatening videos from Atarsa?"

The receptionist nodded with concern.

He held up the phone. "The woman in the videos is Zahra Amadi, also known as Sarvar Rashin. Your boss Shuler used to work for her. Now, I can call my boss to get started on the paperwork for charges obstruction of justice," Ward lied, "or you can get Mr. Shuler now."

"Let me show you to his office!" she sprang out of her seat.

***

Philip Shuler only had a moment or two of disgruntlement when Ward and the receptionist entered without knocking.

"Mr. Shuler, this man is with—is—" the receptionist suddenly realized she hadn't gotten Ward's official affiliation.

"Ward Rutledge," he said to the deeply concerned Shuler, who was in a suit without a jacket. "I'm working out of the Office of the National Counterintelligence Executive." He was indeed working out of their offices. "I'm sorry to interrupt, but we're up against the clock here, and I need you to answer some questions."

"How can I help you?"

He held up the image on his phone.

"This woman, Sarvar Rashin, or maybe you knew her as Zahra Amadi. But you knew her." It wasn't a question.

"I met her only a few times," Shuler said, glancing nervously at his receptionist. "Maybe twice a year, I was at the New Beginnings Foundation for about three years. She came from overseas, one of the Gulf States, I think."

"Try Iran," Ward corrected.

"Okay, maybe Iran," Shuler said, nodding, rapidly becoming a bundle of nerves. "When a benefactor comes with six-figure checks to keep suicide hotlines and counseling programs going in nearly two dozen cities, you don't look that gift horse in the mouth."

"Tell me about anybody else who came with her, worked with her closely," Ward continued, hitting record on the voice recorder in his phone.

"There was another guy, I think. Azi. Azi Dhaka was his name. He was more of a details guy. He stayed a few weeks after she would visit. After we had set up a crisis counseling center, he came in, implemented a new program. He said they had a treatment and counseling method that had been very effective in other countries, and he wanted to try it here."

Ka-thunk. Ward could almost feel the tumblers falling into place in his mind.

"Ah. An Iranian, from a country with a regime that sponsors suicide bombers, comes to you with some new way of dealing with suicidal people. And this didn't smell funny to you at all?"

The blood drained from Shuler's face.

"What did this guy Dhaka want?"

"He, um ..." Shuler gave a nervous look at his receptionist.

Ward snapped his fingers in front of Shuler's eyes. "Don't look at her, look at me!" he barked. "What did Azi Dhaka want?"

"He told us that he wanted us to refer call-ins that met certain parameters to this new initiative, a particular treatment program. Troubled young men. Isolated."

"Where was the treatment center?

"I don't remember the name, I'm sorry—"

Ward slammed his palm flat on the desk. "Don't *lie* to me!"

"Okay, let me think," he said, rubbing his eyes. "I'm not lying to you. The program's name was something Greek. Iso-something. Isoceles. Iso-metric-era, something like that."

"You've been helping a terrorist group, Mr. Shuler," Ward said.

"I swear to you, I had no idea!" Shuler screamed. "Wait, wait, let me check my old e-mails." He turned to a computer and began typing. Ward casually and slowly put his hand by his gun, fearing that Shuler was preparing to destroy some sort of electronic evidence. Ward thought, *That's so cute, he thinks I'm here for court-admissible evidence.*

After a few moments of digging through his Gmail account, he nodded. "Okay, I found it," Shuler said. "Isoptera."

"I need every damn thing you have on Isoptera and the people referred to it," Ward said. He handed him a business card—just a name, cell phone, and e-mail—and wrote down Dee's e-mail as well. "Forward everything you have to these addresses. I really need lists of names, personnel records."

"I don't have—" Shuler looked up and saw the expression on Ward's face. "You know, I might have hard copies, papers from my New Beginnings years in my home office, but that's out in Great Falls."

"Let's go, right now," Ward said. "And I swear, if you try to run away from me once you're behind the wheel, I will catch up and run you right off the road. Are we clear?"

Shuler nodded, eyes wide, wondering if some sort of modern red-bearded Viking warrior had suddenly invaded his life. Ward turned to Shuler's secretary.

"You're probably going to want to clear his schedule."

***

About ninety minutes later, Ward was in the nicest home office he had ever seen, as Schuler sorted through a stack of file folders and papers five inches thick.

"Raquel, we'll talk about my bonus later," Ward said into his phone. "There's a lot to go through here, but I'll bet we just found a bunch of Atarsa's recruits."

"That's terrific," Raquel said. "I have Elaine from the Bureau here."

"Good, the Bureau is probably going to want to check on all of these people." Ward saw Shuler was waving at him from his home printer/copier.

"You need double copies of all of this?" Shuler said.

"Yes," Ward glared.

"Can I get compensated for the paper?" Shuler asked hopefully.

Ward resisted the urge to shoot him. "I'm on the phone with the FBI, and we're deciding whether to charge you with obstruction of justice, so maybe this would be a good time to consider the paper a cost worth swallowing." He rolled his eyes. "Take the business expense deduction!"

Ward hadn't told Shuler that the second set of copies was for him; he would continue his pursuit of the Atarsa members independently of the FBI and the Joint Terrorism Task Force. The sight of the burning school bus in the Atarsa video convinced him a sleeper was operating near his home and family.

"In fact, let me put you on speaker," Ward said. "Shuler, this is Elaine Kopek of the Federal Bureau of Investigation." He figured with Shuler's information, Kopek would be transferred from public affairs to the Joint Terrorism Task Force by the end of the day.

"Tell her what you told me about the profile of troubled youth that this Azi Dhaka guy wanted you to send to their separate treatment center." Ward had learned from Alec that sometimes it paid off to ask the same question multiple times, to see if someone would add more information when retelling it.

"Like I said, young men," Shuler said. "They wanted subjects with anger issues, grievances. The kind of deeply troubled young man you're afraid is going to shoot up a school someday."

Ward felt a flash of anger. "And you just sent them to this other facility, no questions asked?"

"We were told Isoptera's staff had worked with angry young men all over the Middle East, the kind of aspiring jihadist types, and gotten them off the wrong path, off to productive lives." He bristled at Ward's accusatory glare.

"And did you follow up on these angry young men that were sent off to this mysterious Iranian program?"

"Yes, and there were sterling results!" Shuler said defensively. "Gainfully employed, out of trouble with the law, drug-free ... I still can't believe this was connected to terrorism. There was no indication that anyone in Isoptera was even religious!" Shuler scoffed. "You seem to think that I should have suspected terrorism just because this woman was Iranian!"

"No, but it might have seemed a little odd to you that a wealthy Iranian would be so interested in finding violent, angry young men," Ward growled. "Nothing about all this seemed too good to be true?"

Shuler shook his head. "I don't even think any of the young men in the program were Muslim ... They weren't jihadist in their thinking, they were more like ... you know, the Columbine shooters or that nut in Santa Barbara who shot women because they wouldn't go out with him. You know, not terrorists."

Ward shook his head in disgust. "Close enough for my government work. These papers we're going through ... please tell me you kept the names of every person who was referred to this Isoptera."

"I can't be one hundred percent certain," Shuler said quietly. "If the list was kept in one place, I didn't have it. But a lot of the names are in here. I had to be able to demonstrate that we were genuinely referring the callers to counseling centers, in case the IRS doubted we were a genuine charity. Most of these should say where they were referred to." He held up the oldest stack of papers, with the edges dulled.

"Here, here's one of the first ones. Calvin Smith, twenty-five at the time, right here at the end of the column, 'Referred to Isoptera.'"

Ward looked down at the sheet of paper.

"Calvin Smith's dead, Philip," Ward growled. "He was the guy who started stabbing people at the Marriott in Detroit."

Philip Shuler's denial shattered. He looked at the paper, then started rifling through the pages behind it until he could find another. "Reginald Brown."

"He was the guy who stabbed people in Cleveland outside the arena," Ward growled. Elaine's exhale was audible over the phone line. This was it; somehow the previous investigations had missed that both Smith and Brown had been through the Isoptera program—probably because of juvenile records that had been either sealed or expunged. And, she surmised, had most of the Atarsa recruits.

Shuler's hands started shaking and he stumbled over to his desk chair. He wheezed out, "I didn't know!" and then began sobbing.

"Agents should be at the house in about fifteen minutes, Ward," Kopek said. Ward responded affirmatively and signed off. Then he figured he had about fifteen minutes to get through the stack of papers and find every name referred to Isoptera before the Bureau took over the investigation.

Ward thought highly of the FBI, but the thick stack of papers suggested that there were dozens of names—dozens of Atarsa sleepers, waiting for their signal to attack. One of those sleepers was, judging from their threatening video, lurking near the community that was home to his wife and children. And while Ward didn't mind the Bureau arresting almost every last one of the Atarsa sleepers, he was hell-bent that one who had dared threaten his community would be dealt rough justice by his own hand.

CHAPTER 47

TOP SECRET/ /NOFORN/ORCON//MR1

FAX COVER SHEET
Central Intelligence Agency

Washington, DC 20505

March [redacted]

To: Raquel Holtz, [redacted]
From: Merlin, [redacted]

Raquel, I know I'm not in a position to give orders anymore, and I have great faith in your decision-making. But I cannot overstate my sense of risk at sending Katrina to Turkmenistan in these circumstances.

This goes well beyond our discussions that growing swaths of the world are growing more dangerous over time. Start at the Morocco-Algeria border and head east; you won't find a stable safe corner until you reach the Pacific.

But this is a particularly bad neck of the woods, particularly for those of us who care to research long-forgotten history.

Those long-lost cities of Agartha and Shambala. Legendary wild men of the Central Asian plains. The old Silk Road is littered with natural fires that never go out. It's not just the "Gate to Hell" in the Darvaza crater that Alec thinks is the Atarsa hideout. In Azerbaijan, there's a hillside outside of Baku that has been on fire for as long as anyone can remember—it's blamed on gas leaks. The flaming stone at the temple of Yanartas near Antalya, Turkey. They call the fire in the crater of Baba Gurgur in Kurdistan the eternal flame; some theorize it has burned for more than 2,500 years. These places have always been associated with local legends of devils, demons, curses, and misfortune.

If, as we suspect, Atarsa represents not just a new name on a familiar version of modern Islamist jihadism but some dark mutation using its trappings—inspiring fear for the sake of fear, a band of rage-filled serial killers wound up and deployed by a particularly insidious strategic mind who has studied the weaknesses of American society—then we are likely dealing with beliefs, culture, and psychologies that Westerners barely understand. I suspect everyone associated with Atarsa has struggled with their own demons and let them set their path.

I know this sort of talk gets me dismissed as a doddering old man, but I increasingly believe that ignoring all these old myths and legends is an unaffordable luxury. We're fools if we blithely assume these stories that were first told long before you or I were born have no influence on our world today.

Let me hit you with one other local legend, one that might seem particularly pertinent to the moment. Right next door to Turkmenistan is Uzbekistan, where, in 1940, Western scholars discovered the oral history of the Karakalpak people. They shared an epic, 20,000-line poem about a legendary group of warriors, called the Kirk Kuz, who would have been active in the early 1700s. There were forty of these warriors, and they were unparalleled in everything: horse-riding, marksmanship with a bow and arrow, throwing axes and knives, sword-fighting and every martial art imaginable. Strength, agility, cunning, nerves of steel—the DNA of these warriors had to be a double helix of sheer concentrated lethality. They repelled invading hordes and every man in every direction feared the ruthless, silent efficiency of the Kirk Kuz warriors.

What makes the Kirk Kuz different is that they were all women, yet another group that may have inspired the legend of the Amazons. They only left their sisters in death or marriage.

This band of warrior-women kept the peace and defended their land for ages in a region called Samarkand. Which is just down the road from the city of Bukhara.

The tale of the Kirk Kuz would be easier to dismiss as merely a legend if you and I didn't know a woman born in Bukhara who's ruthlessly effective with all weaponry and a modern-day Amazon.

If her lineage is as special as I suspect, perhaps Katrina is indeed just the right person to send to a place called the Gate to Hell. But who could stand alone in the face of those fires?

CHAPTER 48

INTERSTATE 95 BETWEEN FREDERICKSBURG AND RICHMOND, VIRGINIA
WEDNESDAY, MARCH 31

Ward was driving back toward Williamsburg when the radio announced the news that the president would be addressing the country that evening. Within a few minutes, it had leaked: the Pentagon had launched a series of air strikes in Turkmenistan, targeting terrorist training camps used by the group Atarsa.

The president's voice resonated through the speakers in Ward's truck.

"Today, I ordered our great military forces to launch a targeted military strike of fire, fury, and ferociousness. Our target was camps in a remote region of Turkmenistan, camps where Atarsa's leadership planned the recent terror attacks against Americans," the president declared in prepared remarks from Camp David. "It is in the vital national security interest of the United States to decimate terrorists wherever they operate." He deviated from his prepared remarks. "Just terrible people, these guys. Total animals. We're better off with them dead. Totally and completely dead." He returned to the script. "This is only one of many ways we are bringing the full wrath of the American arsenal to our enemies."

Ward wondered if Alec and Katrina were on the ground yet, and if so, what they would find. In the meantime, some Atarsa member was still walking the streets near his family's home, and he knew he had to focus on what he could control, which was when and how that malefactor would meet a terrible fate.

***

PENTAGON BRIEFING
TRANSCRIPT (CONTINUED) 18:34 03–29–21
SECRETARY OF DEFENSE: I have personally reviewed the intelligence, and there is no doubt the sites in the Turkmenistan Desert are the operating bases of individuals connected to the leadership of the terror group. In response to the attacks, our government began a deliberate process, led by the National Security Council, to recommend diplomatic and military options to the president. We met over several days and I spoke with our key allies. We determined that this measured military response could best neutralize the threat posed by those in these camps and made appropriate communications with the Turkmeni government. As always, we examined how best to avoid civilian casualties in the execution of the strike, and our actions were successful.

The air strikes were conducted by a combination of US air assets based out of Bagram Airfield in Afghanistan and part of the NATO training operations in Tbilisi Soganlug Air Base in Georgia, as well as a variety of Tomahawk missiles launched from sea assets.

REPORTER: Mister Secretary, what was the most important objective of the air strike?

SECRETARY OF DEFENSE: To wipe the camp off the face of the earth.

REPORTER: And when you say, "our actions were successful," do you mean—

SECRETARY OF DEFENSE: The face of the earth has now been thoroughly wiped.

***

ASHGABAT, TURKMENISTAN

A half-generation ago, Turkmenistan's president, Saparmurat Niyazov, aspired to turn his country, a largely ignored, mostly poor but oil and gas-rich Central Asian landmass, into "the new Kuwait." A key part of his vision was building a new airport, one he insisted upon designing himself. Leaving basic aeronautic engineering decisions to a man with no experience led to predictable problems, such as the control tower being built on the wrong side of the runway, and the new terminal blocking the view of air traffic controllers when they were trying to guide pilots. The president hand-waved away the warnings, declaring simply, "It looks better this way."

In a country like Turkmenistan, nothing was required to make sense; the arbitrary will of the state claimed supremacy over all other forces, including logic and physics. Authoritarian, paranoid, unpredictable states like this were dangerous from the moment you booked the ticket, as Katrina knew from experience and family history. Katrina wondered if they were a giant involuntary experiment attempting to induce mass psychosis. Like the story of the emperor's new clothes, everyone knew that telling the truth was dangerous and quickly punished, so daily life required insisting outwardly, at all times, that the authorities were correct, and your eyes were lying. And if you did it enough outwardly, did you begin to do it inside as well? At some point did it become easier to believe the lie, even when you knew it was a lie?

Of course, her parents had escaped Soviet Uzbekistan, a country where they were forced to live a lie, or at least outwardly hide signs of their Jewish heritage and faith, to come to America... where she joined the CIA and voluntarily signed on to living a lie, at least when under cover.

She hadn't slept well on the flight to Ashgabat, enduring the nightmare about the Friendly's parking lot again. The mood was the same: dark, twisted; something terrible had happened and she felt hunted. Alec was with her again; the restaurant's windows were, like before, covered in wanted posters. Except now all of them had DEAD written in red letters across the faces.

In her dream, Alec was inexplicably and inappropriately cheery. "I've almost figured it out!" he told her. "I know who did this!" Alec ran around the corner of the restaurant, despite Katrina's cries to him to stop. She followed and found him standing before a giant dumpster—wider and flatter than a real dumpster. "It's in here!" Alec said gleefully, as if he had caught something. Katrina knew that whatever was in the dumpster was certain to kill them.

She had just seen the antennae, as long as fishing poles, emerge from the dumpster and the top of its head with giant compound eyes the size of beach balls when she woke up with a start. She was in the C-17, on final approach to Ashgabat.

***

The tall Turkmeni government agent, whose visage made Leonid Brezhnev look cheery, led a stiff-postured delegation of military and police officials to greet the C-17.

"Eziz Garayev, Ministry of Internal Affairs," the tall man said. Katrina and Alec nodded and introduced themselves. Despite the unfortunate acronym, MIA basically ran anything related to security in the country, combining both the Ministry of National Security, the country's intelligence agency, and the Turkmen national police force.

"We have already secured the site in the desert," Garayev said. "Your country's military offered an unforgettable demonstration of destructive power."

After a moment, he paused and held up a hand and gestured to Alec and Katrina's holsters.

"I do not believe our agreement with your government included your firearms," Garayev said grumpily.

"We're going after terrorists, you can't expect us to go after dangerous people unarmed!" Alec exclaimed in disbelief. He pointed to his left hand. "See this? Got it in Berlin, chasing this Atarsa guy. Intense firefight. Nearly got burned." He pulled up his pant leg, showing where the snake had bitten him. "Brazil. Another one bit me... that guy was a real viper." He rolled up his sleeve, pointed to his elbow. "Huge raid in Mexico City. Guns. A jaguar. Sewer water. By the time all the smoke cleared, there were skulls everywhere." He cracked his neck. "Hear that? Does that ever since last June when I tracked down this one guy, named Victor, out of Latveria—"

Garayev just stared skeptically and cut him off. "My men are more than capable—"

Katrina put a reassuring hand on Garayev's arm, and the Turkmeni officer almost jumped from the physical touch. She leaned in and whispered in his ear: "We know you can and will protect us out there, but this arrangement leaves my partner feeling... dishonored by being entirely dependent upon you for protection."

He furrowed his brow.

"Insufficiently masculine," she said in Russian.

Garayev almost smiled and gave a knowing nod. "I see." He turned to his men and muttered quiet orders in Turkmeni.

"We will release all of your equipment to you, including firearms, after a routine inspection," he offered to Alec. The two men shook hands. The Turkmen took Alec's firearm and his leather messenger bag and quickly inspected two cameras, a series of sealable plastic bags, a blood collection kit, a flashlight and extra batteries, a black light, a watchmaker's loupe, an emergency flare gun. They laughed at the plastic booties that were designed to go over his shoes.

They headed to a small convoy of waiting military vehicles and Toyota Land Cruisers. “He didn’t believe your stories,” Katrina muttered under his breath.

“It was all true!”

CHAPTER 49

INTERSTATE 64, APPROACHING WILLIAMSBURG, VIRGINIA
WEDNESDAY, MARCH 31

Dee and Raquel hadn't liked Ward's insistence that they cross-check his list of names with their databases, overt and covert, checking for ties to Williamsburg. But they had known Ward long enough—and he had proven his willingness to stick his neck out, time after time—that refusing him would bring aggravating consequences. Ward could behave less than fully rationally when he feared his family was endangered.

By the time Ward completed the list, he had forty names, and Shuler said that he was fairly certain the records in his home weren't complete. He estimated that anywhere from sixty to seventy troubled individuals had been referred to Isoptera. He had remembered a few names of referrals that were not in his files: Charles Sullivan, Keith Abse, "Norm Fine." Shuler said he remembered the last one because when he was brought to the program, the guy was neither.

Dee had helpfully explained that "Isoptera" means "equal wings" or "termite" in Greek.

"Could you look beyond the dictionary and see if any of these names live in the James City County school district?" Ward growled. "One of these guys stole a school bus and set it on fire, adding his little bit of nightmare fuel to the Atarsa video. I'm betting he's a local. Cross reference the names we have against—"

"Got it, got it," Dee sang. "DMV records, property records, tax records..."

Ward went over the notes that Shuler had added on the ride to his house in Great Falls. At one point he pulled off at a rest stop to read the stack of papers.

"The ones referred to Isoptera were young males, many but not all white, late teens or early twenties," Ward recalled, speaking to Dee on his hands-free carphone. "Trouble in school or finding or keeping a job, depressed, anger issues. Feelings of envy or a yearning for revenge were not far beneath the surface. Trouble at home, no relationships, few friends, little or no support network. Often obsessed with guns—well, nothing wrong with that—violent video games, movies. Coping with a sense of powerlessness, meaninglessness. Spent enormous amounts of time and energy dwelling on past slights, insults, sense of feeling rejected or humiliated. Constantly cultivating resentment."

"No shortage of those, huh?" Dee said. "I found the MySpace page of one of these guys—that shows you how old he is—but you can get the gist: 'Society locked me in a prison, now I will break down the walls! I lost at life because they cheated! It's time to turn over the board and end their silly game! I will punish them for cheating me out of the life I deserve!' Blah, blah, blah. Lotta 4Chan. Lotta talk about school shooters, praising them as rebels."

"Incels and Columbiners," Ward muttered, more than a little annoyed that modern society had taught him those terms.

Ward could almost hear Raquel looking over Dee's shoulder. "Jesus. They're cultivating homicidal maniacs."

"This is their plot," Ward said. "Gather sixty or seventy rage-filled guys willing to die and indoctrinate 'em. Love-bomb 'em or something."

"Love-bomb?" Dee asked. "I know you've got an extensive home arsenal, but there are some details we don't need to know about—"

"Love-bomb is a technique that cults use for recruits, shower them in attention, praise, validation, maybe even screw 'em, I dunno," Ward continued.

"Should I be worried you know a lot about cult recruitment methods?" Dee asked.

"For a bunch of years, I studied the militia movement as a personal passion," Ward said after a long pause, wondering how much he wanted to discuss Oklahoma City. "It's a short step from there to Waco to Manson to Jonestown. I figure Atarsa would get them good and dedicated to the cause, train them in the basics—hiding a concealed knife, breaking and entering, stuff like that. Then you shut down the program and disappear."

"And then they sit around, waiting to be activated," Raquel surmised. "They activate five and have them kill five people at random. Then within a few days, before the cops can catch any, they send them on their suicide run. They could have used all of them at once, but they want people to feel like the threat keeps growing. They're going to do it again with another five..."

"And with sixty-some guys, they can use five or six guys at a time, for about twelve waves of attacks," Dee shook her head, finally grasping the scale of the unfolding menace. Atarsa was ready to launch attacks week after week, month after month.

"If we've got forty of these names, we can louse up their plans, but we need to stop it cold," Raquel said. "Elaine says the Bureau's going to start full twenty-four/seven surveillance on them as they find them, hoping not to spook anyone not on our list. Then, when they've got as many as possible, take them all down."

CHAPTER 50

ASHGABAT INTERNATIONAL AIRPORT
TURKMENISTAN
WEDNESDAY, MARCH 31

Ashgabat was a surreal expanse of white marble and golden domes, like an ivory-and-gold model of a real city. She felt less directly watched than she expected; maybe her tan skin and careful attention to local attire really was convincing everyone else she was a local. As far as she could tell, tourists from anywhere were rare, and US tourists were exceptionally rare, even before kidnapping Americans had become an unofficial Olympic sport.

Within an hour, the government convoy of Land Cruisers and black SUVs were outside of the city. The Karakum Desert was sparse, empty, and flat. Not much grew between the oven-like days, frigid nights, and periodic blasting winds and dust and sandstorms. A few green shrubs dared expose themselves to the desert sun. One herd of camels went by, with the herder covering his face in a white hood with small eyeholes. Katrina thought it was unnervingly similar to the hoods of the Ku Klux Klan, without the pointed top.

As the sun set to her left, she passed the shell of a snub-nosed Soviet-era Mig-15 jet fighter, abandoned decades ago and stripped of anything useful. Around the bend, off in the distance, in a salt flat that seemed to go on forever, she saw what must have once been a Soviet-era rocket project, gargantuan, perhaps twice as long as the old US space shuttle. Like a giant black thimble on its side, it stood silently, half-completed and then abandoned, long since lost to rust and disrepair. What hadn't been eaten away by the elements made a nice home for birds and other desert critters.

Katrina furrowed her brow. A long time ago, she had wondered about joining NASA or the space program or one of the thriving private space exploration projects. She knew the Russians had attempted to equal the successful Saturn V rockets with enormous rockets of their own, designated the N1 program. The rockets built by the Soviets were gargantuan in scale and technically the most powerful rocket ever built by man. The one little catch was all of that unrivaled fast-burning explosive power proved just about impossible to control. The Soviet space program never actually managed to launch an N1 rocket correctly; the only four ever built all ended up as wreckage in one form or another. The most infamous failure was the second launch in 1969, which cleared the tower . . . and then the rocket suffered sudden massive failure of almost all of the engines, with one lone functioning engine steering the rocket into a quick looping arc, pointing the nose back down toward the earth. The second N1 impacted with the earth, detonating 2,300 tons of propellant fuel, one of the largest non-nuclear explosions in recorded history. Wreckage flew in every direction for six miles and droplets of rocket fuel fell from the sky like intermittent rain for a half-hour afterward. It took a year and a half to rebuild the launch site.

But all of the Soviet N1 rockets were destroyed, she recalled. What was this rusting husk doing out in the middle of central Asia? She shook her head and made a mental note to look into the mystery another day.

***

They drove for another half hour past the old Soviet rocket, then turned away from the highway, onto what could only loosely be called a road—more like a dusty path cleared of brush—until they saw smoke on the horizon. Within a minute, they saw small dark fabric fluttering from a tent post, an inadvertent black flag waving to them.

A small fleet of Turkmeni military vehicles had surrounded the site, and soldiers were picking through the debris.

"They've already taken any useful evidence and intelligence," Katrina said to Alec in Spanish, guessing that Garayev didn't speak the language. Unfortunately, Alec stared back with a furrowed brow, not understanding her. She rolled her eyes again, recalling that just a few days ago, he had insisted to Raquel that he spoke sufficient Spanish to work in Mexico.

She knew Garayev spoke Russian and might speak Turkish. She repeated her frustrated conclusion in French. When Alec shook his head in confusion, she shifted to Japanese. Again, no clue.

"What's left, Klingon?" she fumed, settling for English. "They've already removed anything useful."

Alec nodded. "Ey're-they eeping-kay it-ay as-ay argaining-bay ip-chay." Now she frowned in confusion and took a moment to understand him.

Before them "stood" the remains of a large tent. A few small smoldering patches of black cloth emitted wisps of smoke. Soldiers examined the mundane and thoroughly trashed wreckage of the camp scattered around the site: Tables. Chairs. Cots. One actual bed. What once might have been a power generator.

"A great demonstration of your national arsenal," Garayev said with an approving nod. "You must be quite proud."

Katrina slipped on rubber gloves and walked carefully to the center of the site, a still-smoking crater. After surveying all 360 degrees, she walked slowly, in larger and larger circles, working to the outer edge. Alec took a lot of photographs from the perimeter of the debris field. Suddenly Katrina stopped, looked quite closely at one spot, moved a piece of metal with her foot, and picked something up that had been hidden underneath.

"I think I found something..." she held it up. "Key." It was small, metal, blackened on one side, the blade slightly bent. It was too small to be a car key.

"Filing cabinet?" she wondered as she walked it over to Alec. "Desk drawer? Padlock?"

Alec popped the magnifying lens of the watchmaker's loupe in his right eye and studied the key closely. He attempted to rub away dirt and smudges on the bow, or the part that a person's fingers used to turn the key. "There's something written here... Na... Na-on... Nay-on-hay-thee-a?"

Katrina looked closely and confirmed. "Naonhaithya." Alec put it in a plastic evidence bag and she returned to that point in the debris field.

Within ten minutes, Katrina felt like she had seen enough. She glanced over at Alec and waved her arm at the site like a game show hostess, showcasing the parting gift. She raised her eyebrows and smiled. He understood it as a dare. Alec nodded back, looked around, took a few steps up and down the debris field, then turned back and looked at her. He struck a comic pose of bent arms, extended tongue, and closed eyes. She chuckled and nodded approvingly.

Garayev frowned. The American couple was communicating in an unspoken code that required years of marriage to grasp.

"Mister Garayev, we have a problem," Katrina said firmly. "Something's missing from this site."

Garayev did not respond at first; he merely tilted his head in an unconvincing pose of curious surprise. Finally, after staring in calculated confusion, he replied, "I assure you, nothing was taken."

"She didn't say stolen, she said missing," Alec noted.

"Human remains," Katrina declared. "There was no one here when the missiles hit."

CHAPTER 51

LIBERTY CROSSING INTELLIGENCE CAMPUS
TYSONS CORNER, VIRGINIA
WEDNESDAY, MARCH 31

Raquel sent along all of the appropriate updates up and down the agency's chain of command. Deep down, she knew they would be lost in the intense activity throughout the intelligence community surrounding the US bombings of the Turkmenistan desert.

Finally, she had time to think.

Promoted from the analytical corps, she had been trained to think, study, dissect, and find logic at work—patterns, habits, to see the hidden order within the disorder. Harold Hare had taught her to assume nothing and doubt everything not explicitly verified.

He liked to tell an old joke about CIA analysts. A pair were traveling on a train in Europe's countryside, and passed a field full of sheep.

"Could you imagine having a coat of wool in this summer heat?" the first analyst asked. "It's a good thing those sheep have been sheared."

"Yes, it does look like they've been sheared," the second analyst murmured, "on this side."

Raquel felt like something dark and terrible was at work, trying to stymie them every step of the way. The death toll from

Atarsa's attacks wasn't particularly high. But the group's choice of attacking high-traffic public locations made it likely someone would record it all on their phone—and the media would almost instantly broadcast the images around the world. In years past, Alec and Raquel had argued about how the media should do its job in a world with terrorism. Alec argued the media had a responsibility to show precisely how brutal and evil terrorists could be; a refusal to show terror acts amounted to whitewashing and hiding the truth. Raquel feared that the media showcase rewarded terrorists, turned the news into one of their propaganda videos, and inspired copycats and wannabes. *I told you, Alec*, she thought.

Atarsa's plan was to take the already frayed American social fabric and put it through a woodchipper.

Evacuations of subway stations, hospital wings, skyscrapers, and airport terminals were already becoming depressingly commonplace over every misplaced bag and abandoned backpack. (Raquel wondered if terror groups ever intentionally left backpacks in places just to set off alarms.)

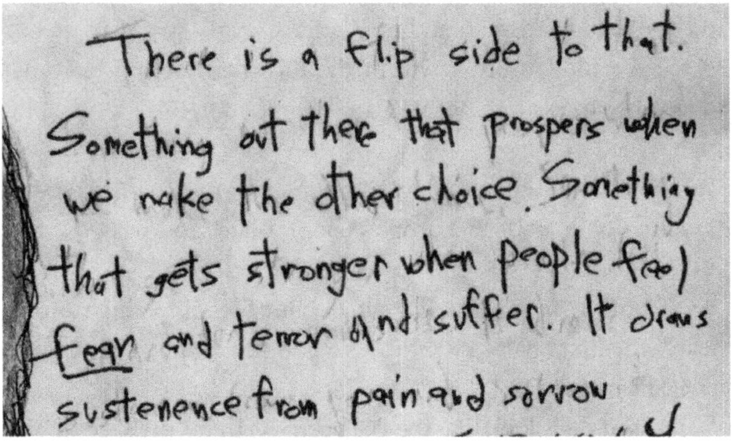
There is a flip side to that.
Something out thee that prospers when
we nake the other choice. Something
that gets stronger when people feel
fear and terror and suffer. It draws
sustenence from pain and sorrow

She looked through the piles of reports on the table next to her desk and dug out her copy of the diary of Francis Neuse.

She found the transcribed section where the mad pharmacologist Neuse said his captors had been demons and tried to explain "who they serve."

"When people feel fear." Now, far too late, the thread was crystal clear; all of Atarsa's actions were designed to spread fear: the randomness of their attacks, the taunting from the television screen, Director Peck's very public panic attack, and Katrina's point that they had no other discernible goals, demands, or agenda. Unlike the Islamists, Atarsa offered no avenue of concession that would make the terror attacks stop.

The only thing we have to fear is fear itself, Raquel thought. She noted how often FDR's quote was repeated, often far outside its original context of the cascading calamity of a financial panic in the markets. Outside the economic realm, there was plenty to fear; that's why even that beloved president made the constitutionally inexcusable decision to send tens of thousands of Americans of Japanese ancestry to internment camps.

You didn't spend your career at the CIA if you didn't love your country, but recent years had given Raquel some nagging fears about America.

Some mornings she looked at the news and wondered if she recognized her country anymore. When the citizenry wasn't gripped by fear, it always seemed angry. Angry at the president, at politicians, at Muslims, gays, transsexuals, gun owners, evangelical Christians, Catholics, celebrities, radio talk show hosts, single moms, drug users, college students who were allegedly "snowflakes," small town bakers, football players, insurance companies, pharmaceutical companies, government bureaucrats, cops, young African-American men, illegal immigrants, legal immigrants, atheists... Oh, she thought, looking at the tiny six-pointed star on her bracelet, and of course, Jews. They always seemed to be the universal scapegoat of every extremist on both sides of the ideological spectrum.

Raquel didn't think of herself as old, but she found herself thinking the kind of thoughts she always associated with old people, such as her parents. She remembered her twenties as an energized time of ambition and determination. (It helped that mentors at the Agency, including Harold Hare, had picked her out early as having enormous leadership capability.) When did Americans get so prone to self-pity, so quick to lash out at others in anger over setbacks?

Her husband, Vaughn, was cool as a cucumber no matter what the day threw at him. Was that trait disappearing? It seemed like a disturbing number of Americans, particularly young men, couldn't handle adversity or setbacks and were quick to look for scapegoats. Young men, killed by police after shooting sprees, left disturbingly similar manifestos, raging at an endless array of personal injustices and pledging to punish those who had what they wanted and that they seemed incapable of obtaining: a satisfying job, a girlfriend, friends, happiness. Their problems were so common as to be nearly universal, but in their eyes, they were historically unprecedented injustices, and the shooters denounced the alleged selfishness of everyone around them while oblivious to their own self-absorption.

For some reason—bad parenting? a materialistic culture? the Internet? a lack of spiritual guidance? a lack of any kind of perspective?—America had become an assembly line of angry young men full of unrealistic expectations, easy pickings for the twisted pied pipers of Atarsa.

If enough Atarsa sleepers slipped through the net, just how would Americans respond? Thankfully every previous terror attack in American history was followed by a massive retaliatory response like on 9/11 or a quick apprehension of perpetrators like in Boston. San Bernardino and Orlando had not set off a wave of terror. But what would happen if attacks kept coming, every few nights, for weeks? Would Americans start to avoid public landmarks and busy city streets? Would they turn on strangers in suspicion? Or would the attacks become so routine that Americans just got used to them?

Raquel allowed herself other ominous thoughts. Katrina and Alec had no guarantee that they would find Sarvar Rashin and Gholam Gul in Turkmenistan. They could be anywhere by now, reorganizing themselves, training another batch of sleepers. They could try to mass-produce the fear toxin used so effectively on Peck.

"Here we go," Dee shouted from the other office, catching Raquel's attention. "I just matched one of the names on the list with a current address in the Williamsburg area. You owe me big time, Ward. Your guy spelled it wrong, but I checked for variations. Norman Fein, F-E-I-N, 1333 Queens Crossing, Williamsburg, Virginia."

Ward hit the accelerator and hoped no state troopers would be along his route.

***

Ward stopped his truck in a neighborhood outside Williamsburg, Druid Hills.

Dee had rapidly put together a fairly detailed biographical file of Norman Fein just from his non-expunged criminal record and court transcripts. Fein lived with his grandmother Tara Whitman, at this address and worked at the local gas station/convenience store. His working-class parents had died in a car accident during his first semester at community college, and Fein moved in with his grandmother. Things got worse fast. He dropped out, started taking drugs, started stealing to support his habit, and faced assault charges for hitting his then-girlfriend. For three years, he rotated between dead-end jobs, short-term jail sentences on multiple counts of assault and possession of controlled substances with intent to distribute, rehab programs, and counseling programs.

Finally, a call to a suicide hotline brought him to the New Beginnings Foundation, which selected him for Isoptera.

According to Fein's parole records, he spent four months in the Isoptera program, which was then operating out of a drug treatment center. He exited sober and a changed man. The parole officer's final report described Fein as "a much more mature, serious, focused young man with a bright future ahead." Fein had worked at the gas station and had been promoted to shift manager.

Parked directly across the street from the house, Ward studied Fein's home. There was a back door and backyard. Dang it, this is where Alec would be handy. Ward liked to tease Alec about his marksmanship and other combat deficiencies compared to a veteran Army Ranger, but Alec could usually hold his own in a fight. Alec was better at improvising cover stories on the fly, asking a lot of questions without seeming nosy, and getting potential foes to underestimate him with an amiable, bumbling persona.

Norman Fein's car was in the driveway, and Dee's NSA friends had determined his phone was inside the house but turned off. Unusual, Ward noted.

The Department of Motor Vehicles photo of Fein showed him in a crew cut, reddish brown hair, long nose, dark eyes. Something about him looked familiar to Ward, but he couldn't place it. Not Fein himself, but the face reminded him of someone. He didn't live that far from this community; had the two men crossed paths before?

Dee had already checked Fein's cell phone and the landline for call records and found them surprisingly quiet in the past few days. She couldn't find any indication that Fein's grandmother owned a cell phone or medic alert bracelet. She noted Tara Whitman's two-decade-old car had expired registration with the state.

"Okay, but Fein's gas station does car inspections," Ward noted. He spotted the grandmother's car halfway down the block in a parking space reserved for property owners when he drove by the house; it looked like it hadn't moved in ages. "He could have inspected it himself."

"Maybe she's gotten too old to drive herself and he just let the registration expire," Dee's voice chirped in the earpiece. Ward grunted.

***

Ward had "borrowed" a Range-R, a handheld radar system used by the FBI, US Marshals Service, and some police forces. The brochure boasted that the device "can 'see' through walls, floors, and ceilings constructed of reinforced concrete, cement block, wood, brick, adobe, glass and other common non-metallic construction materials" with a range of fifty feet. It basically looked like a stud finder. Ward also had his infrared scope. Despite what the movies demonstrated, infrared rarely gave any good view through walls; even a curtain could obscure the heat signature of a human body.

But Ward thought his device was on the fritz. The image on the blurry, Technicolor infrared-vision in the scope made no sense. The figure in the infrared image looked rotund, morbidly obese, body a giant oval. The arms were still skinny, but seemed to be exceptionally low-shouldered, and wearing something badly rumpled or jagged.

Norman Fein's old police mugshot showed a vacant, malignant stare. His much more recent driver's license photo showed him cleaner, no slump in his posture, almost a smile to the camera—like he was laughing at a private joke he refused to share with the DMV. But in both cases, it was a lean, almost lanky figure, nothing like this round silhouette.

Norman—or whoever this was—seemed to be wearing something atop his head, creating two short rods sticking out of his scalp, like bunny ears or antennae. The body was wiggling, in motion, and then Ward's heart skipped a beat. The odd-shaped infrared image, with a head scrunched down and seemingly hunchbacked turned and seemed to look directly at Ward. After a moment of Ward wondering if Norman Fein had seen him, his target got up, went to the bathroom, and then returned to the couch in front of the television.

As the evening progressed, Fein ate food from the fridge, watched some more television, then went to a laptop computer in another room. Ward noticed that there was no indication that his grandmother was in the house.

"Dee, any way we can figure out what he's looking at?" he asked.

Dee checked to see if Fein's computer was infected with the NSA-developed "GUMFISH" malware, but unfortunately for her, it had not. If Fein's computer had that, she could have simply sent some commands to his IP address, activating the malware within his laptop; the camera atop his computer—or tablet or phone—would begin taking pictures and send them to an NSA server.

Her next move used an NSA program called Quantum, a name that Dee always thought must have come from some overeager James Bond fan. When a computer like Fein's laptop connected to a website like CNN.com or the New York Times, it received data from several different sources—the Times server, as well as some banner ads and images that the site's advertisers kept on different servers, as well as some additional code within the page that directed the browser what fonts to use and how to lay out the page. The NSA exploited a vulnerability in that additional code, slipping their own program into the user's computer.

Thus when Fein checked the news websites for more information about the US bombings in Turkmenistan, his computer vacuumed up and executed a special little program from Dee. The program ran through Fein's laptop, targeting a processor called the Cypress EZ-USB. The circuit that ran electricity to the small light next to the camera above the laptop screen was connected to the PD3 port of the Cypress processor. When the PD3 port sent a high signal, it was in standby and the light was off. When the signal was low, the standby order stopped and the light switched on.

A simple insertion of code—0x00c8—reordered the functions of the processor. The camera began normal operation and started sending the signal to an NSA server, but the PD3 port continued to send a high signal. The standby order never stopped, and the computer's light never turned on. And as far as Norman Fein could tell, his computer was not surreptitiously recording him.

When the live video feed from Fein's computer popped up on Ward's phone, he gasped and marveled at how easily Dee had turned the man's own computer into a covert surveillance tool. How many times had the CIA or FBI struggled to get a camera or other recording device into a secure location? Now everyone set up a small camera connected to a global network in their own houses and just assumed they were secure.

"I hope he doesn't start checking out porn," he chuckled. He checked his watch and realized the hour was late.

Knowing that Dee and other personnel back at Liberty Campus were now able to watch his bedroom through the laptop camera, Ward set his phone for an alarm to ensure he would awaken before Fein and slept in the truck.

CHAPTER 52

KARAKUM DESERT
WEDNESDAY, MARCH 31

Garayev insisted that the camp couldn't have been empty when the missiles hit; he insisted the occupants must have been vaporized.

"What, are you saving all the good lies for later on?" Alec scoffed.

"That's not helping, Alec," Katrina gently nudged him and turned her attention to Garayev. "Sir, I've seen the aftermath of a lot of drone strikes. Even if you guys had removed the bodies, or body parts, you wouldn't be able to clean all the blood. It soaks into the ground, fabric, everything."

Alec started writing something down. "Eziz Garayev. I want to make sure that when we tell the president that the Turkmenis lied to us, I spell your name right. But hey, I'm sure this won't turn out badly for you," he scoffed sarcastically. "I mean, it's not like either of our presidents have a reputation for terrible tempers or anything—"

Garayev's face turned red, but Katrina held up a hand, and began speaking in Russian.

"Look, Eziz, we know this wasn't your decision. You've shown us nothing but the respect and courtesy of a true ally since our arrival. I'm looking at this and seeing a good man who's been forced to go along with a bad decision by his superiors, a bad decision that he tried to avert." She knew the Turkmeni soldiers were listening. She raised her eyebrows. "Am I right?"

Garayev looked around. "We are an honorable people." He paused a long time. "But there is a concern that some individuals within our government may have cooperated with Atarsa. It is possible someone warned this camp about the coming strike." He looked at his soldiers. "If so, it would bring great shame to our nation."

Katrina nodded. "We can fix this. Alec and I can send back a very positive report to Washington, saluting your cooperation and honor. In exchange for doing that, we would appreciate if you could arrange a few simple requests in return."

He nodded.

"A Land Cruiser, two AK-74s with suppressors, night vision goggles ... and the right to investigate the nearest villages with no interference from local police for twenty-four hours."

It would take two days of meetings and phone calls, and a lot of debate about the distinction between an American intelligence report that stated "some elements of the Turkmeni government *may have* warned Atarsa" and one that stated "elements of the Turkmeni government *probably* warned Atarsa." But eventually the Turkmeni authorities relented and gave Katrina what she wanted.

CHAPTER 53

DRUID HILLS NEIGHBORHOOD
WILLIAMSBURG, VIRGINIA
THURSDAY, APRIL 1

Ward's phone vibrated before dawn. He awoke with a start, realized where he was, and turned his attention to Fein's house. Fein's car was still in the driveway. No lights were on in the house.

He noticed a Chevy Suburban with tinted windows had arrived and parked itself down the block in the other direction and other side of the street. *Hello, FBI*, Ward thought.

The sun rose, with no other discernable action. Fein's laptop was closed, the camera inoperable. Around eight-thirty a.m., Ward's phone buzzed. "Is Fein still there?" Raquel asked with new urgency.

"Yeah, what's up?" Ward responded. "There's an FBI team here sticking out like a sore thumb, must be the bottom of the barrel team that pulled this duty."

"I called over to the Bureau to let them know that we had our own ongoing independent surveillance," Raquel said. *That explains why they didn't knock on my window during the night*, Ward realized.

"Have you been listening to the car radio or following social media?" Raquel asked.

"No, I'm on stakeout," Ward declared huffily. "That generally involves consistently paying attention to whoever it is you're staking out."

"We're getting word from the target sites—Atarsa tried their attacks this morning. No, this is not an April Fool's Day joke."

Ward swore. He had not expected a morning attack. "Wait, tried?"

"The news isn't that bad. Guy a block away from Ground Zero pulled out a knife, got shot by NYPD before he could stab anybody. In DC, another guy jumped out of a car, tried to attack the kids heading into Sidwell Friends. FBI was already there, tackled him before he could get halfway to the gate. There were stabbings a block away from Independence Hall, Church Street Marketplace in Burlington, and city hall in Peoria, Illinois, but so far, nobody dead. Police, FBI, Homeland Security responded fast."

Ward allowed himself a grim chuckle. "Telling us their next targets was a dumb move."

"I wouldn't bet on them making that mistake again."

"This is good," Ward let his muscles relax slightly. "Their attacks fizzle, right after we bombed the camps in Turkmenistan. Hey, did Katrina and Alec check in yet?" Ward asked.

"Nothing yet," Raquel answered. She paused a moment. "We're still missing a piece of the puzzle. Who's in between the foot soldiers and the masterminds? Where's the middle management? This all gets done with some guy out in Turkmenistan sending postcards?"

In her Tysons Corner office, she shook her head. "They've got to have at least one person stateside. So far, none of the stabbers caught have given anything up."

"Really?" Ward asked.

"Started screaming for lawyers the moment the cuffs came on," she sighed.

Ward chuckled. "I could make 'em talk."

"No, no, don't tell me!" Raquel snapped. "I don't want to know! My next polygraph is going to be bad enough, as is!"

CHAPTER 54

DRUID HILLS NEIGHBORHOOD
WILLIAMSBURG, VIRGINIA
THURSDAY, APRIL 1

Norman Fein didn't leave his house. Dee, remotely monitoring his computer's activity, said he had checked his Internet a few times throughout the day. Through a window, Ward could see a television on.

"This guy needs to grow up, get a job, and start a family," Ward said disapprovingly.

Shortly after one, Ward's phone buzzed again. This time it was Dee.

"Fein still there?" He could tell from her tone something was terribly wrong.

"Hasn't moved all day," Ward said. "I had to get out and stretch my legs, getting cramped. He didn't see me. What's up?"

"Atarsa adapted fast. They just launched another five attacks. Multiple victims. All in restaurants. An Applebee's in Ohio, then Nashville, Jacksonville, Boston and The Palm here in Washington. Hit the lunch crowds. All of them ordered steak, then used the steak knives to stab the patrons around them."

Ward pounded his fist against the top of the steering wheel.

"We can use dogs to sniff for bombs, we can check firearms purchases, but none of that matters with these guys … they just go into a crowded location and we hand them the weapons."

He opened his browser in his phone; the web and social media were already starting to fill with images of the attack, recorded by restaurant patrons with their phones and nearly instantly shared on social media. In Jacksonville and DC, the perpetrators had gone to the restrooms, put on old, off-white Soviet-style rubber gas masks with large, dark, shaded eye lenses, then attacked the patrons with their steak knives. The videos showed patrons shrieking and covered in blood, tables overturning, glasses and plates crashing to the floor.

"Those gas masks—any poison or something?"

"No sign of that yet," Dee answered. "Probably just picked them because they're creepy as hell."

He debated going into the house, grabbing Fein, and squeezing answers out of him. But the guys in the FBI surveillance van probably would have had an issue with that. Atarsa was attacking again, and his butt cheeks were starting to go numb from sitting in the driver's seat of his car for hours upon hours.

CHAPTER 55

LIBERTY CAMPUS
TYSON'S CORNER, VIRGINIA
THURSDAY, APRIL 1

Dee went to the office kitchenette and microwaved some popcorn. Raquel emerged from her series of meetings and told Ward that the orders had not changed: don't interfere with the FBI team; the Bureau had the final call on whether to raid Fein's house.

That decision became a little more difficult shortly after five p.m, when the evening broadcast of WDCW, the Washington-area CW affiliate, was interrupted.

It was a tight, close-in, poorly focused shot of Angra Druj's face.

"We walk by you on the street. We sit next to you on the bus. We are your neighbors. We are behind you on line at the store. We practice sneaking into your homes and workplaces and every place you thought you were safest, leaving little trace. We just move one thing, just a bit ... and we smile, knowing that you will wonder how it moved."

Then they cut to a series of grainy, green-and-white night-vision camera footage, recording a couple sleeping in their bed. The image abruptly cut to more night-vision footage of a children's bunk bed. Then a crib.

The video switched to full-color: A hospital hallway. A hotel hallway. An apartment building. All of these sites were too generic to be identified—which was, of course, the point.

"We are everywhere," she chuckled. "And you never see us."

Finally, the video cut to a hand, holding a piece of paper, depicting a sketch of the Atarsa symbol. The camera panned up ... and down a long open green, visible in the distance was the Wren building on William and Mary's campus.

"You ... are not safe," Druj's voice declared once again.

After watching the video on his phone, Ward's knuckles were white. "Raquel, as soon as the sun's down, I'm taking him out—wait."

Ward had set up a motion detector by the property's back gate, and it was beeping on the laptop computer set up on the passenger seat. He looked up the road and saw no movement in the FBI's Chevy Suburban. The Bureau's D-team had failed to watch the backyard, and Norman Fein had crawled under the fence. Ward had noticed the hole earlier and briefly wondered if some dog had dug his way under it. He quickly surmised it was the work of a two-legged beast.

***

Norman Fein had watched the Atarsa video twice as soon as it was posted to the Internet on news sites, and then closed the lid on his laptop.

Norman had noticed the FBI SUV and concluded he couldn't take his own car or head out the front door. He left the house through the cellar door that led into the backyard, which was surrounded by a wooden fence. He slipped under the fence using the ditch he had dug a week ago and within a few minutes, he was walking down the street, backpack slung over his shoulder.

Norman Fein knew it was his lucky night. His night got even better when a red-bearded gentleman in a baseball cap slowed his F-150 and asked him if he needed a ride.

"Where you headed?" the bearded man asked.

"William and Mary campus," Norman answered.

"Hop in," the man smiled.

Norman Fein smiled back, felt the kitchen knife in his jacket pocket, and felt a little private glee at the way this pickup truck driver had no idea of his true intentions.

He got in and smiled up right up until the moment the man raised his canister of mace and sprayed the entire contents in his face.

"April Fools, dumbass!" the man whispered gleefully.

CHAPTER 56

KARAKUM DESERT
TURKMENISTAN
FRIDAY, APRIL 2

After two and a half days of haggling and negotiating with government officials back in Ashgabat, the Turkmeni authorities outfitted them with their requests. Garayev requested was that the national police be given custody of the key; surely some official was about to be harangued for missing it in the initial inspection of the site. Alec and Katrina spent much of the day driving back down the lonely desert highway, periodically stopping to ensure that they were not being followed. Satisfied, Katrina pulled over and they started checking the vehicle for tracking and listening devices. They found four, left them by the side of the road, and then continued their drive.

A few minutes later, as the sun began to set, they saw a bright orange glow in the sky up over the next hill. Katrina let out a small gasp.

"This is it," she said. The Darvaza crater was beautiful from a distance, an endlessly burning perfect circle carved out of the desert. She quickly understood how the otherworldly anomaly could earn the nickname "The Gate to Hell."

The plan was to use the AK-74s first and their own American-made SIG Sauer P320 Compact pistols only in dire emergency. The idea was that if they left any evidence, it might be mistaken for the work of the Russian-equipped local security forces. The sun set quickly.

Katrina looked down the road in her night vision goggles. Even glancing toward the flaming crater in her peripheral vision offered a near-blinding light. She removed the goggles. She realized that if indeed Jaguar had met Atarsa's leaders at the crater, and anyone from Atarsa was still around this site, their best bet was to approach by foot.

***

When she had just passed the flaming crater, she saw it, on the other side of the crater, reflected by the otherworldly light: A figure. A man.

She hit the ground and yanked Alec down to the ground, wondering if the figure had seen them. A flare of gas burst from the crater, and she saw the figure more clearly—face covered with black scarves, eyes shielded by goggles, dressed all in black or dark gray. The local camel and goat herders she had seen on the drive wore similar robes and hoods, but they were white or off-white, looking unnervingly like desert Klansmen. The wind picked up, and every bit of loose fabric rippled and whipped against him. Katrina contemplated the night vision goggles but found the vision worse in them; in the green light, from this distance, the light of the crater's fires still offered blinding light—the figure just looked like a black beetle standing on its hind legs.

The figure wasn't looking into the crater; he seemed to be scanning the horizon. Then, without warning, he walked—almost scuttled—backward into the darkness.

"You figure anybody with Atarsa would have gotten far from here," Alec said. "Maybe it's just some local checking out why the desert's suddenly crawling with military and police."

"Or maybe Atarsa left a lookout," Katrina said. "This is a really strange, remote place to operate, beyond the fiery view."

"Gate to Hell," Alec declared.

As they circled the crater, they saw no more signs of life, other than the unnerving, otherworldly glow. On the way back to their Land Cruiser, Alec suddenly put out an arm, halting Katrina. She glanced, and he pointed down. A group of camel spiders crept along, directly in front of them. She looked back and realized it was perhaps 100 to 150 spiders, all moving as a cluster. At first glance, the creatures looked like they had ten legs, because of two long "pedipalps," sensors that help them locate prey. The spiders in the group were about four to six inches long; Alec remembered seeing Internet pictures during the Iraq War that claimed spiders three feet long were bedeviling US soldiers. It was all camera tricks and Photoshop, and the camel spiders' bite wasn't deadly. That didn't make them any less spectacularly creepy.

Katrina and Alec watched the creeping cluster of spiders cross their path, headed toward the flaming crater. One by one, the spiders progressed to the edge of the flames, and then, lemming-like, they disappeared over the precipice.

"I'd prefer a black cat," she whispered. Between the chill-inducing Island of the Dolls and the mass suicide of the spider herd, she found herself feeling nostalgic for comparably mundane menaces like ISIS.

They returned to the car, and Alec consulted the map. "Nearest village is Erbent."

They felt the wind pick up, slamming waves of sand against the car windows. It started to ruin visibility. The pair sat there, silently, listening to the wind start to howl. She turned on the night vision goggles again and began peering out in multiple directions. The storm quickly grew stronger, making it almost impossible to see, even with the goggles. Periodically she saw desert critters scurrying to holes, seeking to escape the blowing sand and dust.

"We're not going anywhere until this storm passes," Katrina whispered.

"At least nobody else can come out and get us, right?"

For a moment, Katrina wasn't so sure. Every now and then she thought she saw shapes on the horizon, but then a particularly thick gust of sand and dust would whip through and obscure her vision, and when it cleared, the shapes were gone.

***

The sandstorm kept them stuck by the crater through most of the night. Once it had let up and they could drive again, they made their way to Erbent. They parked the car outside the village, a haphazard collection of small stone and brick structures and more traditional-looking yurts. Dawn was close, but not quite present, just a slight lightening of the Eastern horizon. They got out of the car and felt the chill wind and a spray of sand blown against their faces.

One man led a small group of goats through the dirty street. As they progressed into the heart of the village, something resembling coherent streets formed out of the small square homes and yurts.

An old woman and an old man sat outside one home, its once red-and-white walls faded heavily under endless days and nights of blown sand. Between them was a chessboard and pieces, lit by a lantern. The old woman nodded at Katrina and Alec as they passed, while the old man offered a suspicious stare.

Alec was pretty sure he saw curtains moving in the ramshackle house windows, as barely visible eyes peered out. In the alleys, he saw glowing eyes—perhaps wild dogs.

"Village of the Damned," Alec muttered. "Complete with the Old Folks Home Predawn Chess Club."

"The government razed the neighboring village to the ground," Katrina said. "Probably makes everybody wary of strangers."

As they walked past a group of herdsmen, each readying a sandy-white hood and bulging, circular black goggles around their heads to keep away the blowing clouds of sand and dust, she didn't mind the locals' lack of interest in them.

She walked deeper into the village, breathing softly. Something was wrong. Something was here. If Gul and Rashin were operating out of a base near here, this was the nearest sign of civilization, the easiest place to obtain food and basic supplies. She kept seeing shapes disappear around corners, hearing footsteps, scuttling noises. The village was awakening, and the word that two strangers—one an extremely out-of-place Caucasian man—would spread fast.

"You have a bad feeling about this place like I do?" Alec asked.

She couldn't repress her smile. "We're 120 miles into the desert in a country with a paranoid KGB-trained counter-intel service, and you're just getting a bad feeling now?"

"This is different," he said, trying to get some sand out of his mouth. "You know when you go to someplace where something awful happened a long, long time ago, and it's like you can still feel it? The Budapest Ghetto. The Bataclan Theater in Paris. Ground Zero. You don't feel…" He waved his hand around. "That?"

"No," she said firmly. But something in her tone made Alec think she was trying to persuade herself that she wasn't feeling the ominous presence he described.

There was one obelisk in the center of the village, standing above the tin roofs of the one-story homes and telephone poles. As Alec and Katrina approached, they saw "1931" inscribed at the top. In one corner of the obelisk was a statue of a hooded, sinister figure, clutching his robe to his chest.

"What the hell is that?" Alec gasped. "It looks like the Dark Side of the Force's version of the Washington Monument."

Katrina shook her head in bewilderment. A few lines were etched on one side of the stone tower, but Alec couldn't understand the language.

"The Soviets built this," Katrina whispered, reading the inscription. "It memorializes eleven supporters of socialism killed during the Basmachi Revolt in 1931."

Alec approached the statue with trepidation. Something about it seemed ... radioactive, repellent. "Basmachis the locals?"

Alec continued to glance around. The villagers were awakening, and there was more foot traffic on the dusty paths and spaces between buildings that passed for streets. But no one approached the Americans; no one even seemed to want to make eye contact with them.

"They *were*," Katrina read, emphasizing the past tense. "Moscow decided these people were going to be dragged, kicking and screaming, into the Soviet Empire. The locals didn't like that idea, and they launched a huge, violent uprising, all across this region." She paused. "Family stories got me researching this in high school. The Soviets were brutal. The city of Kokand was burned to the ground with twenty-five thousand dead; destroying the fields allegedly killed another hundred thousand from famine."

Alec stepped back.

"You're telling me ninety years ago, a hundred and twenty-five thousand people were massacred and I've never heard about this? Did this get left out of the history books?"

She looked at him skeptically. "How many of your history books even mentioned Turkmenistan?"

"So ... a hundred and twenty-five thousand people get killed, unacknowledged, unremembered, and instead the Soviets put up a monument to elev—*oh, shi*—" However Alec was going to finish that sentence, it was interrupted as his foot pressed down through some soft ground and he found himself falling into well-hidden pit, covered with soft sticks and dried mud.

"Alec!" Katrina rushed to the edge of the pit. It was a six-and-a-half foot drop into a man-made cave. "Are you all right?"

"That's okay, I didn't need two working ankles," Alec groaned. A steady stream of profanity and the Lord's name emanated from the hole.

"It's still Lent, and I thought you gave up cursing," she said dryly. "I can pull you up!" Katrina extended her arm into the hole.

"Wait," Alec said from below, opening up a flashlight app on his phone.

Before Alec was a small excavated cavern, leading directly below the stone obelisk. It was the size of a small room.

There was another statue below the one erected by the Soviets. It was about five feet tall, carved of marble, and featured a seated, six-armed figure, with a grotesque head that seemed like a cross between an insect and man. The eyes were jet-black cavities shaped like elongated teardrops. The mouth was a hole surrounded by four jagged, dagger-like mandibles. Two of the arms held curved swords above its head, two reached out in a strangely inviting, almost embrace-like pose, and the final two arms rested on the inner thighs, palms up. The figure sat with two long, spindly bent legs sticking out, each appendage ending in a trio of claws.

Without warning, Katrina landed next to Alec and she raised her eyes, let out a short scream upon seeing the statue, and instinctively raised her gun to the statue.

"What in God's name…"

"I know, it's like, Satan's cockroach or something," Alec said.

Katrina's mind reeled, as she contemplated just what abomination the statue was supposed to represent. She remembered Apep from Egyptian mythology, Amatsumikaboshi in Shinto,

Mara in Buddhism, but this didn't quite fit the depictions she remembered of any of them. Whatever this was, it would fit with that crowd of angry, chaotic, demonic figures.

Around the statue were remains of burnt candles, offering urns, and some bones that Alec was... pretty sure weren't human. Goat, probably. Maybe dog.

Katrina raised her phone-light. In the corners she found two smaller statues, each about four feet high, each with similar remains of offerings. One was a human torso with a goat's head and a snake's body below the waist and the other was feminine but scaled, like a lizard or snake.

There were large red symbols written on the floor in a semicircle around the statues.

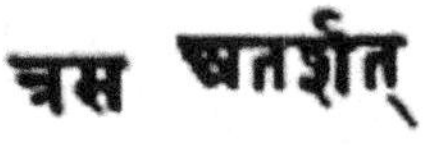

"Atarsa," Katrina whispered.

"This isn't a terrorist group," Alec muttered gravely. "This is a cult."

***

After taking a thorough number of photographs and videos on their phones, Alec hoisted Katrina out of the pit and she helped him climb out. The sun was peeking over the horizon and a few more villagers were moving on the periphery of the square.

"Whaddya figure?" Alec asked, dusting himself off. "Satan's cockroach is down there, that's their God, and either they think they're the... hell-things on the sides, or they're seeking to be reincarnated as them or host beings to them or some such nonsense?"

Katrina didn't have time to respond, as a local man ran up to them and interrupted. He wore a white hood, like a pillowcase with two small eyeholes, and black, circular goggles atop it. The short, skinny man appeared grub-like in his white mask and black eye protection—Katrina wondered if it was the man they had seen at the Darvaza crater the night before. Shouting something incoherent in a deep, guttural, angry rasp, he reached behind his back and drew a foot-long, slightly rusty, curved-blade knife used for skinning animals, and took a swing at Alec's midsection.

"Knife!" Katrina cried, and her hand went to her pistol—but for once, Alec moved faster; Alec already had two hands on Grub—the first hand grabbed the wrist and of the arm holding the knife and the second locked onto his arm at the elbow, seizing control of the man's appendage. Alec brought the grub's arm down onto his knee, digging his thumbs into Grub's inner wrist and the inside of his elbow, and the assailant's wrist reflexively twitched, and the knife tumbled from his grasp.

Grub only swore more furiously, spitting curses in some incomprehensible tongue. His shouting grew louder, angrier, rhythmic—and about one more octave lower. James Earl Jones would have been impressed with his baritone.

"Don't start none, son," Alec growled back, as Grub tried to wiggle his pained arm free. "You know what he's saying?"

"It's not Turkmeni," Katrina said, warily. "It's not Russian, either."

"Not Russian?" Alec said. "How about 'not human'?"

"Khak too saret madar jendeh—" The voice turned from a snarl, and the words became less and less coherent until Grub spat the last word, *"Atarsa!"*

"I understood that!" Alec said.

Grub's arm and shoulder jerked suddenly and uncomfortably, and Alec lost his grasp as the man's arm slipped through his inexplicably torn sleeve. The skin was brown, smooth, and shiny in the morning light, and he held his fingers in three groups—what Alec would have called a "Vulcan Salute." Grub hissed at them—seemingly unbothered by the fact that his arm was now dangling helplessly at his side, and his shoulder, to Alec's layman's eye, appeared to be suddenly dislocated.

It took less than two seconds for Katrina to kick Grub hard, square in the chest, and send him stumbling down into the hole to the hidden pit.

Alec dropped the empty sleeve, exhaled, and looked at Katrina in disbelief. Then they heard Grub screaming below.

"Keep him down there!" Alec shouted. Before she could object, he sprinted off. She looked down and saw Grub's fingers appearing over the edge of the hole, scrambling for a handhold to climb out. Katrina stepped closer and lowered her gun.

"Back. Off." she said in a tone that would be understood in any language. But the man below just shrieked an unnerving, raging scream beneath his mask. Katrina instinctively stepped back and looked around, fearing their altercation was attracting witnesses.

Only a few locals, mostly old women, were looking at her and frowning at the shrieks from the hole. There was no sign of Alec. Katrina didn't like the odds; time wasn't on their side. Whatever represented the local cops or authority in this village, someone would inform them in a matter of moments, and she didn't trust the Turkmenis to honor their previous agreement.

"Come on, Alec, come on," she whispered to herself. Grub's screams were getting lower, reverberating in his chest cavity, echoing in the hole below her.

Alec appeared around a corner, holding a small but seemingly heavy white canister with both hands—a propane tank. Katrina decided she didn't want to know where Alec had stolen it from.

In the pit, Grub had managed to turn over two offering urns and used them as a stepstool to get his head above ground level, flailing at Katrina's feet, seemingly unbothered by her firearm pointed at his head. She stepped back as Alec arrived, carrying the propane tank, and holding it above Grub.

"Catch," Alec said. Then he let go, dropping the canister directly onto Grub. There was a loud *thud*, followed by groaning.

"It's like he's possessed," Katrina said.

"Maybe he is," Alec said, filtering through his satchel. "What do you think happens when you destroy Atarsa's little sacrificial altar down there?"

"I don't know, what?"

Alec removed the flare gun from his satchel. "Let's find out."

Katrina realized Alec had opened the valve on the propane canister before he dropped it into the hole. She turned away as Alec fired in, and within a moment or two, the cavern exploded and flames erupted from the hole, roaring into the sky as high as the obelisk.

Every head in the village turned to the geyser of flame; Alec and Katrina stumbled and scrambled away, glancing back to see the obelisk suddenly plummet down into the earth and tilt diagonally among the pillar of smoke and basket of flames. Somehow, both thought they heard Grub screeching inhumanly through the inferno.

CHAPTER 57

CHICKAHOMINY WILDLIFE AREA, VIRGINIA
FRIDAY, APRIL 2

"My eyes, man, my eyes!" Norman Fein cried when Ward removed the gag and black pillowcase hood an hour later. "I think I'm going to go blind!"

"I don't need your eyes, Norman, I just need your mouth and your mind," Ward said bluntly. "For now."

Once Norman had been thoroughly maced into submission, Ward handcuffed, gagged, and hooded him and stuffed him into the backseat of his truck. He drove to the end of the access road in the dark middle of the Chickahominy Wildlife Area. Ward had used bolt cutters to remove the padlock on a gate that blocked off an access road, and he drove the last few miles with his headlights off. He had dragged the gagged, bound, blindfolded Fein to the spot, a few miles from the charred remains of the school bus. Norman sat on the ground, each arm tied back behind the trunk of a tree and handcuffed. Ward stood above him, lit only by the truck headlights.

"Your grandmother's dead, isn't she?" Ward asked.

Fein just cursed him, but it was confirmation enough for Ward.

"No sign of her at the house. Car still sitting there." He turned and looked hard at Fein. "Let me guess, altercation one day? Did she find you had joined a terror cell, and you just snapped? You and that knife. Couldn't make it look like an accident, didn't report her death. Kept those Social Security checks coming."

Fein just swore back at him. Ward picked up the kitchen knife that Norman had tried to use in his blinded state; he had actually nicked Ward a bit.

"What's with the knives?" Ward asked, contempt dripping with every word. "All of you are using knives."

Norman offered a smug smile.

"Simple, easy to use, easy to hide, found in every house and restaurant in America," he said quietly. "Hold a bomb, hold a gun, people freak out. But you can hold a sharp knife in your hand around complete strangers and no one reacts until the moment you put it into the person next to you." He chuckled. "They taught us, don't worry about getting your weapon, just order the steak."

"Yeah, well, you brought a knife to a gunfight," Ward smirked.

"The Voices need it this way," Norman said. "As Cain slew Abel, that first murder was committed looking into the victim's eyes, smelling the blood, and they drained their goblets, savoring the sweet terror in those final breaths. They need the fear. A bomb works too quick. People walking to the street, gone in a flash? You might as well offer them a buffet of air."

Ward froze for a moment, thrown off and unnerved by the nonsense Norman was spouting. But the moment passed, and he reasserted authority.

"Look, bub, I dragged you out here for a real simple task," Ward said, taking a drag on a cigarette. "Either you tell me who trained you, who you reported to, and anybody else in Atarsa, or I just leave you out here."

Crickets.

"To die of exposure. This is the middle of nowhere, pal, nobody's going to find you out here for weeks."

Still, no words came.

Ward waited about a half minute. "All right, have it your way," he shrugged, then he returned to the back of the truck.

"Wait, wait," Norman said.

"Nah, I gave you your chance. My job's to make sure there's no William and Mary attack, my job's done." He turned the key in the ignition.

"We wait for our signal!" Norman shouted, as the smell of the truck's exhaust hit his nose. "I recorded my video on a burner phone, and—"

"Sounds expensive."

"They gave us money. Cash."

"Who?"

"We record it!" Fein said. "We send the video to an account, then toss it, they take the footage…"

"The only thing that gets you out of this is giving me somebody else to chase," Ward said.

Fein hesitated.

"Who gave you the money? Who told you to record the video?"

"It was a woman," Norman confessed. "Her name was Reese! Reese Scovi or something like that."

"Spell it!" Ward ordered. Norman obeyed.

Here, with barely any light, Ward felt like finally saw him clearly, and recognized why he seemed so familiar. He realized who Fein reminded him of.

McVeigh.

He took one last drag on his cigarette, then felt the temptation to set Fein on fire.

But he resisted that temptation.

"Norman, here's how this is gonna work," Ward said. "I'm going to go looking for this Reese Scovi. After I find her, I'll come back and uncuff you and turn you over to the cops. Until then… you've got some time to think about what you've done."

Norman Fein howled as Ward put the gag back in his mouth.

"Better hope I find her fast."

***

A short time later, Ward was driving back to his home.

"Reese Scovi," Ward said quietly when Raquel answered the phone. "That's the name Fein gave up as his contact."

"Excellent, that name sounds pretty unique," Raquel said, feeling a bunch of muscles in her back, neck, and shoulders finally release tension. "We'll begin working that now. Where's Fein?"

"Where nobody's ever going to find him," Ward said flatly.

There was a long silence on the other end of the line.

"Did you kill him?"

"Not yet," Ward answered quietly.

CHAPTER 58

LIBERTY CAMPUS
TYSON'S CORNER, VIRGINIA
FRIDAY, APRIL 2

Raquel found herself sleeping on the small couch in her office again. She woke up with a crick in her neck and a new-found appreciation for Vaughn's understanding that during any terrorism-related crisis, her schedule would be completely unpredictable.

All across the country, national security, intelligence, and law enforcement officers and their families found their lives disrupted as one spouse or the other found themselves working long shifts, sometimes all night, night after night, grabbling sleep where they could and eating take-out delivered to the office. The CIA, FBI, Homeland Security, local police, military base security personnel—everyone was putting in longer hours and not even asking about when it would end.

Raquel knew it wasn't the best way to run any organization; people needed rest and sleep and time with their families. Those families were, after all, the heart of what they were working so hard to protect. But almost everyone in the ranks had a dedication that bordered on self-destructive. No one wanted to go home while the threat was still out there; everyone wanted to do something to feel useful.

Ward had signed off and returned to his family farm for the night—determined to sleep under the same roof as his wife and children, letting them know he was there with a reassuring snore—and Raquel had filed the appropriate updates and memos and then dozed off on the couch. She awoke six hours later with her sore neck and a full e-mail box. Acting Director Mitchell was having another "all hands" meeting in the seventh-floor conference room. The president was furious that Atarsa's attacks had continued after the air strikes in Turkmenistan.

No time to return home; she would have to wash up in the ladies' room and change into the spare set of office clothes she kept on a hanger behind the door. She grabbed her toiletry bag and stepped out of her office, struck that cubicles and desks were mostly manned and busy, even at this painfully early hour.

She checked again. Still no word from Katrina in Turkmenistan.

CHAPTER 59

CIA HEADQUARTERS
LANGLEY, VIRGINIA
FRIDAY, APRIL 2

The seventh-floor "all hands meeting" was interrupted when somebody declared that Atarsa was broadcasting a signal during a morning newscast of one of the Washington stations. Someone noted that it was the first time Atarsa had interrupted a broadcast in the morning. They were indeed coming much more frequently now. Two of the cable networks agreed to withhold broadcasting a tape of the signal intrusion until intelligence scoured it for messages, but the others insisted that the Atarsa messages were newsworthy and the public had a right to know. After all, tens of thousands of viewers at home were already watching the message, and recordings popped up on social media and YouTube within minutes.

This time, the Atarsa recording featured a camera shot even closer to Angra Druj's face, with almost nothing behind her visible, and the picture quality was much poorer—grainier, with the audio slightly distorted and jumping around. It didn't make her tone any less ominous.

"We have hundreds of devoted, ready to strike, upon our signal, spread across your country," she began. "You have learned our name, Atarsa, and you have recognized that you are on a journey of fear. We are teaching you to fear in new ways, to understand that the threat to you and your families is all around you, and that you will never, ever be safe."

But then she looked down, as if consulting notes, and did something that surprised everyone watching, from the morning news desk, to the viewers at home, to FBI headquarters, to the CIA's operations center.

"To demonstrate our mercy, we will tell you the names and locations of the next five devoted, who are on their way already. Lee Park is planning a stabbing attack in front of Albert Einstein's house in Princeton, New Jersey. Donald Langer is planning an attack on the Erie County Medical Center in Buffalo, New York. Malik Darnell is planning an attack on the Algonquin Hotel in Manhattan. Antonio Genovese is on his way to the Aqua Tower in Chicago. Norman Fein is about to attack the campus of William and Mary University. You have several minutes to catch them."

***

In the next fifteen minutes, American media, law enforcement, and the FBI rose to the occasion. Instantly, people started Googling the names Lee Park, Donald Langer, Malik Darnell, Antonio Genovese, and Norman Fein.

A national manhunt organically grew within minutes, but it proved unnecessary. Police in Princeton arrived within five minutes, backed up by campus police. In Buffalo, police were already at the hospital; in New York City, the two nearest NYPD patrolmen were less than half a block away. Three Chicago police cars arrived at the Aqua Tower, a mixed-use residential skyscraper, within minutes, and the building already had its private security personnel in the lobby.

Albert Einstein's house in Princeton, New Jersey is used as housing for a visiting professor, but the professor and her husband were out of town. Lee Park was crossing the street a block away when a police cruiser roared down the street and veered in front of him. He was stunned, reached for a twelve-inch kitchen knife, but dropped it when he saw the police emerge, guns drawn. He had no idea Atarsa had released a video naming him and his target, or why.

Erie County Medical Center went into immediate lockdown and Donald Langer was surrounded by police the moment he got out of his car in the hospital parking lot. He, too, seemed stunned by the sudden arrival of police, asking them how they knew.

The beat cops standing by the doorway to the Algonquin were a bit irritated when a second squad car identified Malik Darnell walking two blocks away and stopped him. They found a meat cleaver in his messenger bag, but he surrendered peacefully, demanding a lawyer.

Only Antonio Genovese tried to confront the police, and the Chicago Police Department would ultimately rule his effort to stab the approaching officers as another "suicide by cop." He ignored many, many orders to drop his knife.

By nine-thirty in the morning, FBI field offices were happily reporting that four Atarsa attackers had been stopped before attacking any civilians.

But Norman Fein never arrived at the William and Mary Campus, and the local FBI raided his home the moment he was named in the Atarsa message. The FBI team did not find Fein but did find the body of his grandmother stuffed in a crawlspace in the basement. Many found it strange that the Bureau spokesman refused to directly say whether the government knew his current location.

***

Raquel went home for lunch, took a much-needed shower, reconnected with her husband, pledged to do her best to be home for dinner that night, and was back at her office in the early afternoon. She was about to check in on how Dee was doing on the hunt for "Reese Scovi" when her secure line from the FBI rang.

It was Elaine, the voice in the Bureau she trusted more than any other. Elaine Kopek's arrival in the director's office with the list of forty Isoptera treatment center patients, now all suspected Atarsa sleeper agents, earned her a quick promotion. She had moved from the Public Information office to a seat at the primaries table, plugged in to the FBI's Critical Incident Response Group. Unfortunately, her tone was stressed, revealing an overwhelming need to vent. "I think we're about to make a big mistake."

Raquel opened a desk drawer and looked for her non-prescription painkillers. "Now what?"

"Do you guys have any idea why Atarsa ratted out their team today? Our counterterrorism analysts think it's overconfidence, but I'm not buying it. This is part of some trap. Even my husband called me up and quoted that fish-man from Star Wars."

From her FBI office, Kopek glanced again at the paused image on the YouTube video of Andra Druj's most recent message. "There's no mercy in these people. Look at her eyes. They're dead inside. That woman's a ghoul."

"Gul is the boyfriend, that's Sarvar Rashin," Raquel muttered. "No, you're right, it really stinks to high heaven. When I saw the video this morning, I figured these guys would have suicide vests or something, some new trick." Raquel doodled a suicide vest on a yellow legal pad in front of her. Why had Atarsa forsaken so many of the traditional tools of terrorism?

"They're pawns," Elaine said. "You don't mind losing your pawns in chess as long as it's part of a larger gambit, a plan to achieve some larger goal."

"Winning the game," Raquel said.

"The director wants to hold a press availability later today. He thinks these arrests are going to reassure the public."

Elaine's long sigh made clear she thought something would go terribly wrong.

"No, it won't reassure people," Raquel concurred. "Everybody in the country is asking the same question: why did they want us to catch those five?" She couldn't quite hold in a grim smile, knowing Atarsa had no idea that Ward had caught up with Norman Fein overnight and removed that chess piece from the board. If they were monitoring media reports, Atarsa must wonder why Fein had disappeared. For all the moral and legal risks Ward's methods required, the disruption of the enemy's plans and consequential morale hit made it *feel* justified, whether or not it actually was.

"Are they going to round up the rest?"

"We have thirty-one of the forty named Isoptera patients under surveillance," Elaine said. "That's a good start, but if we grab the thirty-one, then maybe the other nine go underground, or go on the run. God knows when we find them. Or maybe the other nine just start stabbing people wherever they are." She didn't have to mention that it was a safe bet Atarsa had at least a few sleeper agents not on the Isoptera list. Within both of their agencies, analysts debated whether Rashin's boast of "hundreds" of agents could possibly be accurate.

"How long do you think they'll wait to see if they can find the others?" Raquel asked.

Elaine was quiet for a moment. "Maybe a day. Not much more than that." She knew all of the teams had been instructed that if they saw their targets preparing for an attack—and at this point, merely going into a restaurant was considered "preparing for an attack"—they should move in and make the arrest. If one team moved, all thirty other teams would move, and the nine teams hunting the remaining names on the list would be alerted as well.

Some FBI lawyers had asked just what charges those suspected Atarsa members would face once they were arrested. After all, no Atarsa attacker yet had used a gun, much less explosives or any other controlled substance or material that violated the law. No one had found any propaganda materials beyond the Isoptera treatment program's brochures, pamphlets, and handouts, which encouraged patients to list their grievances and to think about "a slow, methodical, step-by-step plan, acting with a broad support network, to effectively express those feelings."

The Attorney General pointed out that under that year's National Defense Authorization Act—and basically every version of the act passed since the worst terrorist attack in American history—had declared that "Congress affirms that the authority of the President to use all necessary and appropriate force pursuant to the Authorization for Use of Military Force, includes the authority for the Armed Forces of the United States to detain covered persons, pending disposition under the law of war." In other words, because of suspicions of terrorism, the young men on the Isoptera list could legally be detained indefinitely. Whether the government was willing to take the political heat for locking up American citizens without trial indefinitely was an open question.

CHAPTER 60

FBI HEADQUARTERS
WASHINGTON, DC
FRIDAY, APRIL 2

The FBI director's press conference proceeded as Elaine feared. The director, a square-jawed former agent who was generally liked and respected but a bit more politically attuned than most outside the agency knew, was eager to point to a victory for law enforcement. Unfortunately, he started on an off-note.

"This is, indeed, Good Friday," the director began with a smile. Watching from her office, Elaine put her palm to her face and wondered whether he understood why Christians called the day by that title.

"Atarsa tried to launch a series of attacks today, and law enforcement was able to respond quickly and effectively, resulting in no civilian casualties," he said. "As the threat to harm the American people evolves, we are adapting to confront the challenges, relying heavily on the strength of our federal, state, local, and international partnerships. I salute all of the local law enforcement officers who were the first on scene of today's foiled attacks. Our successes depended on interagency cooperation; I want to salute our partnership with the Department of Homeland Security and the National Counterterrorism Center."

Elaine noted there was a lot of saluting in his remarks.

He elaborated that the names in the Atarsa tape were accurate, and that four individuals had been caught on the way to the mentioned targets with bladed weapons. The director said the whereabouts of the fifth named individual was still under investigation.

When asked why Angra Druj had revealed the names and locations of the attackers, the director responded simply, "That aspect is still under investigation." He ended up giving a variation of those words in response to the next six questions, and finally he realized it was time to wrap it up.

In the FBI Headquarters building, Elaine's phone rang; she recognized the number as her home.

She picked up the receiver and for the second time in the day, her husband imitated Admiral Ackbar and sounded like Winston Churchill underwater: "It's a trap!"

CHAPTER 61

The FBI director timed his press conference to be covered on the early evening newscasts for cities on the eastern seaboard. What he didn't count on was that once again, the Washington-area local broadcast of the national news was interrupted by the chilling face of Angra Druj. This time the camera was tightened in so close to her face that her eyes were almost cut off by the screen: her lips, teeth, and tongue filled it.

"Your leaders seem quite proud of themselves. Let's see how well you do when you only have the names of the perpetrators: Jennifer Brown. Matt Brown. Maria Garcia. Carlos Garcia. Maria Hernandez. James Johnson. Robert Johnson. Maria Martinez. Maria Rodriguez. James Smith. John Smith. Michael Smith. Robert Smith ..."

She recited a hundred names, most of them variations of the most common names in the United States: Smith, Johnson, Garcia, Rodriguez, Taylor, Moore, Thompson, White, and Lee.

She completed her list after five minutes. "These are our members, plotting to strike. They have knives in their kitchens. And they will kill you. Unless you kill them first."

***

Raquel had left early, trying to give Vaughn an actual dinner at home, their first in a week, and debating whether to return to the office in the evening. Her body clock was haywire, and she noticed driving was more difficult. She desperately needed to sleep in her own bed for a long night. Both she and Vaughn were too exhausted to cook and ordered in, but as they began eating, her phone began buzzing again.

They turned on the television in time to see the end of Druj's message.

Tears welled up in Raquel's eyes as she realized what Angra Druj had just unleashed, the revelation of her real motive all along. The day's first message, naming five sleepers before they could strike, was to build credibility for the second. Some unknown percentage of Americans would believe the second, much longer, much less specific list was accurate as well. And now tens of thousands of Americans suddenly stood accused of terrorism in a jittery, angry, frightened country.

Raquel threw the television remote at the screen so hard she cracked it. Vaughn Holtz, the most even-keeled and patient man that Alec and Katrina had ever met, merely shook his head. Raquel's work could, particularly after long stretches of perpetual crises, leave her wound up and frazzled. Vaughn was her rock; Alec joked he had such a cool head, he bled antifreeze. The worse things got, the calmer and quieter he became. He embraced Raquel and said he knew she and the rest could keep things under control.

***

Most of America didn't have Vaughn's cool head.

It became known as the "Night of Sirens." America had roughly thirty-four thousand citizens named Robert Smith, and the vast majority of them were perfectly law-abiding, upstanding citizens. But some of them weren't, and it didn't take much to persuade some paranoid minds that the Rob Smith that lived in the halfway house around the corner or the one who had a drug problem were the next Atarsa sleeper agent waiting to strike. There were more than twenty-seven thousand women named Maria Hernandez in the United States, and most of them were wonderful women. But plenty had behavior to leave their neighbors suspicious: arrests for drug distribution, gang tattoos, a recent conversion to Islam, a public fight.

Any loner or person with a history of odd behavior—or merely behavior that had been perceived as odd—was suddenly seen as not merely weird but perhaps a ticking time bomb. City police departments and local sheriff's offices debated checking in on the known Robert Smiths and other common names that were already on parole or had criminal records, but there were far too many. They didn't have much time to debate that course of action, as the 911 dispatchers suddenly alerted their superiors that the calls were coming in at a pace far too rapid for them to handle, even with the full staff who had been on duty rotations since the Atarsa attacks began.

This Atarsa transmission—quickly given the hashtag #TheParanoiaList on Twitter—finished at roughly 6:35 Eastern time. Within minutes, the 911 switchboards in America's major cities were lighting up, as thousands of Americans suddenly reported that they suspected the Rob Smith and Maria Hernandez that they knew was a terrorist. Shortly after seven p.m., the first reports of gunshots came in at a furious pace.

More than a few Americans, after weeks of feeling helpless and tormented by the videos of horrific stabbings in public places and taunting messages that their families would be murdered in their sleep, set out to confront the Rodriguezes, Taylors, Moores, Thompsons, Whites, and Lees. Most of the Rodriguezes, Taylors, Moores, Thompsons, Whites, and Lees reacted with great indignation and hostility to the pounding fists at their doors. Tempers flared. Punches were thrown. Guns were drawn. The angry crowds, forcing their way into the suspect's home, concluded the presence of sharp kitchen knives was all the evidence they needed.

And some of the Rodriguezes, Taylors, Moores, Thompsons, Whites, and Lees ran when they saw the crowds coming.

***

Vaughn was walking Raquel to her car, ready to kiss her goodbye as she rushed back to Liberty Campus, when the pair heard shouting at a town house down the street.

Neither Raquel nor Vaughn, who had only lived in the Reston Town Center town house condo for two years, had talked much to Ed and Cindy Taylor, the couple that owned the row house down the street. They were a cordial, if not overly friendly, couple in their fifties with a son living at home. He had apparently dropped out of college and battled a drug problem. David Taylor generally dressed in unwashed off-black and could be a bit surly, driving his black Trans Am around the neighborhood, letting it make a roaring noise late at night. Notes left on the Taylors' door about how the late-night engine-revving had woken sleeping babies had not deterred David's behavior.

By now, the previous Atarsa attackers had been described in the media and the profile was clear: Angry loners, with few friends, dead-end jobs, young men who felt powerless over their lives and at some point, fell under the Atarsa spell. After a long stretch of antisocial behavior and criminal behavior as minors, they seemed to walk on the straight and narrow for a longer stretch, quiet and isolated, not attracting attention until they received their "go" signal and suddenly lashed out at innocent people.

Karl Shell, who lived in one of the condos in between Raquel and the Taylors, had gathered several of the neighbors outside the town house on the corner.

"Ed, Cindy, you've gotta bring him out!" He held a wooden baseball bat over his shoulder.

"What the hell are you doing?" Raquel cried. A quartet of disapproving looks turned in her direction. Other neighbors were peeking out their windows, opening their doors, readying their phones. Karl's girlfriend, Stacey, was recording it all with her phone.

"He's one of them, Rachel."

"Raquel," she seethed.

"Karl Shell," he said, extending his hand. She refused to shake it, glaring at his small angry mob of five. He shook his head.

"Look, we all just saw it. You've seen David, the way he acts, the way he looks at all of us. He looks at me like he wants to cut my throat and he looks at Stacey like he's—well, you know the rest." He pointed with his bat. "We're gonna stop the next attack before it happens."

"What the hell are you talking about?" She stared at Karl for a moment and realized there was no reasoning with him.

"I'm calling the cops," she said, reaching for her phone.

"We already did," Karl said. "I want to turn him in." Raquel called 911 herself, and her blood ran cold when the call finally connected, and she got a busy signal. What the hell was going on?

Kevin hit his bat against the Taylors' front door. *Bang, bang, bang.* "Come on, Ed, Cindy. We know he's in there. Don't make us come in."

"That's breaking and entering!" Raquel shouted, trying to reinstate sanity.

"It's a citizen's arrest!" Karl shouted back. "He could be in there stabbing his parents right now for all we know!"

The door opened a crack, and Ed's face and mustache were visible in the space between the door, behind the chain. "Karl, please calm down."

"Open up, Ed!" Karl shouted. "I don't want to have to kick this door down."

Ed shook his head, perplexed, angry, outraged, and sad simultaneously. "Karl... I'm going to have to call the cops."

"We already did!" several people shouted simultaneously. Karl shouted in the space, jamming his foot between the door and the doorframe. "We have to get in there, Ed, your kid's a terrorist!"

"He's nothing of the sort!" Ed shouted back. "Get your foot out of the door!"

"Stop!" Raquel shouted. She was watching the situation spiral out of control right in front of her. She tried again to dial 911 on her phone; this time she was told all circuits were busy.

Instead of stopping, Karl slammed his bat against the door as hard as he could. It splintered a bit, leaving a dent in the door, and Ed backed away from the door.

"We're going in!" Karl shouted. He wound up for another swing, hoping to break the chain.

But before he could swing his bat again, a deafening gunshot rang out, echoing up and down the street. Everyone flinched and instinctively ducked, eyes wide, suddenly terrified, adrenaline pumping, looking around for who had shot the gun.

Raquel turned and was stunned to see Vaughn, holding his own Glock 19 up in the air. He had fired a warning shot straight up.

"That's enough," his voice somehow boomed, even though it was barely above a whisper. "Everybody go back to your homes."

Stacey and the other three neighbors looked at Karl. Stunned, he looked around at everyone else, then he looked down at the broken bat in his hand.

"No lynch mob tonight," Vaughn said, staring at Karl.

Karl shook his head.

"Look, I tried to do something. When that kid in there kills somebody, that's all on you!" he said, pointing at Raquel and Vaughn. He walked back away from the Taylors' door. Ed closed it, and everyone could hear the deadbolt turning. Everyone started walking home and closing their doors, quietly. Within a few minutes, the street was quiet again, except for police sirens in the distance. Raquel hoped it was a delayed response to someone's 911 call, but it was apparently a response to some other similar tense confrontation a few blocks away.

"Are you going to be all right alone here tonight?" Raquel asked Vaughn. He looked at her and let out the smallest of smiles.

"I think I just made that clear," he said. "Will you be?"

She drove to work, listening to news radio. The anchor was trying to keep up with the reports of violence across the country and asked the best expert the station could find at that hour, a retired police chief, if he had ever seen anything like it.

"A little," he said. "First night after the Rodney King verdict, back in '92." He paused, and the station broadcast dead air for an uncomfortably long stretch.

"But this is worse."

***

The violence of the Night of Sirens seemed to have largely calmed by dawn, but it had been a tense eight to ten hours across the country. Police in riot gear had to disperse angry crowds from coast to coast: New York, Philadelphia, Pittsburgh, Atlanta, Milwaukee, Mobile, Tampa, Las Vegas. The sense of anarchy hit worst in cities that had endured long rough patches of high unemployment, racial tensions, and mistrust of the police: Youngstown, Ohio; St. Louis, Missouri; Camden, New Jersey. Once the first wave of violence was reported, more than a few gangs saw an opportunity to take out rivals and have their murders blend in with the wave of violence. More than a few bad jokes comparing the night to "the Purge" floated around social media. The National Guard was called out in fourteen states.

California was hit the worst; the Atarsa message arrived in late afternoon, giving angry crowds daylight hours to assemble and then the cover of darkness to lash out. One angry mob would march down to the nearest police station demanding an immediate roundup of everyone with a name mentioned in the Atarsa message; another crowd of protesters gathered and shrieked that the other side was racist—not really the most accurate denunciation, since Americans of almost every hue and creed matched the names in the message—and the more accurate accusation that the crowds wanted to repeat the shame of the Japanese internment camps during World War Two. The angry mobs brought out the bored and the opportunistic, who were just eager to break things and maybe steal something from a superstore. No matter the crisis, no matter how serious an impending disaster was, somebody was convinced they could get a new flat-screen television out of the mess.

The mayhem-minded gathered in Los Angeles, San Jose, Oakland, Stockton, Santa Ana, Fremont, and Chula Vista, and looting ensued as midnight approached. In San Francisco, Apple and Google ran private buses to get their employees home and found themselves under attack, even though no one could really explain how Google or Apple were responsible for Atarsa's menace. One bandana-masked young man, stopping to speak to a local news crew, explained that if the "fat cats in the tech companies" hadn't invented "all of this stuff," then Atarsa wouldn't be able to interrupt the television signals and threaten them, a justification that revealed the protester/rioter/looter understood absolutely nothing that had happened in recent weeks. Another explained, "the kinds of people in Atarsa are the ones who took our jobs."

Immigrant communities bore a disproportionate brunt of the violence on the Night of Sirens, even though so far none of the attacking Atarsa sleeper agents had been an immigrant. Angra Druj's accented voice was all the justification the angriest xenophobes needed to lash out.

The intelligence officers at Liberty Campus were particularly attuned to the immigrant communities within the United States. Recent immigrants often made excellent sources and could describe all kinds of details in their home countries, in ways that might elude even the best intelligence officer. Case officers sometimes grew attached to these newest Americans, who sometimes traveled back and forth to their home countries, picking up more local gossip and useful information.

It wasn't part of their official duties, but by the early morning hours, the intelligence officers were scouring news reports, both national and local, and social media, tallying up the dreadful costs of what the media had labeled "the Night of Sirens." As of ten a.m., the best estimate was about seventy to eighty people dead, between four and five hundred injured, about sixty cops injured by thrown rocks and other debris, and tens of millions of dollars in property damage. But it was the specific acts that made the night feel like the country was falling apart: some unknown persons set the home of the Garcia family in Baltimore ablaze, burning Carlos, Maria, and their three children to death; a man started randomly shooting people in the street in Newark, and an out-of-control mob beat several people to death in Madison, Wisconsin.

Raquel had seen the looped footage of the Baltimore flames one time too many. She needed to clear her head and got up to walk around the campus. She was surprised to find Patrick Horne, Alec's long-detested rival, standing by the elevators, not pressing a button, staring ahead into the doors blankly. He usually dressed impeccably and never had a hair out of place, but he was starting to show stubble and had bags under his eyes. He didn't move as she approached, lost in whatever thoughts were haunting him at that moment. While Alec loathed Patrick, Raquel found him merely annoying, and she had long since accepted the need to find ways to work with him. But she had never seen him like this; she wondered if he had just learned of the death of someone he knew.

"Patrick, are you all right?" she asked gently, fearing she was about to startle him.

Patrick looked up, and seemed to shake himself out of whatever trance he had been in. "It's bad," he said softly.

"I'm sorry about Peck, I know he was your mentor," she said, trying to figure out what else to say.

"He'll recover," Patrick said, wiping his hand across his face, as if to remove some invisible grime. "No, this was something else last night, I just heard. I grew up outside Boston, little town, still have a lot of friends there. Heard from one this morning. He told me at dawn he went in for his usual breakfast, a McMuffin."

Patrick stood silently for an uncomfortably long time, and Raquel wondered whether he should refer him for immediate counseling.

"He said when he got there, he saw a body hanging from the golden arches. Somebody had strung someone up there in the middle of the night."

CHAPTER 62

KARAKUM DESERT
TURKMENISTAN
SATURDAY, APRIL 3

Alec and Katrina were ten miles out of the village of Erbent before they could even speak of what they had just witnessed. She kept checking the rearview mirrors.

"Atarsa's a cult," Katrina exhaled. "Not that surprising. A lot of terror groups have the same basic structure, psychological appeal, extreme beliefs, apocalyptic worldview."

"Crazy loves crazy." Alec mumbled. He wondered if other people would look at his wife and himself and conclude the same. "If I'm Gul, I'm outta here the moment I hear the US might be bombing. I'm long gone. According to the Iranians, I operate out of Cyprus as well..."

She pulled onto a dirt road that headed toward a railroad track running parallel to the main north-south highway. Then she turned and drove parallel to the tracks.

"If I'm them, I'm changing my identity and maybe even my face. Plastic surgery or something. If we gave Dee the coordinates to the altar underneath that obelisk in the village, the Gate of Hell, and the site that the Tomahawks bombed... any phones that were in more than one of those locations is probably Atarsa," she murmured. Maybe, with a little luck, they could ping a cell phone and find Gholam Gul and Sarvar Rashin.

Knowing that the Turkmen had tipped off the terrorists once, they needed thoroughly secure way to communicate back to Raquel. The only safe bet was probably back on a US Air Force C-17. Luckily, the road ahead revealed farms and signs of civilization, a signal the city was growing closer.

***

The corner of Ashgabat International Airport used for refueling and restocking US Air Force planes was remote from the rest of the facility, by mutual agreement of the Americans and the Turkmeni government. Rackety, dirty tractor-trailers stood silently in a line, and a lone Turkmeni workman—probably a spy—sat in forklift parked in the shadow of the plane. His machine appeared to be held together by duct tape.

Alec and Katrina had to sign a seemingly endless series of documents in Turkmen before they were cleared to step onto the tarmac and speak to the US military personnel.

US Air Force Captain "Big Jim" Richards and Airman Chris Cook did not greet the two Americans cheerily at all.

Richards growled through a strong Texan drawl, "Say that again?"

"We need you to fly us to Cyprus immediately," Katrina said. She looked up at the massive Globemaster C-17, where SPIRIT OF VERNON HARGIS was painted on the cockpit.

"Where were you scheduled to fly?"

The two men spoke simultaneously. "Who the hell are y—" Richards began, before Cook answered, "Incirlik Air Base, Turkey." Richards glared at the junior officer.

"Who the hell are you, and why should we tell you this?" Richards repeated.

Katrina flipped her fake Department of Defense credentials. "We're with Langley. We think two leaders of the Atarsa terror cell are on their way to Cyprus. You're going to have to take us there."

The Air Force pilots exchanged a skeptical glance.

"Do you see an Uber or Lyft logo on the plane behind me, ma'am?" Richards asked sarcastically. "Book yourself a commercial flight."

Katrina burst with exasperation. "You know the guys who have been launching these attacks back in America?! They're on! Their way! To Cyprus!" She pointed three times for emphasis, momentarily acting as if Richards was deaf or slow. "They're gonna have plastic surgery and change their identities and if we don't get there as soon as possible, they will disappear! In the wind! Gone! We will be back to square one!"

"We can't just change where we're going without orders," Richards said.

"You are the only plane we can access right now!" she shouted. Alec was taken aback, momentarily thrown off. The good cop was reading lines from the bad cop's script.

Alec waved his hands. "Okay, okay." He gently turned her away from them, walked her a step or two away, and leaned in close to the two men.

"Gentlemen, we don't have time to argue. You're free to stick to your orders, but if you do, that's going to force our hand." The two Air Force pilots eyed him skeptically. "We're going to have no choice but to ask for help from the Turkmeni Air Force."

Richards let out a laugh. Katrina whipped her head around and wondered if Alec had indeed gone insane while wandering in the desert. There was no way they would tell the Turkmenis anything. Richards and Cook seemed equally shocked by the suggestion.

"Captain" – he glanced down at the uniform – "Richards, am I correct that you're a Texan?" Alec guessed.

"Damn straight," he nodded.

"I cannot believe I'm going to have to tell everyone that the Turkmen helped us catch a terrorist and a Texan would not," Alec shrugged. Richards bristled and scowled. Alec turned and started waving at the Turkmen military soldiers standing by the doors to the terminal building.

He had barely gotten out a *"Hey!"* when Richards grabbed his arm.

"Whoa, whoa, let's hold off on that, son," Richards said. He gave a grumbling look to Cook, who nodded. "We'll get you to Cyprus. Just get on the damn plane."

CHAPTER 63

THE WHITE HOUSE
SATURDAY, APRIL 3

The morning after the Night of Sirens brought the country and the Agency only limited respite. With the National Guard mobilizing into cities coast to coast, Americans took a short break from overtly lashing out at random strangers out of fear and helpless rage and settled for mere suspicious glares. But social media, the nation's seductive accelerant for outrage, exploded with accusations of terrorist affiliations and broad scapegoating of various groups: Iranian Americans, Muslims, Mexicans, white nationalists, ex-cons, violent video game players, millennials and anyone else. The national television media noticed and argued that the government was faltering in the face of a worsening crisis.

This put the already mercurial president into the foulest of moods, and the commander-in-chief dealt with it by chewing out Acting Director Mitchell at the emergency morning cabinet meeting. Now Mitchell was determined to chew out everyone under him, and this meant Raquel's late-morning meeting on the seventh floor did not go well at all. She had very little good news to report. Katrina and Alec had not reported in yet, an uncharacteristically long stretch of silence that increasingly worried her. The CIA's Ashgabat station had no reports of any Americans in Turkmen police custody, but there was no way to keep tabs on every police station in the vast Karakum desert.

Raquel also had to report there was no record of anyone with the name "Reese Scovi" in any government database. Dee and the NSA were running searches of variations of the name in other databases, but couldn't promise results.

The president demanded that the next Atarsa broadcast be their last. Mitchell challenged everyone around the table: stop the terrorizing messages, by any means necessary. Raquel found herself wanting that last phrase in writing.

***

Raquel returned to Liberty Campus to find a marginally rested Dee, lamenting that no news had broken on her end during the meeting. And still no word from Katrina or Alec.

"What's the word from upstairs?" Dee asked.

"The White House is apoplectic. Thirty-nine percent of Americans told a pollster that they were having nightmares about Atarsa and the attacks." She paused. She knew Merlin would call the bombardment of disturbing images a psychic attack upon the American people.

She wondered if Dee could come up with some way to stop Atarsa's messages. "FCC, FBI, Homeland Security—everybody's running around trying to come up with ideas. The military has signal-jamming units, used them to disrupt signals to IEDs in Iraq. They could set them up around the city …"

"Yeah, but once you set up jammers to disrupt any signal on the broadcast station frequency, then the local news affiliates can't do any live remotes," Dee guessed. "Might make it just about impossible to broadcast any signal. And the Atarsa video nightmare gang can just drive up the road to Baltimore or Philadelphia or any other city and start it over again. You can't jam broadcast signals in every city."

She thought for a moment. "And even if we made it impossible to broadcast pirate signals, they could always just go back to uploading YouTube videos and anonymously send them to news stations." *The good old days*, thought Raquel. It was a courier who eventually led the agency to bin Laden's compound in Abbottabad.

Watching the morning news and examining the incoming reports from stations around the world left Dee bereft of her usual bubbly optimism. Raquel knew Dee's mind could be daring and creative but also completely unpredictable—much like the rest of her team. Dee was probably smart enough to figure out a way to stop the Atarsa messages; the only question was whether in the process she would set off some sort of electromagnetic pulse that would blow out half the televisions on the Eastern seaboard or trigger some other comparable catastrophe.

"Dee, if I said I could get you anything you needed . . ." Raquel began, almost afraid to complete that promise, "could you figure out a way to stop these Atarsa messages?"

"Anything?" Dee's eyebrow rose in a manner that Leonard Nimoy would admire. She drummed her fingers on the desk, looked up, nodded her head sideways one way, then the other, thinking through something obscure.

"How far outside legal means can I go?"

Raquel knew that question was coming. Her most recent call with Ward hadn't shed any further details about the fate of Norman Fein.

("Look, Ward, is Norman Fein dead or alive?" she had asked bluntly.

"I really can't say until I take a good look at him," Ward had said evasively. "Think of him as Schrödinger's terrorist.")

Raquel decided she was already in for a penny. Might as well go in for the whole pound. "Theoretically, let's say as far as you need to go," Raquel said.

"I can think of two options," Dee began. "You may want to get me a presidential pardon for Plan B."

Plan B, for "bad," Raquel thought, but Dee was already getting up and setting up a detailed map of the Washington metropolitan area on her largest monitor.

"They started in New York, abandoned their equipment up on the rooftop," Dee reviewed. She looked over the Washington map and started putting little graphics of pushpins in particular spots.

"Moved to the DC area, hijacked the signal of the Fox affiliate, then ABC affiliate, then CW. They haven't moved. Maybe they're local. Maybe they like something about how DC has a whole bunch of broadcast towers close together in Northwest." She placed different-colored pushpins in the spots of the Fox affiliate broadcast tower by the Maryland border in Friendship Heights, the ABC affiliate's broadcast tower farther down by Tenleytown, and the CW affiliate's Hughes Memorial Tower in Brightwood, in central DC.

Raquel looked at the pushpins. "They disrupt the signal here, everyone notices, and the networks quickly take the message national. FBI's put out a BOLO on anything looking like a big network news van, big satellite dish on top."

Dee shook her head.

"They're not going to need something that big. Even a DirecTV-style dish could be big enough if they're close enough to the broadcast tower, a clear line of sight. You could do it from the passenger seat or backseat of a parked car. Might just need to crack the window."

"Could the vehicle be moving?"

Dee held up a finger, then moved her hand around, picturing it in her head. "Maybe, but they would get a clearer signal if they stayed in one place. When we've seen the picture get fuzzy in the past messages, they might be on the move."

Raquel realized how difficult the search for the pirate signal source was. It required searching every car within the line of sight of a tall broadcast tower.

Dee drummed her fingers some more, then nodded. "Raquel, I can absolutely guarantee that I can track them and stop the next intrusion if you give me system access to NORAD's National Capital Region Integrated Air Defense System."

"Oh, is that all?" Raquel looked skeptical. "What, are you going to reenact War Games?"

Dee scoffed, almost plausibly. "You know all that stuff we have to protect the airspace above Washington? Coast Guard helicopters, F-16s, flare cannons? Well, it's all run and organized by some of the most advanced civilian and military radar systems in the world, which can, among other things, track signals. Including broadcast signals."

Raquel squinted at her, suspecting that Dee had already been thinking about not-quite-legal ways to stop the Atarsa messages. The team manager rubbed her temples, contemplating the sort of bureaucratic national security hoops she was about to have to jump through to get Dee the access she wanted. Dee observed her wariness and pressed the sales pitch even harder.

"Get me a bunch of television monitors, let me see the signal from every network in the city. The big local networks they haven't hit yet are CBS, which actually uses an array out in West Virginia, and NBC in Tenleytown. They haven't repeated themselves yet. I'll bet you a doughnut they hit NBC next. And since the NBC local news comes in from a signal inside their own facility, their best chance to override the station signal is when there's a signal coming from somewhere outside NBC Washington—looks like probably the afternoon sports or the basketball game or the national news. Heck, I can almost tell you already when they're going to send the next message."

She checked the local affiliate's Saturday schedule. "They'll either do it... around late afternoon, interrupting the game, or when the national news starts at seven."

Raquel nodded. "I'm going to see if I can get a drone up by the NBC broadcast tower. I'm calling NORAD now."

An aide ran to them, breathless and somewhat confused. "The Air Force says they have a message for you coming from a plane flying out of Turkmenistan!"

***

Alec and Katrina internally fumed that it seemed to take forever for the US Air Force Globemaster C-17 *Spirit of Vernon Hargis* to be cleared for takeoff from Ashgabat. But neither one exhibited their irritation too openly because the last thing they needed was to seem uncharacteristically eager to leave the country. They needed every last i dotted and t crossed, to ensure the Turkmen authorities had no excuses to delay their departure further.

Once Alec and Katrina were in the air, it was a complicated process of connecting the airmen's various superiors to the CIA Headquarters in Langley, where many of the senior officials seemed to have no idea who Alec and Katrina were. It was forty minutes before they could create a secure connection from the plane's communications array to the speakerphone in Raquel's office.

Thankfully, Dee worked fast once they could actually hear each other. They gave Dee precise GPS coordinates of the Atarsa underground altar in the village ruins, the Tomahawk bombing site, and the Darvaza crater and asked if the NSA could track any recurring phone activity in those areas in recent weeks and months. Then Alec asked her to define a word, and she wondered if he really was getting used to thinking of her as Google in the flesh.

"Naonhaithya has two meanings," she reported after a few minutes of searching. "It's a demon in Zoroastrian mythology and the name of a rental boat registered in Tartus, Russian Occupied Zone, Syria. A Poseidon 26. Pretty darn fast."

"Must be how they're getting to Cyprus. But how the heck did they get to Syria?" Katrina said, spreading a map out from the Globemaster's supplies. The National Reconnaissance Office had prepared their best assessment of who controlled what in what was left of Syria. The decision to use a different color for each faction left a crazy quilt, with plenty of overlapping borders—Jackson Pollock as a cartographer. Most ominous were the lengthy light green stretches of the "Toxic Zone," an ungovernable no-man's land allegedly covered in leftover sarin, mustard gas, chlorine gas, Agent 15, and at least a half-dozen other disputed chemical and, some claimed, still-viable biological weapons. The Assad regime never relinquished its claim over territory within the traditional borders, but the fortified, isolated rubble-city of Damascus was effectively powerless over the rest of the country. Tartus, for all intents and purposes, was really governed and run by the Russian Navy.

If Gul and Rashin remained in Tartus, the CIA would have an almost impossible time catching them. Reliable assets on the ground were few and far between. Landing the C-17 there was unthinkable; the Russian military would undoubtedly detain them on some nonsense charges and strip the C-17 down to its airframe, learning everything possible about the US Air Force's technology.

After twenty minutes of discussing the numerous challenges to getting any serious surveillance on the boat docks in Tartus, Dee's voice chirped on the radio. "Hey, I delivered another miracle. I tracked a pair of phones that were in all three of those locations you sent me. They're active, and I just pinged their location. Want to guess where they are?"

"Tartus?" Katrina sighed.

"Sitting on a dock of the bay, watching the tide roll away, in a building across the street from Arwad Harbor, Russian Occupied Zone."

"I'm guessing that introducing them to a Tomahawk missile is out of the question," Alec grumbled.

"The United States military is not about to bomb a densely populated area in Syria that's just over the fence from a Russian naval base," Raquel said over the radio. "We can try to get them when they leave Tartus, or maybe see if the Israelis have any assets that can help, but . . . I really wish we could get them out of there. They could be doing anything over there."

The Air Force had outfitted the C-17 with a satellite-based in-flight wireless system. Alec looked at a Google Maps image of the small pleasure boat harbor, just a little bit south of the massive port that housed Russia's Mediterranean fleet.

"I can get them out," Alec said. "Dee, patch me through to one of those phones."

***

Gul and Sarvar Rashin sat at a table in an outdoor section of a restaurant, overlooking a small harbor. Before their meal, he had briefly stopped at a newsstand and picked up a few international newspapers. The coverage of America's *"Aylat Aldhuer"*—"Night Panic"—was vivid and, to Gul, delightful. A veteran British correspondent in Washington had struggled to bring together the right comparisons to recent American history: the Watts riots, the Rodney King riots, the tense days after 9/11, the chaotic aftermath of Hurricane Katrina . . .

"But those crises brought out the best in many Americans," the octogenarian wrote. "Now, many Americans are choosing to project the faces of their fellow countrymen onto Atarsa.

The captured and killed members of Atarsa have been, so far, white, black, Asian, and Hispanic, ranging from their late teens to early forties. None, so far, appear to be Muslim, and most are described by friends and family as irreligious, with several described as outspoken atheists. Their targets are high-profile but mundane, chosen to maximize the number of Americans who watch in horror and think, 'that could have been me or one of my loved ones.' One is left fearfully wondering whether a confluence of bad influences have conditioned Americans to find ways to blame their fellow citizens for outrages and tragedies. Cynical and exploitative leaders, salacious and conflict-driven news media, outrage and clickbait-chasing social media—a healthy share of the blame goes to all of them. But in the end, it is the American people who are choosing to respond to Atarsa's message of fear in this self-destructive way."

Gul read that and knew the Voices' hunger was finally being satiated.

Seated at the café, Gul felt the hum of his phone in his pants pocket. He removed it, and saw the number was not identified. Like his long-destroyed satellite phone in the Turkmenistan desert, this phone was to be called only in the direst of emergencies. Very few of his associates and comrades had the number to this phone and all of them had been told about the NSA's extensive interception and tracking capabilities. If one had taken the risk of calling him, the matter must be critical.

He switched on the phone but did not say anything.

"Gholam Gul?" The voice was unfamiliar. An American accent.

"Who is this?" he asked in Persian. When that did not generate any response, he repeated it in English.

"This is the man who's going to kill you," the man said, following the threat with a chuckle. "Say hello to Sarvar for me."

Gul looked up and glanced around. Sarvar sensed his tension and began looking around, too, scanning the skies for drones.

"You can't see me, Gul. You're enjoying the coastal breeze in the harbor. Maybe I'm over by the jetty... or maybe I'm by the parking lot. Just kidding, I'm in the restaurant. The seafood's pretty good."

Gul's head swiveled around, trying to see if anyone in the restaurant was on the phone. A few were, but they were speaking in Arabic or Russian—and what they were saying didn't match what he was hearing.

His heart pounded, but Gul calmed himself. "What do you want?"

"I already said I'm going to kill you, Gholam. I think it's pretty obvious that I just like watching you squirm before I do it."

Gul reached across the table to hold Sarvar's hand, awaiting a drone missile at any moment. When nothing happened for a minute, Gul realized he wasn't sitting in the crosshairs. Perhaps the Americans had killed Azi Dhaka and tracked his phone, but he wasn't caught in their net yet.

Gul heard laughter over the line, and he realized that the American was laughing at him.

"My cause will outlive me, American," Gul said firmly.

"Oh, by the way, I also blew up your altar to the Cockroach God or whatever it is in Erbent," the American voice continued. "Gholam—do you mind if I call you 'Goalie'? Goalie, I'm gonna tear apart everything you've ever done. And when I say everything you've ever done, that includes Sarvar. And then I'm gonna kill you. And your last thought is gonna be 'why did I ever mess with the United States of America?'"

Gul hung up. Sarvar threw money on the table and stood up, and Gul did as well, continuing to look around for anyone on a phone. Sarvar already had her hand in her purse, ready to remove a gun. She, too, was frustrated, not seeing anyone who struck her as an immediate threat, unsure whether the Arabs and Russians around her were just checking her out, or eyeing their sudden departure, or watching her because they had hostile intentions, connected to their mysterious caller. The phone buzzed again. It just kept ringing.

Finally, Gul answered. “What?”

“Your old buddies at VEVAK gave you up to us.”

“Ha!” Gul scoffed. “Now I know you’re lying. They would no sooner betray me than the ayatollah.” He walked out of the outdoor patio dining area, into the restaurant, his other hand sliding under his suit jacket, ready to draw the gun holstered in the small of his back at the first sign of trouble. Maddeningly, no signs of trouble manifested themselves. He headed to a back door.

“News flash, Goalie, you’re not as valuable to them as you think you are,” the American teased.

“I salute your ingenuity in finding my phone number, but you clearly have no idea who I am,” Gul said, tense, but strangely intrigued by the taunting phone call. This wasn’t the way the Americans operated, or the Israelis, or MI6. He almost admired the theatricality to this anonymous foe. “No point in hiding it now, I suppose. Lenin said capitalists would sell him the rope he needed to hang them. Your decadent, empty culture and its garden of rage and resentment provide all the foot soldiers I will ever need. My father taught me that, and I follow in his footsteps.”

The alley was clear.

“Aw, here we go. Daddy issues. We should have booked you on Dr. Phil,” the American snorted. “Let me guess, your dad was the one who really shot JFK.”

Gul and Rashin continued to walk quickly, scanning the skies. No drones revealed themselves. Increasingly confident, Gul savored the chance to turn the tables on the smug American.

“Not quite, but we both deeply admired Sirhan Sirhan. My father was a diplomat in the United States around that time—but he was already souring on the shah. Western decadence personified. He took an empire that stood for centuries and turned it into Las Vegas. Big oil, big cars, big Coca-Cola and booze, Western harlots…"

"Goalie, buddy, I've seen your girl Sarvar. You like curves as much as the next man."

This actually made Gul laugh out loud. He straightened himself, wondering if the call was part of some elaborate distraction. Still, his trained eye could see no signs of ambush. He began his preset route to avoid or throw off anyone following him. Sarvar nodded to him and went in a different direction. The plan was to meet again at their docked boat; she, too, would throw her phone onto a passing truck, trying to lure any drones tracking the phone as far from them as possible.

"I'm human. Perhaps it wasn't the vulgar whores of the West that bothered my father, so much as the shah spending a hundred million dollars on a party, dining on peacock and drinking champagne from Baccarat crystal glasses, while our people lived in poverty. My father went to Basra, to meet with an exiled holy man, Ruhollah Musavi. You know him today as the Ayatollah Khomeini. Long before he returned to Iran, the Ayatollah sent my father to America, to begin our first campaign against the Great Satan."

"This would have been what, the seventies?" the American guessed. "What, did your dad invent disco or something?"

"I marvel at your culture, so decadent and distracted that it managed to largely ignore and forget his campaign of terror," Gul sneered condescendingly. He now felt assured that whoever was taunting him could not launch a strike from a drone. "My father spent years training any radical he could find to build bombs. He and his protégés blew up the top floor of a skyscraper in Pittsburgh. He taught some group in Oregon how to cultivate salmonella—they made hundreds of people sick. He trained Croatian nationalists who bombed the Statue of Liberty. He struck at some of your most iconic symbols, and most of your countrymen simply forgot about it."

***

In the cockpit of the C-130, Alec looked at Katrina. He was embarrassed that he couldn't tell whether Gul was bluffing.

"Look, Goalie, I don't think anything your dad ever did mattered that much," Alec taunted. "How long do you remember a mosquito bite?"

There was silence on the other end. Alec smiled at Katrina, sensing he had really gotten under Gul's skin.

"My American friend, I've never seen a mosquito kill a dozen people with a bomb in a locker at LaGuardia Airport." Alec's blood ran cold. Katrina saw her husband's expression change completely—she didn't remember anything about LaGuardia Airport being bombed, but clearly it meant something to Alec. She reached out and shook him out of his momentary trance.

***

On the streets of Tartus, headed back toward the docks, Gul wondered if the connection to the anonymous American had been lost. Finally, he heard that voice again.

"I can't wait to kill you," the American whispered.

"I don't think you'll ever see me," Gul chuckled again. "Well done finding my phone number, but this is goodbye." He tossed his phone into the back of a passing truck.

***

The line went dead.

"What is it?" Katrina asked. "What is it about LaGuardia?"

"LaGuardia was bombed in 1975," Alec said softly. "Killed about a dozen, injured about a hundred. Dad told me the story. He was supposed to fly out that night on a business trip, his cab turned around when they heard they shut down the airport."

The C-17 worked its way around Iranian airspace, crossing Azerbaijan into Armenia. The next hour of the flight was relatively quiet, until Katrina discovered something on her laptop and began hitting the side of the plane in frustration.

"Please stop hitting my plane, ma'am!" Richards barked.

Katrina muttered an apology and turned to Alec. "Remember those blueprints for the old plane, the Trident? The ones that Rat had, that we thought didn't mean anything?" Alec nodded. She held up her laptop, and showcased a satellite image.

"Nicosia International Airport in Cyprus. It's been abandoned since the war in 'seventy-four. There's a Cyprus Airways Trident that's been sitting on the tarmac for decades, just falling apart and collecting dust."

"That explains the operating manual Rat had," Alec said, thinking back to the singed papers from the Berlin hostel room. "Gul and the gang have somebody fixing that plane for them."

"Their that's their get-out-of-Dodge plan," Katrina concluded. "Get on, take off, freak out every member of the UN peacekeeping force in Cyprus, and then land somewhere else." She thought for a moment. "And somewhere along the line, they're going to get plastic surgery. They know we're after them, they know we know their faces, so they're going to reinvent themselves. New identities. This al-Qaeda guy, Luia Sakka, did it a bunch of times."

"I'm gonna get you, Sakka," Alec murmured. Katrina didn't get the joke. "This is great. We've got them, as long as we can get to that plane before they do!"

They reconnected to Raquel's office and brought her up to speed.

"There's a dozen airports and airfields within an hour's flight that are closed, no longer used, abandoned, private airfields," Raquel sighed. "They walk off the plane, get new faces, new names, new passports, and then they're gone."

Alec looked at the Air Force pilots in front of him and wondered how much they were hearing and understanding. He hoped they could somehow metaphorically step on the gas and get them to Cyprus faster. After Katrina explained the need for speed, Richards looked at his charts and started calculating how quickly Gul and Rashin could get to Cyprus.

"Distance from Tartus to the Cyprus coast is about 130 miles, say 140 nautical miles. Maximum speed of their boat is forty-five knots, that's about fifty miles an hour, let's say they take three hours, maybe four."

"Probably going to take them longer," piped up Cook from the copilot's chair. "There's a serious thunderstorm forming, and you almost never see that at this time of year. Must be global warming or something."

"Or something," Alec muttered.

***

Alec crossed himself. "If you're up there, God, now would be a nice time to help out," Alec whispered.

Oh, sure. Now you call.

"A guilt trip is not help," Alec told the voice in his head. "I'm trying to protect your creations. Could you at least pretend to be interested? Bad enough you created a world with evil nut-jobs like this running around."

You would complain if I had created a world of always-noble automatons, missing free will.

"There's a lot of doubt around here about whether you're all-good or all-powerful, because you can't be both."

You've got the same free will that they do. What do you have, stumps at the ends of your arms? I gave you a body. I gave you a mind. I gave you Katrina.

Alec pursed his lips. "Fair point."

Get to it.

CHAPTER 64

LIBERTY CROSSING INTELLIGENCE CAMPUS
TYSONS CORNER, VIRGINIA
SATURDAY, APRIL 3

NBC's coverage of the Georgetown—Saint John's University men's basketball game began at three p.m. Eastern. There had been debate about canceling it after last night's violence, but eventually authorities agreed that the normality of sports might bring some comfort to a shocked country. The entire game was played without incident, although the crowd was sparse for the first half as fans encountered delays going through the metal detectors as part of the new security measures. When NBC switched to the local news at six p.m., Dee told everyone to expect an Atarsa signal interruption within thirty to thirty-five minutes.

Surely enough, shortly after the national newscast from New York began that evening at six-thirty, viewers in the Washington area suddenly saw increasing static on the NBC signal. The visual images and sound grew more and more disrupted and inaudible until, a few moments later, Angra Druj's face appeared on screens again. Tens of thousands of viewers shuddered, taking pictures of their television screens and sharing the invasive spectral image on social media.

What the viewers at home didn't know was that at that moment, sitting behind her console and computers at the Liberty Campus complex offices, Dee executed an electronic program of hot pursuit. Her triangulation with the various radar and other sensor arrays within the Washington area did not take long, barely a minute and a half into Druj's recitation of all the ways Americans would find their loved ones brutally murdered.

"Homing in on the signal," Dee announced as Raquel looked over her shoulder. "Tracking. Real close to the broadcast tower..." She checked the coordinates against her map. "Got it. Parking lot of the National Presbyterian Church. It's right next door to NBC's complex."

Dee typed furiously, opening new windows, typing in new codes, hitting enter, fingers a blur on the keyboard.

They went right back to where they poisoned the director, Raquel noted. She began barking orders to the assembled staffers. "Get the location to MPD and FBI, they must have somebody close by."

Dee emphatically hit the enter key and smiled. "Actually, they wo—" she began.

"We spotted them with the drone!" another technician interrupted with a shout. "I'm putting it on the big screen!"

The black-and-white live video feed came up on main screen in the bull pen. A black van with a sliding panel door was parked in the corner of the church parking lot. The panel door was open, and two figures, a man and a woman, were holding a small dish, perhaps two feet across, aimed at the NBC broadcast tower.

"Boy, are they in for a rude surprise," Raquel finally allowed herself a smile. "Enjoy the broadcast, Atarsa, because it's your last."

But the euphoric moment was suddenly interrupted by loud screaming and swearing in the office adjacent to their bull pen of cubicles and desks. Raquel felt like her attention was being pulled in a million directions at once. She glanced at the screen showing the live feed of the Atarsa message, but it was just Angra Druj damning the West in her ghostly tone.

A DNI staffer burst into the room.

"Somebody says they just saw a missile flying over the Potomac!" he cried, eyes bulging.

"What?" Raquel cried in disbelief.

"Visuals confirm something flying up the Potomac really fast, social media's going nuts, gotta be Atarsa!" The other room burst with gasps, expletives, and cries. "Headed toward Northwest!" someone shouted. Someone yelled for NORAD and other air defense, but among the cacophony, Raquel heard one voice cutting through it all because of how soft it was—almost a mumble.

"That wasn't Atarsa," Dee had murmured.

Raquel's head snapped around. Dee hadn't just . . .

"What did you just say?"

Dee simply pointed up at the screen and shrugged. A second later, on the black-and-white screen, the black van suddenly exploded, disappearing in a white flash. The entire office gasped again, until someone let out a thrilled, *"Yeah!"* and pumped his fist madly.

On the monitors tuned to the local NBC broadcast signal, the Atarsa message abruptly ended, returning to the regular NBC nightly news broadcast from New York.

Everyone stood silently, looking around in confusion.

"What the hell was that?"

Another intelligence liaison shouted from elsewhere in the office. "NORAD's reporting they just had an unauthorized missile launch at Joint Base Anacostia!"

"Wasn't really that unauthorized," Dee mumbled quietly, rubbing her hand over her mouth as she spoke.

"What . . . did . . . you . . . just . . . do?" Raquel whispered.

Dee looked sheepish.

"It's not hard to reprogram a missile to home in on a particular signal's location," she said quietly. "Back in the Persian Gulf war, they had to warn all the network correspondents about what frequencies they used, otherwise the US Tomahawks might land in Bernie Shaw's lap. Over at Joint Base Anacostia Bolling, they've got a SLAMRAAM—Surface Launched Advanced Medium Range Anti-Aircraft Missile—designed to shoot down any plane veering off course from Reagan National or some other plane on a suicide course. It didn't take a lot to get that system to track the source of the broadcast, and to... well, basically treat the source of the signal the way it would treat a plane coming in on a suicide course."

Raquel blinked, still coming to terms with what she had just heard.

"You just *blew up* the Atarsa van?!?" Raquel exclaimed. She tried to organize the million emotions running through her, and concluded that for now, disbelief would take priority.

"I promised you I could stop the broadcasts," Dee said. "And you didn't really specify any limits as to how I could stop them."

Raquel's eyes bulged, and she fumed, as she contemplated how she could even begin to explain an unauthorized missile launch and strike in the middle of Washington DC—into a church parking lot, for Christ's sake!—to her superiors and, at some point, how those superiors could explain that act to the American public.

She stepped closer to the large screen, showing the signal from the drone. The van's roof had been completely blown off... it was a mass of flaming shrapnel with four wheels. There was no way either figure seen within could have possibly survived. She turned back to Dee.

"You..." Raquel gasped, holding on to her sanity by her fingernails. She pointed an angry finger at Dee. "You have been hanging around with Ward and Alec for too long! They're rubbing off on you!"

Dee pointed her finger back. "As far outside the law as I needed to go! You said it yourself!" she shouted indignantly. "I told you I was going to need a presidential pardon beforehand!"

"I said theoretically!" Raquel shouted back. "I thought you meant breaking into some database or something! You said no war games!"

"This isn't 'war games'! This is just killing some people by pressing buttons!"

Then she realized how inappropriately casual that sounded. "Okay, that came out wrong."

Another staffer shouted to interrupt: "Raquel, it's Director—I mean, Acting Director Mitchell. He says it's urgent!"

"I'll bet it is." Raquel walked over to the nearest secure phone and picked up the receiver, punching up the right line. How on earth could she even begin this conversation? She remembered his furious challenge in the morning's meeting.

"Directorate of Any Means Necessary, Raquel speaking."

***

There was a lot of yelling on that phone call, followed by a lot of yelling on the Agency's seventh floor, followed by a lot of yelling in the White House. One person who surprised everyone by not yelling was the President of the United States, who seemed pleased with the newfound ability to announce on Twitter to the American people that the evening explosion in a usually quiet corner of Northwest Washington represented the US Government striking back at Atarsa and destroying their ability to send the threatening messages. Yes, the sight of the incoming missile and sudden explosion had caused quite a few car accidents throughout Northwest Washington, particularly up and down Nebraska Avenue, and at least a dozen emergency room visits. The whiplash personal injury lawsuits wouldn't be sorted out for years. But thankfully, the only two dead bodies in Washington this evening were Atarsa's propaganda wing, now burnt to a crisp.

The cable news networks and the big broadcast networks again interrupted their prime-time programming, but their reports were almost joyous. A few cell phones had recorded glimpses of the missile flying over DC, and the sudden mini-mushroom cloud of smoke formed by the van's destruction. A few guest analysts and senators calling in to the programs pointed out that the US government had just killed American citizens without a trial on American soil using a method similar to a drone strike, something a previous attorney general had promised to never, ever, ever do.

The public didn't get to see the Defense Department's reaction to someone—even another federal agency tasked with national security duties—remotely taking over one of their air defense systems and launching a missile without their consent. The secretary of defense spat hot fire in the National Security Council's emergency conference call. Among the recommendations from the joint chiefs for the appropriate consequence for this act was prosecution, incarceration, drawing and quartering, and "shipping that CIA hacker to Gitmo."

Dee wasn't physically dragged up to the director's office on the seventh floor, but she felt like she might as well have, escorted by two beefy uniformed Federal Protective Service officers. Acting Director Mitchell was in video conference in the director's conference room, and more than a few generals and National Security Council staffers couldn't hide their skepticism that the woman who had just launched the missile was relatively young and pretty, the kind of woman who could be dancing in a Target commercial for Christmas sales.

"Miss Alves, as you can probably gather, your little stunt with NORAD's systems has a lot of people very upset right now," Mitchell began, a human teakettle about to bubble over. "I've pointed out to our counterparts in the Pentagon that if they really want to prosecute you, that will require a long public trial discussing exactly how vulnerable our local air defense systems are to a remote takeover, a prolonged and detailed humiliation that would probably end a lot of careers." He shifted in his seat.

"While they contemplate the ramifications of pursuing charges, I figured I should ask you if you have one reason why I shouldn't have you arrested right now."

He noticed a disapproving stare from Raquel, sitting next to Dee. The director of the Central Intelligence Agency had to balance a lot of unaligned duties in his job, and if protecting the American people was the top priority, then number one-A was protecting his own people. The CIA was the universal scapegoat, demonized for being too reactive or too active, too reckless or too timid, too invasive or insufficiently thorough, too tied up in bureaucratic knots and red tape or too arrogantly convinced that no laws applied to itself. Everyone else in the federal government, or perhaps in America, liked to point the finger at the Agency when things went wrong. The agency's rank and file couldn't speak publicly to defend themselves, for obvious reasons. It was the job of the director to remind everyone else—other agencies, Congress, the media, even the president—that yes, we did brief you on that. Yes, you did ask us to do that, even if it's politically inconvenient to acknowledge that now. Yes, we warned you about the risks; yes, we informed you about the contrary evidence.

The CIA director had to stand up for his people, because no one else would. And right now, in Raquel's eyes, Mitchell was coming dangerously close to throwing Dee under the bus. The dynamic between Raquel and Alec and the rest of the team worked so well because she could tear them a new one over their mistakes—and she did so, regularly—but she relentlessly defended them among her peers and superiors. They never spoke of it directly, but it was clear. The team was like family—"friends are the family that you choose," Alec had said—and a bit like the old mafia, Raquel never chose anyone else over the family.

She knew she had a uniquely challenging position—to take their unorthodox methods and clear out a path for them to do what they did best, within an organization whose incentive structure increasingly punished risk. She thought Mitchell was going to give them a longer leash, but now she had her doubts, watching him trying to placate a line of DoD officials who looked angrier than a YouTube video comments section.

Raquel, Mitchell, and the rest of the room expected Dee to argue her missile launch was a necessary step to save lives. But she went in a completely different direction.

"No one's had any luck getting any of the arrested Atarsa sleepers to talk, right?" she asked. Mitchell grunted affirmatively.

"One of our officers got the name 'Reese Scovi' as the handler for one of the sleepers—maybe all of them," Dee said cheerfully. "That name didn't match any public record, so I expanded the parameters for variations. A few hours ago, I found one hit in the Census records for 'Fabrice Vuscovi.'"

Raquel's head snapped around. Another little development that Dee had neglected to mention immediately. Dee looked down at her yellow legal pad.

"Turns out that despite 'Fabrice' being a man's name, Fabrice Vuscovi is a woman. Born in Silver Spring, Maryland. Thirty-five-year-old licensed psychiatrist, traveled to Iran, Turkmenistan, and Cyprus six years ago. Closed private practice a year ago, sold her house six months ago, mail is sent to a P.O. Box. But her name is still on the property records for an out-of-business nursery and garden supply place on Route 50 in Fairfax County."

"That's practically our backyard," Mitchell gasped. He turned to his Bureau liaison. "How long will it take to get an FBI team to that site?"

"No need," Dee said. "I texted it to Ward Rutledge shortly after I found it, he'll be there any minute."

And with that, almost everyone in the room quickly forgot about how upset they were about the unauthorized NORAD missile launch that had occurred ninety minutes ago.

***

It was once a fair-sized greenhouse, series of sheds, and a garden supply store. But that "once" had to have been three or four years ago. Ward had brought his flashlight, a hunting knife, and three guns. Once he saw the overhead lights flickering in the greenhouse, he figured his night was getting easier. A Prius had been parked at one end of the parking lot, which now had a healthy crop of weeds emerging from cracks in the pavement. Ward crept over and quietly punctured all four tires. Fabrice Vuscovi was not going to drive away from him tonight.

After carefully entering and scanning the greenhouse for any signs of human life, he was disappointed. The flickering light left a strobe effect, but the illumination was sufficient to see most of the greenhouse was a mess: overgrown weeds, plants hanging, ranging from wildly overgrown to dying, pots of every shape and size everywhere. Water dripped from the misting system and pooled at his feet in puddles.

On the far side of the long room, he saw a table and plants, clipboards, a ruler, beakers, a mortar and pestle. Clearly, someone had been working over on that far side. He heard a distant rumble of thunder; it was a little unseasonal for a thunderstorm, and the constant flicker of the lights made Ward wonder whether he was seeing lightning outside.

The hairs on the back of his neck went up. The thunder's slow tumbling noise would cover up the sound of anyone approaching, and he was quick to turn back every few seconds. Dang it, this was another time where Alec would be useful. If Raquel knew he was here, she would have been screaming bloody murder, livid that he hadn't waited for backup or the FBI. On the other hand, he had figured out how to get Norman Fein to talk when every other law-abiding official had failed. He had generated this lead himself, and he felt adamantly that he had earned the first shot at catching this Fabrice Vuscovi woman. He would try his best to take her in alive. That didn't mean unscathed, of course, as he examined all the pruning shears, blades, and other tools piled in the gaps between the tables. Vuscovi apparently wound up these killers and set them loose, putting as much blood on her hands as theirs.

Another rumble of thunder, and now Ward was convinced he hadn't seen lightning outside. Was it a recording? Some sort of auditory trick? He kept checking his back, careful, peering around corners, certain he wouldn't let himself get ambushed. Where he heck was she? Ward felt his heart pumping, the beat seeming to throb in his ears. Adrenaline surged. Ward thought he had long since acclimated to life-and-death moments, the sense of hunting and being hunted, so why was he suddenly so nervous, on edge?

And then he saw it, before he heard it: the misting system was turned on, and a gentle hiss announced that something had been flowing through it all along. Ward rubbed his fingers against his skin, feeling faint moisture, and smelled. Something sweet, but distinctly unnatural.

Chemicals. Gas.

They're hitting me with what the same drug they hit the director with, he thought, wondering how long he had until the chemical hit his brain and altered his perception, overtaking his self-control and ability to control his fear, or perhaps the drug would just knock him out so that suddenly, without warning, everything would just sto

CHAPTER 65

VAROSHA TURKISH REPUBLIC OF NORTHERN CYPRUS
SATURDAY, APRIL 3

Varosha was, long ago, a beautiful beach resort, the playground of the rich and famous, a Greek-influenced pleasure port—the French Riviera of Cyprus. Brigitte Bardot posed in a bikini there, and if ever there was compelling evidence of God's love for man and his desire for his creations to be happy, it was the sight of Bardot in a bikini. The Greek coastal resort of Varosha was a Technicolor dream—aqua blue waters, ochre sand, pink flowers, tangerine beach umbrellas, and smiling, happy people, swimming, sunbathing, drinking, and carousing—all the joys of life, compressed into one slightly hedonistic, glamorous corner.

Then in 1974, long-simmering tensions between Greek and Turkish Cypriots finally boiled over. A group of the island's Greek Cypriot military officers, allied with Greece's military junta, launched a coup and burned down the presidential palace. Once they had taken over, the military began carrying out the early moves from a depressingly familiar playbook: censor the independent press, search homes and seize weapons, arrest and kill known supporters of the previous regime. Most consequential, the brutal new rulers threatened the enclaves of Turkish Cypriots scattered throughout the island.

Five days later, the nation of Turkey gave their answer to the threat to their ethnic compatriots: about three thousand troops, twelve tanks, twenty personnel carriers, and twelve howitzers landed in the early morning hours on the largely unguarded northern coast of Cyprus. The new military junta seemed unprepared for this wave or the nearly forty thousand additional troops lining up behind them; Greek Cypriot forces couldn't muster any significant resistance until late morning. The first Greek Cypriot forces to respond found they had more cannons than tractors to pull them, and were strafed by Turkish air forces.

On August 20, 1974, tens of thousands of Varosha Greek Cypriot residents awoke to the terrifying news that war was almost literally at their doorstep. They fled, grabbing only what they could carry. They left their homes, businesses, stores, and the once-luxurious hotels on the beachfront abandoned, doors unlocked. They were right to flee; a few Turkish bombs and artillery took chunks out of buildings like bites from a giant monster. Within a few days, the Turkish army controlled the area; they walled off the entire neighborhood behind barbed-wire and chain-link fences and lines of rusting oil barrels.

The shooting stopped, but the relationship between the new "Turkish Republic of Northern Cypru" and the southern Greek Republic of Cyprus remained tense. Months under the new separation stretched into years. In 1984, the United Nations ruled that only the original inhabitants could legally occupy any land within Varosha; Turkey had no interest in handing back prime property without concessions, so the small resort city remained walled off. Red FORBIDDEN ZONE signs warned trespassers that the Turkish guards' orders were to shoot on sight. The military authorities barred visitors or inspections.

And in those empty buildings and streets, nothing happened, decade after decade. The only glimpse of Varosha came from the occasional daring photographer who snuck past the fences and snapped shots of the ultimate ghost town, depicting a small city frozen in time. A car dealership with "new" 1974 models sat untouched. Towers of once-gorgeous beachfront balconies succumbed to rust. Bottles, glasses, and empty plates stood on café tables, covered in dust. Long-since-spoiled food sat in kitchen cupboards. Clothing displays remained in store windows. It was as if some strange bomb had suddenly removed all the people, but left almost all of the buildings standing, a modern Pompeii.

Varosha was, in many ways, a dangerous spot for Sarvar Rashin and Gholam Gul to come ashore. But the whispering Voices had urged them to this spot, and the no-man's-land between the Turkish and Greek Cypriot rivals seemed to please the voices. This place represents a future, the voices told Rashin and Gul. Your triumph.

The Voices had guided them to sort through a long list of European, Russian, and Turkish plastic surgeons willing to travel, take cash, and not ask too many questions, and led them to Solak Osman.

They had led them to Force Commander Julian Veer, who had acquiesced to their disguised requests, deeming them odd but unlikely to threaten the security of the United Nations Peacekeeping Force in Cyprus.

The reports of the storm approaching from the south kept the local navies and coast guard patrols at bay. Rashin and Gul's boat, the *Naonhaithya*, cut through the waves like a knife, and once their GPS indicated they were at the edge of international waters, they switched to their inflatable Zodiac boat.

***

If some cheerful nuts wanted to fix up the husk of the Cyprus Airways airliner that had been sitting on the tarmac of the long-abandoned Nicosia International Airport as part of a documentary on aviation engineering, what did UN Force Commander Veer care? The work had been slow and methodical; only God could know where they were finding the parts for an airliner that went out of service two generations ago.

Tonight Veer had much bigger problems to worry about. For the past month, incendiary graffiti had cropped up on both sides of the border. His blue-helmeted team didn't usually spend a lot of time focusing on what was, in all likelihood, the work of angry teenagers. But the graffiti was followed by reports of shots fired across the border. Thankfully, the locations of the alleged shots were far from known Greek Cypriot or Turkish Cypriot military forces. But three nights ago, a Greek Cypriot border patrol officer claimed he had been shot at by a sniper.

Both sides elevated their alert status and the rhetoric from politicians in North Nicosia and Nicosia had grown louder in recent days. Veer found it bitterly ironic that both national leaders had used the same phrase, "we will not let this insulting provocation stand." Already tonight Veer's men heard reports of explosions on each side, trying to determine if they were fireworks or artillery. Veer had the distinct feeling radicals on either side—or both sides—were trying to provoke an all-out shooting war. Thunder from the approaching storm created more booms, more tense questions of whether the divided island was about to erupt.

And now this American C-17, somehow horrifically off-course from its filed destination of Incirlik, Turkey, was requesting an emergency landing.

***

"US Air Force C-17, this is United Nations Air Traffic Control," Alec heard the voice, with a strong British accent, and it reminded him a bit of Basil Fawlty. "We are preparing to clear a flight path for you to Lacarna International Airport."

"No can do, good buddy, I'm carrying some very sensitive, highly classified material and equipment and I am not authorized to land this at a civilian airport," Richards improvised. Alec and Katrina nodded approvingly.

They could hear the UN air traffic control officer sigh. "Is this a bloody emergency?"

"Sir, I'd like to avoid a crash landing *and* not get thrown in the brig for endangering classified information," Richards answered. "We're on course for Nicosia, inbound, ten minutes."

"Negative, US Air Force C-17. That airport hasn't been used in years."

"Is the runway flat? Because that's all I need."

"I repeat, negative, US Air Force C-17. I'm arranging a corridor for you to divert to Royal Air Force Akrotiri," the air traffic controller said with audible impatience.

"That's a little far, I'm going to stick to Nicosia," Richards answered. "We've had issues with unresponsive ailerons. Right now it's a straight, short shot to the main runway."

"Are you listening, you bloody stubborn Yank?!" the control officer snapped. "Nicosia Airport has been shut down and abandoned for decades. There is no electricity there, no fuel, no maintenance or air crews. You'll be stuck there once you land. I'm not even sure the runway lights still work. Wait."

They heard the control officer ask, "Are you sure?"

"Well, this is bizarre. I'm told the runway lights just went on at Nicosia."

Katrina and Alec looked at each other. The lights hadn't suddenly come alive to help their "emergency" landing; they were turned on because the Atarsa flight was ready to take off.

***

The deal for Solak Osman was generous. A $75,000 fee up front and airfare to Ercan International Airport. His employers had already arranged a rental car, and with it, instructions to drive to the United Nations Protected Area on the site of the old Nicosia International Airport. He was to introduce himself at the gate as Solak Osman, the producer of a documentary film about restoring the long-abandoned Cyprus Airways Trident, coming to review the work of his documentary team.

There he would meet Kolak, the supposed documentary filmmaker who had handled all the arrangements; Naresh, the pilot; and Bahadur, the bald, mustached, barrel-chested engineer who looked like he wrestled animals in his spare time.

Osman's journey ran relatively smoothly, until the guard at the checkpoint entrance to the United Nations Protected Area shook his head and said that the documentary crew was supposed to have left hours ago.

"We're in elevated alert status, we can't have civilians running around the airport unaccompanied," the guard said firmly.

With tensions on the island rising tonight, the civilians should have left. The United Nations commanders had grown increasingly laid back about civilians on the compound; about a decade ago, an outdoor concert, a "peace symphony," featuring many Greek Cypriot musicians and one Turkish Cypriot musician, was held in front of the terminal building's ghostly façade. Another photographer had brought old Cyprus Airlines employees to pose in front of their now-crumbling workplaces in their old, ill-fitting uniforms, making some sort of grand statement about the tragic division of the island.

Osman had some improvisational skills. He showed the man his airline ticket stub and said he was exhausted, but he had driven here straight from the airport because that damn filmmaker had been avoiding his calls and he wanted to see just what the hell his investment in the documentary was getting him. Osman whined and pleaded and made enough of a nuisance of himself that the guard finally relented and told Osman to go to the documentary film crew and tell them they were supposed to leave more than an hour ago. The guard debated calling for a team to escort the documentary crew off the base, but the elevated alert status meant everyone had other duties.

That was all Osman needed. He drove out to the tarmac and saw the restored Trident under a few floodlights. Kolak greeted him; Naresh and Bahadur were conducting the final inspection. Osman was welcomed aboard, and inspected the surgical table built onto the plane with a gyroscopic stabilizer. He had described what he needed, in great technical detail, to the Iranian man and woman, and they had met every last one of his specifications. Within an hour, the couple would join them; his assignment was to give them distinctly different appearances. The instruction was to make their faces "more Western." Behind the surgical bay Osman saw cameras and the equipment used to make official passports. Osman couldn't read the faded plaque that read "Property of the Syrian Government" in Arabic.

Within an hour or two, the man and woman would walk off the plane with completely new identities … and he would walk off the plane a half-million dollars richer.

***

Kolak, Naresh, and Bahadur felt slightly tense as they saw a United Nations–labeled jeep approaching their site. They exhaled and smiled as Sarvar Rashin and Gholam Gul emerged from the jeep, in not particularly well-fitting uniforms, identifying them as part of the UN Peacekeeping force.

"Somewhere on this island there are two very unlucky soldiers," Kolak laughed. "Shall I salute?"

Instead Gul embraced his old Iranian VEVAK comrade and turned to Naresh and Bahadur. The three men bowed to Rashin and assured them everything was ready.

"Luck is with us and against us," Kolak summarized. "The authorities have been cooperative and barely paid attention to us. Tensions between the Cypriots were bad when we arrived and are worse now. Just one spark could ignite an ugly border skirmish." He cast a careful glance at Sarvar. When they had laid out this plan, she assured Kolak that at the key moment, both sides would be itching for war. Was it clairvoyance? Or had she somehow helped feed the tensions on the island?

"Good work," Gul said. "You've arranged to ignite that spark if needed?"

"Absolutely," he nodded. "The bad luck is the storm. You can feel the wind picking up already. It could make our flight out of here difficult."

"I am ready," Naresh said tersely. Gul put a hand on his shoulder and nodded with confidence.

Dr. Osman stepped forward, greeted the two arrivals professionally and studied their faces; he had much to work with. Sarvar Rashin was particularly beautiful; he would strive to preserve some of that beauty. They climbed aboard.

***

Across the tarmac, United Nations troops turned in surprise. The documentary team and their engineering team had managed to get the plane's engines revving in the previous nights, but it had never moved. It hadn't moved in decades. And now it was suddenly jolting forward, lurching, shaking, moving away from its comfortable longtime home next to the terminal and toward the long, empty runway.

The staffers and peacekeeping troops started shouting; this wasn't scheduled or planned and no one had been notified.

In the cockpit, Gul, out of the ill-fitting stolen military uniform and back in his all-black outfit, sat next to Naresh in the pilot's seat. He couldn't help but chuckle at the seemingly hapless United Nations peacekeepers trying to run toward the runway and waving their arms. The fools. His team had operated right under their noses the entire time. His chuckle turned into a full laugh. Nicosia International Airport was about to have its first departure in decades. He looked back over his shoulder at Sarvar, who had changed, with little modesty, out of her uniform into a tight, dark-green jumpsuit. Their eyes met and she smiled at Gul; it was a triumphant moment. Within a few months, with new faces, they would reconstitute Atarsa, recruit more troubled minds, and set forth new wind-up toys of death into public squares of the West. What was left of the United States and Europe would once again find itself under siege by angry young men lashing out through violence in public places, and the people of the West would turn against themselves in fear. The Voices would be pleased.

The Trident completed its slow turn so that the nose was parallel to the runway, and Naresh pushed the lever forward to increase the thrust from the engines. He looked at the instruments, looked up, and then suddenly his eyes went wide. "*What the hell is that?*" he screamed in Persian.

Coming right at them, down the runway, was a US C-17 Globemaster cargo plane, at an exceptionally high speed, in a giant airplane game of chicken.

***

In the opposing cockpit, Richards and Cook had managed to get the massive C-17 down on the runway—no easy task—and Alec and Katrina sat behind them, bracing themselves with one arm and pointing out the cockpit window at the Cyprus Airways Trident directly ahead of them.

"Hit them! Hit them!" Katrina screamed.

"Do you want to die?" Richards shouted.

"We need that plane disabled!" Alec shouted. "I don't care how you do it, just do it!"

The plane violently bounced down the uneven, rocky, long-unused runway, on a collision course with the resurrected Cyprus Airlines plane ahead.

***

In the other cockpit, Naresh, Gul, Sarvar, and Kolak screamed a cacophony of expressions of disbelief, rage, and fear. How could a plane be landing at this runway at the precise moment they were to take off?

"Can't go around—" Naresh tried to scream above the din, realizing there was almost no way to avoid a collision. He tried to steer left, but the plane, a hybrid of modern avionic equipment inside an ancient husk, wasn't built to turn on a dime. The enormous, four-engine C-17 was barreling down at them like a giant gray whale, massive fins angled to the ground, ready to flop upon them and crush them under its mighty weight. The sight of the C-17 filled the cockpit windows, getting larger and larger, until it was clear impact was inevitable.

"How?!" Sarvar screamed.

Impact was seconds away, Gul saw the small American flag insignia on the side of the approaching cockpit, he realized how.

"The Americans," he whispered. "Those fuc—"

Too late.

***

Once Richards knew a collision was unavoidable, he steered left as well, trying to at least avoid a head-on crash. Finally, the two fuselages weren't perfectly aligned, and instead were parallel. If the two planes had only consisted of the fuselages, the horrible wreck could be avoided. But it was too late: The plane's wings clipped each other; the Trident's tore off like tin foil, the C-17's tip sheared off, and the two planes, crippled, careened off in different directions.

***

Inside both planes, the collision felt like the entire room had been punched, picked up, thrown down, and stepped on. Heads slammed against cockpit chairs.

Inside the Trident, Gul never awoke because he had managed—just barely—to not lapse into unconsciousness. He did feel like his internal organs had tried to bounce out of his body, and had only been held inside by the lap and chest belt straps. Was it the wind knocked out of him? He coughed.

Was there gas leaking from the wing? Would the plane burst into a fireball soon?

He looked around in tearful frustration. He managed to get out of his cockpit seat. Beside him, in the pilot's seat, Akash held his head and moaned. He might have a concussion, Gul concluded. Kolak was groaning, saying he thought his rib cage was broken. Sarvar was at least able to walk and had painfully, slowly undone her seat belt.

Looking out the cockpit door that hung open, he saw Osman and Bahadur's bodies, out of their seats, lying motionless, the surgical bay a mess of violently tossed equipment. He called their names and heard no answer. Osman dead—this meant no plastic surgery. Poor Bahadur, he had spent so much time figuring out what it would take to make a plane rise from the dead. Better that he enjoy his final rest than see his work torn to pieces around him.

Gul looked at Sarvar as she rose from the chair and turned to stumble her way out of the cockpit. This was a disaster; their final battle was coming much sooner than they had ever expected. Akash and Kolak were trying to will themselves out of the cockpit chairs, with little success. Perhaps they would be able to stumble out of the plane and run, perhaps not. In all likelihood, they would be found by the UN peacekeepers, which meant they could he hospitalized and treated, but also arrested.

"The second plan," Gul painfully whispered to Sarvar.

She nodded. There was no way to avoid it now. "Send the signal, and we can try to get off the base, get off Cyprus some other way."

He nodded, although he doubted there would be any escape this time.

His bag in the compartment behind the cockpit had been tossed around violently during the collision, but the phone within it was intact.

They had to get to get away from the plane, to a spot with a strong wireless signal. From there, Gul and Sarvar could record their final message. It would activate every last Atarsa sleeper waiting in the United States. Their last act would be launching attacks nineteen through sixty-six—forty-seven devoted followers, in forty-seven different locations across the continental United States. Atarsa's sleepers would charge into public squares, schools, hospitals, train stations, churches, and movie theaters, stabbing people until they were stopped. It would be terrifying.

His plan had been to peel off the Band-Aid slowly, to subject his enemies to an excruciatingly slow and steady stretch of pain and suffering. Now he would tear it off all at once, a burst of the same pain flooding the system all at once. This was not how he wanted his last battle to end, but it would be appropriately spectacular.

***

Alec hadn't been knocked out often in his life, but he hated the feeling each time. It was as if his mind was a television and someone had changed the channel without warning. One moment he was in the plane, then a half-awake, half-dreaming state, with noise all around him, a throbbing pain in the back of his head and a sudden confusion. It felt like being in bed, but he didn't remember going home and going to sleep. And what had happened in Cyprus? *How did I get home unless... I'm not at home.* He jerked his head and realized his head had been hanging down, and his vision came into focus. Still in the cockpit. In pain. How much time had passed?

"Katrina?"

Alec looked over at the other seat in the cockpit behind the pilots and his heart stopped. Katrina sat motionless and silent in her chair.

He snapped off his seat belt and reached for her—she was breathing. A moment later, she groaned.

Alec swore. He looked up and down, and didn't see anything sticking out of her. He pinched her thigh and she squirmed. Good, he thought, no paralysis. She groaned again. She closed her eyes tightly, but he used his fingers to open her eyelid. She weakly groaned in objection.

"If I had to guess, your head hit on something and you have a concussion," Alec said. He knew his assessment was a hope as much a diagnosis. She mumbled something that sounded like an incredibly implausible insistence she was fine.

"Yeah, that's what all the quarterbacks say," Alec said.

Richards coughed in the cockpit seat. "Well, I just broke a two-hundred-million-dollar plane. I'm sending the repair bill to Langley."

Cook also groaned. Alec stood up and realized he was in the least pain out of the quartet. He suddenly smelled jet fuel. That's a bad sign.

"I've got to get you guys out of here," he said. He looked out the cockpit windows, trying to get a sense if anyone was rushing to approach the C-17. He couldn't see where the Cyprus airliner was. The collision must have prevented their takeoff, but where were they?

He carefully unbuckled Katrina and began the process of trying to lift her in his arms. The doorway to the cockpit was not particularly wide, and he was going to have a tough time carrying her through it.

***

He had to gingerly try to carry Katrina down the flight of internal stairs, and stumble over to the main entry doorway. The door opened out and down, with the door forming the "integral air stairs," a little stairway down to the tarmac. He heard Richards and Cook starting to follow behind them.

The door opened. Outside in the night, Alec was frustrated that no one had run up to the damaged C-17. Their plane had just crashed on an airstrip in United Nations territory—where the hell was everyone? He saw some movement behind parked trucks on the parallel access road beyond the runway.

"I could have ordered a pizza by now," he grumbled, before hearing gunshots.

He instinctively tumbled to the ground, taking Katrina with him. Alec refocused his attention to his left. About thirty yards away, he saw a blue-beret-clad United Nations peacekeeper lying on the tarmac, holding a bloody thigh. A second peacekeeper was similarly on the ground, lying flat, entirely without any cover or anywhere to hide.

Cook and Richards hit the deck as well.

Farther down the airstrip, he saw the Trident, freshly shorn of one wing. A man and a woman ran toward the dark terminal building across the runway. There was shouting by the far edge, and Alec realized there *had* been a response team from the peacekeepers on the base, approaching both planes, and then someone had come out of the Trident and started shooting. The United Nations team had been taken surprise by the first shots, but they had scrambled for cover and were shouting into radios for armed response teams.

After twenty seconds, when no further shots had been fired, Cook and Richards began crawling on their bellies toward Alec and Katrina. Alec looked across the tarmac.

He was certain it was Gul and Sarvar running toward the darkened terminal building. It stood in the night, a long-forgotten and abandoned monument to 1960s architecture, with most of the letters stop the roof missing: NI O INTE N IO AI P RT

Alec watched them run . . . and then smiled.

He turned to Cook and Richards. "Can I trust you guys to get her to a medic?" He checked Katrina's pulse and breathing again, then turned his attention to her holster and removed her pistol. He grabbed the extra clips.

"Where the hell are you going?" Cook asked. Alec pointed toward the terminal building.

"There are a couple of heads over there I've gotta get mounted and stuffed," he said.

***

Getting inside was no problem; the windows of the terminal building had been smashed decades earlier. Sarvar and Gul simply stepped through the empty space where a window once stood. Once inside, they realized they were stepping on decades of pigeon droppings, crusted upon the floor. Their feet stuck with every step.

Sarvar went deeper inside, knowing that it was just a matter of time before someone from the United Nations peacekeepers would track them down. Everything depended upon getting that message out. They crept past faded tourism and cigarette billboards from a half-century ago.

The wall had once been decorated with blue and black airliner silhouettes; now it was faded and scratched. Wallpaper peeled from the walls. Gul proceeded inward, past what had once been "Health Control," and checked his wireless signal. Not as strong as he needed for a message as important as this. They heard glass breaking behind them.

***

Alec looked at his bloody shin and sighed. Next time, he swore, he would just step over the broken glass window instead of trying to dramatically leap over it.

He scrambled to a corner and looked at his leg. Not as bad as he had feared. He had been bitten by a snake, swum in Mexico's filthiest waters, incinerated some human cockroach, survived a plane crash, and now broken glass sliced up his shin. The universe seemed to be conspiring in a far-reaching effort to cut him off at the knees.

He saw movement out the corner of his left eye, and swiveled, pointing his gun. There it was again, something moving, fairly high in the darkness of that corner of the terminal entryway. He fired a single shot, and *the pop* echoed and reverberated throughout the terminal building.

So much for the element of surprise, he thought.

A moment later, the source of the movement fluttered out of the shadows: a barn owl, common to Cyprus. Farmers and conservationists welcomed the bird to protect carob trees. Alec found himself wishing he had killed the damn bird.

***

Gul and Sarvar froze when they heard the shot, but realized it was a significant distance away from them in the terminal hall. They scrambled around a corner and ducked into what had once been a duty-free shop, shelves now empty and broken. He turned to her and whispered, "We'll need that distraction you promised."

She nodded. She held up her phone and determined the signal was strong enough to send a text, if still a little iffy for Gul's all-important video message. She pressed a series of buttons, and sent two messages.

Two angry old men awaited the signal. She couldn't suppress a chuckle; this little precaution had taken so little money, so little equipment. Just a propane canister, nails, ball bearings, some basic electronics, and the right cold-hearted elderly men. The Voices had guided her, finding the perfect prospect living bitterly and alone in the Alaykoy neighborhood, just northwest of Nicosia Airport. When obtaining an actual mortar was deemed too dangerous and likely to attract attention, Sarvar had instructed the hard Turkish Cypriot how to assemble a giant makeshift slingshot in his backyard. He didn't need perfect aim; the long rubber tubing would hurl his propane tank-bomb high into the air. He believed he would send it across the border into Kokkinotrimithia, hitting the damn Greeks. Sarvar knew the old man's projectile was far too heavy to arc across the border. Much to the old fool's horror, his bomb would fall out of the sky in some

Turkish Cypriot neighborhood intersection, just outside the UN Compound gates.

The surrounding Turkish Cypriot authorities wouldn't know that, of course.

What the hard Turkish Cypriot didn't know was that Sarvar had made the same deal—even buying the same equipment—with a hard Greek Cypriot in the neighborhood of Egkomi, just south and east of the airport. His projectile would also fall short, most likely landing in the neighborhood of Agios Dhometios.

And within a few minutes, the two armies on each sides of the border would fire in response, each convinced the other had just fired a mortar.

***

Broken glass.

Alec peered around a corner and thought he saw movement about halfway down the terminal, in what had been a duty-free shop, when he was distracted by the sound of a distant explosion. Alec briefly froze in terror, worrying that the C-17 had exploded. But from his glances through the broken windowpanes, he could see that both planes remained in place, no carrot-colored glow of exploding gas tanks. No, that boom seemed too far off, somewhere to the west, beyond the airport.

Less than a minute later, a second boom, from the other side of the airport. What the hell was going on out there? Now gunfire, farther away. He wiped the sweat from his brow and eyes.

***

Gul and Sarvar shared one last passionate kiss, and went their separate ways. They knew that without extraordinary luck, they would never see each other again.

***

The accelerating noise of gunfire and explosions convinced Alec no one would hear the sound of his footsteps, and he advanced more confidently. Alec quickly peeked around the corner and saw her: Sarvar Rashin, looking away, peering around another distant corner. There was no sign of Gul, but Alec figured he would come running as soon as his woman was down. Good.

Alec raised his gun, lined up Sarvar Rashin's head square in his sights, and pulled the trigger with great satisfaction. A second later, he winced as his shot went significantly lower than he expected. Still, by his standards, it was a good-enough shot, ripping through Sarvar's hand holding her gun. It blew off her ring finger, and her gun clattered to the floor. She howled in pain and turned to him with a hiss.

Alec exhaled and decided that if anyone asked, he would say he had deliberately aimed for her hand.

"Hands up!" he ordered, holding his gun steady with both hands, ready to put the next shot through her head, or at least somewhere closer to it. "Well, what's left of that hand."

Arm trembling, she did so, glaring at him, full of hate.

Alec found her hateful visage pleasing; her monotone warnings on the seemingly endless terror videos struck him as smug. "Sarvar Rashin. Do you remember your first words in that first message?"

Sarvar stared back and didn't hesitate. "You brought this on yourself."

Alec chuckled. "That will do, too, but I was thinking of, 'you are not safe.'"

"Who are you?" she demanded.

Alec smiled. "I'm the goddamn consequences."

It would have been a fantastic moment, and he would have felt awesomely victorious pulling the trigger again at her center mass if the wall next to them hadn't suddenly exploded, knocked to pieces by a Greek Cypriot—fired mortar landing outside. Alec was knocked across the room, pelted with pieces of concrete, inhaling and choking on dust, slamming against the floor and painful shock waves reverberating from his shoulder to his fingertips and up and down his spine and back and down to his legs and toes like a slinky. Alec's ears rung and he wiped dust from his eyes. What the hell was that, a grenade?

Then Alec heard another high-pitched whistle of a mortar landing, and another explosion, the sound of pieces of gravel and dirt and whatever had just been there crumbling and landing everywhere. The floor shook, and he could hear faraway gunfire picking up.

He wiped his eyes again. Where the hell was Sarvar? He looked—not where she was a moment ago. He silently swore to himself. He looked around. Where the hell was his gun? He felt around. No sign of it. He made a fist and pounded the floor in frustration. *Got to move. Got to move!*

***

Richards and Cook kept their heads on a swivel, confused and incredulous that the urban neighborhoods around the airport had suddenly become a war zone. One howitzer had fired from the Greek side, slamming into the wall of the main terminal building behind them. With their wounded compatriot safely moved behind a truck as cover, the blue-beret-clad UN troops were now running around and shouting orders, seeming to forget about the three Americans outside the crashed C-17. Richards and Cook had carried the groggy, mumbling Katrina farther away from the C-17 and looking in vain for decent cover.

"What the hell is this?" Cook shouted. "Heck of a time for Greece and Turkey to go to war!" The gunfire was thankfully distant, but the howitzer had demonstrated that death could fall out of the sky at any moment.

Across the runway, they saw two figures stumble out of the Cypriot airliner and hobble toward the airport building.

"That's bad," Cook said. "With those two in there..."

Richards finished his thought. "It's four against Alec. He's a goner."

Beneath them, Katrina's eyes snapped open.

***

Alec mumbled one profanity after another. Like that sock that went missing in the dryer, his gun seemed to have just slipped into another dimension during the explosion. Maybe Sarvar had somehow grabbed it, but considering her not-so-suppressed rage of a moment ago, she seemed like the type who would shoot him the moment she had the chance. She, too, seemed to have completely disappeared. Hearing noise from upstairs, separate from the gunfire outside, he scrambled down a hall, looking for the nearest doorway.

The small room had once been a workshop. Alec looked forlornly, thinking what he could do with a crowbar, or just getting close enough to put the claw end of a hammer through her skull. Unfortunately, the workshop had long been stripped of anything useful decades ago. The room just held a dust-covered worktable, a few boards and planks, tin cans full of rusty bolts and wing nuts—useful fodder for a bomb if he could find any explosive. Dang it, this was the sort of situation where Ward was practically MacGyver. Alec thought about the time in Spain when Ward had used an industrial spring and a ballpoint pen to shoot a guy's eye out. Ward loved to tell that story every time he saw *A Christmas Story* on television.

Alec looked behind the workbench. Something glinted in the light from his phone—something long and metal—rusted in some spots, but it would do.

***

The room was once a small office; now it simply housed a rusted metal folding table and provided a home for varieties of mold and mildew growing on the walls. It was all Gholam Gul really needed, though. Up on this level, the phone's signal seemed strong enough. He was, as far as he could tell, live-streaming from a Facebook account. Fabrice Vuscovi or the broadcast team would have to check the account, set up under a fake identity. But eventually, this message would go out. And when it did, he would unleash chaos across the United States.

Gul kneeled before his phone, hoping to be seen clearly and centered. He wished he had brought a stand or tripod; he had to balance his phone on its side. Still, as long as the signal was strong enough and the message went through, it would work. He held his gun in his hand at his side, knowing that someone was still chasing him. He had heard gunshots, a cry of pain from Sarvar, and then an explosion. The mortar that hit another part of the airport was unnervingly close.

He hit "go live."

"This is our moment, Atarsa. We have made them bleed, and yet they have not yet bled enough. They are gasping for air, clutching their wounds, feeling their vision go blurry, gripped by fear..." He realized he was partially describing himself at that moment. Something hit the airport terminal building hard—could it possibly have been a mortar?—and he wondered if he would ever see her again.

From the moment she had stepped into Gholam Gul's life, Sarvar pulled at him, as if he wore an invisible leash around his neck. She seduced him because he had wanted so badly to be seduced, convinced him that together they could tear the world down to its foundations, and rebuild it as they wished. She convinced him that VEVAK was wasting his talents; he spent years there secretly arranging the tools and resources to begin this campaign. The ayatollahs built arsenals to oppose the Great Satan, but were too afraid to use them. Gul would show that with simply enough nerve and a few hundred thousand dollars, he could cripple America.

Through her, he had begun to hear the Voices. Gul didn't understand everything about the Voices, but he knew enough. The Voices growled, their throats rippling with hunger, demanding sustenance in the form of fear from others. He knew they had existed as long as there had been people, and that while they seemed to have no tangible presence, he could feel their influence, in strokes of luck and coincidence and the actions of others. He knew schizophrenics could hear the Voices and that the West's foolish modern science dismissed them as insanity. He knew that the more Atarsa attacked, the clearer the Voices came, as if that abundance of fear was strengthening them.

Gul knew Rashin was much stronger than he was, that she heard the Voices much more clearly, and he suspected they whispered more to her than to him. He might die, quite soon, but she would figure out a way to carry on their work. He adored her.

"Now we tear America apart, and curse its sinful peoples to an eternity of fear and mistrust, a life of perpetual threat. We have adhered to the power of unity, as all of the great teachers instructed. The Old Ones, the Voices, are pleased with the nourishment we have offered. Go forth, my children. Strike now, where they least expect, in their beds, in their houses, in their schools and workplaces, let every corner of their wretched land be drenched in blood, and let them tremble in their homes; their gods will fall, and Aka Manah will enjoy eternal sustenance. We have introduced them to fear, brought fear into their homes and dreams, wrapped them in fear, violated them with fear—"

He was so focused on his phone that he didn't see the figure rushing at him through the doorway. Gul looked up, just in time to see a Caucasian man swinging a four-foot span of pipe and bringing it down hard against Gul's hand holding the gun, right on the wrist. Pain shot up and down Gul's arm as his trapezium, trapezoid, and scaphoid bones shattered upon the impact. He let out a howl and the gun dropped from his grip.

***

The small phone camera eye saw Gul look up and a long, metal pipe come down on his arm. Alec, just off screen, brought the pipe up again and slammed it up underneath Gul's chin—breaking the jaw and pushing his teeth up into the roof of his mouth. Gul staggered backward and stumbled, giving Alec just enough space to get into a batting stance and swing with all his might, right at face level. The camera captured the blood and teeth suddenly flying across the room, then the impact of Gul's body on the floor caused the phone to topple to the ground, the camera facedown on the table.

Alec placed his foot on Gul's neck. He leaned down, eyes glaring at the bloody, confused face.

"You want fear, Gul?" Alec spat. "Fear us."

Groaning, blinded, gasping to breathe, nasal passages and mouth filling with blood, Gul's hand flailed around, hoping to grasp his gun. Alec raised the pipe above his head and slammed it down on the crown of Gul's head, as hard as he could. Gul's skull fractured instantly. Alec raised the pipe and slammed it down again, like a lumberjack chopping wood.

"Feel this!" Alec screamed, eyes welling with tears.

It was fifteen or twenty strikes, pummeling Gul's head over and over and over again, so badly that brain matter was visible. Alec, breathing heavily, finally stopped when his arms and shoulders were sore. Gul's head looked like a cracked egg beneath him.

"That's for Sarina," he whispered.

Alec looked up and realized the phone might still be broadcasting and smashed it with the pipe; it shattered and pieces flew around the room.

With Gul a bloody mess at his feet, he looked down. After a moment, he awkwardly laughed and dropped the pipe. Then he felt a sudden exhaustion and leaned on the table. He let out a mad giggle and stumbled to his knees. He couldn't quite suppress a sob, relief and rage that the world had driven him to this point, a little unnerved that beating Gul's head into a pulp had felt so satisfying. He gasped for air, regaining control of himself from the wave of emotions. Whatever he had done, it was finally over. Finally, finally, finally over.

And then he felt a gun at the base of his neck.

"Mister Consequences." Sarvar.

Alec screamed a word that started out as a profanity and just turned into a primal howl of frustration. How the hell had she crept up on him so quietly?

"This will be your last lesson," she said, pressing the gun hard against the top of his spine. She looked down at the unrecognizable scarlet glob that was once the face of her lover.

"You think you are the consequence," she moved the gun slightly down, between his shoulders. "Today you experience your own consequences. I'm trying to decide whether to kill you or leave you paralyzed."

"I'll bleed out either way, so the joke's on you."

"The joke?" Sarvar asked. "Let me give you a final lesson from the Voices. There is no consequence, no cosmic justice. Only chaos. The persistence of life's random injustice means there is no justice. The perpetual destruction of innocence means there is no innocence. Everything you stand for is an epic lie, meant to soothe you as you avert your eyes from reality. Your life, everything you do, is the joke. Your final thoughts will be acceptance of this—and the realization that when you are gone, your wife will learn that as well."

He realized she must have noticed his wedding ring.

"I'd try to bribe you with this ring, but you're short one ring finger," Alec taunted.

"One of my fingers will shatter your wife's world," Sarvar hissed. "Let your last thought be of the pain she'll endure."

"You don't know her!" Alec shouted with a defiant laugh. "She's as hard as a ... brick. She won't waste time shedding a single tear until she's put you down. See what I just did to your boyfriend there?" Alec hoped Sarvar would look down, be distracted, lash out, or something, but he felt the gun against his neck, steady. "That's nothing compared to her. She's a modern samurai. You'll never see her coming, and she will make ... you ... hurt."

"And how does she cope with that curse, a natural gift for the art of murder?"

Alec heard a gunshot, but it came from too far away to be from Sarvar. He felt the gun slide back from his neck, down his back, and to the floor. He twisted around and saw two holes in Sarvar Rashin's head—one where the round had entered, and a messier one where it had departed, carrying a lot of brain matter with it.

"I'm learning to live with it," he heard Katrina say from the doorway.

CHAPTER 66

ROUTE 50
FAIRFAX COUNTY, VIRGINIA
SATURDAY, APRIL 3

Ward awoke, realizing he hadn't even finished his thought before passing out in the greenhouse. He found himself shaking... He reached for his gun and realized he couldn't move his arms. He was seated in a chair, and felt his hands tied behind him—plastic ties. Somebody had the audacity to bind him with his own zip-ties while he was unconscious.

Even worse, his gun was missing. In fact, all of his guns were missing. When he felt particularly unnerved about where he was heading, such as the excursion to the greenhouse, Ward liked to carry a SIG Sauer, a Glock, and a Smith & Wesson 380 in an ankle holster. He felt pain on the side of his face and wondered if his head had ricocheted off one of the metal greenhouse tables when he fell down. *Make it even easier for them*, Ward fumed, pulling against the plastic restraints. He looked around and realized he wasn't in the greenhouse anymore—he had been moved to a large, almost entirely empty supply shed behind the greenhouse.

A lone lamp stood beside him the corner, the shade tilted to illuminate him and shine in his eyes whenever he looked up. His pupils couldn't seem to adjust—beyond the light in his eyes, the rest of the room was pitch black.

"Ward Rutledge," a voice in the darkness whispered.

Ward felt his heart pounding, ready to burst out of his chest, and his clothes were wet with sweat. His hands were still shaking. He coughed. Gas, he remembered. The greenhouse suddenly stank of something—some sharp, earthy smell, something between topsoil and honey and freshly cut wood.

He saw movement in the dark corner of the greenhouse.

Francis Neuse's fear drug, Ward realized. *They aerosolized it and hit me with it.*

"Ward Rutledge ..." the voice whispered again. Damn it, they must have taken his wallet and ID.

"What do you want?" Ward barked, looking around. The only light came from that standing lamp, plugged into the corner, casting harsh light upon him and not much anywhere else in the room.

He saw more movement in the dark, but it seemed to be scuttling, animal-like, not moving like a person. A dog? A crab? But the whisper was coming from there. *Heck, maybe I'm hallucinating all this,* Ward realized.

"Your fear ..." the voice said, only slightly louder.

"Yeah, well, I've seen worse than you," Ward grunted. He tried to force his heart to stop beating so fast and hard, felt the sweat trickling down his forehead, neck, and back, and tried to sit up. She had bound his legs with multiple plastic ties. Good. He could wiggle around a bit. The chair was wooden. Maybe he could smash it against the wall and it would break apart, freeing his hands.

"No, you haven't," the voice responded. And then he heard a buzz.

And then, before him, was a giant termite-woman.

It seemed impossible: something distinctly feminine in its mannerisms and voice, but was simply not human; giant eyes, wiggling mandibles, no discernable clothing, creating a strange effect with the feminine curvature, her chest a twin-lumped thorax, her hind now a gigantic segmented abdomen reaching all the way down to the floor. Some exterminator's commercials from years ago had imagined human-sized insects trying to sneak into a house, and Ward wondered if somehow he was encountering some giant animatronic puppet, but there were no strings. She waddled closer on ugly, spindly, long legs; additional mandibles extended from within her mouth, letting out a clearly inhuman hiss.

Ward screamed. A lot.

He kicked his legs back in horrified desperation. He rocked the chair back and to the side, into the standing lamp, knocking it to the floor and knocking off the dusty lampshade. The lighting in the room changed for the brighter. As far was Ward could tell, he was beset by a six-foot-tall queen termite.

"We've been hard at work for a long time," the buzzing voice of the termite woman said. "You fear being too late to stop us. You are indeed too late. Your society is in a state of decay. Easy pickings for us. We're already in the woodwork. We're already inside the walls."

Ward rocked back and forth and backed himself to the lamp. His bulk obscured the light, and the Termite's features were again hidden in darkness.

"I'm not too late..." Ward whispered defiantly. He wasn't quite sure if it was a boast, self-reassurance, or a prayer.

"Your culture gives birth to our drones," the termite said.

Her giant insect head leaned down, antennae nearly touching Ward's sweaty forehead.

"Everything you've spent a life building—and your fathers and your grandfathers—is about to fall apart, right before your eyes," she continued. "We've been inside. Using you. Consuming you from within. Changing you to suit our purposes. It's going to look like you, but it won't be you anymore. You won't recognize your allies as you watch them betray you, one by one. Betraying everything they ever claimed to stand for."

"No," was all Ward could muster. He pressed hard against the lamp behind him, as he remembered a line from a book:

"Humanity is inconceivable without heroes; we are not egalitarian members of an ant farm, shuttling from cradle to grave, indistinguishable from one another and easily replaceable."

"We're so … close … already," the termite gleefully hissed.

The Queen Termite was quite stunned when Ward's hand came free and punched her in one of her giant compound eyes—the hot plastic from his cuff burned her and his wrist as well. While she had been approaching, whispering, he had been pressing his plastic cuffs against the hot lightbulb. His wrists were scorched, but his hands were free, and he intended to beat the living hell out of the impossible beast before him.

Ward yanked hard and pulled the plastic binding around his feet down and off the chair leg. He hit the termite again. Scrambling to a wall, he found a hand rake—he turned and swung it—metal pierced flesh and ripped. He heard a garbled, twisted, inhuman scream, a buzzing hum twisted around a woman's soprano, until it gurgled and coughed and spat.

Ward blinked and looked down. A woman lay on the floor, bleeding badly across her lower neck. Her top was black with yellow trim and two-toned reddish-blond hair with black roots and dark eyeshadow, wearing giant round black sunglasses. She wasn't a Termite Queen, just a woman. The hallucination had ended.

He slumped to the floor, exhausted.

He realized he should start searching for his guns and phone, but the sound of the sirens suggested he would soon have help looking for them.

He smiled, then giggled. His mission was complete. He let his head fall back to the floor, and closed his eyes, feeling relaxed for the first time in weeks.

Then his eyes popped open. He suddenly remembered he needed to tell someone where to find Norman Fein in the woods.

CHAPTER 67

DULLES INTERNATIONAL AIRPORT
MONDAY, APRIL 5

Upon stepping off the plane, Alec succumbed to the temptation to put down his carry-on bags, get on all fours, and kiss the ground.

"What are you doing?" Katrina asked quietly, mildly embarrassed, averting her face from the people around them staring in bewilderment.

"The hostages did this in 1981," he answered, rising to his feet. "A good tradition for when an American escapes an Iranian trap."

He looked up and felt surprise at what he saw: Ward, Raquel, and Dee waiting for them, along with several men in dark suits who did a terrible job of hiding their government affiliation.

Ward ran to Alec as he emerged through the doorway and hugged him, nearly bowling him over.

"Thank God you're all right, man!" he said. "I leave you for a few days and you nearly get yourself killed in a plane crash *and* executed! We're never doing that again."

Alec nodded. "We're all right," he said, giving Katrina a grateful look, knowing that she was all that prevented him from coming home in a coffin and becoming another star on the wall of the lobby of CIA Headquarters. "Knocked around, but in one piece."

"Nice shooting over there," Raquel said, giving Katrina a hug. "I wish I could let you rest up, but Mitchell wants you debriefing him personally and immediately." She looked toward Alec. "Both of you."

Alec's back straightened. Finally, an invitation to the exalted ground of the seventh floor. He grinned and turned to Ward.

"What's this I heard about you squishing a bug or something?"

***

Alec found the debriefing felt uncomfortably similar to a trial. A variety of old men that he didn't recognize lined both sides of the table, with Acting Director Mitchell sitting at the head. At his left, Patrick Horne glared at Alec with seething disapproval. He felt like it was every uncomfortable judgment rolled into one—a job application, a loan application at the bank, and biopsy test results from the doctor's office—before an irritable panel of senior citizens who had already repeatedly told you to stay off their lawn.

After Katrina and Alec completed detailing every moment on the ground in Turkmenistan and Cyprus, filling in the gaps in the local agency station reports, Mitchell's face cycled through several dozen emotions and he rubbed his temples for thirty seconds or so.

"When I talk to the president an hour from now, he is going to want to know … is the threat contained?"

Raquel raised a hand and turned the room's attention to a PowerPoint she had prepared and loaded onto the room's computer and display monitors.

"Our best estimate is that the Isoptera program recruited about sixty young men and set them up as Atarsa sleeper agents. Five were killed in the first round of attacks—Detroit, Beverly Hills, et cetera. Four were captured in the second round of attacks, the ones where they posted the video of the targets a few days beforehand—Sidwell Friends and the rest. Five more were killed or apprehended after the restaurant stabbing attacks in Columbus, Nashville, Jacksonville, Boston, and Washington. Three more were caught in Princeton, Manhattan, and Buffalo. A fourth was shot by police in Chicago. There was a fifth attacker . . ." She looked over at Ward, who refused to let her take any heat for his actions.

Ward interrupted. "I intercepted Norman Fein as he was preparing an attack on the William and Mary campus."

Mitchell put his finger to his chin. "And what did you do with him, Mr. Rutledge?"

Ward looked for the right words. "The woods are dark and scary, sir, very easy to get lost out there."

The FBI representative at the other end of table cleared his throat. "The information I have here from the Virginia State Police is they're treating him for exposure and dehydration. They found him gagged and bound to a tree."

Ten heads turned to Ward in unison, all sharing the same skeptical and disapproving look.

"There are a lot of ways something like that could have happened," Ward said, waving his hand. "Camping trip gone wrong. Really elaborate hide-and-seek. Bondage games."

The old men around the table shook their heads in disapproval.

Raquel continued. "In the past forty-eight hours, the FBI rounded up an additional forty young men who went through the Isoptera program."

Two of the old men at the table had been tallying the sums themselves on paper in front of them.

Mitchell looked at them. "By my math, that's fifty-five arrested or killed. If our best estimate is there are sixty of these nut jobs out there . . ."

Raquel nodded in disappointment. "We cannot say with any certainty that there are no more Atarsa sleepers remaining. The best guess of our analysts is that anywhere from three to ten remain."

Mitchell sat back in his chair and let out a long sigh.

"There's one key point to remember," Katrina said, pointing to the timeline of the attacks. "All of Atarsa's attacks were carefully scheduled and organized with great discipline. Starting from the New York broadcast, to the poisoning of Director Peck, to the submission of video clips from others ... No one from the second wave did anything until the first wave was done. No one from the third wave did anything to even arouse suspicion until the second wave of attacks failed. And so on."

"Fein would have been part of the fourth wave," affirmed Ward. He shot a defiant look at the FBI liaison. "Lucky for us, he got a little tied up."

"The signal hijackings were the 'go' signal to each wave of attackers," Katrina said confidently. "Without a new 'go' signal, the remaining Atarsa sleepers may never 'awaken.' At the very least, we can be reasonably comfortable that those three to ten sleepers out there are waiting for a launch signal that will never come."

Mitchell chewed this over.

"And we feel confident telling the president that the signal hijackings are finished because you blew up a church parking lot, am I correct, Ms. Alves?"

Dee shrunk in her chair. He made her elimination of the Atarsa broadcast operation sound so *wrong*. "Yes, sir. Many frightened commuters, some automobile accidents, but no civilian casualties. Well, no major civilian casualties. I mean, really major."

"What about this Azi Dhaka figure connected to the charity?" Mitchell asked.

Katrina looked at a detail of the description of Azi Dhaka, only about five feet tall. Grub, the hooded figure who had screamed at them after they found the Atarsa alter in the village, was about that height.

"We encountered a man in the village of Erbent who may have been Azi Dhaka," Katrina stated.

"He drew a knife on us, we subdued him and then grilled him," Alec elaborated.

"Grilled him? You didn't mention an interrogation over there," Patrick Horne objected.

"No, I mean, he was literally grilled in a propane gas explosion," Alec answered. "Or if you prefer, flame-broiled."

Mitchell looked down at the text he was supposed to read aloud to the president. "This 'Angra Druj,' Sarvar Rashin woman can't record any new videos … because Ms. Leonidivna shot her in the head." He nodded to himself, suspecting the president would find that development satisfying.

"Through it," Alec corrected.

"Angra Druj had a gun to someone else's head. Deadly force was necessary and justified," Katrina said firmly. She looked at Alec, who returned her look with another expression of sheepish gratitude. Mitchell exhaled in what seemed like frustration, and Alec bristled.

"And the ringleader, this former Iranian propaganda officer whose dad worked for Khomeini …" He shot an exasperated look at Alec. He turned the page of the report and winced at a photo of what was left of Gul, taken at the airport. "Jesus Christ, Alec, you knocked him around like he was a … a …" Words failed the director.

"Piñata?" Alec offered. Mitchell shot him a look that shut him up for once.

The director looked down at his yellow legal pad. "This all began, what, a month ago, with Rafiq Tannous coming to

Berlin and telling Katrina that Akoman had a mole in this agency. Did you ever encounter anything to support that claim?"

An awkward silence followed. Finally Raquel answered, "You mean besides the fact that you're sitting at the head of the table right now instead of Peck?"

Mitchell recoiled. "Are you suggesting—"

"Not at all, sir," Raquel said, raising her hands. "I'm simply saying that if Atarsa had a mole, it would make targeting Director Peck much easier."

Everyone briefly looked at everyone else around the table with suspicion.

Mitchell looked over his list. "Fein, in the hospital. The broadcast team, dead. Druj, dead. Gul, dead."

Ward cleared his throat. "Sir, Fabrice Vuscovi, who was coordinating the sleeper agents, is in Inova Fairfax Hospital's intensive care unit with a severe laceration to her throat from a hand rake and massive blood loss. But she's not dead!" He gleefully held up two fingers to Alec, raised his eyebrows, and mouthed the word *two!*, boasting he had managed to not kill either Atarsa operative he had encountered.

Mitchell stared at Ward with a withering stare for ten seconds, and then gave him sarcastic slow applause.

"You five really put me in an impossible situation," Mitchell fumed. "Sure, you guys cut a path through Atarsa, but you left a trail of bodies halfway across the globe leading right back to this agency! I'm supposed to go to the White House, and the Hill, and our foreign partners, and now I've got to explain that we've been—"

"With all due respect, sir, how prepared was this agency and this administration?" All the heads in the room snapped to Katrina, the figure least expected to interrupt Mitchell. "How prepared were you?"

Raquel was too surprised to offer any disapproving look. Heck, Katrina was the last person in the world to ever be openly insubordinate, but she never took any grief from anyone, either.

"Atarsa managed to override broadcasting signals, poison your predecessor, and unleash a multi-week campaign of terror on American soil," Katrina spoke to the man who was her boss with a tone of confident command. "They planned this and prepared for *years*. They figured out exactly how to play our media and play our culture to maximize the psychological impact of their attacks. They studied the curdling milk of our culture and exactly how to turn Americans against each other in an unthinking rage. They blindsided everyone, and we started out ten steps behind them. If anybody else in the entire national security community had done a better job at any point, we might not have had to kill everyone we did. And this is with us getting lucky, over and over again! This agency and this administration have to recognize that the way they currently do things, by the time they notice the problem, all the good options are gone."

Mitchell looked like he had been slapped.

"Considering the scale of this threat, and the exceptional efforts we had to make to eliminate that threat, you have only one appropriate response." Katrina leaned forward. "Gratitude."

Mitchell looked more than a little chastened. He nodded.

"All of you fought through hell out there," he said, quietly at first, finding his voice. "I don't want it to seem like I've forgotten that. And your point, that perhaps we've grown far too reactive instead of proactive with threats . . . well, there are days I would agree with that."

He looked down and checked his watch.

"I have to get to the White House soon," Mitchell said. "Rest assured, you'll all be recognized and commended. We're just going to have to make sure we're all on the same page moving forward. Thank you." He nodded, and they rose.

Mitchell turned to Raquel. "Stay."

***

In the hallway outside, Patrick Horne made the most cursory of polite nods to Katrina and then scoffed audibly loud enough to an aide, looking at Alec, "Unbelievable."

Alec stopped and turned. "Yes, that's right, Patrick," he said, smiling softly. "My team *is* unbelievable."

"Lucky you didn't get yourself and everyone else killed," Patrick said. He turned to Katrina. "Watch yourself with this guy, Katrina," he warned. "Hope it's worth the risk to your life and career in exchange for..." He let the unfinished sentence hang in the air like a dare, as if what Alec could possibly offer her was unimaginable.

After a long pause, she finished his sentence.

"Full support in everything that I do, and absolute faith in me, even when I don't have it in myself?" She glanced at Alec and smiled. "Yes. It's worth it."

Shaking his head in disbelief, Patrick turned and started walking down the hall with his aide.

"Oh, hey, everybody, party at our house, Saturday!" Alec called down the hall. "All of you guys are invited! Deputy directors, executive directors, liaisons..." His voice trailed off as he continued. "All of you old men who hate me."

"Kind of you to include Patrick," Katrina noted dryly.

"Oh, Patrick's not invited, I just want him to know where everybody is going to be having fun without him."

***

After the others had left and the conference room had cleared, Mitchell removed a folder from his stack, one that included everything he wouldn't be telling the White House.

"No word on this Mexican Jaguar character either, hm?"

"Everything we have suggests Juan Lopez is in the wind," she shook her head sadly. "For now."

Mitchell picked up three pages stapled together, reread a section, and shook his head with amused incredulity.

"I am not telling the president that one of our paramilitary officers claims he saw a giant termite-woman in the greenhouse."

"Completely understandable, sir," Raquel said. "The explanation is pretty simple: he was hit with the toxin they used on Director Peck." It wasn't the slightest of lip bites that gave her away; Mitchell knew it was a lie before she said it.

"Yeah, that explanation would work really well if I hadn't already seen the crime lab team's evaluation of the greenhouse and Rutledge's post-incident medical evaluation indicating he was never exposed to any hallucinogenic substances."

Raquel looked down.

"Horne double-checked. Don't withhold things like that from me," Mitchell glared. "If Rutledge had a stress-induced hallucination in the field, we can deal with it."

She nodded and kept to herself the nagging question of how Ward, who had seen all kinds of intense combat situations in his adult life, and who had never given any indication of a propensity to hallucinations before, would have one now. And why out of all possible hallucinations, Ward saw a bug, while halfway around the world, Alec and Katrina had described an insect-like demonic figure at an underground altar, or the raspy inhuman sound coming from the Atarsa cultist in the Turkmen village. Or former director Peck's strange comment during his breakdown about someone being a "bug." Or the nightmare Katrina had described to her about a creature with antennae—or her previous, eerily prophetic dream about someone being hung from a McDonald's sign.

Because Ward's vision had to be a hallucination. Surely.

CHAPTER 68

APRIL 10

The party at Alec and Katrina's house represented the revival of a long-dormant tradition. As if she hadn't been good enough at everything else under the sun, Katrina cooked up an Uzbeki storm, and Alec basically loaded up a supermarket shopping cart at Total Wine and the local ABC store. (He did this even though Ward said he knew people in his neck of the woods who made their own artisan organic moonshine.) It was far too much for the two dozen or so guests. Alec made a point of inviting as many coworkers and friends as possible, many more than the house could hold, to ensure everyone felt welcome. Experience taught him that the full list never showed. Perhaps most important, he had invited the neighbors. (Alec had figured out neighbors never complained about a party's noise if they were invited.) Former colleagues scattered in dangerous, far-flung corners of the world such as Pakistan, Ankara, the Balkans, London, Houston, Tallahassee, Ottawa, and Connecticut RSVPed that they would be there in spirit. Both friends with security clearances and without knew the general gist—if Alec and Katrina were throwing a party, then something, somewhere in the world had gone really well, and it was time to scan the foreign news wires for confirmation some notorious radical had met an untimely end.

Five days earlier, the president strode out along a long red carpet and stopped at a lectern in the East Room of the White

House and announced with a smile that "the United States has completed simultaneous operations that eliminated all of the remaining Atarsa senior leadership." The commander-in-chief credited the operation to "a small team of Americans from the Air Force and other government agencies" for intercepting the leaders as they attempted to flee from an airport in Cyprus. POTUS thanked the United Nations and the Turkish and Greek Cypriot governments for their "extensive cooperation." (In fact, neither government had cooperated much beyond letting US personnel leave the country and slightly less than the maximum imaginable amount of public complaining about the secrecy concerning what had just happened in their jurisdiction.)

The ten minutes of live, prime-time remarks also credited the FBI for swift work in tracking down Atarsa's sleeper agents and warned that while the threat of terrorism could never be said to be completely eliminated, this particular terror group had just suffered "a grievous blow, from which they are unlikely to ever recover." Leaders in both parties quickly agreed to just forget about the FBI director's press conference from last month, touting the arrests of four Atarsa sleepers, had inadvertently played directly into the terror group's plans. The White House press secretary said she could offer no new information about the NORAD missile strike in northwest Washington, the "unrelated" crash of an Air Force supply plane in Cyprus and the sudden explosion of violence all over Mexico as the Craneos and Damascos cartels fought an unexpected turf war. The White House press corps furiously demanded answers until the president went on a tirade on Twitter and then the cable news networks debated his as-yet-unproven accusation that a prominent news anchor often critical of the president was being treated for erectile dysfunction.

In Alec and Katrina's house, they moved the furniture back against the walls to form the traditional makeshift dance floor, but it didn't take long for a joyously heated, semi-sober argument about the playlist to break out. Alec had launched the playlist with Thin Lizzy's "The Boys Are Back in Town," but Katrina pointed out that it wasn't merely the boys who were back. They were placated once it was agreed that the second song would feature her, Dee, and Raquel singing a karaoke version of "Girls Just Want to Have Fun."

Defiant exuberance was the theme of the playlist, featuring Tom Petty's "I Won't Back Down," Twisted Sister's "We're Not Gonna Take It!," A-Ha's "Take On Me," X-Ambassadors' "Renegades," Fall Out Boy's "Immortals," and then Alien Ant Farm's cover of "Smooth Criminal." Ward selected the Bloodhound Gang's "Fire Water Burn," leading an enthusiastic, rousing chant of support of rooftop arson. Elaine declined to sing to "Come On Eileen" by Dexy's Midnight Runners. Alec crooned an off-key version of Chris Isaak's "Baby Did a Bad Bad Thing" to Katrina.

Alec was about to express his yearning to be an infamous and feared punisher of the world's wicked through Chris Cornell's "You Know My Name" when Raquel suddenly looked with concern at her phone. She said she had to step out for a moment, and briefly, Katrina wondered if some new crisis had arisen at the most inconvenient time.

"Nope, an old friend just texted he's in town," she said. "He's unexpectedly close by." And with that Raquel headed out the front door.

No sooner than the door closed than Ward, having consumed a healthy serving of moonshine, began to half-sing, half-yell boasts about how he had just saved the world, and how "hunting season" was now year-round.

"I had strings, but now I'm free," Alec sang. "There are no strings on me."

It took only a few moments for the men's half-drunken boasting to spur Katrina to switch the Bose stereo system to a new song, U2's "Window in the Skies." Thankfully, it didn't take much to get the inebriated Alec to shift to a raucous "Can't you see what love has done?" chorus.

***

The black Lincoln Town Car was just idling at the curb; the rear doors were unlocked. Raquel opened the door.

Raquel had not seen Merlin in a long time.

He was now completely bald, bespectacled; he looked like a good character actor waiting to be cast in the film version of a Dickens novel, or the wise old grandpa making nickels appear out of a toddler's ear in a Miracle hearing aid commercial. Raquel was glad to see him again, but part of her was saddened and a little frightened to see how much former CIA deputy director Harold Hare had aged. No doubt many suspected that he had gone senile years ago. He was in a tuxedo, somehow fitting his magician nickname.

"Glad you could spare a few minutes," Merlin chuckled.

"You know I'd rearrange anything for our chats," she said. "Obviously you knew I was at Katrina's. Nice tux, is it prom night?"

Hare laughed heartily. "Mitchell's got some big black-tie dinner downtown for the previous administration's movers and shakers. He brought us out of the Crotchety Spy Retirement Home for Old Timer's Day at the ballpark."

Merlin had encouraged her to set up Alec and Katrina's team years ago. Now, with the Atarsa crisis resolved, she felt like pushing Merlin on a suspicion that had been building, month by month, year by year.

"Why is it every time I talk to you, I feel like you know something you're not sharing?" she asked. "I mean, I know you're withholding something. What I can't figure out is why."

Merlin nodded, exhaled, then looked out the window.

"How many people at the agency believe in God?" Merlin asked.

"You know we don't ask about that," Raquel answered. "That's just asking to get sued."

"It's hard for a nonbeliever to understand a believer," Merlin shrugged. "Because of this, a lot of people over in that building, smart and skilled as they are, don't understand half of what our enemies are fighting for. And if you don't understand the psychology of your enemies, I'm not sure you can really understand what you're fighting for."

This answer didn't satisfy her. "Theology?"

"I've spent my life researching this, asking these questions," Merlin answered. "And everything you faxed me in the past weeks just offered further confirmation. Are you still blacking out sections of my memos as you read them?"

"Old habits die hard," she responded. "Some of the things you write shouldn't be seen by anyone."

The pair chuckled that they were the last two people in America who faxed each other documents the old-fashioned way, and felt confident that their communications would remain secure, less because of their electronic encryption than because no one else in the world still remembered how to operate a fax machine.

Raquel had a nagging suspicion the conversation would turn in this direction. Aging had made Merlin increasingly less focused on the here and now and more focused on the hereafter. Part of her dreaded it and part of her knew she had to entertain Merlin's crazy notions after everything she had seen, read, and heard in the past month.

Merlin closed his eyes and pictured some of the half-blacked-out classified documents she had faxed him the past weeks.

He pictured his desk with the documents: "Francis Neuse believed he had been kidnapped by demons and that kindness or cruelty generated nourishment for angels and demons. Sure, you can dismiss him as crazy, but when he says his captors had skulls for faces, how do you know he wasn't looking at their souls?"

"Harold," she scoffed. But she made a mental note that his photographic memory of the memos should dispel any claims of senility for a while.

"Jaguar in Mexico, all that Aztec worship stuff he had in his place... the gang that's into Santa Muerte. Even if you think all their strange gods don't exist, the fact that they believe in that guardian spirit, that force watching over them, influences their behavior. It makes them take risks they otherwise never would. Once you stop looking for literal angels and demons and you simply look for human behavior driven by a great illumination or a great darkness, all of a sudden you see signs everywhere."

There it was, she realized.

"But you want me to accept it's more than just belief, don't you?" Raquel poked. "You think this thing, this attack, Atarsa, all of this... was some force beyond humanity trying to influence us, push us to some bad end."

"Not just that," Merlin said. "I think we had something unseen behind us, too, pushing us to stop them every step of the way. We had our own improbable luck out there. Any one of them could have suffered a fatal snakebite on that island in Brazil. I notice that the report said the goon in Mexico missed Alec at close range when he was standing in front of a mural of the Virgin Mary. Katrina had to make a hell of a shot in that airport – a peaceful neutral ground between countries representing two great faiths. The Atarsa plane could have taken off a few minutes earlier. Some might call all of those... miracles."

Raquel shook her head skeptically.

Merlin was undeterred.

"I think this is just one more chapter in a fight that goes back throughout human history. And the fight and our role in it aren't even close to being done. This isn't just you, me, and a few others, trying to make sense of a world that seems stranger every day, evil men and evil acts that seem like something out of another time, terror-minded bands that seem all-too-literally demonic, stopped by only unimaginably selfless courage. It's this sense that whatever's going on, it's accelerating, getting more dangerous, more extreme, building to some … bigger clash …"

Raquel felt a shudder. Sure, Merlin liked to drink deeply from the cups of religion and mysticism and myth and superstition, but that ominous vibe struck a chord deep in her gut. Life had once seemed so normal, so comparably calm, so happily obsessed with irrelevant nonsense. But that awful Tuesday decades ago seemed to have opened up Pandora's box: terrorism, war, invasions, insurrections, chemical weapons, radical groups of every kind, splintering political and global factions, barbaric torture, sections of the map written off as ungovernable and uncontrollable, the slow-motion collapse of the international order. And now a twisted cult of Zoroastrian demon-worshippers, using not much more than troubled youth and steak knives, had managed to shake American society to its core.

She remembered reading that during the development of the first atomic bomb in the United States during World War Two, some of the world's most brilliant scientists had serious fears about what would happen when man split an atom. Edward Teller feared that the reaction might ignite the atmosphere with a self-sustaining fusion reaction of Nitrogen nuclei—in other words, an ever-expanding fireball that would consume not just the test site but speed out all across the skies of the American Southwest and perhaps incinerate the entire planet. At the Trinity test, all of the scientists knew they were about to change the world in ways they could not fully comprehend beforehand. After the mushroom cloud rose, J. Robert Oppenheimer famously quoted a line from the Bhagavad Gita, a Hindu scripture, "Now I am become Death, the destroyer of worlds." More Westerly-focused theological minds among the scientists wondered if splitting the atom represented man cracking open God's work, and in so tearing the curtain that obscured creation from its Creator—or the earthly realm from heaven and hell.

In that greatest of cities, on that worst of all possible Tuesday mornings, the collapse that shook the earth and every American's soul was powerful enough to be measured in megatons, both literal and figurative. Raquel found herself wondering if the divine and the demonic were a little closer to the human heart ever since. She had certainly witnessed enough impossibly evil horror, and enough impossibly noble courage and compassion, in the two decades since.

Merlin leaned forward.

"In all this, rational, smart, professional, analytical, previously atheist, non-snake-handling, no Ouija boards, no healing crystals, no alien abductions, people with access to all of the best information from the widest and most thorough collection of sources . . . we look at the world and all of its terrible conflicts between the good and the evil, and we see . . ."

She waited for him to finish the sentence. She wasn't ready to say it.

"Something greater at work. Maybe God and the Devil. Maybe angels and demons. But something . . . with the light and the dark."

She sat back and contemplated. After a long while, she glanced back at Merlin.

"We can't tell them. Not yet."

ABOUT THE AUTHOR

Jim Geraghty is an award-winning senior political correspondent at *National Review*. His work has also appeared in *The Philadelphia Inquirer*, *The New York Sun*, *The Washington Times* and *The Washington Examiner*. His journalism has taken him from the reopening of the anthrax-fumigated Hart Senate Office Building on Capitol Hill to firing an Israeli-made fully-automatic Uzi at the National Rifle Association's range in Fairfax, Virginia to debating the constitutionality of NSA surveillance methods at the Heritage Foundation. He spent two years in Ankara, Turkey working as a foreign correspondent and studying anti-Americanism, democratization, Islam, Middle East politics, and U.S. diplomatic efforts and has also filed dispatches from Great Britain, Germany, Egypt, Italy, Israel, Spain, and Jordan. He is also the author of the novel *The Weed Agency*, which was a *Washington Post* bestseller, and the nonfiction books *Voting to Kill* and *Heavy Lifting* with Cam Edwards.